A Very Personal Assistant

JESSICA HART

MARGARET MAYO

NINA HARRINGTON

MILLS & BOON

First published in Great Britain 2013
by Mills & Boon, an imprint of Harlequin (UK) Limited,
Eton House, 18-24 Paradise Road, Richmond, Surrey TW9 1SR

A VERY PERSONAL ASSISTANT
© by Harlequin Enterprises II B.V./S.à.r.l 2013

Oh-So-Sensible Secretary, The Santorini Marriage Bargain and *Hired: Sassy Assistant* were published in Great Britain by Harlequin (UK) Limited.

Oh-So-Sensible Secretary © Jessica Hart 2010
The Santorini Marriage Bargain © Margaret Mayo 2009
Hired: Sassy Assistant © Nina Harrington 2009

ISBN: 978 0 263 90498 7
ebook ISBN: 978 1 472 00819 0

05-0213

Printed and bound in Spain
by Blackprint CPI, Barcelona

OH-SO-SENSIBLE
SECRETARY

BY
JESSICA HART

OH-SO-SENSIBLE SECRETARY

BY

JESSICA HART

Jessica Hart was born in West Africa, and has suffered from itchy feet ever since, travelling and working around the world in a wide variety of interesting but very lowly jobs, all of which have provided inspiration on which to draw when it comes to the settings and plots of her stories. Now she lives a rather more settled existence in York, where she has been able to pursue her interest in history, although she still yearns sometimes for wider horizons. If you'd like to know more about Jessica, visit her website www.jessicahart.co.uk

For Nikki at 2DC,
with many thanks for all her work on the website

CHAPTER ONE

EVERYTHING was in place. A sleek computer sat on my desk, humming gently. A notebook and freshly sharpened pencil were squared up to one side of a high-tech phone, but otherwise the desk was empty, the way I like it. I can't bear clutter.

There was only one thing missing.

My new boss.

Phin Gibson was late, and I was cross. I can't bear unpunctuality either.

I had been there since eight-thirty. Wanting to make a good impression, I'd dressed carefully in my best grey checked suit, and my make-up was as subtle and professional as ever. Rattling over the keyboard, my nails had a perfect French manicure. I was only twenty-six, but anyone looking at me would know that I was the ultimate executive PA, cool, calm and capable.

I might have *looked* cool, but by half past ten I certainly wasn't feeling it. I was irritated with Phin, and wishing I had bought myself a doughnut earlier.

Now, I know I don't look like the kind of girl with a doughnut fetish, but I can't get through the morning without a sugar fix. It's something to do with my metabolism (well, that's my story and I'm sticking to it), and if I don't have something sweet by eleven o'clock I get scratchy and irritable.

OK, even *more* irritable.

Chocolate or biscuits will do at a pinch, but doughnuts are my thing, and there's a coffee bar just round the corner from Gibson & Grieve's head office which sells the lightest, jammiest, sugariest ones I've ever tasted.

I'd fallen into the habit of buying one with a cappuccino on my way into work, and waiting for a quiet moment to get my blood sugar level up later in the morning, but today I'd decided not to. I wasn't sure what sort of boss Phin Gibson would prove to be, and I didn't want to be caught unawares with a sugar moustache or jammy fingers on our first day working together. This job was a big opportunity for me, and I wanted to impress him with my professionalism.

But how could I do that if he wasn't there?

Exasperated, I went back to my e-mail to Ellie, my friend in Customer and Marketing.

No problem, Ellie. To be honest, I was glad of something to do. There's a limit to what you can do as a PA without a boss—who STILL hasn't appeared, by the way. You'd think he could be bothered to turn up on time on his first day in a new job, but apparently not. Am already wishing I was back in the Chief Executive's office. I have a nasty feeling Phin and I aren't going to get on, and unless

——Original Message——
From: e.sanderson@gibsonandgrieve.co.uk
To: s.curtis@gibsonandgrieve.co.uk
Sent: Monday, January 18, 09:52
Subject: THANK YOU!

Summer, you are star! Thank you SO much for putting those figures together for me—and on a Friday afternoon, too! You saved my life (again!!!!!).

Any sign of Phin Gibson yet??? Can't wait to hear if he's as gorgeous as he looks on telly!
Exx

'Well, well, well…Lex must know me better than I thought he did.'

The deep, amused voice broke across my exasperated typing and my head jerked up as I snatched my fingers back from the keyboard.

And there—at last!—was my new boss. Phinneas Gibson himself, lounging in the doorway and smiling the famously lop-sided smile that had millions of women, including my flatmate Anne, practically dribbling with lust.

I'd never dribbled myself. I'm not much of a dribbler at the best of times, and that oh-so-engaging smile smacked a little too much of I'm-incredibly-attractive-and-charming-and-don't-I-know-it for my taste.

My first reaction at the sight of Phin was one of surprise. No, thinking about it, surprise isn't quite the right word. I was *startled*.

I'd known what he looked like, of course. It would have been hard not to when Anne had insisted that I sit through endless repeats of *Into the Wild*. It's her flat, so she gets control of the remote.

If you're one of the two per cent of the population fortunate enough never to have seen it, Phin Gibson takes ill-assorted groups of people to the more inhospitable places on the planet, where they have to complete some sort of task in the most appalling conditions. On camera.

According to Anne, it makes for compulsive viewing, but personally I've never been able to see the point of making people uncomfortable just for sake of it. I mean, what's the point of hacking through a jungle when you can take a plane?

But don't get me started on reality TV. That's another thing I can't bear.

So I was braced against the extraordinary blue eyes, the shaggy dark blond hair and the smile, but I hadn't counted on how much bigger and more *immediate* Phin seemed in real life. Seeing him on the small screen gave no sense of the vivid impact of his presence.

I'm not sure I can explain it properly. You know that feeling when a gust of wind catches you unawares? When it swirls round you, sucking the air from your lungs and leaving you blinking and ruffled and invigorated? Well, that's what it felt like the first time I laid eyes on Phin Gibson.

There was a kind of lazy grace about him as he leant there, watching me with amusement. So it wasn't that he radiated energy. It was more that everything around him was energised by his presence. You could practically see the molecules buzzing in the air, and Phin himself seemed to be using up more than his fair share of oxygen in the room, which left me annoyingly short of breath.

Not that I was going to let Phin guess *that*.

'Good morning, Mr Gibson,' I said. Minimising the screen just in case, I took off the glasses I wear for working at the computer and offered a cool smile.

'Is it possible that *you're* my PA?' The blue eyes studied me with a mixture of surprise, amusement and appreciation as Phin levered himself away from the doorway and strolled into the room.

'I'm Summer Curtis, yes.'

A little miffed at his surprise, and ruffled by the amusement, I pushed back my chair so that I could rise and offer my hand across the desk. *Some* of us were professional.

Phin's fingers closed around mine and he held onto my hand as he looked at me. 'Summer? No.'

'I'm afraid so,' I said a little tightly. I can't tell you how many times I've wished I was called something sensible, like Sue or Sarah, but never more than at that moment, with those blue eyes looking down into mine, filled with laughter.

I tried to withdraw my hand, but Phin was keeping a tight hold on it, and I was uncomfortably aware of the firm warmth of skin pressed against mine.

'You are *so* not a Summer,' he said. 'I've never met anyone with a more inappropriate name. Although I did know a girl called Chastity once, now I come to think of it,' he added. 'Look at you. Cool and crisp. Conker-brown hair. Eyes like woodsmoke. What were your parents thinking when they called you Summer instead of Autumn?'

'Not about how embarrassing it would be for me to go through life named after a season, anyway,' I said, managing to tug my hand free at last. I sat down again and rested it on the desk, where it throbbed disconcertingly.

'I must thank Lex,' said Phin. To add to my discomfort, he perched on my desk and turned sideways to look at me. 'He told me he'd appointed a PA for me, but I was expecting a dragon.'

'I can be a dragon if required,' I said, although right then I felt very undragon-like. I was suffocatingly aware of Phin on the other side of the desk. He wasn't anywhere near me, but his presence was still overwhelming. 'I'm fully qualified,' I added stiffly.

'I feel sure Lex wouldn't have appointed you if you weren't,' Phin said.

He had picked up my pencil and was twirling it absently

between his fingers. It's the kind of fiddling that drives me mad, and I longed to snatch it from him, but I wasn't that much of a dragon.

'What's your brief?' he added, still twirling.

'Brief?'

The look he shot me was unexpectedly acute. 'Don't tell me Lex hasn't put you in here to keep an eye on me.'

I shifted uncomfortably.

'You're the most sensible person around here,' had been Lex Gibson's exact words when he offered me the job. 'I need someone competent to stop that idiot boy doing anything stupid. God knows what he'd get up to on his own!'

Not that I could tell Phin that. I admired Lex, but I wondered now if he was quite right. Phin didn't seem like an idiot to me, and he certainly wasn't a boy. He wasn't that much older than me—in his early thirties, perhaps—but he was clearly all man.

'Your brother thought it would be helpful for you to have an assistant who was familiar with the way the company operates,' I said carefully instead.

'In other words,' said Phin, interpreting this without difficulty, 'my brother thinks I'm a liability and wants you to keep me in order.'

I'd leapt at the chance of a promotion, even if it did mean working for Lex Gibson's feckless younger brother. Perhaps I should just explain, for those of you who have just jetted in from Mars—well, OK, from outside the UK—Gibson & Grieve is a long-established chain of department stores with a reputation for quality and style that others can only envy. The original, very exclusive store was in London, but now you'll find us in all the major British cities—setting a gold standard in retail, as Lex likes to say.

The Grieves died out long ago, but the Gibsons still have

a controlling share, and Lex Gibson now runs the company with an iron hand. As far as I knew, Phin had never shown the slightest interest in Gibson & Grieve until now, but, as heir to a substantial part of it, he was automatically a member of the board. He was coming in right at the top, and that meant that his PA—me—would be working at the most senior level.

I gathered the idea was for Phin to spend a year as the public face of Gibson & Grieve, so even though the job wasn't permanent it would look very good on my CV. And the extra money wouldn't hurt, either. If I was ever going to be able to buy my own place I needed to save as much as I could, and this promotion would make quite a difference to my salary. I'm someone who likes to have a plan, and this job was a major step on my way. I might not be thrilled at the thought of working for Phin Gibson, but it wasn't an opportunity I was prepared to lose.

I couldn't dream about a future with Jonathan now, I remembered sadly, and that left buying my own flat the only plan I had. I mustn't jeopardise it by getting on the wrong side of Phin, no matter how irritatingly he fiddled.

'I'm your personal assistant,' I assured him. 'It's my job to support you. I'm here to do whatever you want.'

'*Really?*'

'Of course,' I began with dignity, then saw that his eyes were alight with laughter. To my chagrin, I felt a blush steal up my cheeks. It was just a pity my plan involved working with someone who was clearly incapable of taking anything seriously. 'Within reason, of course.'

'Oh, of *course*,' Phin agreed, eyes still dancing.

Then, much to my relief, he dropped the pencil and got up from the desk. 'Well, if we're going to be working together we'd better get to know each other properly, don't you think? Let's have some coffee.'

'Certainly.' Making coffee for my boss. That I could do. Pleased to be back in proper PA mode, I swung my chair round and got to my feet. 'I'll make some right away.'

'I don't want you to make it,' said Phin. 'I want to go out.'

'But you've just arrived,' I objected.

'I know, and I'm feeling claustrophobic already.' He looked around the office without enthusiasm. 'It's all so… sterile. Doesn't it make you want to shout obscenities and throw rubbish everywhere?'

I actually winced at the thought.

'No,' I said. Gibson & Grieve had always been noted for its style and up-market image. The offices were all beautifully designed and gleamed with the latest technology. I loved the fact that this one was light and spacious, and free as yet of any of the clutter that inevitably accumulated in a working office. 'I like everything neat and tidy,' I told Phin.

'You know, I should have been able to guess that,' he said in a dry voice, and I suddenly saw myself through his eyes: crisp and restrained in my grey suit, my hair fastened neatly back from my face. In comparison, he looked faintly un-kempt, in jeans, a black T-shirt and a battered old leather jacket. He might look appropriate for a media meeting, but it was hardly appropriate for an executive director of a company like Gibson & Grieve, I thought disapprovingly.

Still, I had no doubt he was even less impressed by me. I would have bet on the fact that he thought me smart, but dull.

But then maybe all men thought that when they looked at me. Jonathan had, too, in the end.

I pushed the thought of Jonathan aside. 'We can go out if you'd rather,' I said. 'But don't you at least want to check your messages first?'

Phin's brows rose. 'I have messages?'

'Of course. You're a director and a board member,' I pointed out. 'We set up a new e-mail address for you last week, and you've been getting messages ever since. I'm able to filter them for you, and you have another address which only you will be able to access.'

'Great,' said Phin. 'Filtering sounds good to me. Is there anything important?'

'It's all important when you're a director.' I couldn't help the reproving note in my voice, but Phin only rolled his eyes.

'OK, is there anything *urgent*?'

I was forced to admit that there wasn't. 'Not really.'

'There you go,' he said cheerfully. 'I didn't think I'd need a PA, but Lex was right—as always. You've saved me wading through all those e-mails already. You deserve a coffee for that,' he told me, and held open the door for me. 'Come on, let's go.'

It was all going to be very different now, I thought, stifling a sigh as we headed down the corridor to the lift. I was used to working for Lex Gibson, who barely stopped working to sip the coffee Monique, his PA, took in to him.

Lex would never dream of going out for coffee, or bothering to get to know his secretaries, come to that. I was fairly sure he knew nothing about my private life. As far as Lex was concerned you were there to work, not to make friends, and I was perfectly happy with that. I didn't want to get all chummy with Phin, but for better or worse he was my boss now, so I could hardly refuse.

'Where's the best place for coffee round here?' Phin asked when we pushed through the revolving doors and out into the raw January morning. At least it wasn't raining for once, but I shivered in my suit, wishing I'd bothered to throw on my coat after all.

'Otto's is very good,' I said, hugging my arms together. 'It's just round the corner.'

'Better and better,' said Phin. 'Lead the way.' He glanced down at me, shivering as we waited to cross the road. 'You look cold. Would you like to borrow my jacket?'

The thought of his jacket, warm from his body, slung intimately around my shoulders, was strangely disturbing—quite apart from the fact that it would look very odd with my suit. 'I'm fine, thank you,' I said, clenching my teeth to stop them chattering.

'Let's step on it, then,' he said briskly. 'It's freezing.'

The warmth and the mouth-watering smell of freshly baked pastries enveloped us as we pushed through the door into Otto's. Inside it was dark and narrow, with four old-fashioned booths on one side and some stools at a bar in the window.

The coffee and sandwiches were so good that first thing in the morning and at lunchtime there was always a long queue out of the door, but it was relatively quiet now. We lined up behind three executives exuding testosterone as they compared bonuses, a German tourist, and a pair of middle-aged women carrying on a conversation that veered bizarrely between some terrible crisis that a mutual friend was enduring and whether a Danish pastry was more or less fattening than a blueberry muffin.

Phin picked up a tray and hustled me along behind them. 'What about something to eat?' he said. 'I'm going to have something. I'm starving.'

I eyed the doughnuts longingly, but there was no way I was going to eat one in front of him. 'Just coffee, please.'

'Sure?' I could almost believe he had seen the yearning in my eyes, because he leant suggestively towards me. 'You don't want a piece of that chocolate cake?' he said, rolling the words around his mouth suggestively. 'A scone with cream? One of those pastries? Go on—you know you want to!'

I gritted my teeth. 'No, thank you.'

'Well, you're a cheap date,' he said. 'I'm going to have one of those doughnuts.'

I had to press my lips firmly together to stop myself whimpering.

Ahead, Otto's ferocious wife, Lucia, was making coffee, shouting orders back to Otto, and working the till with her customary disregard for the service ethic. Lucia was famous for her rudeness and the customers were all terrified of her. I've seen senior executives reduced to grovelling if they didn't have the correct change. If the coffee and the cakes hadn't been so good, or if Lucia hadn't been so efficient, Otto's would have closed long ago. As it was, she and the café had become something of a local institution.

'Next!' she snarled as we made it to the top of the queue, and then she caught sight of me and smiled—a sight so rare that the executives now helping themselves to sugar stared in disbelief.

'Back again, *cara*?' she called, banging out old coffee grounds from the espresso machine. 'Your usual?'

'Yes, thanks, Lucia.' I smiled back at her, and then glanced at Phin, who was watching me with an oddly arrested expression. 'And…?' I prompted him.

'Americano for me,' he supplied quickly, before Lucia got impatient with him. 'No milk.'

'Why are you looking at me like that?' I asked Phin as I slid onto a shiny plastic banquette. Otto's wasn't big on style.

'I'm curious,' he said, transferring the cups to the table and pushing the tray aside.

'Curious?'

'Perhaps intrigued is a better word,' said Phin. 'You know, I've dodged guerrillas in South America, I've been charged at by a rhino and dangled by a rope over a thousand-foot crevasse, but I found Lucia pretty scary. She had every single person in that queue intimidated, but you she calls *cara*. What's that about?'

'Oh, nothing,' I said, making patterns in the cappuccino froth with my teaspoon. 'I wrote her a note once, that was all.'

'What sort of note?'

'I noticed that she wasn't here one day, mainly because the queue doesn't move nearly as fast when she's not around. I asked why not, and she told me she'd had to go back to Italy because her father had died. I wrote her a short note, just to say that I was sorry. It wasn't a big deal,' I muttered. I was rather embarrassed by the way Lucia had never forgotten it.

Phin looked at me thoughtfully. 'That was a kind thing to do.'

Feeling awkward, I sipped at my coffee. 'I didn't do much,' I said. 'Anyone can write a note.'

'But only you did.'

He picked up his doughnut and took a big bite while I watched enviously. My mouth was watering, and I was feeling quite light-headed with the lack of sugar.

'Want a bit?' he asked, offering the plate.

I flushed at the thought that he had noticed me staring. 'No...thank you,' I said primly.

'Sure? It's very good.'

I *knew* it was good. That was the trouble. 'I'm sure.'

'Suit yourself.' Phin shrugged, and finished the doughnut with unnecessary relish.

The more he enjoyed it, the crosser I got. What sort of boss was this, who dragged you out to coffee, tried to force-feed you doughnuts and then tortured you by eating them in front of you?

Scowling, I buried my face in my cappuccino.

'So, Summer Curtis,' he said, brushing sugar from his fingers at last. 'Tell me about yourself.'

It sounded like an interview question, so I sat up straighter and composed myself. 'Well, I've been working for Gibson & Grieve for five years now, the last three as assistant to the Chief Executive's PA—' I began, but Phin held up both hands.

'I don't need to know how many A levels you've got or where you've worked,' he said. 'I'm sure Lex wouldn't have appointed you if he didn't trust you absolutely. I'm more interested in finding out what makes you tick. If you're going to be my personal assistant I think we should get to know each other personally, and your work experience won't tell me anything I really need to know.'

'Like what?' I asked, disconcerted.

Phin sat back against the banquette and eyed me thoughtfully. 'Like your pet peeves, for instance. What really irritates you?'

'How long have you got?' I asked. 'Sniffing. Jiggling. Mess. Smiley faces made out of punctuation marks. Phrases like "Ah…bless…" or "I love her to bits, but…" Men who sit on the tube with their legs wide apart. Unpunctuality. Sloppy spelling and misuse of the apostrophe—that's a big one for me.' I paused, aware that I might have been getting a bit carried away. 'Do you want me to go on?'

'I think I might be getting the picture,' he said, his mouth twitching.

'I'm a bit of a perfectionist.'

'So I gathered.' I could tell he was trying not to laugh, and I was beginning to regret being so honest.

'You did ask,' I pointed out defensively.

'I did. Maybe I should have asked you what you *do* like.'

'I like my job.'

'Being a secretary?'

I nodded. 'Organisations like Gibson & Grieve don't work unless executives have proper administrative back-up. I like organising things, checking details, pulling everything together. I like making sure everything is in its right place. That's why I like filing. I find it satisfying.'

Phin didn't say anything. He just looked at me across the table.

'I'm sorry,' I said, putting up my chin. 'I do. Shoot me.'

He grinned at that. 'So…an unexpectedly kind, nitpicking perfectionist with an irrational prejudice against poor punctuation and a bizarre attachment to filing. I think we're getting somewhere. What else do I need to know about you?'

'Nothing.'

'Nothing? There must be more than that.'

I drank my coffee, unaccountably flustered. I was more thrown than I wanted to admit by the blueness of his eyes, by that lazy smile and the sheer vitality of his presence. There was a whole table between us, but I was finding it hard to breathe.

'I really don't know what you want me to tell you,' I said. 'I'm twenty-six, I share a flat in south London with a friend, and my life is the exact opposite of yours.'

His eyes gleamed at that, and he leant forward. 'What do you mean?'

'Well, you come from a wealthy family whose stores are a household name,' I pointed out. 'You make television programmes doing the kind of things the rest of us would never dare to do, and when you're not skiing down a glacier or hacking through a jungle you're at all the A-list parties— usually with a beautiful girl on your arm. The closest *I* get to an A-list party is reading about one in *Glitz*, and I'd rather stick pins in my eyes than set foot in a rainforest. We don't have a single thing in common.'

'You can't say that,' Phin objected. 'You don't really know anything about me.'

'I feel as if I do,' I told him. 'My flatmate, Anne, is your biggest fan, and after listening to her talk about you for the past two years I could take a quiz on you myself.' I pushed my empty cup aside. 'Go on—ask me. Anything,' I offered largely, and even gave him an example. 'What's your latest girlfriend called?'

A smile was tugging at the corner of Phin's mouth. 'You tell me,' he said.

'Jewel,' I said triumphantly. 'Jewel Stevens. She's an actress, and when you went to some awards ceremony last week she wore a red dress that had Anne weeping with envy.'

'But not you?'

'I think it would have looked classier in black,' I said, and Phin laughed.

'I'm impressed. Clearly I don't need to tell you anything about myself, as you know it all already. Although I think I should point out that Jewel *isn't*, in fact, my girlfriend. We've been out a couple of times, but that's all. There's no question of a real relationship, whatever the papers say.'

'I'll tell Anne. She'll be delighted,' I said. 'She's got a very active fantasy life in which you figure largely, in spite of the fact that she's very happy with her fiancé, Mark.'

'And what do you fantasise about, Summer?' asked Phin, his eyes on my face.

Ah, my fantasies. They were always the same. Jonathan realising that he had made a terrible mistake. Jonathan telling me he loved me. Jonathan asking me to marry him. We'd buy a house together. London prices being what they were, we might have to go out to the suburbs, and even pooling our resources we'd be lucky to get a semi-detached house, but that would be fine by me. I didn't need anywhere grand. I just wanted Jonathan, and somewhere I could stay.

I realise a suburban semi-detached isn't the stuff of most wild fantasies, but it was a dream that had kept me going ever since Jonathan had told me before Christmas that he 'needed some space'. He thought it was better that we didn't see each other outside the office any more. He knew how sensible I was, and was sure I would understand.

I sighed. What could I do but agree that, yes, I understood? But I lived for the brief glimpses I had of him now, and the hope that he might change his mind.

Phin was watching me expectantly, his brows raised, and I had an uneasy sense that those blue eyes could see a lot more than they ought to be able to. He was still waiting for me to answer his question.

Jonathan had been insistent that we keep our relationship a secret at the office, so I hadn't told anyone. I certainly wasn't going to start with Phin Gibson.

'I want a place of my own,' I said. 'It doesn't have to be very big—in fact I'll be lucky if I can afford a studio—but it has to be mine. It has to be somewhere I could live for ever.' I glanced at him. 'I suppose you think that's very boring?'

'It's not what I was expecting, and it's not a fantasy I understand, but it's not *boring*,' said Phin. 'I don't find much boring, to tell you the truth. People are endlessly interesting, don't you think? Obviously not!' he went straight on, seeing my sceptical expression. 'Well, *I* find them interesting. Why is it so important for you to have a home of your own?'

'Oh…I moved around a lot as a child. My mother has always been heavily into alternative lifestyles, and she's prone to sudden intense enthusiasms. One year we'd be in a commune, the next we were living on a houseboat. When my father was alive we had a couple of freezing years in a tumbledown smallholding in Wales.'

It was odd to find myself telling Phin Gibson, of all people, about my childhood. I didn't normally talk about it much—not that it had been particularly traumatic, but it was hard for most people I knew to understand what it was like growing up with a mother who was as charming and lovely and flaky as they come—and there was something about the way he was listening, his expression intent and his attention absolutely focused on me, that unlocked my usual reserve.

'Wales was the closest we ever got to settling down,' I told him. 'The rest of the time we kept moving. Not because we had to, but because my mother was always looking for something more.

'Basically,' I said, 'she's got the attention span of a gnat. I lost count of the schools I attended, of the weird and wonderful places we lived for a few months before moving on.'

I turned the cup and saucer between my fingers. 'I suppose it's inevitable I grew up craving security the way others crave excitement. My mother can't understand it, though. She's living in a tepee in Somerset at the moment, and for her the thought of buying a flat and settling down is incomprehensible. I'm a big disappointment to her,' I finished wryly.

'There you are—we've something in common after all,' said Phin, sitting back with a smile and stretching his long legs out under the table. 'I'm a big disappointment to my parents, too.'

CHAPTER TWO

I LOOKED at him in surprise. 'But you're famous,' I said. I'd known Lex wasn't impressed by his younger brother, but had assumed that his parents at least would be pleased by his success. 'You've had a successful television career.'

'My parents aren't impressed by television.' Phin smiled wryly. 'They think the media generally is shallow and frivolous—certainly compared to the serious business of running Gibson & Grieve. Lex and I were brought up to believe that the company was all that mattered, and that it was the only future we could ever have or ever want.'

'When did you change your mind?'

'When I realised that there wasn't really a place for me here. Lex is older than me, and anyway he had Chief Executive written all over him even as a toddler. Gibson & Grieve was all he ever cared about.'

It was my turn to study Phin. He was looking quite relaxed, leaning back against the banquette, but I sensed that this wasn't an easy topic of conversation for him.

'Didn't you ever want to be part of it, too?'

'As a very small boy I used to love going into the office,' he admitted. 'But as I got bigger I didn't fit. I was always being told to be quiet or sit still, and I didn't like doing either of those things. I wanted to skid over the shiny floors, or play football, or fiddle with the new computers. After a while I stopped going.'

Phin's smile was a little crooked. 'Of course it's easy now to see that I was just a spoilt brat looking for attention, but at the time it felt as if I were reacting against all their expectations. Lex was always there, doing what he should, and there never seemed any point in me doing the same. I got into as much trouble as I could instead,' he said. 'My parents were beside themselves. They didn't know what to do with me, and I didn't know what to do with myself. I don't think they ever thought I would get a degree, and I took off as soon as I'd graduated. I suspect that they were glad to be rid of me! I mean, what would they have done with me at Gibson & Grieve? I didn't fit with the image at all!'

No, he wouldn't have done, I thought. In spite of its commitment to style, Gibson & Grieve was at heart a very solid, traditional company—it was one of the reasons I liked it—and Phin would have been too chaotic, too vibrant, too energetic to ever properly fit in.

'So what did you do?' I asked, wondering how he was going to fit in now that he was back.

'I messed around for a few years,' he said. 'I worked my way around the world. I didn't care what I did as long as I was somewhere I could keep my adrenalin pumping—skiing, sailing, white-water rafting, climbing, sky-diving…I tried them all. I spent some time in the Amazon and learnt jungle survival skills, and then I got a job leading a charity expedition, and that led onto behind the scenes advice on a reality TV programme.'

He shrugged. 'It seems I came across well on camera, and the next thing I knew they'd offered me my own programme, taking ill-assorted groups into challenging situations.'

And I knew what had happened after that. It had taken no time at all for Phin Gibson to become a celebrity, almost as famous as Gibson & Grieve itself.

'And now you've joined the company,' I said.

'I have.' Phin was silent for a moment, looking down at his hands, which lay lightly clasped on the table, and then he looked up at me and the blueness of his eyes was so intense that I actually drew a sharp breath.

'Last year I took a group of young offenders on a gruelling trek through Peru,' he said.

I remembered the programme. I had watched it with Anne, and even I had had to admit that the change in those boys by the end of the trek was extraordinary.

'I recognised myself in them,' Phin said. 'It made me think about how difficult it must have been for my parents. I guess I'd grown up in spite of myself.'

His mouth quirked in a self-deprecating grin, then he sobered. 'My father had a stroke last year as well. That put a new perspective on everything. It seemed to me that it was time to try and make some amends. My mother has got it into her mind that all Dad wants is for me to settle down and take up my inheritance at Gibson & Grieve.'

He sighed a little. 'To be honest, it's a little hard to know exactly what Dad wants now, but he did manage to squeeze my hand when my mother told him what she had in mind. Basically, a certain amount of emotional blackmail is being applied! In lots of ways it's worse for Lex,' Phin went on thoughtfully. 'He stepped into my father's shoes as Chief Executive, and he's been doing a good job. Profits are up. Everyone's happy. The last thing he wants is me muddying the waters. In the end he suggested that we capitalise on my "celebrity", for want of better word, and make me the new face of Gibson & Grieve. You know we've just acquired Gregson's?'

He cocked an eyebrow at me and I nodded. The acquisition had made the headlines a few months ago when it happened.

'Supermarkets are a change of direction for us,' Phin went on. 'Our brand has always been up-market, even exclusive, and we need more of a popular, family-friendly image now. Lex seems to think I can help with that, and I agreed to see how it went for a year initially, on condition that I could finish a couple of filming commitments.'

I smoothed my skirt over my knees. I was feeling a bit bad, if you want the truth. I'd dismissed Phin as a spoilt celebrity and assumed that he was choosing to dabble in the family business for a while. I hadn't realised that he was under some pressure.

'It makes sense for you to be Director of Media Relations,' I offered.

'I think we all know how little that means,' said Phin, leaning across the table, and I found myself leaning back as if pushed there by the sheer force of his personality. 'Lex's idea is to shunt me off and just wheel me out to be photographed every now and then. As far as he's concerned all the media relations will be done by his PR guy…what's his name? John?'

'Jonathan Pugh.'

Just saying his name was enough to bump my heart into my throat, and my tongue felt thick and unwieldy in my mouth. I wondered if Phin would notice how husky I sounded, but he didn't seem to.

'Yep, that's him,' was all he said, sitting back again. 'A born suit.'

I bridled at the dismissive note in his voice. I'd been quite liking Phin until then, but I was very sensitive to any criticism of Jonathan. At least Jonathan dressed professionally, unlike *some* people I could mention, I thought, eyeing Phin's T-shirt disapprovingly.

'Jonathan's very good at his job,' I said stiffly.

'Lex wouldn't employ him unless he was,' said Phin. 'But if he's that good there won't be much left for me to do, will there? I'm not going to spend a year opening stores and saving Lex the trouble of turning up at charity bashes.'

'Then why come back if you're not going to do anything?' I asked, still ruffled by his dismissal of Jonathan.

'But I am going to do something,' he said. 'Lex just doesn't know it yet. If I'm going to be part of Gibson & Grieve, I'm going to make a difference.'

Oh, dear. I had a nasty feeling this was the kind of thing Lex had meant when he had told me to stop Phin doing anything stupid.

'How?' I asked warily.

'By increasing our range of fair trade products. Promoting links with communities here and overseas. Being more aware of environmental issues. Developing our staff and providing more training. Making *connections*,' said Phin. 'We're all part of chain. It doesn't matter if we're picking tea in Sri Lanka, stacking it on the shelves in Sheffield or buying it in Swindon. We should be celebrating the connections between people, not pretending that the only thing that matters is underlying operating profit or consensus forecasts.'

I was secretly impressed that Phin even knew about consensus forecasts, but I couldn't see any of this going down well with Lex.

I nibbled my thumb. It's a bad habit of mine when I'm unsure. 'And you haven't discussed any of this with your brother yet?'

'Not yet, no,' he said. 'I wanted to get to know you first.'

'Me?' I was taken aback. 'Why?'

'Because if I'm going to get anything done I need a team. I need to be sure that we can work together, and that we share the same goals.'

The blue, blue eyes fixed on me with that same unnerving intensity. 'You've been working for Lex, and I know his staff are all very loyal to him. I'm not trying to take over, but there's no use pretending he's going to share my ideas, and I don't want to put you in a difficult position. If you'd rather not work with me to change things, this is the time to say, Summer. I'm sure Lex would give you your old job back if you wanted it, and there'd be no hard feelings.'

I'll admit it. I hesitated. There was part of me that longed to go back to the Chief Executive's office—which buzzed with drive, where everyone was cool and efficient, and where there was no Phin Gibson with his unsettling presence and alarming ideas about change. I didn't like change. I'd had enough of change as a child. I wanted everything to stay the same.

But this was my big chance. When Anne got married I was going to have to move out of the flat. With my new salary I might be able to save enough to put down a deposit on a place of my own by then. It was only for a year, too, I reminded myself. When it was up, I'd be in a good position to get another job at the same level in spite of my age. It would be worth putting up with Phin until then.

So I met the blue eyes squarely. 'I don't want my old job back,' I said. 'I want to be part of your team.'

I was sorting through the post the next morning when Phin appeared. Late again. Hadn't he ever heard of a nine-to-five day at work?

He had spent no more than a couple of hours in the office after we had got back from Otto's, before disappearing to a meeting with his producer.

'But I've read all my e-mails, you'll be glad to hear,' he said as he left. 'I take back everything I said about never being bored. All that corporate jargon puts me to sleep faster than a cup of cocoa. I'm never going to make it through a meeting if these guys actually talk like that.'

It would be nice to think he would ever be there to *go* to a meeting, I thought crossly.

It was after ten, and I had been in a dilemma about when to have the doughnut I'd bought earlier at Otto's. Having forgone my treat the day before, I was determined not to miss out again, but I wanted a few minutes to myself, so that I could enjoy it properly. I needed Phin to be in his office, so that I knew where he was.

Not knowing when he might appear had been making me twitchy, so when Phin strolled in and wished me a cheerful good morning I glared at him over the top of my glasses.

'Where have you been?' I demanded.

'You know,' Phin confided, 'that librarian thing you've got going really works for me.'

'What librarian thing?' I asked, thrown.

'The fierce glasses on the chain, the scraped back hair, the neat suit…' He grinned at my expression, which must have been dumbfounded. That's certainly how I felt. 'Please say you're about to shake out your hair and tell me you're going to have to be very strict with me for being late!'

I'd never met anyone like Phin before, and I was completely flummoxed. 'What on earth are you talking about?'

'Never mind,' he said. 'I was just getting a bit carried away there. What was it you wanted to know again?'

'I was wondering where you'd been,' I said tightly. 'It's after ten. I was expecting you here an hour ago at least.'

'I went into the Oxford Street store to see how things are going,' said Phin casually, picking up the post from my desk and leafing idly through it. 'I thought it would be an idea to meet the staff and hear what they think, and it was very useful.' He looked up at me, his eyes disconcertingly blue and amused. 'Why? Should I have asked permission?'

I pressed my lips together. 'It's not a question of permission,' I said. 'But there's no point in having a PA unless you let me know where you are. I need to be able to make appointments for you, and I can't do that if I've no idea when you're going to turn up.'

'Who wants an appointment?'

'Well, no one, as it happens,' I was forced to admit. 'But they might have done. It's a matter of principle.'

'Principle? That sounds serious.' Phin dropped the post back onto the desk and without thinking I squared up the pile, looking up when he sucked in his breath alarmingly.

'What's the matter?' I asked, startled.

'I don't know…' He was squinting at the pile I'd tidied. 'I think those papers at the bottom might be half a millimetre out of alignment.'

'Sarcasm—excellent,' I said. Sarcastically. That was all I needed. 'Thank you so much.'

He held up his hands. 'It's nothing, honestly. Just one more service we offer.'

My lips tightened. I tried to pick up the conversation. 'Perhaps we should agree a system.'

'A system,' said Phin, testing the word as if he'd never heard it before. 'Fine. What sort of system?'

'If you let me have your mobile number, so that I can get

hold of you if I need to, that would be a start. And then perhaps we could sit down and go through your diary.'

'Absolutely. Let's do it.' He clenched his fist and punched it in the air, to demonstrate an enthusiasm I was perfectly aware he didn't feel. 'Let's do it now, in fact.'

'Fine.'

We exchanged mobile numbers, and then I carried the diary into his office. I would put all the details on the computer later, but it was easier at this stage to use an old-fashioned hard copy.

I sat down with the diary on my knee, while Phin fished out a personal organiser and leaned back in his chair so that he could prop his feet on the desk.

'What do you want to know?'

'I'd better have everything.' I smoothed the page open, admiring in passing how nice my hands looked. I take care of my nails, and today they were painted a lovely pale pink called Dew at Dawn. 'If you're the face of Gibson & Grieve, you'll be expected to appear at various functions and I'll need to know when you're available.'

'Fair enough.'

He had an extraordinarily complicated social life, with two or three events an evening as far as I could make out. I couldn't help comparing it with my own , which largely consisted of painting my nails in front of the television, watching Anne getting ready to go out with Mark and feeling miserable about Jonathan.

'This is great,' said Phin when we'd finished. 'I never need to remember anything by myself ever again. Maybe I won't mind being an executive after all. What else is there to do?'

'There's a meeting to discuss the new media strategy at

half past ten,' I said, handing him a folder. 'Your brother suggested you went along if you were here on time. I've noted all the salient points, and included copies of recent minutes so you know the background.'

'Salient points?' he echoed, amazed. 'I didn't realise people still said things like that any more!'

I chose to ignore that, and looked pointedly at my watch instead. 'You should get going. You've only got a couple of minutes and you don't want to be late.'

'You mean *you* don't want me to be late,' said Phin, but he swung his legs down from the desk.

I could hardly wait for him to go. I practically shoved him out of the door towards the lifts. Lex's office was on the floor above, and as soon as I saw him step into the lift I scurried down the corridor to the kitchen to make myself some coffee.

My office, and Phin's of course, was in a prime location on the corner of the building, with fabulous views of Trafalgar Square, but more importantly we were at the end of the corridor, which meant that nobody dropped in just because they were passing.

Even so, I closed the door as a precaution and prepared to enjoy my doughnut in private. I settled happily behind my desk with my coffee and cleared a space. Eating a doughnut could be a messy business. Perhaps that was why it always felt faintly naughty to me.

At last. I pulled out the doughnut and took a bite, mumbling with pleasure as my teeth sank into the sugary dough.

And then froze as the door opened and Phin came in. 'I forgot that file—' he began, and then it was his turn to stop as he took in the sight of me, sitting guiltily behind my desk, doughnut in hand and mouth full.

His eyes lit with amusement. 'Aha! Caught red-handed, I see.'

Blushing furiously, I dropped the doughnut and brushed at the sugar moustache I could feel on my top lip. 'I thought you'd gone,' I blustered, mortified at having been caught in such an unprofessional pose.

'Now I know why you were so keen to get rid of me,' said Phin. 'This is a new side to you. How very, very unlikely. Who would have thought that sensible Summer Curtis would have a doughnut addiction!' He leant conspiratorially towards me. 'Does anyone else know?'

'It's not an *addiction*,' I said, trying for some dignity. 'I just work better if I've had some sugar in the morning.'

'Well, I'm delighted to find that you've got a weakness. I was finding all that perfection just a little intimidating.' He grinned. 'It's good to know that when it comes down to it you can't resist temptation either.'

Of course, then I had to prove him wrong.

The next day, when I called in to buy my usual cappuccino on my way into work, I refused the doughnut Lucia offered and felt virtuous. This would be the start of a new regime, I vowed. I didn't need a sugar fix, anyway. That was just silly. I would stick to coffee—a much less embarrassing habit and one that was less likely to lead to humiliation.

And I made it all the way to the lifts before I started to regret my resolution. Why shouldn't I have a mid-morning snack? It wasn't as if eating a doughnut was immoral or illegal. I blamed Phin for making me feel guilty about it. It was more satisfying than blaming myself.

Already I could already feel the craving twitching away in the pit of my stomach, making me tense. It didn't bode well for the rest of the day, and I hoped everyone would give me a wide berth. I wasn't known for my easygoing attitude on the best of days, and I had a feeling this most definitely wasn't going to be a good one.

At least Phin managed to turn up before ten o'clock, looking distinctly the worse for wear.

'I hope I get a gold star for turning up early,' he said.

I thinned my lips, still illogically determined to blame him for my doughnut-less day. 'I'd hardly call ten *early*,' I said repressively.

'It is for me.' Phin yawned. 'I had a very late night.'

I wondered how much his lack of sleep was due to the beautiful Jewel Stevens. According to last night's *Metro*, the two of them were 'inseparable'. Not that I was scouring gossip columns for news of my new boss, you understand. In spite of taking a book to read on the tube every day, I somehow always ended up devouring the free paper on the way home. When it's pressed into your hand, it seems rude not to.

Phin's name just happened to catch my eye—honest. There had even been a picture of him at some party, with Jewel entwined around his arm. I know I'm in no position to talk about stupid names, but really…Jewel? I'd put money on the fact that she was christened Julie. In the picture Phin had a faintly wary look, but that might have been the flash. He certainly didn't look as if he were pushing her away.

Why would he? She was dark and sultry, with legs up to her armpits, a beestung mouth and masses of rippling black hair. Every man's fantasy, in fact.

I felt vaguely depressed at the thought, and then worried by the fact that I was depressed—until I realised it must just be the lack of sugar getting to me.

'No, really, though. I'll be fine,' said Phin, when I failed to offer the expected sympathy. 'There's no need to make a fuss.'

I sighed and narrowed my eyes at him.

'I can tell that deep down you're really worried,' he said, and when I just looked back at him without expression he wisely took himself off into his office.

'I'll survive,' he promised, just before he shut the door. 'But if I don't, you're not to feel bad, OK?'

All was quiet for nearly an hour. I was betting that he had gone to catch up on his sleep on one of those sofas, but frankly I was glad to get rid of him for a while. I tried to soothe myself with a little filing, but a few days wasn't long enough to generate much of a backlog, and I couldn't stop thinking about how good a doughnut would taste with a cup of coffee.

Perhaps Phin was right. Perhaps I really was addicted, I fretted. I even considered sneaking out to Otto's, but couldn't take the chance of Phin waking up and finding me gone. I'd never hear the end of it.

The more I tried not to think about doughnuts, the more I wanted one, and it was almost a relief when Phin buzzed me. Yes, buzzed me—like a real executive! Maybe he would get the hang of corporate life after all.

'It's almost eleven,' came his voice through the intercom. 'Am I allowed to have coffee yet?'

'Of course,' I said, glad of the distraction from my dough-nut craving, and relieved to be able to act as a normal PA for a change. 'I'll bring you some in.'

'Bring yourself some, too. We need to do some planning. You'll like that.'

Planning. That sounded more like it. I switched my phone through, wedged my notebook under my arm, and took in a pot of coffee and two cups on a tray.

I half expected to find Phin lying on one of the sofas, but he was sitting behind his desk, apparently immersed in something he was reading on the computer screen. He looked up when I pushed open the door with my elbow, though, and got to his feet.

'Let's make ourselves comfortable,' he said, guiding me over to the sofas and producing a familiar-looking paper bag from a drawer. 'I thought we'd have a little something with our coffee,' he said, waving it under my nose.

He'd brought two doughnuts.

It was all I could do not to drool. I've no idea what my expression was like, but judging by the laughter in the blue eyes it was a suitable picture.

'*Now* aren't you sorry you weren't more sympathetic?' he asked as he set the doughnuts out on a paper napkin each.

I eyed them longingly. 'I've just decided to give them up,' I said, but Phin only clicked his tongue.

'You can't do that just when I've found a weakness I can ruthlessly exploit,' he said. 'Besides, you told me yourself you needed a sugar fix in order to concentrate. You'll just get grumpy otherwise.'

Unfortunately that was all too true.

'Take it as an order, if that helps,' he said as I hesitated. 'Keeping me company on the doughnut front is compulsory. If I'd been able to appoint my own PA I'd have put it in the job description.'

What could I do? 'Well, if you insist…' I said, giving in.

I sat on one sofa, Phin sat on the other, and we bit into our doughnuts at the same time.

I can't tell you how good mine tasted. I laughed as I licked sugar from my fingers. 'Mmm…yum-yum,' I said, and then stopped as I saw Phin's arrested expression. 'What?'

'Nothing. I was just realising I hadn't heard you laugh yet,' he said. 'You should do it more often.

My eyes slid away from his. 'It's easy to laugh when you're being force-fed doughnuts,' I said after a tiny pause. I was very aware of him watching me, and I licked sugar from my lips with the tip of my tongue, suddenly uncomfortable as the silence stretched.

I cleared my throat. 'What exactly did you want to plan?' I said.

'Plan?' echoed Phin, sounding oddly distracted.

'You said we needed to do some planning,' I reminded him.

'Oh, yes…' He seemed to recover himself. 'Well, I had a chat about my role here with Lex last night, and we discussed things in a civilised manner.'

'Really?'

'No, not really. We had a knock-down-drag-out fight, and shouted at each other for a good hour. It didn't quite come to fisticuffs, but it was touch and go at one point. Just like being boys again,' he said reflectively.

I couldn't imagine anyone daring to shout at Lex, but then Phin was a self-confessed adrenalin junkie and obviously thrived on danger.

'What happened?' I asked a little nervously. I hoped Phin hadn't enraged his brother so much that we would be both be out of a job.

'I'd like to claim utter victory, but I'd be lying,' Phin admitted. 'Lex wasn't budging when it came to renegotiating our suppliers, but he did agree eventually that I could start to build up links with communities overseas. In return I had to promise to co-operate fully on the PR front. Apparently he's lined up a feature in *Glitz* already.'

Phin shrugged as he finished his doughnut and brushed the sugar from his hands. 'So, not everything I wanted, I'll admit, but it's a start.'

'Well…good,' I said, feeling a little uncertain. 'What happens next?'

'We'd better keep Lex quiet about the PR,' he decided. 'Make arrangements for that interview, and talk to Jonathan Pugh about what they want.'

Talk to Jonathan! *Talk to Jonathan.* My stomach clenched with excitement. I had a reason to go and talk to Jonathan! My handwriting was ridiculously shaky as I made a note, although there was no chance of me forgetting that particular task.

Phin was talking about a trip to Cameroon he was planning but I hardly listened. I was too busy imagining my meeting with Jonathan.

This would be my first chance to talk to him properly since that awful evening when he had told me it 'wasn't working' for him. I had seen him around the office, of course, but never alone, and I was sure that he was avoiding me. I'd been holding onto the hope that if we could just spend some time together again he would change his mind.

I would play it cool, of course, I decided. Surely he knew that I was the last person to make a fuss? I would be calm and reasonable and undemanding. What more could he want? *I've missed you, Summer,* I imagined him saying as the scales dropped from his eyes and he realised that I was just what he needed after all. *You've no idea how much.*

But if he had missed me, why hadn't he told me? I puzzled over that one. OK, maybe he had just been waiting for the right moment. Or he'd thought I was busy.

It even sounded lame in my fantasy, which wasn't a good sign.

I suddenly realised that Phin had stopped talking and was looking at me enquiringly. 'So what do you think?' he asked.

'Um…sounds good to me,' I said hastily, without a clue as to what he'd been talking about. 'Great idea.'

His brows lifted in surprise. 'Well, that's good. To be honest, I didn't think you'd go for it.'

'Oh?' I regarded him warily. That sounded ominous. 'Er…what exactly didn't you think I'd like?'

'Staff development in Cameroon,' he prompted, but his eyes had started to dance.

'What?'

Phin tried to look severe, but a smile tugged at the corner of his mouth. 'Summer, is it possible you weren't listening to a word I was saying?'

I squirmed. 'I may have got distracted there for a moment or two,' I admitted feebly.

He tutted. 'That's not like you, Summer. After I gave you sugar, too! I've just explained about my plan to take a group from Head Office to Cameroon for a couple of weeks, to help build a medical centre in one of the villages I know there. It's a great way to start forging links between the company and a community, and everyone who goes will get so much out of it. But you don't need to worry about it yet. You'll have plenty of time to prepare.'

'Hold on,' I said, alarmed by the way this was going. 'Me? Prepare for what?'

'Of course you'll be coming, too,' said Phin, with what I was sure was malicious pleasure in my consternation. 'We're a team, remember? This is our scheme. It's important that you're really part of it. What better way than to go as part of the first group, to find out what it's like out there?'

CHAPTER THREE

'YOU'RE not serious?'

'I'm always serious, Summer,' said Phin. His face was perfectly straight, but I've never seen anything less serious than the expression in the blue eyes right then.

I stared at him, aghast. 'No way am I going to Africa!'

'Why on earth not?'

'I don't like bugs.'

'There's more to the rainforest than bugs, Summer.'

'The rainforest?' My eyes started from my head. How much had I missed here? 'Oh, no. No, no, no. The jungle? No way. Absolutely not.'

'You'd like it.'

'I wouldn't,' I said, still shaking my head firmly from side to side. I'd seen him leading those poor people through enough rainforests on *Into the Wild* to know just what it would be like. They spent their whole time struggling through rampant vegetation, or slithering down muddy slopes in stifling humidity, so that their hair was plastered to their heads and their shirts wringing with sweat.

There was almost always a shot of Phin taking off his shirt and rinsing it in the water. Anne's favourite bit, in fact. Whenever they reached a river she'd sit up straighter and call out, 'Shirt alert!' and sigh gustily at the glimpse of Phin's lean, muscled body.

I didn't sigh, of course, but I did look, and even I had to admit—although not to Anne, of course—that it was a body worth sighing over if you were into that kind of thing.

But I certainly wasn't prepared to trek through the rainforest myself to see it at first hand.

'It sounds awful,' I told Phin. 'Hot and sweaty and crawling with insects…ugh.'

He leant forward, fixing me with that unnerving blue gaze. 'You say hot and sweaty, Summer,' he said, rocking his hand in an either/or gesture. 'I say heat and passion and excitement.'

Heat. Passion. Excitement. They were so not me. But something about the words in Phin's mouth made me shift uneasily on the sofa. 'And what on earth makes you think I would like that?' I asked, with what I hoped was a quelling look.

'Your mouth.'

It was a bit like missing a step. I had the same lurch of the heart, punching the air from my lungs, the same hollowness in the stomach. My eyes were riveted to Phin's, and all at once their blueness was so intense that I felt quite dizzy with the effort of not tumbling into it.

'It just doesn't go with the rest of you,' he went on conversationally, while I was still opening and closing the mouth in question. 'You're all cool and crisp and buttoned up in your suit. But that mouth…' He put his head on one side and studied it. 'It makes me think there's more to you than that. It makes me think that you might have a secretly sensual side… Am I right?'

'Certainly not,' I blustered, unable to think of a suitably crushing reply. 'I can assure you that there isn't a single bit of me that wants to go to the rainforest.'

Phin clicked his tongue and shook his head sadly.

'Summer, Summer…I never thought you'd be a coward. Isn't it time you stepped out of your comfort zone and explored a different side of yourself?'

'I'm not into exploration,' I said coldly. 'That's the thing about comfort zones. They're comfortable. I've got no intention of making myself *un*comfortable if I don't have to.'

'But I'm afraid you *do* have to,' said Phin. 'You're on my team, and my team is going to Cameroon, whether you want to or not. So you'd better get used to the idea.'

I looked mutinously back at him. He was smiling, but there was an inflexibility to his jaw, a certain flintiness at the back of the blue eyes, that gave me pause and, like the coward Phin called me, I opted out of an argument just then.

I was sent off to liaise with Human Resources and find candidates for the first staff development trip. Phin said that he would organise everything at the Cameroonian end, but it would be my job to sort out flights, insurance, and all the other practicalities involved in taking a group of people overseas.

I didn't mind doing that as long as I didn't have to go myself. Still, he could hardly force me onto the plane, could he? I would be able to get out of it somehow, I reassured myself, and in the meantime I was much more excited about organising the *Glitz* interview. This was the chance I had dreamed about. At last I had a real reason to be in touch with Jonathan again.

Putting Africa out of my mind, I sat down to compose an e-mail to him. My heart was beating wildly at the mere thought of seeing him again, and I didn't trust my voice on the phone.

All I had to do was suggest that we meet the next day to discuss the *Glitz* feature, but you wouldn't believe how long it took me to produce a couple of lines that struck just the right balance between friendliness and cool professionalism.

I knew Jonathan would want to get involved. *Glitz* was

stacked at every supermarket checkout in the land, and a positive piece about Phin taking up a new role at Gibson & Grieve would be fantastic publicity for us. Jonathan wouldn't let a PR opportunity like this go past without making sure Phin's office—i.e. me—was onboard.

Sure enough, he came back straight away.

Good idea. 12.30 tomorrow my office? J

Not a long message, but I read it as carefully as the floweriest of love letters, desperate to decipher the subtext.

Good idea… That was encouraging, wasn't it? I mean, he could have just said *OK*, couldn't he? Or *fine*. So I chose to see some warmth there. Also, he'd signed it with an initial. That was an intimate kind of thing to do. Not as good as if he'd added a kiss, of course, but still better than a more formal *Jonathan*.

But the bit that really got my heart thumping with anticipation was the time. Twelve-thirty. Was it just the only time he could fit me in, or had he chosen it deliberately so that he could suggest lunch?

Naturally I spent the entire afternoon composing a suitable reply. The resulting masterpiece ran as follows: 12.30 tomorrow fine for me. See you then. S. And, yes, my finger did hover over the *x* key for a while before I decided on discretion. I didn't want to appear too pushy. Jonathan would hate that.

I discarded the idea of suggesting lunch myself for the same reason. But just in case Jonathan *was* thinking that we could discuss a PR strategy for Phin over an intimate lunch somewhere, I was determined to be prepared. Normally I'm very confident about putting outfits together, but I spent hours that night, dithering in front of my wardrobe, unable to decide what to wear the next day.

'What do you think?' I asked Anne.

I had dragged her away from yet another repeat of *Into the Wild*—wasn't there anything else on television?—so she wasn't best pleased. She sprawled grouchily on the bed.

'What I *think* is that you're wasting your time,' she said frankly. 'Face it, Summer, Jonathan's just not that into you. He's already made that crystal-clear.'

'He might change his mind,' I said, and even I could hear the edge of desperation in my voice.

'He won't,' said Anne, who had never liked Jonathan. 'Why can't you see it?' She sighed at my stubborn expression. 'For someone so clear-thinking, you're incredibly obtuse when it comes to Jonathan,' she told me. 'It's not like he ever made any effort for you, even when you were seeing each other. Why was he so keen to keep your affair a secret? It wasn't like either of you were involved with anyone else.'

'Jonathan didn't think it was appropriate to have a relationship in the office,' I said primly.

'You weren't *having* a relationship,' said Anne, exasperated. 'That was the whole point. You weren't even having much of an affair. You were just sleeping together when it suited Jonathan. If he'd been really keen on you he wouldn't have cared who knew. If he'd loved you he would have wanted to show you off, not hide you away as if he was ashamed of you.'

'Jonathan's not the kind of person who shows off,' I said, aware that I sounded defensive. 'I like that about him. He's sensible.'

'I think you're mad!' she said, throwing up her hands. 'I can't believe you spend every day with a hot guy like Phin Gibson and you're still obsessing about Jonathan Pugh!'

'Phin's not that hot,' I said, dismissing Anne's objections as I always did. 'And anyway, he's my boss. And we all know his idea of commitment is making it through to dessert without feeling trapped. I'm certainly not going to waste my time falling for him. That really would be mad! Now, concentrate, Anne. This is important. The twinset or the jacket?'

I held them on hangers in each hand. The cropped jacket was one of my favourites, a deep red with three-quarter-length sleeves, a shawl collar and a nipped-in waist. 'Too smart?' I asked dubiously. 'I don't want to look as if I'm trying too hard. But maybe the cardigan is a bit casual for the office?'

I'd bought the twinset with my Christmas bonus. A mixture of angora and cashmere, it was so beautifully soft I hadn't been able to resist it. I liked to take it out and stroke it, as if it were a kitten. To be honest, I wasn't sure that the colour— a dusty pink—was quite *me*, and I never felt entirely comfortable with the prettiness of it all, so I'd never worn it to the office. It was very different from my usual smartly tailored look, but perhaps different was what I needed.

Anne agreed. 'The twinset,' she said without hesitation. 'It's a much softer look for you, and if you leave your hair loose as well it'll practically scream *touch me, touch me*. Even Jonathan won't be able to miss the point.'

The hair was a step too far for me. If I turned up at work with my hair falling to my shoulders *everyone* would get the point. I might as well hang out a sign saying 'On the Pull'. So I tied my hair back as usual, but made up with extra care and painted my nails a pretty pink: Bubblegum—much nicer than it sounds. I wore the twinset, with a short grey skirt and heels just a little higher than usual.

Phin whistled when he came in—late, as usual—and saw me. 'You look very fetching, Summer,' he said. 'What's the occasion?'

'No occasion,' I said. 'I just felt like a change of image.'

'It's certainly that,' he said. 'You look very…touchable. How many people have stroked you to see if that cardigan is as soft as it looks?'

'A lot,' I said with a sigh. I'd lost count of the women who'd stroked my arm and ooh-ed and aah-ed over its softness. I couldn't blame them, really. Wearing it was like being cuddled by a kitten. 'It's a bit disconcerting to have perfect strangers running their hands down your arm.'

'But you can understand why they do,' said Phin. 'In fact, I'm sorry, but I'm just going to have to do it myself. I don't count as a perfect stranger, do I?' Without waiting for my reply, he smoothed his own hand down from my shoulder to my elbow, and I felt it through the fine wool like a brand. 'Incredibly soft,' he said, 'and very unexpected.'

Funny—I'd never felt anyone else's stroke quite like that. My skin was tingling where his fingers had touched me. I swallowed.

'I think I'll go back to a suit tomorrow.'

'That would be a shame,' said Phin. 'I like this new look a lot.'

Now all I needed was for Jonathan to like it, too. If the cardigan had the same effect on him, it would be worth feeling self-conscious now.

For the first time I realised that Phin didn't look quite his normal self either that morning. There was a distinctly frazzled air about him, and his shirt was even more crumpled than usual. Probably partying all night again with Jewel, I thought unsympathetically.

I was sure of it when he suggested having coffee immediately. 'In keeping with today's theme, I've bought Danish pastries for a change,' he said. 'I'm badly in need of some sugar!'

'Hangover?' I asked sweetly.

'Just a very fraught morning,' said Phin with a humorous look. 'I never thought I'd be glad to say I had to go to the office!'

He didn't say any more, and I didn't ask. I was too busy checking the clock every couple of minutes and willing the hands to move faster.

I decided that if Jonathan didn't suggest lunch, I would. I would make it very casual. *Do you want to grab a sandwich while we're talking?* Something like that.

I mouthed the words as my fingers rattled over the keyboard. The trouble was that I didn't do casual very well. Look how astounded everyone was when I appeared in a cardigan.

I knew the words would come out sounding stiff and awkward if I didn't get it right, but how was I supposed to practise when Phin was in and out of my office every five minutes, asking how to send a fax from his computer, wanting to borrow my stapler, giving me the dates for the Cameroon trip—about which I was still trying to keep a *very* low profile.

'You know, you could just buzz me and I'd come in to you,' I said, exasperated, in the end.

'I'd rather come out,' said Phin, picking up a couple of spare ink cartridges from my desk and attempting to juggle them. 'I feel trapped if I have to sit down for too long.'

I detoured back from the photocopier to snatch the cartridges out of the air. I put them in a desk drawer and shut it firmly as I sat down.

'Why don't you go for a walk?' I suggested through clenched teeth.

'It's funny you should say that. My producer just e-mailed me to say that we're going back to finish filming in Peru next week, so I'll be doing the last part of the trek again. I'll be away about twelve days.' Now he had my stapler in his hand,

and was holding it out to me like a microphone. 'Do you think you'll miss me?'

'Frankly, no,' I said, taking the stapler from him and setting it back on the desk with a click. I glanced at the clock. Just past midday! I didn't have long. 'Are you going out for lunch?' I asked hopefully.

'I haven't got any plans,' said Phin. 'I might just—'

That was when my mother rang. As if I didn't have enough to cope with that morning!

'I just *had* to tell you,' she said excitedly. 'A new galactic portal is opening today!'

I love my mother, but sometimes I do wonder how we can possibly be related. I'd suspect a mix-up in the hospital if I hadn't been born into a commune, with who knows how many people dancing and chanting and shaking bells around my mother. It must have been the most godawful racket, and if had been me I would have told them all to go away and leave me to give birth in peace. But of course Mum—or Starlight, as she prefers to be called nowadays—was in her element. The wackier the situation, the more she loves it.

I pinched the bridge of my nose between thumb and forefinger. I knew better than to ask what a galactic portal was.

'That's great, Mum,' I said. 'Look, I can't really talk now—'

But she was already telling me about some ceremony she had taken part in the night before, that apparently involved much channelling of angels and merging of heart chakras.

'Such a beautiful spiritual experience!' she sighed. 'So empowering! The energy vibrations now are quite extraordinary. Can't you *feel* them?'

I resisted the urge to bang my head against my desk.

'Er, no—no, I can't just this moment,' I said, aware that Phin was eavesdropping. I couldn't imagine him caring about the fact that this was obviously a personal phone call, but I hoped he couldn't hear anyway. My mother was deadly serious but, let's face it, she could sound nuts.

'That's because you're not open to the energy, darling,' my mother told me reproachfully. 'Have you been entering the crystal the way I showed you? You must let the love flow through your chakras.'

'Yes, yes, I will,' I said, one eye on the clock. After dragging all morning, it was suddenly whizzing round. If I wasn't careful, I'd be late for Jonathan. 'The thing is, Mum, I'm actually quite busy right now. Can I call you later?'

I'd finally managed to give her a mobile phone, which I paid for by direct debit. I knew she would never keep it topped up herself. My mother preferred spiritual forms of communication to the humdrum practicalities of paying phone bills or keeping track of credit.

'That would be lovely, darling, but I'll be seeing you soon,' she said. 'I'm coming to London, so we can talk properly then.'

Another time I would have been alarmed at her casual mention of a London visit, but I was desperate to get her off the phone before my meeting with Jonathan.

'That's great,' I said instead. 'Bye, then, Mum.'

I caught Phin's eye as I put the phone down. 'That was my mother,' I said unnecessarily.

'Is everything OK?'

'Oh, yes, fine,' I said airily. 'A new galactic portal is opening. You know how it is.'

'Blimey.' Phin sounded impressed. 'Is that good or bad?'

'I've no idea. Whatever it is, it seems to be keeping my mother busy.' I glanced at the clock again. Twelve-fourteen. I should think about getting ready.

I gathered my papers into a file and stood up. Only sixteen

minutes and I'd be alone with Jonathan for the first time in weeks. I couldn't wait.

Edging round the desk, I opened my mouth to tell Phin that I was going to a meeting, but before I could make my escape I saw consternation on his face as he looked over my shoulder. I turned to see Jewel Stevens framed in the doorway.

To say that she came in wouldn't do her justice. You could tell that she was an actress. I felt that there should have been a fanfare—or possibly the theme tune from *Jaws*—as she waited until all eyes were on her before making her entrance.

'Hi, baby,' she cooed, her sultry brown eyes on Phin. I was fairly sure that she hadn't registered my existence.

'Jewel!' The appalled expression I had glimpsed had vanished, and he was once more Mr Charm. 'What are you doing here?'

She pouted at him, sweeping a glance up from under impossibly long lashes. 'I just wanted to make sure you weren't too cross with me after this morning.'

'No, no,' said Phin easily. 'I never liked that dinner service anyway.'

Jewel laughed, delighted at her own power, and then her voice dropped seductively. 'I came to make it up to you. To see if you missed me after last night.'

You had to hand it to her. Completely ignoring my presence, she wound her arms around his neck and kissed him on the mouth. And I don't mean a casual peck. I mean a full-on passionate kiss with tongues—well, I assume with tongues. It certainly looked that kind of kiss.

Anyway, by the time she had finished she was plastered all over him and twirling her tongue in his ear. Yuck. I can't bear anyone touching my ears—I'm funny like that—and it made me queasy just looking at her. Just as well I hadn't had my lunch yet.

I averted my gaze. No wonder Phin was looking tired this morning!

'What say we go back to my place?' Jewel was saying huskily. 'We can spend the afternoon together. Just wait until you see what I've got for you, tiger,' she whispered suggestively in his ear, and then—and I swear I'm not making this up—she growled.

Oh, please. I rolled my eyes mentally, only to catch Phin's gaze over her shoulder. He grimaced at me and mouthed an unmistakable *Help!*

I was half tempted to leave him to it, but there was such naked appeal in his eyes that I relented. 'You haven't forgotten your twelve-thirty meeting, have you?' I asked clearly.

'God, yes, I have!' Phin sent me a grateful look as he disentangled himself from her—which took some doing, I can tell you. Managing to free a hand, he slapped his head. 'I'm sorry, Jewel. I can't.'

Jewel's beautiful face darkened. 'Do you have to go? Meetings aren't important. What's it about?'

Another agonised look at me. 'You need to discuss PR strategy,' I supplied obediently.

'Yes, that's right. PR. So I'm afraid it *is* important.' Phin spread his hands disarmingly.

'Then I'll wait for you in your office.' She was twining herself around him again. Honestly, the woman was like an octopus. Phin would just manage to prise one of her hands away and the other would already be sliding round him.

'I think you'd get very bored, Jewel,' he said. 'It's likely to be a long meeting. We're going out to lunch. In fact, we'd better go—hadn't we, Summer?'

I looked at the clock. 'Definitely,' I said, picking up the file. I didn't care what he did with Jewel, but I was meeting Jonathan at twelve-thirty if it killed me.

Jewel's beautiful sullen mouth was turned down. 'When will you be finished?'

'I'm not entirely sure,' said Phin, steering her towards the door. 'I'll give you a ring, OK?'

Still pouting, Jewel insisted on another kiss before she would let him go. 'See you later then, tiger.' She smirked, and sashayed off towards the lifts.

There was silence in the office. I looked at Phin. 'Tiger?'

He had the grace to squirm. 'Believe me, Jewel's the tiger. I'm the baby antelope here.'

'I'm sure you fought madly.'

'If I'd known what I was getting into I would have done,' he said frankly. 'I mean, she's gorgeous, and I've got to admit I was flattered when she made a beeline for me, but she gives a whole new meaning to high-maintenance. Talk about a prima donna! I must have withdrawn my attention for about ten seconds this morning, while I made myself some toast, and my eardrums are still ringing! She was throwing plates at the walls—it was like Greek night down at the local kebab shop. I'm buying plastic ones next time. I never thought I'd say it, but it was a real relief to come into the office and find you as cool and calm as ever.'

I certainly hadn't been feeling cool and calm, I thought, but could only be glad my fluttery nerves hadn't shown.

'Anyway, I owe you one,' he said. 'If you hadn't rescued me I'd have been dragged back to her lair and spat out later, an empty husk of a man.'

'Call it quits for the doughnuts,' I said. I looked at my watch and my heart gave a lurch. Twelve twenty-five. 'I'd better go.'

Phin peered round the doorway to check if Jewel was still waiting for the lift. Apparently she was, because he withdrew his head hastily. 'I might as well come, too,' he said.

I looked at him in dismay. I didn't want him muscling in on my *tête-à-tête* with Jonathan! 'I don't think you'll find it very interesting,' I tried, but Phin was already hustling me down the corridor away from the lifts.

'We'll take the stairs,' he muttered. 'Isn't your meeting about PR, anyway?' he went on once safely out of Jewel's sight. 'I should know what's going on.'

'I'll fill you in on the details afterwards,' I tried.

'No, I'd better come. I wouldn't put it past Jewel to come back and surprise me,' said Phin, with an exaggerated grimace of fear. 'And where would I be without you to rescue me?'

If I resisted any more, Phin would start wondering why I was so keen to be on my own with Jonathan, and that was the last thing I wanted. I could hardly refuse to take my own boss to a meeting, after all, but I was rigid with disappointment as we made our way up to Jonathan's office on the floor above.

Not that Phin seemed to notice. He was in high good humour, having escaped Jewel's clutches, and he breezed into Jonathan's office and completely took over the meeting. I had no need to bring out my line about grabbing a sandwich.

'Let's talk over lunch,' said Phin, and bore us off to a wine bar tucked away in a side street between Covent Garden and the Strand.

So much for my date with Jonathan. I walked glumly beside Phin, listening to him setting out to charm Jonathan, who was obviously delighted at Phin's unexpected appearance. I was feeling pretty miserable, if you want the truth. I couldn't fool myself that there had been even a flash of disappointment from Jonathan because he wouldn't be meeting me alone.

Still, I found myself grabbing onto pathetic crumbs of comfort—like the way he arranged for me to sit next to him at the table. Later, of course, I realised it was so that he could sit face to face with Phin, on the other side, but at the time it was all I had to hang on to.

Not that it did me much good. I wanted to concentrate on Jonathan, but somehow I couldn't with Phin sitting across the table exuding such vitality that even after what had obviously been a heavy night with Jewel everyone else seemed to fade in comparison to him. Whenever I tried to slide a glance at Jonathan my eyes would snag instead on Phin's smile, or Phin's solid forearms, or his hands that fiddled maddeningly with the cutlery as he talked and gesticulated.

The two men couldn't have been more of a contrast. Jonathan was in a beautifully cut grey suit, which he wore with a blue shirt and dotted silk tie. Anne would have looked at him and said conventional and boring, but to me he was mature and professional. Unlike Phin, whose hair could have done with a cut and who was wearing a casual shirt and chinos in neutral colours and yet still managed to look six times as colourful as anyone else in the room.

'*Glitz* are planning a major spread,' Jonathan was explaining to Phin. 'It's a great opportunity for us to promote a more accessible image. Market research shows that Gibson & Grieve are still seen as elitist, so for the new stores we need to present ourselves as ordinary and family-friendly. Your image as a celebrity will be very valuable to us, but up to now you've been associated with the wild. What we want is to associate you with the home, and we'd like *Glitz* to interview you at your house, so that their readers get an idea of you in a domestic setting.'

Jonathan paused delicately. 'If you have a girlfriend, it

would be very good to get her involved as well—perhaps even give the impression that you're thinking of settling down. I did hear that you're going out with Jewel Stevens…?' He trailed off, more than a touch of envy in his tone.

Phin's eyes met mine. 'I'm not involving Jewel,' he said with a grin. 'It might give her all the wrong ideas—and besides, I wouldn't have any crockery left by the time *Glitz* turned up. I'm reduced to eating off paper plates as it is!'

'She sounds very feisty,' said Jonathan. I don't know if he was aiming for a man-about-town air or humour, but either way it didn't quite work.

I glanced at Phin and away again.

'Feisty is one way of putting it,' he said. 'Sorry, Jonathan, but I'm going to have to do this as single guy.'

Jonathan looked disappointed. I got the feeling that he would have liked to have talked more about Jewel. 'Well, perhaps you could give the impression that you're thinking of settling down without mentioning any names,' he suggested.

'I'll do my best.'

'What about your house? Do we need to redecorate for you?'

'Redecorate? I thought the article was supposed to be showing me as I am at home?'

'No, it's to show you at the kind of home we want readers to associate with Gibson & Grieve,' Jonathan corrected him. He turned to me. 'Summer, you'd better check it out. You'll know what needs to be done.'

'She'll just tidy me up,' Phin protested.

'Summer's very competent,' said Jonathan.

Competent. You know, when you dream of what the man of your dreams will say about you, you think about words like *beautiful, amazing, sexy, passionate, incredible*. You never long for him to tell you're competent, do you?

'No redecorating,' said Phin firmly. 'If you make it all stylish it'll look and seem false, and that would do our image more harm than good. Summer can come and keep me on the straight and narrow in the interview, but I'm not changing the house. If you want readers to see what my home is like, we can show them. It's not as if I live in squalor.'

My only hope was that Phin might leave us after lunch, but, no, he insisted on walking back with us. So I never had one moment alone with Jonathan. I had to say goodbye to him in the lift as Phin and I got out on the floor below.

And that was my big date that I'd looked forward to so much. A complete waste of make-up. Jonathan hadn't even commented on my cardigan.

Phin looked nervously around the office when we got back. 'She's gone—phew!' He wiped his brow in mock relief. 'Thanks again for earlier, Summer. It's good to know you can lie when you need to! If Jewel comes in again, I'm not here, OK?'

I was too cross about Jonathan to be tactful. I was even beginning to feel some sympathy for Jewel. At least she had the gumption to go for what she wanted. Jonathan evidently found her feistiness appealing. Perhaps I should have tried smashing a few plates.

'If you don't want to see her again, you should tell her yourself...tiger,' I said sharply, and Phin winced.

'I'll try,' he said. 'But Jewel isn't someone who listens to what she doesn't want to hear. Still, I'm going away in a few days,' he remembered cheerfully. 'She'll soon lose interest if I'm not around.'

CHAPTER FOUR

HE LEFT for Peru a week later. 'How long will you be away?' I asked him.

'We should be able to wrap it up in twelve days.' Phin looked up from the computer screen with a grin. 'Why? Do you think you'll miss me after all?'

'No,' I said crushingly. 'I just need to know when to arrange a date with *Glitz*.'

But the funny thing was that I *did* miss him a bit. I realised I'd got used to him being in the office, managing to seem both lazy and energetic at the same time, and without him everything seemed strangely flat.

I told myself that I enjoyed the peace and quiet, and that it was a relief to be able to get on with some work without being teased or constantly interrupted by frivolous questions or made to stop and eat doughnuts—OK, I didn't mind that bit *so* much. I had a whole week without Phin juggling with my stapler and my sticky note dispenser, or messing around with the layout of my desk, which I know quite well he only did to annoy.

He was always picking things up and then putting them down in the wrong place, or at an odd angle, and he seemed to derive endless amusement from watching me straighten them. Sometimes I'd try and ignore it, but it was like trying to ignore an itch. After a while my hand would creep out to rearrange whatever it was he had dislodged, at which point Phin would shout, 'Aha! I knew you couldn't do it!'

I mean, what kind of boss carries on like that? It was deeply unprofessional, as I was always pointing out, but that only made Phin laugh harder.

So all in all I was looking forward to having the office to myself for a few days, but the moment he'd gone I didn't quite know what to do with myself.

That first morning on my own I went down to the kitchen to make myself some coffee. I'd got out of the habit of buying myself a doughnut, I realised. Phin always bought them now, and I'd forgotten that I wouldn't have anything to have with my coffee. It wouldn't kill me, but the lack of sugar just added to my grouchiness as I carried my mug back to my desk.

Khalid from the postroom was just on his way out of my office. 'I've left the mail on your desk,' he told me. 'You've got a Special Delivery, too.'

I'd ordered a scanner the day before. The supplies department must have moved quickly for once, I thought, but as I set down my mug I saw a small confectionery box sitting in front of my keyboard. 'Summer Curtis, Monday' was scribbled on the top. Not a scanner, then.

Puzzled, I opened it up. Inside, sitting on a paper napkin, was a doughnut.

There was a business card, too. I pulled it out. It had Phin's name and contact details on one side. On the other he had scrawled, 'I didn't want to think of you without your sugar fix. P x'

My throat felt ridiculously tight. Nobody had ever done anything as thoughtful for me before.

Of course it didn't mean anything, I was quick to remind myself. It was just part of Phin's pathological need to make everyone like him. His charm was relentless.

But still I found myself—annoyingly—thinking about him, about where he was and what he was doing, and when I picked up the phone and heard his voice my heart gave the most ridiculous lurch.

'Just thought I'd check in,' said Phin. 'I hardly know what to do with myself. I'm so used to you telling me what to do and where to be all day. I've got used to being organised. Are you missing me yet?'

'No,' I lied, because I knew he'd be disappointed if I didn't. 'But thank you for the doughnut. How on earth did you organise it?'

'Oh, that was easy. I had a word with Lucia—who, by the way, smiled at me the other day, so you're not the only favourite now—and I asked her to send you a selection, so that you get something different every day I'm away. I think we're in a doughnut rut.'

'I like my rut,' I said, but I might as well have spared my breath. Phin was determined that I would try something different.

Sure enough, the next day an apricot Danish arrived at half past ten, and even though I was determined not to like it as much as a doughnut, I had to admit that it was delicious.

The next day brought an almond croissant, and the one after that an apple strudel, and then an éclair. Pastries I'd never seen before appeared on my desk, and I found myself starting to glance at the clock after ten and wondering what I'd have with my coffee that day. I'd try and guess what would be in the box—vanilla turnover? *Pain au chocolat?*—but I never got it right.

Inevitably word got round about my special deliveries. I wasn't the only one who was guessing. I heard afterwards they were even taking bets on it in Finance.

'I wish my boss would send me pastries,' my friend Helen grumbled. 'You'd think in Food Technology it would be a perk of the job. You are lucky. Phin's so lovely, isn't he?'

I heard that a lot, and although I always said that he was a nightmare to work for, the truth was that I was finding it hard to remember just how irritating he was. When he walked into the office the following Tuesday, my heart jumped into my throat and for one panicky moment I actually forgot how to breathe.

He strolled in, looking brown and fit, his eyes bluer than ever, and instantly the air was charged with a kind of electricity. Suddenly I was sharply aware of everything: of colour of my nails flickering over the keyboard—Cherry Ripe, if you're interested—of the computer's hum, of the feel of the glasses on my nose, the light outside the window. It was as if the whole office had snapped into high definition.

'Good morning,' I said, and Phin peered at me in surprise.

'Good God, what was that?'

'What was what?' I asked, thrown.

'No, no…it's OK. For a moment there I thought I saw a smile.'

'I've smiled before,' I protested.

'Not like that. It was worth coming home for!' Phin came to sit on the edge of my desk and picked up the stapler. 'I'm not going to ask if you missed me because you'll just look at me over your glasses and say no.'

'I would have said a bit—until you started fiddling,' I said, removing the stapler from his grasp and setting it back into its place. 'But now I've remembered how irritating you are.'

Deliberately, Phin reached out and pushed the stapler out of alignment with one finger. 'Irritating? Me?'

'Stop it,' I said, slapping his hand away. I straightened the stapler once more. 'Haven't you got some other trip to go on? I'm sure they must need you in Ulan Bator or Timbuktu or somewhere.'

'Nope. Next time you're coming with me.' He had started on the scissors now, snapping them at me as he talked. 'So, what's the news here?'

'We've set up your *Glitz* interview for Thursday,' I told him. 'The interviewer is called Imelda Ross, and she's bringing a photographer with her. They'll be at your house at ten, so can you please make sure you're ready for them?'

'That's an appointment, not news,' he said. 'What's the gossip? Has Lex run off with a lap dancer? Has Kevin been caught siphoning funds to some offshore bank account?' Kevin was our Chief Financial Officer and famously prudent.

'Nothing so exciting, I'm afraid. Everyone's been doing what they always do.'

Actually, that wasn't *quite* true. Jonathan was looking much more relaxed these days. I had shared a lift with him a few days earlier, and instead of being stiff and awkward he had smiled and chatted about the spell of fine weather.

I'd replayed the conversation endlessly, of course, and was hugging the hope that he might be warming to me again. Between that and Phin's pastries I'd been happier than I'd been for ages—but I didn't think that would be of much interest to Phin, even if I had been prepared to confess it, which I wasn't.

'According to the gossip mags, Jewel Stevens has got a new man,' I offered instead.

'*Has* she? Excellent! I was hoping she'd lost interest.'

'She rang looking for you a couple of times, but I didn't think you'd want to speak to her in Peru, so I said you were out of contact.'

'Summer, you're a treasure,' he told me, putting down the scissors at last and digging around at his feet. 'So, even though you haven't missed me, you deserve a reward,' he said as he produced a paper bag. 'I've brought us something special to celebrate my return.'

The 'something special' turned out to be a cream doughnut each. 'I didn't feel we knew each other well enough to tackle one of these before,' he said as I eyed it dubiously, wondering how on earth I was going to eat it elegantly.

'I defy you to eat one of these without making a mess,' Phin added, reading my expression without any difficulty.

I couldn't, of course. I started off taking tiny nibbles, until he couldn't bear it any more.

'Get on with it, woman,' he ordered. 'Stop messing around at the edges. Take a good bite and enjoy it! That's not a bad recipe for life, now I come to think of it,' he said, watching as I sank my teeth obediently into the middle of the doughnut and cream spurted everywhere. 'The doughnut approach to living well. I might write a book about it.'

'Make sure you include a section on how to clean up all the mess,' I said, dabbing at my mouth with my fingers, torn between embarrassment and laughter. I spotted a blob of cream on my skirt. 'Ugh, I've got cream *everywhere*!'

'The best things in life are messy,' said Phin.

'Not as far as I'm concerned,' I said, as I carefully wiped the cream from my skirt. 'But maybe I'll make an exception for cream doughnuts. It was delicious!'

With a final lick of my fingers, I got to my feet. 'I'd better get back to work,' I said.

Phin got up, too. His smile had faded as he watched me eat the doughnut, and his expression was oddly unreadable for once. He was looking at me so intently that I hesitated.

'What?' I asked.

'You've missed a bit,' he said and, reaching out, he wiped a smear of cream from my cheek, just near my mouth. Then he offered me his finger to lick.

I stared at it, mesmerised by the vividness with which I could imagine my tongue against his finger. I could practically taste the sweetness of the cream, feel the contrast between its smoothness and the firmness of his skin, and a wave of heat pulsed up from my toes to my cheeks and simmered in my brain. For one awful moment I was afraid that the top of my head would actually blow off.

Horrified by how intimate the mere idea seemed, and about Phin—my boss!—of all people, I found myself taking a step back and shaking my head at the temptation.

Phin's eyes never left my mouth as he licked the cream off himself.

'Yum, yum,' he said softly.

I know, it doesn't sound very erotic, but my heart was thudding so loudly I was sure he must hear it. My pulse roared in my ears and I had a terrible feeling that I might literally be steaming. I had to get out of the room before Phin noticed.

I cleared my throat with an effort. 'I…er…I should let you get on. Haven't you got a meeting now?'

'I have?'

'Yes, in HR. You wanted me to set it up for you, to talk to Jane about staff development and the Cameroon trip. It's in the diary.' I could feel myself babbling as I backed away towards the door. 'I'll forward the e-mail to you…'

Somehow I made it back to my desk, and had to spend a few minutes just breathing very carefully.

I felt very odd, almost shaken. I had never thought about Phin that way before. I had never thought about Jonathan like that either, to be honest. I loved Jonathan, but he was safe. This wild pounding of my blood felt dark and rude and dangerous, and I didn't like it.

I pulled myself together at last. A momentary aberration, I told myself. A huge fuss about nothing. I mean, we hadn't even touched. A flick of Phin's finger against my cheek. That was all that had happened. Nothing at all, in fact.

I was just…hot. Was this what a hot flush was like? I wondered wildly. If so, I wasn't looking forward to the menopause at all.

Jittery and unsettled, I took myself off to the Ladies' to run cold water over my wrists. Someone had once told me that was the best way to cool yourself down, and I had no intention of splashing cold water all over my make-up. I wasn't in *that* much of a state.

I met Lex's PA, Monique, on her way in at the same time. Typical, isn't it, that the moment you're desperate to be alone people you don't normally see for ages start popping out of the woodwork? This wasn't even Monique's floor.

I was afraid that she would comment on how hot and flustered I looked, but fortunately she didn't seem to notice anything amiss. Reassured, I stopped to chat.

See, I told myself, all I needed was a little normality. It was a relief to talk about ordinary stuff, and I began to feel myself again.

'So what's the gossip?' I asked Monique, remembering Phin's question earlier. Monique was famously discreet, but if she did have any news it would be good to be able to pass a titbit on to Phin. At least it would be something to say other than *Could we try that cream on the finger thing again?*

'Funny you should say that.' Monique glanced around and lowered her voice, even though there was no one else in there with us. 'Have you seen Jonathan recently?'

Phin and the cream were instantly forgotten. 'A couple of times,' I said, as casually as I could. My poor old heart was working overtime this morning. Now it was pattering away at the mention of Jonathan. 'Why?'

'He's a changed man, isn't he?'

I thought of how relaxed he had looked the last time I'd seen him. 'He seems to be in a good mood.'

'Yes, and we all know why now!'

'We do?' I asked cautiously.

Monique grinned. 'Our steady, sensible Jonathan is in love.'

Not content with pattering, my heart pole-vaulted into my throat, where it lodged, hammering wildly. 'In love?' I croaked.

She nodded. 'And with Lori, of all people! I wouldn't have thought she was his type at all, but they're all over each other and they're not even bothering to try and hide it. Oh, well, at least he's happy.' She looked at her watch. 'I'd better get on. Lex will be wondering what's happened to me.'

There was a rushing in my ears. I think I must have said something, but I've no idea what, and Monique waggled her fingers in farewell as she hurried off, oblivious to the fact that my world had come crashing down around me.

Shaking, feeling sick, I shut myself in a cubicle and put my head between my knees. *I mustn't cry, I mustn't cry, I mustn't cry,* I told myself savagely. I had the rest of the afternoon to get through, and if I cried my mascara would run and everyone would know my heart was broken.

I don't know how long I sat there, but it can't have been

that long. I knew I had to get back. Lifting my head, I drew long, painful breaths to steady myself. I could do this.

Thank God for make-up. I reapplied lipstick very carefully and studied my expression. My eyes held a stark expression, but you'd have had to know me very well to spot that anything was wrong. Inside I felt ragged and raw, and I walked stiffly, so as not to jar anything, but outwardly I was perfectly composed.

I made it back to my desk and sank down in my chair, staring blankly at the computer screen. I just had to sit there for another few hours and then I'd be able to go home. Phin had gone out to his lunch with Jane, the director of HR, so I was spared him at least. Those blue eyes might be full of laughter but they didn't miss much.

By the time he came back it was after four, and I had had plenty of time to compose myself. I ached all over with the effort of not falling apart, and my brain felt as if it had an elastic band snapped round it, but I was able to meet his gaze when he came in.

'How was your meeting?' I asked, knowing Phin would never guess what it cost me to sound normal.

'Very useful. Jane's great, isn't she? We talked about Cameroon and she's all for a trial visit to see—' He broke off and frowned. 'What's the matter?'

'Nothing.' My throat was so tight I had to force the word out.

'Don't try and deny it,' said Phin. 'That stapler is a milli-metre out of alignment. And…' he peered closer '…yes, I do believe that's a chip in your nail polish!' The laughter faded from his voice and from his face. 'Come on, I can see in your eyes that something's wrong. What is it?'

'It's…nothing.' I couldn't look at him. I stared fiercely away, pressing my lips together in one straight line.

'You're not the kind of person that gets upset about

nothing,' he said gently. Going back to the door, he closed it. 'Tell me,' he said.

There was a great, tangled knot of hurt in my throat. I knew if I even tried to say Jonathan's name I would break down completely, and I wasn't sure I could bear the humiliation. 'I…can't.'

'OK,' he said. 'You don't need to say anything. But we're going out. Get your coat.'

I was too tired and miserable to object. He took me to a dimly lit bar, just beginning to fill with people leaving work early. Like us, I supposed. We found a table in a corner and Phin looked around for a waiter.

'What would you like?' he asked. 'A glass of wine?'

God, I was so predictable, I realised. No wonder Jonathan didn't want me. Even Phin could see that I was the kind of girl who sensibly just had a small glass of white wine before going home. I was boring.

'Actually, I'd like a cocktail,' I said with a shade of defiance.

'Sure,' said Phin. 'What kind?'

I picked up the menu on the table and scanned it. I would love to have been the kind of girl who could order Sex on a Beach or a Long Slow Screw Against a Wall without sounding stupid, but I wasn't. 'A pomegranate martini,' I decided, choosing one at random.

His mouth flickered, but he ordered it straight-faced from the waiter, along with a beer for himself.

When it came, it looked beautiful—a rosy pink colour with a long twirl of orange peel curling through it. I was beginning to regret my choice by then, but was relieved to take a sip and find it delicious. Just like fruit juice, really.

I was grateful to Phin for behaving quite normally. He chatted about his meeting with Jane, and I listened with half an ear as I sipped the martini which slipped down in no time. I even began to relax a bit.

'Another one?' Phin asked, beckoning the waiter over.

About to say that I shouldn't, I stopped myself. Sod it, I thought. I had nothing to go home for. 'Why not?' I said instead.

When the second martini arrived, I took another restorative pull through the straw and sat back. I was beginning to feel pleasantly fuzzy around the edges.

'Thank you,' I said on a long sigh. 'This was just what I needed.'

'Can you talk about it yet?'

Phin's voice was warm with sympathy. The funny thing was that it didn't feel at all awkward to be sitting there with him in the dim light. Maybe it was the martini, but all at once he felt like a friend, not my irritating boss. Only that morning the graze of his finger had reduced me to mush, but it was too bizarre to remember that now.

I sighed. 'Oh, it's just the usual thing.'

'Boyfriend trouble?'

'He's not my boyfriend any more. The truth is, he was never really my boyfriend at all,' I realised dully. 'But I loved him. I still do.'

In spite of myself, my eyes started to fill with tears. 'He told me before Christmas that he wanted out, that he didn't think it was working,' I went on, my voice beginning to wobble disastrously. 'I'd been hoping and hoping that he'd change his mind, and I let myself believe that he was beginning to miss me, but I just found out today that he's going out with Lori and he's mad about her and I don't think I can bear it.'

I couldn't stop the tears then. It was awful. I hate crying, hate that feeling of losing control, but there was nothing I could do about it.

Phin saw me frantically searching for tissue, and silently handed me a paper napkin that had come with the bowl of nuts.

'I'm sorry, I'm sorry,' I wept into it.

'Hey, don't be sorry. It sucks. Who is this guy, anyway?' he said. 'Do you want me to go and kill him for you? Would that help?'

'I don't think Lex would be very pleased if you did.' I sniffed into the napkin. 'He'd have to find a new PR person.'

Phin's brows crawled up to his hairline. 'Are we talking about *Jonathan Pugh*?'

I could see him trying to picture Jonathan's appeal. I know Jonathan isn't the sexiest looking guy in the world, but it was about more than looks.

'Jonathan's everything I ever wanted,' I told him tearfully. 'He's a bit older than me, I know, but he's so steady, so reliable. He seems reserved, but I always had the feeling that he'd be different in private, and he is. I never thought I'd have a chance with him, but then there was the summer party…'

I'll never forget my starry-eyed amazement when Jonathan came over to talk to me, and suggested going for a quiet drink away from all the noise. I'd been bedazzled by all my dreams coming true at once.

'I was so happy just to be with him,' I told Phin. Now I'd started talking, it was as if I couldn't stop. I had to blurt it all out. I gulped at my martini. 'I'd never been in love before, not like that, and when I was with him it felt like I had everything I'd ever wanted. I didn't mind that he wanted to keep our relationship a secret—to me that was just him being sensible, and I loved him for that, too. But he's not being sensible with Lori,' I said bitterly. 'He's not keeping *her* a secret. He doesn't care who knows how he feels about her.'

My mouth began to tremble wildly again. 'It wasn't that he

didn't want to have a proper relationship. He just didn't want *me*. He wanted someone like Lori, who's pretty and feminine.'

'I bet she isn't prettier than you,' said Phin.

'She is. If you saw her, you'd know.'

I'd never liked Lori. She's the kind of woman who gives the impression of being frail and shy and helpless, but who always manages to get her own way. Men hang around, asking her if she's all right the whole time. As far as I knew Lori had no female friends—always a bad sign, in my opinion—but even I had to admit she was very pretty. She was tiny, with a tumble of blonde curls, huge blue eyes and a soft, breathy little voice.

Phin wouldn't be able to resist her any more than Jonathan had.

'OK, maybe she's pretty,' Phin allowed, 'but you're *beautiful*, Summer.'

'I'm not.' I blew my nose on the napkin. 'I'm ordinary. I know that.'

He laughed at that. 'You are so not ordinary, Summer! You've got fantastic bones and beautiful skin and your eyes are incredible. And don't get me started on your mouth… Your trouble is that you don't make the most of yourself.'

'I do,' I protested, still tearfully. 'Look at me.' I gestured down at my suit. Even in the depths of my misery I knew it was better not to draw attention to my face right then. I'm not a pretty crier. Maybe the likes of Lori can cry without their skin going blotchy and their eyes puffy and their nose running, but I couldn't. 'I always take trouble over my clothes,' I pointed out. 'I never go out without make-up. What more can I do?'

'You could let your hair down sometimes,' said Phin, lifting a hand as if to touch it, but changing his mind at the last minute. 'It looks as if it would be beautiful, thick and silky. It would make you look more…' he searched for the right word '…accessible,' he decided in the end, and I remembered what Anne had said about changing my image by letting my hair hang loose.

But what difference would it have made? 'What's the point in looking accessible when I'm boring?' I asked despairingly. 'Jonathan still wouldn't want me.'

'He must have wanted you at some point or he wouldn't have got involved with you in first place.'

'No, he didn't.' I was just starting to accept the truth. 'I flung myself at him, and I must have been convenient, but he never meant it to be more than that. He didn't want *me*. And why should he? I'm boring and sensible and practical,' I raged miserably, remembering now—too late—some of the things Jonathan had said. In hindsight, it was all so obvious. Only I hadn't wanted to see the truth before.

'Jonathan doesn't want someone as competent as he is. He doesn't want someone who can look after herself. He wants someone needy and feminine—like Lori. Someone he can look after. But I can't do needy. I'm too used to dealing with everything, ever since I was child. I can't help it, but Jonathan thinks it makes me bossy. He used to make comments about it. I thought he was being affectionate, but now I wonder if it really bothered him. Funny how a man is never bossy, isn't it?' I added in a bitter aside. 'A man is always assertive or controlling, but never, ever bossy.'

'I don't think you're bossy,' said Phin. 'You're practical, which is a very different thing.'

'Jonathan thinks I am. He just got bored with me. All that time I was telling myself how much I loved him, he was losing interest. I should have realised that he hadn't invested anything in the relationship. He didn't even leave a toothbrush at my flat. When he ended it, there was nothing to discuss.'

Oh, dear, here came the tears again. I groped around for the wet napkin until Phin found me another, and I scrubbed furiously at my cheeks before drawing a shuddering breath.

'When Monique told me about Lori today, it just made me realise what a fool I've been about everything,' I said. 'I'd had this dream in my head for so long, and it was all wrapped up with being with Jonathan and feeling safe, but I should have known it was too good to be true,' I said wretchedly. 'He'd never want someone like me.'

'But you still want him?'

I nodded. 'I love him,' I said, my voice catching.

'Then I think you should go out and get him back,' said Phin. 'I didn't have you down as someone who would give up as easily as that. What have you been doing since you split up?'

'Nothing.'

'Precisely, and look where it's got you. You're miserable, and Jonathan's dating a woman named after a truck. Lori? I mean, how serious can he be?'

I looked at him. 'That's a pathetic joke,' I said, but I managed a watery smile even so.

'I'm just saying you shouldn't give up,' Phin said. 'Your trouble is that you're too subtle. I had lunch with you both the other day, and I didn't have a clue that there had been anything at all between you. I wouldn't be surprised if Jonathan thinks you don't care one way or the other. I suggest we have another drink,' he went on, gesturing for the waitress to bring another round, 'and plan your strategy.'

I considered that, my brow creased with the effort of thinking after two martinis. 'You think I should tell Jonathan how I feel?'

'Absolutely not!' Phin tutted. 'Really, Summer, you haven't got a clue, have you? If you get heavy on him he'll panic and think you're about to drag him off to the suburbs via the nearest registry office—which is what you want, of course, but this is not the time to tell him that. You've got to reel him in first.'

'Well, what do you suggest, if you're such an expert?' I asked, wiping mascara away with the napkin. What was the point of waterproof mascara if you couldn't cry? I would have to write and complain. 'If I tell him how I feel, I'm too intense. If I don't, he won't notice because I'm so boring and predictable.' I lapsed back into gloom once more.

Another beer and a fresh martini were placed on the table. Phin pushed my glass towards me. 'For a start, you've got to get this idea that you're boring out of your head,' he told me sternly. 'You're smart, you're funny—not always deliberately, I'll grant you—and you're sexy as hell.'

CHAPTER FIVE

I STARED at him. *Sexy?* I was sensible, practical, reliable. Not sexy.

Jewel was sexy, pressing herself against him and sticking her tongue in his ear. Not me, with my glasses on a chain and my neat suits. Phin was either being kind or making fun of me.

For a fleeting moment I remembered the way I had felt as he'd wiped that blob of cream from my cheek, but then I pushed the memory aside. It was too incongruous.

'All you've got to do is make Jonathan appreciate what an incredible woman you are,' said Phin.

Yeah, right. 'How?' I asked, with a trace of sullenness. 'He never appreciated how "incredible" I was before.'

'Make him jealous,' said Phin promptly. 'I know guys like Jonathan. Hell, I *am* a guy like Jonathan, and if I saw you with another man I'd be intrigued at the very least. I guarantee Jonathan would start to remember what he saw in you if there's another guy sniffing around and making it obvious that he thinks you're incredible.'

'Well, yes, brilliant idea,' I said, picking up my glass. The third martini was definitely kicking in now. 'There's just one problem. I don't have another guy.'

'Start dating again,' said Phin, as if it was obvious.

'Oh, sure,' I said sarcastically. The martinis had made me bolshy, but it was better than snivelling. 'That's easy. I'll just snap my fingers and produce a man.' I patted my pockets. 'I'm sure I left one or two lying around somewhere…'

Phin looked at me appreciatively. 'I see you're feeling better,' he said. 'Look, it can't be that hard for a girl who looks like you to find a guy. Go and stand at the bar and smile, and I bet they'll be falling over themselves. Better still, eat a cream doughnut.'

There was a tiny silence. I flickered a glance at Phin. He was smiling, but the blue eyes held that odd expression again—the one that made me feel as if the world was tilting out of kilter.

'You have no idea, do you?' he said.

I swallowed. I didn't want to remember that disconcerting wave of heat. I didn't want to think about what it meant.

'I don't think it would be that easy,' I told him, my eyes sliding away from his. 'And even if I *did* find a boyfriend who wouldn't mind the fact that I don't actually want to be with him, when would Jonathan ever find out?'

'I see what you mean. Someone at work would be better.'

'Except if it was someone at work Jonathan would just feel sorry for him.' My confidence was crumbling again. Quick, it was time for another gulp of pomegranate martini.

'Not if it was obvious he was mad about you.'

'Oh, so now I have to find a boyfriend who can act, too? I'd have to hire him, and where do you suggest I look?'

'What about right here?'

I looked around the bar. 'How do I know if any of these guys can act? Well, the barmen are probably resting actors, but I'd never dare talk to them—they're far too cool.'

'No, *here*,' said Phin, tapping his chest.

My jaw dropped. *'You?'*

'There's no need to look like that! I'm perfect.'

'I know you think so,' said the third martini, and Phin grinned.

'I do think so, and so will you if you think about it,' he said. 'Jonathan can hardly not notice if you're with me, and I think you'll find I'm not a bad actor. They still talk about my Ugly Sister in the school pantomime and, according to my mother, I stole the show in the nativity play as the sheep that fell over when it tried to kneel in front of the manger.'

'I don't know why you're not in line for an Oscar,' I said, 'but why would you want to squander your great talent on me?'

'I like you,' said Phin simply, 'even if you are a bit sharp with me sometimes. If I can help you, I will. Besides, it might work out quite well for me from a PR point of view.'

I frowned. 'How do you work that out?'

'Think about it. Jonathan was very keen to push my family credentials in the *Glitz* interview. How better to do that than pretend I'm about to settle down with you? You can hang around and look good for the article, which means that even if Jonathan hasn't got the idea before, he definitely will then. A double whammy.'

He sat back smugly while I sipped my martini and considered what he had said. Surely it couldn't be as easy as Phin seemed to believe?

'What about Jewel?' I prevaricated.

'What about her? You said yourself that she's been going out with someone else, poor guy. I'm well out of that one!' said Phin. 'I wouldn't have had a plate left in the house. But now I come to think of it,' he went on, 'it might not be a bad idea to let her see I'm unavailable now. Just in case she's thinking she might pick up where we left off before I went to Peru.'

'I can't believe you'd have much trouble finding someone

else to make sure she gets the point,' I demurred. 'There must be much more likely types who would give the impression that you're ready to settle down.'

'I wouldn't want to give anyone the wrong idea,' said Phin, not bothering to deny it. It would have been annoying if he had, but I was annoyed anyway. 'I'm not the settling down kind,' he said. 'At least with you we'd both know it was just a pretence.'

I blame it on the pomegranate martinis, but it was starting to make a weird kind of sense.

'No one would believe that I was really your girlfriend,' I said. 'You're used to going out with actresses and models.'

'Which is why they'll think I'm serious if they see me with you.'

My, this was doing wonders for my ego.

'It would only be for a few weeks,' Phin was saying. 'You wouldn't have to do much. Just be seen out at a few parties with me and hang around looking like a girlfriend for the interview. Then we can seem to break it off later, so I can carry on avoiding commitment while you walk off into the sunset with Jonathan.'

'Do you really think it would make a difference with Jonathan?' I asked wistfully.

'Listen, do you really want him back or not?'

'I really do.'

'Even though he's made you feel boring and unlovable?'

'I love him,' I said, dangerously close to getting weepy again.

'OK,' said Phin, 'if Jonathan is what you really want, then I think you deserve what you want. The first thing is to make him realise that you're not boring at all, that you're quite capable of being spontaneous when you've got the right incentive. Make him think that it's *his* fault you never had much fun with him—which it probably is, by the way. We're going to convince him that we're having a raging affair, and he's sure to sit up and take notice.'

'How do we go about having an affair?' I said doubtfully. I couldn't see myself being convincing as someone in the throes of a raging affair somehow. It wasn't the kind of thing I would do. It wasn't the kind of thing I liked, to be honest. It smacked too much of losing control and abandoning yourself. I liked things calm and steady and *safe*.

'Well, let's see,' said Phin with a grin. 'I could take you back to my place. We'll say it's just for a drink, but we won't be able to keep our hands off each other. The moment we're through the front door I'll start kissing you, and you'll kiss me back. You'll fall back against the door and pull me with you—'

'I don't mean really have an affair,' I interrupted, scarlet. I was horrified at how vividly I could imagine it, and there was a strange thumping deep inside me. Jonathan had never lost control like that. I was beginning to feel very odd, but I hoped very much that was down to the martinis. 'I meant… how would we make everyone believe it? We can hardly send round an e-mail announcement that we're sleeping together.'

Phin didn't seem to think that would be a problem. 'We'll go to a couple of parties, maybe leave work together—or even better arrive together—and word will get round in no time. If you can contrive to blush whenever my name is mentioned in the Ladies', or wherever you girls all congregate, so much the better. And remember how besotted I'm going to be with you,' he went on. 'I won't be able to keep my hands off you—especially when Jonathan is around. I don't think it will take long before he gets the point.'

I buried my nose in my martini, trying not to wonder what it would be like to have Phin putting his arm around me, sliding his hand down my back. Would he twine his fingers around mine? Would he stroke my hair?

Would he *kiss* me?

The breath rushed out of my lungs at the thought. *Would* he? And if he did what would it be like?

My heart was thudding painfully—ba-*boom*, ba-*boom*, ba-*boom*—and I had to moisten my lips before I could speak. This was about Jonathan, remember?

'But if Jonathan thinks I'm with you, he'll assume I'm not interested in him any more,' I objected.

'Once he starts paying attention—and he will—you'll have to let him know that you just might be tempted away from me. If you can do it without seeming too keen. You might have to spend some time alone together…' Phin snapped his fingers. 'Of course! Jonathan can come to Cameroon. If you can't seduce him back on a steamy tropical night, Summer, I wash my hands of you!'

I thought about it as I sucked on the long curl of orange peel which was all that was left at the bottom of my glass. Apart from the reminder of Cameroon, which I'd been rather hoping he'd forgotten about, I was struggling to think of a good argument as to why Phin's idea wouldn't work.

The third martini wasn't helping. I was feeling distinctly fuzzy by now, and finding it hard to concentrate.

Phin followed my gaze to the empty glass. 'Had enough?' he asked, and I bridled at the humorous understanding in his voice.

A sensible girl would say yes at this point, but being sensible hadn't got me anywhere, had it?

'No,' I said clearly. Well, it was *meant* to sound clear. Whether it did is doubtful. 'I'd love another one.'

One of Phin's brows lifted. 'Are you sure?'

'Absho—absolutely sure.'

'It's your hangover,' he said, the corner of his mouth quirking in that lop-sided smile of his. He beckoned the waitress over. 'Another pomegranate martini for my little lush here, and I'll have another half.'

I waited until she had set the glasses on the table. Part of me knew quite well that Phin's plan was madness, but I hadn't been able to come up with a single argument to convince him how ridiculous the idea was.

'Do you really think it would work?' I asked, almost shyly.

'What's the worst that could happen if it doesn't?' Phin countered. 'You'd be in the same situation you are now, but at least you'll know you did everything you could to make your dream come true. That has to be better than just sitting and watching it disappear, doesn't it? And, if nothing else, we'll have promoted the family image of Gibson & Grieve with this interview. As a good company girl, I know you'll be glad to have done your bit!'

He was watching my face.

'It's a risk,' he said in a different voice, 'but you don't get what you really want without taking chances.'

I looked back at him, biting my lip.

'So,' he said, lifting his glass, 'do we have a deal?'

And I, God help me, chinked my glass against his. 'Deal,' I said.

'Good morning, Summer!' Phin's cheery greeting scraped across my thumping head.

'Not so loud,' I whispered, without even lifting my head from the desk, where I'd been resting it ever since I'd staggered into work twenty minutes earlier. Late, for the first time in my life. I would have been mortified if I had had any feelings to spare. As it was, I had to save my energy for basic survival. Breathing was about all I could manage right then, and even that hurt.

'Oh, dear, dear, dear.' I could picture him standing over me, blue eyes alight with laughter, lips pursed in mock reproach. 'Is it possible you're regretting that last martini?'

I groaned. 'Go away and leave me to die in peace!'

'Aren't you feeling well?' Phin enquired solicitously.

'How could you possibly have guessed that?' I mumbled, still afraid to move my head in case it fell off.

'I'm famed for my powers of deduction. The FBI are always calling me up and asking me to help them out.'

I didn't even have the energy to roll my eyes. 'How many martinis did you make me drink last night?'

'Me? It wasn't me that insisted on another round, or the next, or the next… I asked you if you were sure, and you said that you were. Absolutely sure, you said,' he reminded me virtuously, and I hated the laughter in his voice.

I only had the vaguest memory of getting home the night before. Phin. A taxi. Anne's astonished face as I reeled in the door.

'Oh, God…I'm going to be a statistic,' I moaned into the desk. 'I'll be one of those moody binge drinkers we're always hearing about who throw away their entire careers.'

'You don't think you might be exaggerating just a teeny bit?' said Phin. 'Letting your hair down once in a while isn't the end of the world.'

It certainly felt like the end of the world to me. I'd never been closer to pulling a sickie. I couldn't even *imagine* a time when I would feel better. My forehead stayed where it was, pressing into the desk. 'If you knew how awful I felt, you wouldn't say that.'

'You were great fun,' he offered, but that was no consolation to me then. 'You were the life and soul of the bar by the time I managed to bundle you into a taxi. It's one of the best nights I've had in a long time. I think I'm going to enjoy going out with you.'

'I'm not going out ever again,' I vowed.

'You'll have to. How else will everyone know how in love we are?'

Very cautiously, I turned my head on the desk and squinted up at him. 'Please tell me last night was all a bad dream.'

'Certainly not!' said Phin briskly. 'We had a deal. You drank to it—several times, if I recall. Besides, we're committed. I met Lex on my way in and asked if I could take you to some drinks party he's having on Friday.'

'*What?*' Horrified, I straightened too suddenly, and yelped as my head jarred.

'Our cunning plan is never going to work if you hide away,' Phin pointed out, sitting on the edge of my desk and deliberately pushing a pile of square-cut folders aside. I was in such a bad state that I didn't even straighten them, and he looked at me in concern.

'Jonathan will be there,' he added, to tempt me, but I was beyond comfort by then.

'Oh, God.' I collapsed back onto the desk. 'What did Lex say? He must have been horrified.'

'Not at all. He was surprised, sure, but he said falling for you could be the most sensible thing I'd ever done.'

'I can't believe I let you talk me into this,' I moaned.

'Now, come along—you'll feel better when you've had some sugar,' said Phin, jumping off the desk. 'I'll go and make some coffee, and you can have your doughnut early.'

Oddly enough, I *did* feel a bit better after something to eat.

My head was still thumping, but at least it didn't feel as if it was about to fall off my neck any more.

Gingerly, I settled down at my computer and managed a few e-mails, although the clatter of the keyboard made me wince and I had to type very, very slowly, while Phin drip-fed me coffee and tried to rouse me by pretending to put files away in the wrong drawer.

'Don't torture me,' I grumbled. 'I thought you were supposed to be in love with me?'

'That's true. I should think of a truly romantic gesture to show what you mean to me. I could start putting my books in alphabetical order, or using a square rule to tidy my desk.'

'Why don't you try leaving *my* desk alone, for a start?' I said, swatting his hand aside as he made to pick up my calculator.

'Aha, I see you're feeling better!'

'I'm not. I'm a sick woman. I can't take any more.'

The words were barely out of my mouth before 'more' arrived—much more—in the shape of my mother.

She wafted in the door, beaming. 'Summer, darling, *there* you are!'

'Mum!'

It was Phin's turn to gape. *'Mum?'*

I couldn't blame him for looking staggered. No one ever believes she's my mother. You'd never think she was in her forties. She's got long red hair, shining eyes and a clear happy face. There's something fey, almost childlike, about her. I've never seen her in a scrap of make-up, she wears sandals and flowing ethnic skirts, and she always looks wonderful.

And, while she may be deeply into all things spiritual, she's not immune to flattery either. The smile she gave Phin was positively flirtatious. 'I hope I'm not interrupting?'

'Of course not,' said Phin, leaping forward to shake her hand. 'I'm Phin Gibson.'

'And I'm Starlight,' she told him.

They beamed at each other. I judged it was time to put a stop to their mutual love-in.

'I wasn't expecting you,' I said.

'I did tell you I was coming to London,' she reminded me.

She *had* said something, I remembered too late. 'I didn't realise it would be so soon.'

'It was an impulse.'

When had it ever *not* been an impulse? I thought wearily.

'We were gathered the other evening, channelling, when we were all seized by the same idea. It was the most extraordinary coincidence, so we knew that it had to be meant! Each of us felt our guardian angels were telling us to follow the ley lines into London…and now here we are!'

'What about the shop?' I asked, my heart sinking. A couple of years ago she had decided that she would open a New Age shop in Taunton. I'd been all for the idea of her settling to a job, so I'd helped with the practicalities of arranging the lease and sorting out a set-up loan. Mum had been full of enthusiasm for a while, but I hadn't heard much about it recently. Obviously she was into something else now.

Sure enough, she waved all talk of the shop aside. 'This is more important, Summer. We've been walking between the worlds at the powersites along the ley line. The earth needs it desperately at the moment. Only by channelling the energy and letting the Divine Will flow through us can we help to heal it.'

'Someone told me there's a ley line running right along the Mall to Buckingham Palace,' said Phin, sounding interested. 'Is that right?'

'It is.' She beamed approvingly at him. 'And this building sits on the very same line! I'm getting good vibes here.'

I dropped my head into my hands. My hangover had come back with a vengeance. I wasn't up to dealing with my mother today. I wished Phin would stop encouraging her.

Meanwhile my mother had turned her attention back to me. 'Your aura is looking very murky, Summer. Haven't you been using the crystals I sent you? If only I had some jade with me. That's very calming for irritability.'

'I'm not irritable, Mum,' I said—irritably. 'I've just got a bit of headache.'

'I sense your energy is all out of balance.' She tutted. 'You need to realign your chakras.'

'Right, I'll do that. Look, Mum, it's lovely to see you, but I have to get on. Where are you staying? We could meet up this evening.'

Her face fell. 'Jemima is going to regress tonight. Her spiritual journeys are always *so* interesting,' she told Phin. 'Last time she was reborn as one of Cleopatra's maids. It was quite an eye-opener.'

'I can imagine,' he said. 'You wouldn't want to miss that, so why don't I take you both out to lunch?'

'Oh, but—' I began in dismay, but neither Phin nor my mother were listening.

'I know a vegan restaurant just round the corner,' he was telling her, having accurately guessed her tastes. 'They do a great line in nut cutlets.'

How Phin came to know a vegan restaurant I'll never know, as I'd had him down squarely as a steak and chips man, but sure enough, tucked away a block or two from the office, there was a little café. Before I knew it, we were tucking into grilled tofu, bean ragout and steamed brown rice, and my mother, blossoming under Phin's attention, was well into her stride with stories about my childhood. I gazed glumly into my carrot juice and wished for the oblivion of another martini.

'She was such a funny little thing,' Mum told Phin. 'Always worrying! Ken and I used to joke that her first words were "Have you paid the electricity bill?"' She laughed merrily.

'Ken was my father,' I explained to Phin. 'He died when I was nine.'

'Such a spiritual man!' My mother sighed. 'I know I should be glad he's moved on to a higher astral plane, but I still miss him sometimes. We were totally in harmony, physically and spiritually.'

'You're lucky to have had that,' said Phin gently. 'It's quite rare, I think.'

'I know, and I'm so glad dear Summer is going to have the same feeling with you.'

I looked up from the alfalfa sprouts I was pushing around my plate, startled. 'Er, Mum, I think you've got wrong end of the stick. Phin's my boss.'

I might as well have spared my breath. 'His colours are very strong,' she said, and turned to him. 'I'm getting a lot of yellow from you.'

'Is that good?' asked Phin, as if he was really interested.

'In positive aspects, absolutely. Yellow is a warm colour. It relates to the personality, the ego.'

'No wonder you've got so much of it,' I said snippily, but Phin held up a hand.

'Hold on, I get the feeling your mother really understands me.'

'Yellow is how we feel about ourselves and about others.' Did I tell you Mum is a colour therapist? 'It tells me that you're confident and wise and positive about life.'

'And you thought I was just like everyone else,' Phin said to me. 'What about Summer? Is she as wise as me?'

'Summer has a cool aura,' said Mum, well away now. 'She's got a lot of indigo and blue. That means she's fearless and dutiful and self-sacrificing, but she's also kind and practical.'

Phin nudged me. 'Bet you wish you were wise, like me!'

'You're a very good match,' Mum said, and I scowled.

'How do you work that out? Yellow and blue are quite different.'

'But when you put them together they make green,' said my mother. 'That's the colour of balance and harmony.' She smiled at us both. 'Green relates to the heart chakra, too. When it comes to giving and receiving love, it's the perfect combination.'

'Thank you for not laughing at her,' I said to Phin when my mother had drifted off to prepare for the evening's regression. I fingered the clear crystal pendulum ("Very good for energy tuning") that she had pressed on me before she left. 'I know she's a bit wacky, but…'

'But she's so shiningly sincere you can't help but like her,' said Phin. 'What's not to like about someone who loves life as much as she does?'

As we walked back to the office I tried to imagine Jonathan sitting down to grilled tofu with my mother. I'd never really talked to him about my childhood. I'd had the feeling he'd be appalled by her flaky ideas, and I was absurdly grateful to Phin for seeing her good side.

'It must have been hard for you, losing your father when you were so young.' Phin broke into my thoughts. 'Did you miss him?'

'Not that much,' I said honestly. 'We were living in a

commune then, and there were lots of other people around. Besides, we weren't allowed to be sad. We had to rejoice that he had ascended to a higher plane.'

I shook my head, remembering. 'I think it must have been much harder for my mother. They do seem to have really loved each other, and I suspect she threw herself into the spiritual side of things as a way of coping. She's got a very flimsy grasp on reality, and sometimes she drives me mad, but at least she's happy.' I sighed. 'And who am I to say what she should or shouldn't believe?'

'I can't see you in a commune,' Phin commented.

'I hated it, but, looking back, it was the best place for Mum,' I said reflectively. 'I wish she'd join another. At least then someone else would worry about the day-to-day things.'

'Like paying the electricity bill?'

'Exactly. They were both hopeless with money, and just couldn't be bothered with things like bills, so the electricity was always getting cut off. They thought it was funny that I used to fret, but if I didn't sort out the practicalities no one else would.'

'Sounds like they were the opposite of my parents,' said Phin, as we waited to cross the road at the lights. 'They were both obsessed with financial security. They thought that as long as they could pay for us to go to "good" schools and we had everything we wanted they would have done their duty as parents.'

He grinned at me suddenly. 'We're an ungrateful generation, aren't we? My parents did their best, just like yours did. It's not their fault that we want different things from them. Mine drive me mad, just like your mother does you, but that doesn't mean I don't love them. The truth is that there's part of me that still craves their approval. Why else would I be at Gibson & Grieve, getting in Lex's way?'

'At least you're trying,' I said. 'My mother would be delighted if I gave up my job to channel angels or dowse for fairy paths. I don't think she even knows what "career" means.'

We were passing a burger bar just then, and as the smell of barbecued meat wafted out Phin stopped and sniffed appreciatively. 'Mmm, junk food…!' His eyes glinted as he looked down at me. 'Are you still hungry?'

'What? After all those delicious alfalfa sprouts? How can you even ask?'

We took our burgers away and sat on the steps in front of the National Gallery, looking down over Trafalgar Square. It was a bright February day, and an unseasonal warmth in the air taunted us with the promise of spring.

I was certainly feeling a lot better than I had earlier that morning. I was still a bit fuzzy round the edges but my headache had almost gone. Perhaps my mother's crystal was working after all.

'What are you doing?' Phin demanded as I unwrapped my burger and separated the bun carefully.

'I don't like the pickle,' I said, picking it out with a grimace and looking around for somewhere to dispose of it.

'Here, give it to me,' he said with a roll of his eyes, and when I passed it over he shoved it into his own burger and took a huge bite.

'See—we're like a real couple already,' he said through a mouthful.

I wished he hadn't reminded me of the crazy pretence we'd embarked upon the night before. I couldn't believe I'd actually agreed to it. I kept waiting for Phin to tell me that it was all a big joke, that he'd just been having me on.

'Did you really tell Lex that we were going out?'

'Uh-huh.' He glanced down at me. 'I told him that we were madly in love.'

I wanted to look away, but my eyes snagged on his and it was as if all the air had been suddenly sucked out of my lungs. Held by the blueness and the glinting laughter, I could only sit there and stare back at him, feeling giddy and yet centred at the same time.

It was a very strange sensation. I was acutely aware of the coldness of the stone steps, of the breeze in my face and the smell of the burger in my hands.

I did eventually manage to wrench my gaze away, but it was an effort, and I had to concentrate on my breathing as I watched the tourists milling around the square. They held their digital cameras at arm's length, posing by the great stone lions or squinting up at Nelson on his column. A squabble erupted amongst the pigeons below us, and my eyes followed the red buses heading down Whitehall, but no matter where I looked all I saw was Phin's image, as if imprinted behind my eyelids: the mobile mouth with its lazy lop-sided smile, the line of his cheek, the angle of his jaw.

When had he become so familiar? When had I learnt exactly how his hair grew? When had I counted the creases at the edges of his eyes?

There was a yawning feeling in the pit of my stomach. Desperately I tried to conjure up Jonathan's image instead, but it was hopeless.

'What did Lex say?' I asked, struggling to sound normal. 'Did he believe you?'

'Of course he did. Why wouldn't he?'

'You've got to admit that we make an unlikely couple.'

'Your mother doesn't think so,' Phin reminded me.

'My mother believes that fairies dance around the flowers at dawn,' I pointed out. 'The word "unlikely" doesn't occur in her vocabulary.'

'Well, Lex didn't seem at all surprised—except maybe that you would fall in love with me.' Phin crumpled the empty paper in his hand. 'He seemed to think that you were too sensible to do anything like that. He's obviously never seen you drinking pomegranate martinis!'

I flushed. If I never touched a martini again, it would be too soon.

'I would have thought he'd be more surprised that you'd be in love with *me*,' I said, finishing my own burger.

Phin shrugged. 'I'm always falling in and out of love. I suspect he's more worried that I might hurt you. He knows I'm not the settling down type. When you dump me for Jonathan, he'll probably be relieved.'

CHAPTER SIX

THE *Glitz* interview was scheduled for the next day.

Phin lived just off the King's Road, in one of those houses I have long coveted, with painted brick and colourful doors. That morning, though, I was in no mood to admire the prettiness of the street, or the window boxes filled with early daffodils that adorned the cottages on either side. I was feeling ridiculously nervous as I stood on the steps outside his door— a bright red—and I wasn't even sure why.

Except that's not quite true. I *did* know why. It was because of this crazy pretence we had agreed on. I couldn't understand how I had let myself get sucked into it. It was utter madness. *And* it would never work. I should just accept that Jonathan didn't love me and move on.

But instead I was committed to pretending to be Phin's girlfriend. It was too late to change my mind. Phin had told Lex that we were madly in love—just imagining a conversation like that with our dour Chief Executive made my mind boggle—and now everybody knew.

Phin had rested his hand against casually against my neck as we'd waited for the lifts on our way back from Trafalgar Square. I knew he was only doing it so that Michaela at Reception would see and pass the word around—she had, and

I'd only been back at my desk five minutes when Ellie was on the phone demanding to know what was going on—so there was no reason for my nape to be tingling still, no reason for me to be tense and jittery.

But I was.

Well, I had to get on with it. Drawing a deep breath, I rang the bell.

The door opened as suddenly as a slap, and there was Phin, smiling at me, in faded jeans and a T-shirt. His feet were bare, his hair rumpled, and he was in need of a shave. He looked a mess, in fact, but all at once there wasn't enough air to breathe and my mouth dried.

I badly wanted to retreat down the steps, but pride kept me at the top. 'Hi,' I said, horrified to hear how husky my voice sounded.

'Hey,' said Phin, and before I realised what he meant to do he had kissed me on the mouth.

It was only a brief brush of the lips, the casual kind of kiss a man like Phin would bestow a hundred times at a party, but my pulse jolted as if from a massive bolt of electricity. So that's what it's like being struck by lightning. I swear every hair on my body stood up.

'What was that for?' I asked unsteadily.

'Just getting into character,' he said cheerfully. 'I hadn't realised the perks of promoting G&G's family-friendly image until now. Who would have thought it would be so much fun keeping Lex happy?'

He stood back and held the door open. 'Come on in and see where we're having our wild affair.'

We won't be able to keep our hands off each other. I remembered Phin answering my stupid question about how we would go about having an affair. *The moment we're through*

the front door I'll start kissing you, and you'll kiss me back.
You'll fall back against the door and pull me with you...

Now I couldn't help glancing at the door as I passed, couldn't help imagining what it would be like to feel the hard wood digging into my back, the weight of Phin's body pressing me against it, his mouth on mine, his hands hot and hungry.

I swallowed hard. I had no intention of giving Phin the satisfaction of knowing how that casual kiss had affected me, but it was difficult when I still had that weird, jerky, twitchy, shocked feeling beneath my skin.

It wasn't a very big house. Clearly it had once been a cottage, but the kitchen had been extended at the back with a beautiful glass area, and on a sunny February morning it looked bright and inviting.

'Nice house,' I managed, striving for a nonchalant tone that didn't quite come off.

'I can't take any credit for it,' said Phin. 'It was like this when I bought it. I wanted somewhere that didn't need anything doing to it. I'm not into DIY or nest-building.'

'Or tidying, by the looks of it,' I said as I wandered into the living room. Two smaller rooms that had been knocked into one, it ran from the front of the house to the back, where dust motes danced in the early spring sunshine that shone in through the window.

It could have been a lovely room, but there was stuff everywhere. A battered hat sat jauntily on the back of an armchair. The sofa was covered with newspapers. Books were crammed onto a low table with dirty mugs, empty beer cans and a water purification kit.

I clicked my tongue disapprovingly. 'How on earth do you ever find anything?'

'I've got a system,' said Phin.

'Clearly it doesn't involve putting anything away!'

He made a face. 'There never seems much point. As far as I'm concerned, this is just somewhere to pack and unpack between trips.'

'What a shame.' It seemed a terrible waste to me. 'I'd love to live somewhere like this,' I said wistfully. 'This is my fantasy house, in fact.'

'The one you're saving up for?'

The chances of me ever being able to afford a house in Chelsea were so remote that I laughed. '*Fantasy*, I said! I'm saving for a studio at the end of a tube line, which will be all I can afford. And I'll be lucky if I can do that with London prices the way they are. But if I won the Lottery I'd buy a house just like this,' I said, turning slowly around and half closing my eyes as I visualised how it would be. 'I'd paint the front door blue and have window boxes at every window.'

'What's wrong with red?'

'Nothing. It's just that when I was a kid and used to dream about living in a proper house it always had a blue door, and I always swore that if I ever had a home of my own the door would be blue. I'd open it up, and inside it would be all light and stripped floorboards and no clutter...like this room could be if there wasn't all this mess!'

'It's not messy,' Phin protested. 'It's comfortable.'

'Yes, well, comfortable or not, we're going to have to clear up before Imelda and the photographer get here.'

I started to gather up the papers scattered over the sofa, but Phin grabbed them from me. 'Whoa—no, you don't!' he said firmly. 'I'll never find anything again if you start tidying. I thought we agreed the idea was to let readers see me at home?'

'No, the *idea* is that readers have a glimpse of what their lives could be like if only they shopped at Gibson & Grieve all the time,' I reminded him. 'You're a TV personality, for heaven's sake! You know how publicity works. It's about creating an image, not showing reality.'

Ignoring his grumbles, I collected up all the mugs I could find and carried them through to the kitchen. I was glad to have something to do to take my mind off the still buzzy aftermath of that kiss. I was desperately aware of Phin, and the intimacy of the whole situation, and at least I could try and disguise it with briskness.

'We'll need to offer them coffee,' I said, dumping the dirty mugs on the draining board. 'Have you got any fresh?'

'Somewhere…' Phin deposited a pile of newspapers on a chair and opened the fridge. It was like a cartoon bachelor's fridge, stacked with beers and little else, but he found a packet of ground coffee, which he handed to me, and sniffed at a carton. 'The milk seems OK,' he said. 'There should be a cafetière around somewhere, too.'

It was in the sink, still with coffee grounds at the bottom. I dreaded to think how long it had been there. Wrinkling my nose, I got rid of the grounds in the bin and washed up the cafetière with the mugs.

'What sort of state is the rest of the house in?' I asked when I had finished.

'I haven't quite finished unpacking from Peru,' Phin said as he opened the door to his bedroom.

'Quite' seemed an understatement to me. There were clothes strewn everywhere, along with various other strange items that were presumably essential when you were hacking your way through the rainforest: a mosquito net, a machete, industrial strength insect repellent. You could barely see that it was an airy room, sparsely but stylishly furnished, and dominated by an invitingly wide bed which I carefully averted my eyes from.

Phin had no such qualms. 'That's where we make mad, passionate love,' he said. 'Most of the time,' he added, seeing me purse my lips and unable to resist teasing. 'Of course there's always the shower and the sofa—and remember that time up on the kitchen table…?'

'It sounds very unhygienic,' I said crisply. 'I'd never carry on like that.'

'You would if you really wanted me.'

'Luckily for you,' I said, 'I'm only interested in your mind.'

'Don't tell *Glitz* that,' said Phin, his eyes dancing. 'You'll ruin my reputation.'

'They're not going to be interested in our sex life, anyway.'

'Summer, what world are you living in? That's *exactly* what they'll be interested in! They're journalists on a celebrity rag. I can tell you now this Imelda won't give two hoots about our minds!'

I lifted my chin stubbornly. 'The interview is supposed to be about you as a potential family man, not as some sex symbol.'

'You know, sex is an important part of marriage,' he said virtuously. 'We don't want them thinking we're not completely compatible in every way.'

'Yes, well, let's concentrate on our compatibility in the living room rather than the bedroom,' I said, closing the bedroom door. 'We'll just have to hope that they don't want to come upstairs.'

Anxious to get away from the bedroom, with all its associations, I hurried back downstairs.

'We're going to have to do something about this room,' I decided, surveying the living room critically. 'It's not just the mess. It looks too much like a single guy's room at the moment.'

I made Phin clear away all the clutter—I think he just dumped it all in the spare room—while I ran around with a vacuum cleaner. It didn't look too bad by the time I'd finished, although even I thought it was a bit bare.

'It could do with some flowers, or a cushion or two,' I said. 'Do you think I've got time to nip out before they get here?'

'Cushions?' echoed Phin, horrified. 'Over my dead body!'

'Oh, don't be such a baby. A couple of cushions wouldn't kill you.'

'Cushions are the beginning of the end,' he said mulishly. 'Next thing I know I'll be buying scented candles and ironing my sheets!'

'Sheets feel much nicer when they're ironed,' I pointed out, but he only looked at me in disbelief.

'I might as well be married. I've seen it happen to friends,' he told me. 'They meet a fabulous girl, they're having a great time, and then one day you go round and there's a cushion sitting on the sofa. You know it's the beginning of the end. You can count the days before that wedding invitation is dropping onto your mat!'

I rolled my eyes. I was feeling much better by that stage. I always find cleaning very comforting.

'Oh, very well, it's not as if we're supposed to be married,' I conceded. 'You'll just have to look as if you're keen enough on me to be considering a cushion some time soon.'

'I think I can manage looking keen,' said Phin, and something in his voice made me glance at him sharply. Amusement and something else glimmered in the depths of those blue eyes. Something that made my breath hitch and my heart thud uneasily in my throat. Something that sent me skittering right back to square one.

I moistened my lips, and cast around wildly for something to say. 'Shouldn't you go and change?' To my horror, my voice sounded high and tight.

'What for?' said Phin easily. 'They want to see me at home, don't they?'

'Well, yes, but you might want to look as if you've made a bit of an effort. You haven't even got any shoes on. You look as if you've just rolled out of bed,' I said, and then winced inwardly, wishing I hadn't mentioned bed.

'That's what we want them to think,' said Phin. 'And, now you come to mention it, I think you're the one who needs to do something about your appearance.'

'What do you mean?' Diverted, I peered anxiously into the mirror above the mantelpiece. Anne and I had spent hours the evening before, going through the clothes heaped on my bed and trying to pick just the right look. It had to be sexy enough for me to be in with a remote chance of being Phin's girl-friend, but at the same time I wanted it to fit with Gibson & Grieve's new family-friendly image.

'And you mustn't wear black or white next to your face,' Anne had said bossily. 'It's very draining in photographs. You want to look casual, but sophisticated, elegant, but colourful, sexy, but sensible.'

In the end we had decided on a pair of black wool trousers with a silky shirt I had worn to various Christmas parties the previous December. It was a lovely cherry-red, and I had painted my nails with Anne's favourite colour, Berry Bright, to match. I had even clipped my hair up loosely, the way I wore it at the weekend. I thought I looked OK.

'What's wrong with how I look?' I asked.

'You look much too neat and tidy,' said Phin, putting his hands on either side of my waist. 'Come here.'

'What are you doing?' I asked nervously as he drew me towards him.

'I'm going to make you look as you've just rolled out of bed, too. As if we rolled out of bed together.'

Lifting one hand, he pulled the clip from my hair so that it slithered forward. 'You shouldn't hide it away,' he said, twining his fingers through it. 'It's beautiful stuff. I thought it was just brown at first, but every time I look at it I see a different colour. Sometimes it looks gold, sometimes chestnut, sometimes honey. I swear I've even seen red in there…it makes me think of an autumn wood.'

I was speechless—and not just because of his closeness, which was making me feel hazy. No one had ever said anything like that to me before. I didn't want to look into his eyes to see if he was joking or not. I was afraid that if I did I would lose what little grip I still had on my senses.

'Very poetic,' I managed.

'But it'll look even more beautiful tousled up,' said Phin— and, ignoring my protests, he mussed up my hair before turning his attention to my shirt. 'And, yes…I think we'll have to do something about this, too. There are just too many buttons done up here, and they're all done up the right way! That won't do at all.'

Very slowly, very deliberately, he undid the first two buttons and looked down at me, his eyes dark and blue.

'No, you still look horribly cool,' he said, which must have been a lie because my heart was thundering in my chest and I was burning where those blunt, surprisingly deft fingers had grazed my skin. I opened my mouth, but the words jammed in my throat, piling into an inarticulate sound that fell somewhere between a squeak and a gasp. He was barely touching me, but every cell in my body was screaming with awareness and I couldn't have moved if I had tried.

'I may have to work a bit harder on this one…' he went on

and, bending his head, he blew gently just below my ear. The feel of it shuddered straight down my spine and clutched convulsively at its base. In spite of myself, I shivered.

'Mmm, yes, this may just work,' said Phin, pleased, and then he was trailing kisses down my neck, warm and soft and tantalising.

I really, *really* didn't want to respond, but I couldn't help myself. It was awful. It was as if some other woman had taken over my body, tipping her head back and sucking in her breath with another shudder of excitement.

My heart was thudding in my throat, and I could hear the blood rushing giddily in my ears.

'You see where I'm going with this,' murmured Phin, who was managing to undo another couple of buttons at the same time. 'I mean, we did discuss how important it was to make it look as if we found each other irresistible, didn't we?'

'I think that's probably enough buttons, though,' I croaked as he started on the other side of my neck. His hair was tickling my jaw and I could smell his shampoo. The wonderfully clean, male scent of his skin combined with the wicked onslaught of his lips was making my head spin, and I felt giddy and boneless.

Perhaps that was why I didn't resist as Phin steered me over to the great leather sofa. There was no way my legs were going to hold me up much longer, and as we sank down onto the cushions I felt as if I were sinking into a swirl of abandon.

'OK, no more buttons,' he whispered, and I could feel his lips curving against my throat. 'But…I…don't…think… you…look…*quite*…convincing…enough…yet.'

Between each word he pressed a kiss along my jaw until he reached my mouth at last, and then his lips were on mine, and he was kissing me with an expertise that literally took my breath away. Since I'm being frank, I'll admit that it was a revelation. I'd never been kissed so surely, so thoroughly, so completely and utterly deliciously. So irresistibly.

I certainly couldn't resist it. I wound my arms around him, pulling him closer, and kissed him back.

It wasn't that I didn't know who he was or what I was doing, but I thought… Well, I don't know what I thought, OK? The truth is, I wasn't thinking at all. I was just *feeling*, the slither of the satiny shirt against my skin, the hardness and heat of his hands on me as he pushed the slippery material aside.

Just tasting…his mouth, his skin.

Just hearing the wild rush of my pulse, the uneven way he said my name, my own ragged breathing.

Just *touching*—fumbling at his T-shirt, tugging it up so that I could run my hands feverishly over his smoothly muscled back, marvelling at the way it flexed beneath my fingers. I let them drift up the warmth of his flanks and felt him shiver in response.

What can I say? I was lost, astonished at my own abandon, and yet helpless to pull myself back.

Or perhaps I'm not being *entirely* honest. I was aware at one level of my sensible self frantically waving her arms and ordering me back to safety, but Phin's body felt so good, so lean and hard as it pressed me into the sofa, and his mouth was so wickedly enticing, that I ignored her and let my fingers drift to the fastening of his jeans instead.

Afterwards, I could hardly believe it, but the truth is that there was a moment when I *did* know that I'd regret it later, and I still chose the lure of Phin's hands taking me to places I'd barely suspected before. I succumbed to the excitement rocketing through me, and if Imelda and the photographer hadn't arrived just then who knows where we would have ended up?

Except I do know, of course.

What I don't know is whether that would have been a good thing or a bad thing. I'm pretty sure I would have enjoyed it, though.

As it was, the piercing ring of the doorbell tore through the hazy pleasure and brought me right back to earth with a sickening crash.

I jerked bolt upright. 'Oh, my God, it's them!'

Frantically I tried to button up my shirt and shove it back into my trousers at the same time as pushing my hair behind my ears. 'What were we *doing*?'

Phin was infuriatingly unperturbed. He was barely breathing unsteadily. 'Well, I don't know about you, but *I've* been doing my bit for our pretence—and with all due modesty, I think I've excelled,' he said, and grinned as his eyes rested on my face. I dreaded to think what I looked like. 'Now you really *do* look the part.'

The bell rang again, more stridently this time. 'Ready?' asked Phin, and without waiting for me to answer strolled to open the door.

I could hear him exchanging chit-chat with Imelda and the photographer in the narrow hallway as I desperately tried to compose myself. I was horrified when I looked in the mirror to see that my hair was all over the place, my eyes huge and my lips swollen. I hardly recognised myself. I looked wild. I looked wanton.

I looked *sexy*.

I looked the part, just like Phin had said.

The next moment Phin was ushering Imelda into the room. She stopped when she saw me. 'Hello,' she said, obviously surprised.

'Hello,' I said weakly, and then remembered—far too late, I know—that I was the one who had set up this interview. I cleared my throat and stepped forward to shake her hand. 'We've spoken on the phone,' I said. 'I'm Summer Curtis— Phin's PA.'

'Ah.' Imelda looked amused, and when I followed her gaze I saw that she was looking at my shirt, which I had managed to button up all wrong in my haste.

Flushing, I made to fix the top button, and then realised that I was just going to get into an awful muddle unless I undid them all and started again. As Phin had no doubt intended.

'Not just my PA,' said Phin, coming to put his arm round my waist and pulling me into his side.

'So I see,' said Imelda dryly.

Her elegant brows lifted in surprise. I didn't blame her. She must have known as well as I did that I wasn't exactly Phin's usual type, and I lost confidence abruptly. We'd never be able to carry this off. Not in front of someone as sharp as Imelda.

'Shall I make coffee?' I asked quickly, desperate to get out of the room. My heart was still crashing clumsily around in my chest, and I was having a lot of trouble breathing. I felt trembly and jittery, and I kept going hot and cold as if I had a fever.

Perhaps I *did* have a fever? I latched onto the thought as I filled the kettle with shaking hands. That would explain the giddiness, the way I had melted into Phin with barely a moment's hesitation. My cheeks burned at the memory.

Not just my cheeks, to be honest.

When I came back in with a tray, having taken the opportunity to refasten my shirt and tuck myself in properly, Phin was leaning back on the sofa, looking completely relaxed. He pulled me down onto the sofa beside him. 'Thanks, babe,' he said, and rested a hand possessively on my thigh.

Babe? Ugh. I was torn between disgust and an agonising

awareness of his hand touching my leg. It felt as if it were burning a hole through my trousers, and I was sure that when I took them off I would find an imprint of his palm scorched onto my skin.

'So, Phin,' said Imelda, when we had got the whole business of passing around the milk and sugar out of the way. 'It sounds as if you're making a lot of changes in your life right now. Does your new role at Gibson & Grieve mean you're ready to stop travelling?'

'I won't stop completely,' he said. 'I've still got various programme commitments, and besides, I'm endlessly curious about the world. There are still so many wonderful places to see, and so many exciting things to do. I'm never going to turn my back on all that completely. Having said that, my father's stroke did make me reassess my priorities. Gibson & Grieve is part of my life, and it feels good to be involved in the day to day running of it. It's time for me to do my part, instead of leaving it all to my brother.

'And then, of course, there's Summer.' He lifted my hand and pressed a kiss it. His lips were warm and sure, and a shiver travelled down my spine. I did my best to disguise it by shifting on the sofa, but I saw Imelda look at me. 'She's changed everything for me.'

'You're thinking of settling down?' She made a moue of exaggerated disappointment. 'That's another of the most eligible bachelors off the available list!'

'I'm afraid so,' said Phin, entwining his fingers with mine. 'I was always afraid of the idea of settling down, but since I've met Summer it doesn't seem so much like giving up my freedom as finding what I've been looking for all these years.'

You've got to admit he was good. No one could have

guessed he'd been ranting about cushions and commitment only a few minutes earlier.

Imelda was lapping it all up, while I sat with a stupid smile on my face, not knowing what to do with my expression. Should I look besotted? Shy? Smug?

'You're a lucky woman.' Imelda turned to me. 'What's it like knowing that half the women in the country would like to be in your place?'

I cleared my throat. 'To be honest, it hasn't sunk in yet. It's still very new.'

'But it feels absolutely right, doesn't it?' Phin put in.

He was doing so much better than me that I felt I should make an effort. 'Yes,' I said slowly, 'funnily enough, it does.'

And then, bizarrely, it didn't seem so difficult. I smiled at him, and he smiled back, and for a long moment we just looked at each other and there was nothing but the blueness of his eyes and the thud of my heart and the air shortening around us.

It took a pointed cough from Imelda to jerk me back to reality. With an effort, I dragged my eyes from Phin's and tried to remember what I was supposed to be talking about. Phin, that was it. Phin and me and our supposed passion for each other.

'We're so different in lots of ways,' I told Imelda, and the words seemed to come unbidden. 'Phin isn't at all the kind of guy I thought I would fall in love with, but it turns out that he's exactly right for me.'

'So it wasn't love at first sight for you?'

'No, he was just…my boss.'

'And what made the difference for you?'

Images rushed through my head like the flickering pages of a book. Phin smiling. Phin wiping cream from my cheek. Phin pulling the clip from my hair. Phin's mouth and Phin's hands and the hard excitement of Phin's body.

'I…I don't know,' I said hesitantly. 'I just looked at him one day and knew that I was in love with him.'

I thought it was pretty feeble, but Imelda was nodding as if she understood and looking positively dewy-eyed.

I was all set to relax then, but that was only the beginning. I still had to endure an excruciating photo session, posing cuddled up to Phin or looking at him adoringly, and my nerves were well and truly frayed by the time it was over. I tried to get out of the photographs, pleading that the article was about Phin, not me, but Imelda was adamant.

'All our readers will want to see the lucky woman who has convinced Phin Gibson to settle down,' she insisted.

I can tell you, I didn't feel very lucky by the time we'd finished. I was exhausted by the effort of pretending to be in love with Phin, while simultaneously trying to convince him that all the touching and kissing was having no effect on me at all.

But at last it was over. We waved them off from the steps, and then Phin closed the door and grinned at me. 'Very good,' he said admiringly. 'You practically had me convinced!'

'You didn't do badly yourself,' I said. 'You weren't lying when you said you were a good actor.'

No harm in reminding him that I knew he *had* been acting.

'If you can fool a hard-boiled journalist like Imelda, you should be able to fool Jonathan,' Phin said.

Why hadn't I remembered Jonathan before? I wondered uneasily. Jonathan was the reason I was doing this. I should have been thinking about him all morning, not about the sick, churning excitement I felt when Phin kissed me.

'Let's hope so,' I said, as coolly as I could. I looked at my watch. 'We'd better get back to the office.'

'What's the rush? Let's have lunch first,' said Phin. 'We should celebrate.'

'Celebrate what?'

'A successful interview, for one thing. Promoting Gibson & Grieve's family image. And let's not forget our engagement.'

'We're not engaged,' I said repressively.

'As good as,' he said, shrugging on his jacket and slipping a wallet into the inside pocket. He held the door open for me. 'You're now officially the woman who's convinced me to settle down.'

'You may be settling down, but I'm certainly not spending my life with anyone who calls me babe!'

Phin grinned at me as he pulled the door closed behind him. 'It's a mark of affection.'

'It's patronising.'

'Well, what would you like me to call you?'

'What's wrong with my name?'

'Every self-respecting couple has special names for each other,' he pointed out.

We walked towards the King's Road. 'Well, if you have to, you can call me darling,' I allowed after a moment, but Phin shook his head, his eyes dancing.

'No, no—darling is much too restrained, too *ordinary*, for you. You're much sexier than you realise, and we need to make sure Jonathan realises, too. Shall I call you bunnikins?'

'Shall I punch you on the nose?' I retorted sweetly.

He laughed. 'Pumpkin? Muffin? Cupcake?'

'*Cupcake?*'

'You'd be surprised,' said Phin. 'But you're right. I don't see you as a cupcake. What about cookie?'

'Oh, please!'

'Or—I know! This is perfect for you, and in keeping with the baking theme…cream puff?'

'Don't you dare!'

'Cream puff it is,' said Phin, as if I hadn't spoken. 'All crispy on the outside, but soft and delicious in the middle. It couldn't be better for you,' he said. 'That's settled. So, what are you going to call me?'

I looked at him. 'You really—*really*—don't want to know,' I said.

CHAPTER SEVEN

PHIN only smiled and took my hand. 'Come along, my little cream puff. Let's go and find some lunch. If you don't want to celebrate our non-engagement, let's just celebrate the fact that it's a beautiful day. What more reason do we need, anyway?'

I tried to imagine Jonathan suggesting that we celebrated the fact that the sun was shining, but I couldn't do it. It wasn't that he was a killjoy. Jonathan would celebrate a promotion, a rise in profits, a successful advertising campaign, perhaps. But a lovely day? I didn't think so.

And if he did celebrate he would want to plan it. Jonathan would book the very best restaurant, or order the most expensive champagne. He wouldn't just wander along the King's Road the way Phin did, and find the first place with a table in a sunny window.

But that was why I loved Jonathan, I reminded myself hastily. I loved him precisely because he *wasn't* spontaneous, because he was the kind of man who would think things through and plan them sensibly, instead of dropping everything when the sun came out, and because he didn't act on a whim the way my mother and Phin did.

On the other hand, I have to admit that I enjoyed that lunch—although that may have been largely due to the large glass of wine that came with it. I asked for water, but the wine came, and then it seemed too much of a fuss to send it back, so I ended up drinking it. I'm not used to drinking in the middle of the day, and I could feel myself flushing, and laughing a lot more than I usually do.

Perhaps it was relief at having got through the interview. Perhaps it was the sunshine.

Or perhaps it was Phin sitting opposite me, making me believe that there was nowhere else he would rather be and no one else he would rather be with. Having spent months having to be grateful for any time Jonathan could spare me, it was a novel sensation for me to be the focus of attention for a change.

It was so little, really—to feel that Phin saw *me* when he looked at me, that he was listening, really listening, to what I was saying—but I'd have been less than human if I hadn't responded, and I could feel myself unfurling in the simple pleasure of having lunch with an attractive man on a sunny day.

It was very unlike me. I'm normally very puritanical about long lunches in office time. I wasn't myself that day.

I felt really quite odd, in fact. Fizzy, is the best way to describe it, as if that kiss had left all my senses on high alert. I was desperately aware of Phin opposite me, scanning the menu. I could see every one of the laughter lines around his eyes, the crease in his cheek, and that dent at the corner of his crooked mouth which always seemed on the point of breaking into a smile.

I was supposed to be looking at the menu, too, but I couldn't concentrate. My eyes kept flickering over to him, skittering from the prickle of stubble on his jaw to his hands, to his throat and then back to that mobile mouth. And my own mouth dried at the memory of how excitingly sure his lips had been.

My whole body still seemed to be humming with the feel of his hands, of his mouth, but at the same time it seemed hard to believe that we could have kissed like that and yet be sitting here quite normally, as if nothing had happened at all. I shifted uncomfortably as I remembered how eagerly I had kissed Phin back. What must he think of me?

On the other hand, it hadn't been a *real* kiss, had it? It hadn't meant anything. Phin had made it clear enough that he had only been kissing me for effect, and I wondered if I ought to make it clear that I had been doing the same. And, yes, I know, that wasn't exactly how it was, but a girl has her pride.

Or perhaps I should pretend to ignore the whole issue?

I was still dithering when Phin looked up from the menu. 'Have you decided? I'm going to have a starter, too. I don't know about you, but all that kissing has given me an appetite!'

Now that he had raised the subject, I thought I might as well take the opportunity to make my position quite clear.

'Speaking of kissing,' I said, and was secretly impressed at how cool I sounded, 'perhaps we ought to discuss what happened earlier. I understand *why* you kissed me—' I went on.

Phin's brows lifted and his smile gleamed. 'Do you, now?'

'Of course. It created a convincing effect for Imelda, and I can see that it worked, but I hope there won't be any need to repeat it,' I said, at my most priggish.

Much effect it had on Phin. 'Now, there we differ, cream puff, because I hope there *will*. I enjoyed that kiss very much. Didn't you?'

My eyes darted around the table and I longed for the nerve to lie.

'I just don't want to lose sight of what we're trying to do here,' I said evasively. 'And don't call me cream puff.'

'That wasn't quite an answer to my question, though, was it?' said Phin with a provocative smile.

I might have known he wouldn't let me get away with it.

We locked eyes for a mute moment, until he gave in with a grin and a shake of his head.

'Look, don't worry. I haven't forgotten that for you this is about getting Jonathan back.'

'And it's promoting Gibson & Grieve,' I added quickly, not wanting it to be all about me. 'Not to mention keeping Jewel at arm's length!'

'All very fine causes,' Phin agreed with a virtuous expression. 'But since we're going through this pretence, it seems to me we might as well enjoy it. We're not going to look like a very convincing couple if we never touch each other, are we? Touching is what couples do.'

Jonathan and I had never touched in public. But then we hadn't been a real couple, had we?

'OK,' I said, 'but only when necessary.'

'Only when necessary,' he confirmed, and held up crossed fingers. 'Scout's honour. Now, let's get serious and talk about lunch…'

I felt that I had made my point, and after that I was able to relax a little. I suppose that glass of wine helped, too. I don't remember what we talked about—just nonsense, I think—but I was still in an uncharacteristically light-hearted mood when we made it back to the office.

We waited for a lift in the glossy atrium, with the sun angling through the building to lie across the floor in a broad stripe. Phin was telling me about a disastrous trip he'd been on for one of the *Into the Wild* programmes, where everything that could possibly go wrong had done, and I was laughing when the lift pinged at last and the doors slid open to reveal Lex and Jonathan.

There was a moment of startled silence, then they stepped out. I had a sudden image of myself through Lex's eyes, flushed and laughing and dishevelled. Somewhere along the line I had mislaid my clip, and my hair was still tumbling to my shoulders. In my silky red shirt I must have looked almost unrecognisable from my usual crisp self.

My smile faded as I encountered first Lex's stern gaze, then Jonathan's astounded look.

'Hello,' said Phin cheerfully. 'Don't tell me you two are sloping off early?'

'We've got a meeting in the City.' Pointedly Lex looked at his watch and, like Pavlov's dog, I looked at mine, too. My eyes nearly started out of my head when I saw that it was almost three o'clock. How had it got that late?

'I see you're not letting your new position here change your work ethic,' he added, with one of his trademark sardonic looks.

Phin was unperturbed. 'Less of the sarcasm, please,' he said. He was the only person I knew who wasn't the slightest bit intimidated by Lex. I suppose it helped that Lex was his brother. 'I'll have you know we've been busy promoting Gibson & Grieve all morning.'

'It's some time since morning,' said Lex, less than impressed.

'We've been recovering from the stress of persuading the media of my family friendly credentials. Summer did an absolutely brilliant job.'

I wished he hadn't mentioned me. Lex's cold grey gaze shifted back to me, and it took all I had not to squirm. I was unnervingly aware of Jonathan's astounded gaze fixed on me, too. I managed a weak smile.

'Remarkable,' was all Lex said.

'Isn't she?' said Phin fondly, putting an arm around me and pulling me against him. I could feel the heat and weight of his hand at my waist, making the slippery material of my shirt shift over my skin. 'That's just what I've been telling her.'

'We're so late,' I wailed as soon as we got in the lift. I could feel myself winding rapidly back up to my usual self. I was *never* late. Well, there had been yesterday, after the pomegranate martinis, but that had been exceptional circumstances. I couldn't believe that I had actually sat there in the sun and let time tick by without even thinking about getting back to the office.

'We're not late,' said Phin. 'We haven't got any appointments this afternoon.'

'I should have been back earlier,' I fretted, remembering Jonathan and Lex's raised brows. 'I wish they hadn't seen me like this,' I said as I tugged my shirt into place. 'I look so unprofessional.'

'Nonsense. You look fantastic,' said Phin. 'We couldn't have planned it better if we had tried. Did you *see* Jonathan's expression?'

I nodded. 'He was horrified,' I said gloomily.

'He wasn't horrified. He was absolutely amazed.' Phin spoke with complete authority. 'He looked at you and saw exactly what he could have had if he'd ever taken the trouble to kiss you senseless on a sofa and then take you out to lunch. He didn't like me touching you either,' he added.

'How on earth do you know that?'

'It's a guy thing.' Phin smiled smugly. 'Trust me, Summer, our little plan is working already.'

I know I should have been delighted, but actually I spent the rest of the afternoon feeling scratchy and unsettled. It was impossible to concentrate. It wasn't fair, the way Phin could be so casual about it all. How could he kiss me like that and then turn round and sound pleased at the idea of handing me on to someone else?

Easily, of course. It was a guy thing, just like he had said. Phin was perfectly happy to enjoy a kiss, or a long lunch, as long as there was no suggestion of any long-term commitment.

I'm not the settling down type, he had said. Well, no surprises there. And no reason for his cheerful admission to leave me feeling not *depressed*, exactly, but just a bit…flat.

I told myself not to be so silly.

So there we were, in this ridiculous situation, working together as boss and PA during the day, and at night pretending to be madly in love.

Whenever I stopped to think about what we were doing I wondered what on earth had possessed me to agree to such a thing, so it was easier to carry on as if it were perfectly normal to spend your days talking to your boss about brand marketing or strategic development or the logistics of taking twenty people to Africa to help build a medical centre, and your nights holding his hand and leaning into his warm, solid body as if you knew it as well as your own.

It was a strange time, but the funny thing was it really did seem quite normal after a while. I couldn't understand why everybody else didn't see through the pretence right away, but they all seemed to accept it without question. It was bizarre.

I was so unlike Phin's normal girlfriends, most of whom he still seemed to get on excellently with. To a woman, they were lushly glamorous and prone to extravagant kisses, with much 'mwah-mwah' and many 'darlings' scattered around. Next to them, I felt prim and boring. I tried to loosen up, but every time Phin put his arm around me or took my hand my senses would snarl into a knot and I would prickle all over with awareness. It wasn't exactly relaxing.

The first night we appeared as a couple we went to a party,

to launch some perfume, I think. Something unlikely, anyway. I can remember wondering why on earth Phin had been invited, but he seemed to be on hobnobbing terms with all sorts of celebrities. That was also the first time I realised quite how many ex-girlfriends he had, and I was glad I hadn't done anything silly like let myself wonder if that kiss might have meant something to Phin, too.

Still, I was nervous. It was all so strange to me, and I was feeling very self-conscious in a short dress with spaghetti straps which I had borrowed from Anne. It showed rather more flesh than I was used to, and when Phin let his hand slide down my spine I shivered.

He clicked his tongue. 'You're too tense,' he murmured in my ear. 'You're supposed to like me touching you.'

'Anyone would be tense, meeting all your ex-girlfriends like this,' I said out of the corner of my mouth, while keeping my smile fixed in place. 'They're all wondering what on earth you're doing with me.'

'Their boyfriends aren't.' His smile glimmered as he ran a knuckle along the neckline of my dress. 'You look delectable, in a behind-closed-doors kind of way.'

I hated the way every cell in my body seemed to leap at his touch. It made it very hard to remember that I was in control.

'What kind of way is that?' I asked, squirming at the breathlessness in my voice.

'You know—all cool on the surface, but making every man feel that if only he were lucky enough to get you on your own you'd be every hot-blooded male's fantasy.'

'Oh, please,' I said edgily, moving away from him. 'And stop stroking me!'

'Nope,' said Phin as he pulled me easily back against him. 'You're my girlfriend, and I can't keep my hands off you!'

'You've clearly got the same problem with your ex-girlfriends too,' I said waspishly. 'I notice you're still very touchy-feely with them.'

'Could it be that you're jealous, cream puff?'

'I'm hardly likely to be jealous, am I? I'm just keeping in character, like you. I'm sure if I really was your new girl-friend I wouldn't want to see quite how chummy you still are with them.'

'I'm just saying hello to old friends.'

I sniffed. 'I can manage to say hello to friends without sticking my tongue down their throats!'

'You do exaggerate, Summer—' Phin began, amused, and then broke off. 'Uh-oh. Do you see who I see?'

I followed his gaze to where Jewel Stevens was wrapped around a young guy who looked vaguely familiar to me. I wondered if I'd seen him on television. He was very pretty, but had a vacuous look about him.

'That's Ricky Roland,' said Phin in my ear. 'He's a rising star, they say, and just as well if he's going to get involved with Jewel! He'll be able to afford a new dinner service. I wonder how many plates he's got left?'

'She's coming over,' I hissed as Jewel somehow spotted Phin and made a beeline for him, abandoning poor Ricky with barely a word. Phin promptly put his arm around my waist and pulled me closer, so that I was half in front of him like a shield.

'Phin, darling, where have you *been*?' she cried as she came up—and, completely ignoring my existence, she gave him a smacking kiss on the lips.

'Peru,' he said, keeping a firm hold of me.

'What on earth for?' said Jewel, but didn't bother to wait for his reply. She glanced languidly around at the party. 'This is all very tedious, isn't it? We're all going on to a club after this if you want to come.'

'Not tonight, thanks, Jewel,' said Phin, his smile steady but inflexible. 'I'm taking Summer home. You remember Summer, don't you?'

Jewel's eyes flicked over me as if I was something unpleasant Phin had brought in on the bottom of his shoe. 'No.'

Charming, I thought. 'I'm Phin's PA,' I reminded her.

'And so much more than that, too,' said Phin.

At that, Jewel's gaze sharpened, and she looked from Phin to me, and then back to Phin again. 'You and…Sunshine, or whatever her name is?' she said incredulously.

'Yes,' said Phin blandly. 'Me and Summer.'

Disconcertingly, Jewel began to laugh. 'You and your little secretary…isn't that a bit of a cliché, darling?'

Phin's arm tightened around me, but his voice was admirably even. 'That's the thing about clichés,' he said. 'They're so often true.'

'Well, if you say so.' Jewel was evidently unconvinced. Her brown eyes rested speculatively on me once more, and I could practically hear her thinking that I was too boring to hold Phin's attention for more than five minutes. 'How very odd,' she said.

And then she leant forward to Phin and did her ear licking trick again. *Bleuch*. 'When you're bored and want some excitement again, give me a call,' she said huskily, only to shriek and leap back as I moved, managing to stand on her foot and spill my glass of champagne all down her fabulous dress at the same time.

It was quite a clever move, even if I say so myself. Subtle, but effective.

'Oh, I'm *so* sorry,' I said insincerely as she glared at me.

I could feel Phin's body shaking with suppressed laughter. 'How clumsy of me.'

I could see Jewel debating whether to make a scene, but in the end she just sent me a poisonous look and kissed Phin once more. On the mouth, this time, which was a fairly effective retort of her own.

'You know where to find me when you change your mind, darling,' she said to him.

My lips thinned as she prowled off to reclaim Ricky Roland, who was making the big mistake of talking to a pretty girl about his own age. I didn't fancy his chances of keeping the rest of his plates intact.

'*When!*' I huffed. 'She's got a nerve, hasn't she? Not even *if* you lose interest in me!'

'Yes, but the round definitely went to you, with the champagne spilling trick,' said Phin, letting me go at last. 'That was an excellent impression of a jealous girlfriend, Summer. I didn't think you had it in you!'

'I don't think it convinced Jewel,' I said. 'She clearly didn't believe for a moment that you'd be interested in anyone as boring as me!'

'No? Well, her style is much more obvious than yours.'

'You can say that again!'

He studied me for a moment. 'Personally, I think that restrained look is good for you. It's classy. On the other hand, it *would* look more natural if you could be a little more relaxed.'

'What do you mean?'

'We may have to do something about making you look a *little* less like a librarian who's strayed into an orgy,' said Phin. 'It works for me—don't get me wrong!—but other people might wonder eventually why you're so tense with me.'

'Maybe they'll think I'm shy,' I said, on the defensive. I

knew I looked uptight—I *felt* uptight—but then so would you if you had to snuggle up to Phin while Jewel stuck her tongue down his ear, and I wasn't used to parties where you fell over a celebrity every time you turned round.

'You can get away with being shy tonight, but the next time we go out you'll need to loosen up a bit.'

'How do you suggest I do that?' I snapped, annoyed because I knew he was right.

'I'm not sure yet,' said Phin. 'I'll give it some thought.'

But, apart from Jewel, everyone seemed to accept our supposed relationship with an extraordinary lack of surprise. Monique, Lex's PA, whom I'd always admired for her perspicacity, even told me that she thought Phin and I were a perfect match!

'You're just right for each other,' she said when we met in the corridor one day, on my way back from making coffee. 'He's so lovely, isn't he?' she went on, while I was still boggling at the idea that anyone could think Phin and I were right for each other when it must be blindingly obvious that we were completely different.

'Lex is always baffled by him, but Phin is a huge asset to Gibson & Grieve if only he'd recognise it. He's one of those people that just has to walk into a room and everyone relaxes, because you know he'll be able to defuse any situation and charm everyone so they'll all go away feeling good about themselves, whatever's been decided.'

I did some more boggling then. Relaxed was the last thing I felt with Phin. He was too unpredictable. One minute he'd be sitting lazily with his feet up on the desk, the next he'd be fizzing with energy. I never knew when he was going to appear or what he was going to do.

Whenever Phin was around I felt edgy, jittery. My pulse

was prone to kicking up a beat at the most inexplicable moments. All he had to do was stretch his arms above his head and yawn, or look at me with that smile twitching at his mouth, and my heart would start to thump and an alarming shivery feeling would uncoil in my belly and tremble outwards, until my whole skin prickled with awareness. It was very disturbing.

Relaxed? Ha!

'How are *you* anyway, Monique?' I asked, sick of being told how wonderful Phin was.

'Fantastic,' she said, beaming. 'In fact…' She checked to make sure no one else was around. 'I'm not telling many people yet, as it's early days, but I'm pregnant!'

I was delighted for her. I knew that Monique and her husband had been hoping for a baby for a while now. 'Monique, that's wonderful news! Dave must be thrilled.'

'He is. Lex is less so, of course,' she said, with a wry roll of her eyes.

Monique adored her boss, but she had no illusions about him. With Lex it was business all the way, and babies just didn't enter the equation.

'He was grumbling just this morning that if I'd told him earlier he would never have let you go and work for Phin— and what a shame that would have been!' She hesitated. 'I don't suppose you'd want to go back to Lex's office now, but he'll be looking for someone he trusts to cover my maternity leave, so if you're interested there might be an opening in a few months.'

'*Really?*'

'The baby's due in September, so I'll work up until August,' she said. 'Talk it over with Phin and see what he thinks. If you're spending all your time together, it might not be a bad thing to work in different offices…but you'd obviously want to vet any new PA!' Monique could obviously see the thoughts whirling in my brain. 'Maybe I shouldn't have said anything? I was just being selfish. It would make it so much easier for me if I could reassure Lex that you'd look after him while I'm away, that's all.'

'I'll definitely think about it,' I promised.

Thoughtfully, I carried the coffee back to my office. To be Lex's PA—the most senior in the company…! Only temporarily, of course, until Monique came back. But what a thing to have on my CV. It would be an extraordinary opportunity, and one I could only ever have dreamed of up to now.

It was hard to believe that only a month ago I had felt utterly hopeless. Now I not only had the prospect of a fantastic promotion, but there was even a real chance of getting back together with Jonathan. Or so Phin seemed to think—and, much as I hated to admit that he was right, I had to admit that Jonathan had been much more friendly the last few days. He had taken to dropping by the office on the slimmest of pretexts, and telling me how nice I looked if we met by the lifts.

It was all very confusing. Everything was changing so quickly I didn't know what to think any more.

I should be excited. I knew that. In a few months' time I could be back with Jonathan and working with the Chief Executive—and Phin… Well, this had only ever been meant as a temporary exercise anyway. Phin would move on. He'd go back to making television programmes and I wouldn't see him any more. There would be no more jitteriness, no more exasperation, no more teasing. No more doughnuts. And that would be fine, I told myself. It would all work out perfectly.

But there was a sick feeling in the pit of my stomach all the same.

'What's up?' said Phin, when I took in his coffee. It was uncanny the way he always knew if something had happened, no matter how smooth I made my expression.

So I told him what Monique had said. 'Typical Lex,' was his comment, when he heard about his brother's response to the news that his PA was having a much longed for baby. 'He's got no idea. You'd think he could be happy for her before he thought about how her pregnancy will affect Gibson & Grieve!'

'Monique doesn't really mind,' I said, a little uncomfortably. 'She knows what he's like. The normal rules don't apply to someone like Lex.'

'Well, they should,' said Phin. He was leaning back, twirling a pen between his fingers. 'So what about you?' he asked, blue eyes suddenly intent. 'Do you really want to work for a man who wouldn't know what a doughnut was, let alone think about buying you one?'

'It would be a good career opportunity for me.' Unable to bear it any longer, I held out my hand for the pen, and after a stubborn moment he surrendered it, dropping it into my open palm.

'At least I wouldn't have to put up with your endless fiddling any longer,' I said, putting the pen back into its holder. 'And it might be easier when our supposed romance falls through,' I added. 'It would look a bit odd if we carried on working together perfectly happily when…if…'

'When you're back with Jonathan?' Phin finished for me.

There was an unusual note in his voice that made me look sharply at him.

'Even if that doesn't happen, we can't carry on like this indefinitely,' I pointed out.

'Then we'll have to make sure it does happen,' he said, swinging his feet off the desk abruptly. 'Maybe it's time to intensify our campaign. When's the launch party for the *Charmless Chef*?'

The *Charmless Chef* was Phin's own title for a series of TV food programmes that Gibson & Grieve were sponsoring that spring. It was actually called *Hodge Hits*, after the presenter, celebrity chef Stephen Hodge. Hodge was famously rude, and prone to the most appalling temper tantrums. Very early in his career he had discovered that the worse he behaved, the more audiences would want to watch him and the more he would be paid.

This meant Gibson & Grieve would get even more publicity from their sponsorship of the programme, and a fabulous party had been planned to mark the launch and appease his monstrous ego. All senior staff were on a three line whip to turn up and do whatever it took to keep Stephen Hodge happy. Except Lex, of course. He hated socialising, and only went out when absolutely necessary. On this occasion Phin was lined up to represent him and make a speech.

'It's on Friday,' I said.

'Jonathan will be there, won't he?'

'Of course. He negotiated the deal with Stephen Hodge,' I reminded Phin.

'In that case you'll have to pull out all the stops. You always look smart, but on Friday you've got to look stunning. Take tomorrow off and buy a special dress if you have to, but wear something that will knock Jonathan's socks off.'

'He'll be too busy with Stephen Hodge to notice me,' I protested, but Phin refused to listen to any objections.

'If you get the right dress he'll notice you, all right,' he said. 'Besides, I have a cunning plan up my sleeve to relax you.'

'What sort of plan?' I asked suspiciously. I had tried to loosen up whenever we'd been out together, but it was almost impossible when every cell in my body jolted if Phin so much as grazed me with his touch.

'I'll explain on Friday,' he said. 'The launch is at seven, isn't it? We might as well go straight from here.'

Which is how I ended up changing in the directors' bathroom that Friday evening. I'd brought my dress in on a hanger, and carried shoes and make-up in a separate bag.

I had put the need to look stunning to Anne, who had borne me off late-night shopping the night before, and bullied me into buying the most expensive dress I'd ever owned. Even though I felt faintly sick whenever I thought about my credit card bill, I couldn't regret it. It was *so* beautiful.

I don't really know how to begin to describe it. It was red, but not that hard pillarbox red that's so hard to wear. This was a softer, deeper, warmer red—a simple sleeveless sheath, with a layer of chiffon that floated and swirled as I walked. I wasn't used to such a plunging neckline, and with bare shoulders and a bare back I felt a lot more exposed than usual, but it was the kind of dress you couldn't help but feel good in.

I'd painted my toenails a lovely deep red—Ruby, Ruby— to match my fingers, and slipped my feet into beautiful jewelled sandals. My hair was swept up into a clip, and I thought it looked elegant like that, but I hesitated as I studied my reflection, remembering Phin's librarian comment. On an impulse I pulled the clip out and shook my hair free, and then I walked back into the office before I could change my mind.

Phin was there, adjusting his bow tie, but his fingers froze when he saw me. There was a moment of stunned silence. 'Dear God,' he said blankly.

My confidence promptly evaporated. 'What's wrong with it?' I asked, looking down at my lovely dress. I'd been so sure he would like it.

'Nothing's wrong.' Phin cleared his throat. 'Nothing at all. You look…incredible.'

He sounded a bit odd, I thought, but he had said I looked incredible. 'Shall I order a taxi?' I asked after a moment.

'No, it's all sorted,' he said, still distracted. 'A car's waiting downstairs.'

'Oh. Well, shall we go, then?'

Phin seemed to pull himself together. 'Not quite yet, CP,' he said, making a good recovery. 'We need to put my cunning plan into action first.'

'CP?' I echoed blankly.

'Cream…' He waited expectantly for me to supply the rest. Puff, in fact. I sighed.

'Oh, for heaven's sake,' I said crossly. 'Will you *stop* with the silly names? Now, what *is* this plan of yours?'

'It's really quite simple,' said Phin, coming towards me. 'I'm going to kiss you.'

CHAPTER EIGHT

'KISS me?' The world titled disconcertingly beneath my feet, and it took me a moment to realise that the air was leaking out of my lungs. I drew in a hissing breath, glad of the steadying effect of the oxygen. We had been through this before, I remembered. 'What kind of plan is that?'

'A good one,' said Phin.

'We agreed that you would only kiss me again if it was necessary,' I reminded him, backing away. My voice was embarrassingly croaky, but under the circumstances—i.e. pounding heart, racing pulse, entrails squeezed with nerves or, more worryingly, anticipation—I didn't think I did too badly.

'I think it *is* necessary,' he said.

I had ended up against the desk, the wood digging into the back of my thighs. 'There's no one else here,' I pointed out bravely. 'How can it be necessary?'

Phin kept coming until he was right in front of me. 'That's the whole point,' he said.

'I've been thinking about it. If we kiss before we go out every time you'll get used to it. It'll just seem part of the evening, like putting on your lipstick—although you might think about doing that *after* we kiss next time. You'll look much more relaxed after a kiss,' he went on. 'Remember how well it worked before the *Glitz* interview?'

'We're not kissing like that again!' My eyes went involuntarily to the sofas on the other side of the room. If we ended up on one of those we'd never get to the party.

'Maybe not *quite* like that,' Phin agreed. A smile hovered around his mouth. The mouth I was doing my level best not to look at. 'Not that it wasn't very nice, but what we want now is for you to feel more comfortable. Once kissing me feels normal, you'll stop feeling so tense whenever I touch you.'

'It's not going to feel normal tonight.'

'No, but I can tell you that if you go to the party in that dress, looking thoroughly kissed, it won't just be Jonathan I'll be fighting off with a stick,' Phin promised.

Jonathan. The thought of him steadied me. Jonathan was the reason I was wearing this dress...wasn't he?

'Go on, admit it,' said Phin. 'It's a good plan, isn't it?'

I eyed him dubiously. I couldn't help remembering the last time we had kissed. I had got carried away then, and I didn't want that to happen again. On the other hand, I didn't want to admit to Phin that I was nervous about losing control. Somehow I had to pretend that it wasn't that big a deal.

'It might work,' I conceded, and he grinned.

'Come along, then—pucker up, cream puff,' he said. 'The sooner we get it over with, the sooner we can get to the party.'

'Oh, very well.' I gave in. 'If you really think it'll help.'

Maybe it *would* help, I told myself. Instead of constantly wondering what it would be like to touch him again, I would know.

So I stood very still and lifted my face for Phin's kiss, pursing my lips and closing my eyes.

And willing myself not to respond.

Nothing happened at first, and, feeling foolish, I opened my eyes again in time to see him brush my hair gently back over my shoulders. Then very slowly, almost thoughtfully, he slid his hands up the sides of my throat to cup my face. His eyes never left mine, and I felt as if I were trapped in their blueness. My heart was slamming against my ribs.

My mouth felt dry, and I had moistened my lips before I realised what an inviting gesture it was.

Phin smiled. We were so close I could see every eyelash, every one of the tiny creases in his lips, the precise depth of the dent at the corner of his mouth, and I felt dizzy with the nearness of him.

By the time he lowered his head and touched his mouth to mine my blood was thumping with anticipation, and I couldn't help the tiny gasp of relief that parted my lips beneath his.

I willed myself to stay still and unresponsive. All I had to do was stand there for a few seconds and it would be over. How difficult could it be?

You try it. That's all I can say. Try not responding when a man with warm, strong hands twines his fingers in your hair and pulls you closer. When a man with warm, sure lips explores your mouth tantalisingly gently at first, then more insistently. When he smells wonderful and tastes better.

When every kiss pulls at a thread inside you, unravelling you faster and faster, until the world rocks and your bones melt and the only way to stay upright is to clutch at him and kiss him back.

'That's better,' murmured Phin when he lifted his head at last.

I was flushed and trembling, but I was glad to see that his breathing wasn't quite steady either.

'There—it wasn't so bad, was it?' he added, sliding his hands reluctantly from my hair.

'It was fine,' I managed, hoping my legs were going to hold me up without him to hang on to. I was very glad there was a car waiting downstairs. It was going to take all I had to get to the lift, and I was in no shape to trek to the tube—even if my shoes had been up to it.

For reasons best known to the television company, the launch party for *Hodge Hits* was being held in the Orangery at Kew Gardens. I'd never been before, and it looked so beautiful with that row of high arched windows that I actually forgot my throbbing lips and crackling pulse as I looked around me.

The room was already crowded, but I caught a glimpse of Stephen Hodge, surrounded by groupies as always, wearing his trademark scowl. He had long hair that always looked as if it could do with a good wash, and he was very thin. There's something unnatural about a thin chef, don't you think? I suspected that Stephen Hodge never ate his own food and, having seen some of his more innovative recipes, I didn't blame him.

'Now, be nice,' said Phin, seeing my lip curl.

'That's good, coming from you,' I countered. 'Are you sure you've got the right speech with you?'

He'd tried a scurrilous version on me earlier, which had been very funny but which was unlikely to go down well with either Hodge or Jonathan, who had been instrumental in setting up the sponsorship. I was hoping that he had a suitably bland alternative in his pocket somewhere, but with Phin you never knew.

'Don't worry, I've got the toadying version right here,' he said, patting his jacket. 'Besides, you're not in PA mode tonight. You're my incredibly sexy girlfriend and don't you forget it. Talking of which—' he nudged me '—look who's heading our way. Or rather don't look. You're supposed to be absorbed in me.'

I risked a swift glance anyway, and spotted Jonathan, pushing his way through the crowd towards us. He had Lori with him, looking tiny and delicate in a sophisticated ivory number. I immediately felt crass and garish in comparison, but it was too late to run away.

'Remember—make him jealous,' Phin murmured in my ear.

There was no way Jonathan would even notice me next to Lori, I thought, but I turned obediently and slid my arm around Phin's waist, snuggling closer and smiling up at him as if I hadn't noticed Jonathan at all.

Perhaps that kiss had worked after all. It felt oddly comfortable to be leaning against Phin's hard, solid body—so much so, in fact, that when Jonathan's voice spoke behind me I was genuinely startled.

'I'm glad you're here, Phin,' Jonathan began. 'I just wanted to check everything's under control. We want to kick off with your speech, and then Stephen's going to—'

He broke off as his gaze fell on me, and I gave him my most dazzling smile. 'Summer!'

'Hi, Jonathan,' I said.

Gratifyingly, he looked pole-axed. 'I didn't recognise you,' he said.

Beside him, Lori raised elegant brows. 'Nor did I. That colour really suits you, Summer.'

'Thank you,' I said coolly. 'You look great, too.'

Jonathan was still watching me with a stunned expression. Funny, I had dreamt of him looking at me just that way, but now that he was doing it I felt awkward and embarrassed.

'You look amazing tonight,' he said, and all I could think was that it wasn't fair of him to be talking to me like that when Lori was standing right beside him.

'Doesn't she?' Phin locked gazes with Jonathan in an unspoken challenge, and slid his hand possessively beneath my hair to rest it on the nape of my neck.

I could feel the warm weight of it—not pressing uncomfortably, but just there, a reassuring connection—and I had one of those weird out of body moments when you can look at yourself as if from the outside. I could see how easy we looked together, how right.

Jonathan and Lori had no reason not to believe that we were a real couple. They would look at us and assume that we were used to touching intimately, to understanding each other completely. To not knowing precisely where one finished and the other began, so that there was no more me, no more Phin, just an us.

The thought of an 'us' made the world tip a little. Abruptly I was back in my body, and desperately aware of Phin's solid strength beneath my arm, of the tingling imprint of his palm on my neck.

There *was* no us, I had to remind myself. I only just stopped myself shaking my head to clear it. Everything about the party seemed so unreal, but I was bizarrely able to carry on a conversation with Jonathan and Lori while every cell in my body was straining with Phin's closeness.

True, it wasn't much of a conversation. Some small talk about Stephen Hodge and his vile temper. I complimented Lori on her earrings, she mentioned my shoes, but all I could really think about was the way Phin was absently stroking my neck, his thumb caressing my skin.

Every graze of his fingertips stoked the sizzle deep inside me, and I was alarmingly aware that it could crackle into life at any time. If I wasn't careful there would be a *whoosh* and I would spontaneously combust. That would spoil Stephen Hodge's party all right.

I had to move away from Phin or it would all get very messy. Straightening, I made a show of pushing my hair behind my ears. 'Um…isn't it time for your speech?' I asked him with an edge of desperation.

'I suppose I'd better throw a few scraps to the monster's ego,' sighed Phin. 'He hasn't been kow-towed to for all of thirty seconds! Where would you like me to do it, Jonathan?'

'We've set up a podium,' said Jonathan. 'I'd better go and warn Stephen that we're ready to go.'

'Lead on,' said Phin, and held out his hand to me. 'Are you coming, CP?'

Jonathan looked puzzled. 'CP?'

I smiled uncomfortably as I took Phin's hand. 'Private joke,' I said.

After that, we had to kiss every time we got ready to go out. 'Come here and be kissed,' Phin would say, holding out his arms. 'This is the best part of the day.'

I was very careful to keep reminding myself that those kisses didn't mean a thing, but secretly I found myself looking forward to them. I always tried to make a joke of it, of course.

'Oh, let's get it over with, then,' I'd say, putting my arms briskly around his neck, but there was always a moment when our determined jokiness faded into something else entirely, something warm and yearning—the moment when I succumbed to the honeyed pleasure spilling along my veins, to the tug of longing and the wicked crackle of excitement between us.

I would like to say that it was me who put an end to the kiss every time, but I'd be lying. It was almost always Phin who lifted his head before I remembered that it was only supposed to be a quick kiss and thought about pulling away.

'We're getting good at this now,' Phin would say. I noticed, though, that the famous smile looked a little forced, and he was often distracted afterwards.

The theory had been that the more we kissed, the easier it would get. But it didn't work like that. It got more and more difficult to disentangle those kisses from reality, harder and harder to remember that I wanted Jonathan, that Phin was just amusing himself.

To remember why we had to stop at a kiss.

And the worst thing was that there was a bit of me that didn't want to.

Whenever I realised that I'd give myself a stern ticking off. This would involve a rigorous reminder of all the reasons why it would be stupid to fall for someone like Phin. He wasn't serious. He wasn't steady. He didn't want to settle down. I'd end up hurt and humiliated and I'd have no one to blame but myself.

Much—*much*—more sensible to remember why I had loved Jonathan. Why I *still* loved him, I'd have to correct myself an alarming number of times.

Jonathan was everything Phin wasn't. He was everything I needed.

I just couldn't always remember why.

Ironically, the harder I tried to remind myself of how much I wanted Jonathan, the more often Jonathan found excuses to drop into the office.

'You can't tell me our plan's not working now,' Phin said to me one evening as we sipped champagne at some gallery opening. 'Jonathan's always sniffing around nowadays. I trip over him every time I come into office. I notice he was there again this afternoon.'

He sounded uncharacteristically morose, and I shot him a curious look.

'He just came to see what I knew about the Cameroon trip,' I said uncomfortably, although I had no idea why I felt suddenly guilty.

'Ha!' said Phin mirthlessly. 'Was that all he could think of as an excuse?'

'It wasn't an excuse,' I said.

I had the feeling Jonathan was looking forward to going to Africa about as much as I was. I'd tried everything I could to get out of the trip, but Phin was adamant. The flights were booked for the end of March, and I was dreading it.

It was so *not* my kind of travelling. I like city breaks—Paris or Rome or New York—and hotels with hairdryers and mini bars, all of which were obviously going to be in short supply on the Cameroon trip. We'd had to be vaccinated against all sorts of horrible tropical diseases, and Phin had presented us all with a kit list so that we'd know what to take with us. Hairdryers didn't appear on it. I would be taking a rucksack instead of a pull-along case, walking boots in place of smart city shoes.

'And don't bother with any make-up,' Phin had told me. 'Sunblock is all you'll need.'

I was taking some anyway.

I don't suppose Jonathan was bothered about the make-up issue, but he was clearly anxious about the whole experience. Phin had presented the trip as a staff development exercise, and I suspected Jonathan didn't want to be developed any more than I did.

'I'm really glad you're going to be in same group when we go to Africa,' he had said to me, only that afternoon.

Phin was eyeing me moodily over the rim of his champagne glass. 'Nobody could be *that* worried about going to Africa. He just wants to hang around and talk to you.' He scowled at me. 'I hope you're not going to give in too easily. Make him work to get you back!'

'Look, what's the problem?' I demanded. 'Isn't the whole

idea that Jonathan starts to find me interesting again? Or did you want to spend the rest of your life stuck in this pretence?'

'It just irritates me that he's being so cautious.' Phin hunched a shoulder. 'If you'd been mine, and I'd realised what an idiot I'd been, I wouldn't be dithering around talking about malaria pills, or whether to pack an extra towel, and how many pairs of socks to take. I'd be sweeping you off your feet.'

It wasn't like Phin to be grouchy. That was *my* role. The worst thing was that there was a bit of me that agreed with him. But I had no intention of admitting *that*.

'Yes, well, the whole point is that you're *not* Jonathan,' I said. 'Yes, he's being careful—but that's only sensible. As far as he knows I'm in love with his boss. It would be madness to charge in and try and sweep me off unless he was sure how I felt.'

I lifted my chin. 'And I wouldn't *want* to be with someone that reckless,' I went on. 'I'd rather have someone who thought things through, who saw how the land lay, and then acted when he was sure of success. Someone like Jonathan, in fact.'

And right then I even believed it.

Or told myself I did, anyway.

Now, I know what you're thinking, but you have to remember how clear Phin always made it that he would never consider a permanent relationship. He liked teasing me, he liked kissing me, and we got on surprisingly well, but there was never any question that there might be more than that.

I'm not a fool. I knew just how easy it would be to fall in love with him. But I knew, too, how pointless it would be. I might grumble about him endlessly, but it was fun being with Phin. Much to my own surprise, I was enjoying our pretend affair.

But I wouldn't let myself lose sight of the fact that the security I craved lay elsewhere. I was earning better money now, and could start to think about buying a flat. Lori, I'd heard, was back with her old boyfriend and, whatever I might say to Phin, I knew Jonathan was definitely showing signs of renewed interest in me. Somewhere along the line I'd lost my desperate adoration of him, but he was still attractive, still nice, still steady. I could feel safe with Jonathan, I knew.

I had never had a better chance to have everything I wanted, and I wasn't going to throw it away—no matter how good it felt being with Phin.

I had run out of excuses. Hunched and sullen, I sat in the departure lounge at Heathrow, nursing a beaker of tea. It was five-thirty in the morning, and I didn't want to be there. I wanted to be at home, in bed, soon to begin my nice, safe routine.

I did the same thing every day. I woke up at half past six and made myself a cup of tea. Then I showered, dried my hair and put on my make-up. I took the same bus, the same tube, and stopped at Otto's at the same time to buy a cappuccino from Lucia.

You could set your watch by the time I got to the office and sat down behind my immaculately tidy desk. Then I'd sit there and savour the feeling of everything being in its place and under control, which lasted only until Phin appeared and stirred up the air and made the whole notion of control a distant memory.

'It's a rut,' Phin had said when I told him about my routine.

'You're missing the point. I *like* my rut.'

'Trust me, you're going to like Africa, too.'

'I'm not,' I said sulkily. 'I'm going to hate every minute of it.'

And at first I did.

We had to change planes, and after what seemed like hours hanging around in airports it was dark by the time we arrived at Douala. The airport there was everything I had feared. It was hot, crowded, shambolic. There seemed to be a lot of shouting.

I shrank into Phin as we pushed our way through the press of people and outside, to where a minibus was supposed to be waiting but wasn't. The tropical heat was suffocating, and the smell of airport fuel mingled with sweat and unfinished concrete lodged somewhere at the back of my throat.

Through it all I was very aware of Phin, steady and good-humoured, bantering in French with the customs officials who wanted to open every single one of our bags. He was wearing jungle trousers and an olive-green shirt, and amazingly managed to look cool and unfazed—while my hair was sticking to my head and I could feel the perspiration trickling down my back.

There were twelve of us in our group. Hand-picked by Phin, together we represented a cross-section of the headquarters staff, from secretaries like me to security staff, executives to cleaners. I knew most of the others by sight, and Phin had assured us we would be a close-knit team by the time we returned ten days later. I could tell we were bonding already in mutual unease at the airport.

'Everything's fine,' Phin said soothingly as we all fretted about the non-appearance of the mini-bus. 'It'll be here in a minute.'

The minute stretched to twenty, but eventually a rickety mini-bus did indeed turn up. It took us to a strange hotel where we slept four to a room under darned mosquito nets. There were tiny translucent geckos on the walls, and a rattling air-conditioning unit kept me awake all night. Oh, yes, and I found a cockroach in the shower.

'Tell me again why I'm supposed to love all this,' I grumbled to Phin the next morning. I was squeezed between him and the driver in the front of a Jeep that bounced over potholes and swerved around the dogs and goats that wandered along the road with a reckless disregard for my stomach, not to mention any oncoming traffic.

'Look at the light,' Phin answered. To my relief we had slowed to crawl through a crowded market. 'Look at how vibrant the colours are. Look at that girl's smile.' He gestured at the stalls lining the road. 'Look at those bananas, those tomatoes, those pineapples! Nothing's wrapped in plastic, or flown thousands of miles so that it loses its taste.'

His arm lay behind my head along the back of the seat, and he turned to look down into my face. 'Listen to the music coming out of the shops. Doesn't it make you want to get out and dance? How can you *not* love it?'

'It just comes naturally to me,' I muttered.

'And you're with me,' he pointed out, careless of our colleagues in the back seat.

I was very aware of them—although I couldn't imagine they would be able to hear much over the sound of the engine, the music spilling out of the shacks on either side of the road and the children running after us shouting, 'Happy! Happy! Happy!'

'We're together on an adventure,' said Phin. 'What more could you want?'

I sighed. 'I don't know where to begin answering that!'

'Oh, come on, Summer. This is fun.'

'You sound just like my mother,' I said sourly. 'This reminds me of the way Mum would drag me around the country, telling me how much I should be loving it, when all I wanted was to stay at home.'

'Maybe she knew that you had the capacity to love it all if only you'd let yourself,' said Phin. 'Maybe she was like me and thought you were afraid of how much love and passion was locked up inside you.'

It certainly sounded like the kind of thing my mother *would* think.

'Why do you care?' Cross, I lowered my voice and looked straight ahead, just in case anyone behind was listening or had omitted to put lip-reading skills on their CV. 'We don't have a real relationship, and even if we did it would only be temporary. You can't tell me you'd be hanging around long enough to care about my *capacity* for anything.'

There was a pause. 'I hate waste,' said Phin at last.

I had thought the road from Douala was bad, but I had no idea then of what lay ahead.

After that little town, the road deteriorated until there wasn't even an attempt at tarmac, and a downpour didn't exactly improve matters. Our little convoy of Jeeps lurched for hours over tracks through slippery red mud. We had to stop several times to push one or other of the vehicles out of deep ruts gouged out by trucks.

'This is what it's like trying to get *you* out of your rut,' Phin said to me with a grin, as we put our shoulders to the back of our Jeep once more. His face was splattered with mud from the spinning tyres, and I didn't want to think about what I looked like. I could feel the sprayed mud drying on my skin like a measles rash.

'Of course it's harder in your case,' he went on. 'Not so muddy, though.'

We were all filthy by the time we reached Aduaba—a village wedged between a broad brown river and the dark green press of the rainforest. There was a cluster of huts, with mud daub walls and roofs thatched with palm leaves, or occasionally a piece of corrugated iron, and what seemed like hundreds of children splashing in the water.

My relief at getting out of the Jeep soon turned to horror

when I discovered that the huts represented luxury accommodation compared to what we were getting: a few pieces of tarpaulin thrown over a makeshift frame to provide shelter.

'I'm so far out of my comfort zone I don't know what to say,' I told Phin.

'Oh, come now—it's not that bad,' he said, but I could tell that he was enjoying my dismay. 'It's not as if it's cold, and the tarpaulin will keep you dry.'

'But where are we going to sleep?'

'Why do you think I made you buy a sleeping mat?'

'We're sleeping on the *ground*?'

His smile was answer enough.

I looked at him suspiciously. 'What about you?'

'I'll be right here with you—and everyone else, before you get in a panic.'

I opened my mouth, then closed it again. 'Does Lex know the conditions here?' I demanded. I couldn't believe he would have put his staff through this if he'd had any idea of what it would be like.

'I shouldn't think so,' said Phin cheerfully. 'The conditions aren't bad, Summer,' he went on more seriously. 'This isn't meant to be a five star jolly. It's *meant* to be challenging. It's all about pushing you all out of your comfort zones and seeing what you're made of. It's about giving you a brief glimpse of another community and thinking about the ways staff and customers at Gibson & Grieve can make a connection with them.'

I set my jaw stubbornly, and he shook his head with a grin. 'I bet,' he said, 'that you'll end up enjoying this much more than going to some polo match, or having a corporate box at the races, or whatever Lex usually does to keep staff happy.'

'A bet?' I folded my arms. 'How much?'

'You want to take me on?'

'I do,' I said. 'If I win, you have to…'

I tried to think about what would push Phin out of *his* comfort zone. I could hardly suggest he settled down and got married, but there was no reason he shouldn't commit to something.

'…you have to agree to get to work by nine every day for as long as we're working together,' I decided.

Phin whistled. 'High stakes. And if I win?'

'Well, I think that's academic, but you choose.'

'That's very rash of you, cream puff! Now, let's see…' He tapped his teeth, pretending to ponder a suitable stake. 'Since I know I'm going to win, I'd be a fool not to indulge a little fantasy, wouldn't I?'

'What sort of fantasy?' I asked a little warily.

'Do you care?' he countered. 'I thought you were sure you weren't going to enjoy yourself?'

I looked at the tarpaulin and remembered how thin my sleeping mat had looked. There was no way Phin would win this bet.

'I am sure,' I said. 'Go on—tell me this fantasy of yours.'

'We're at work,' he told me, his eyes glinting with amusement and something else. 'You come into my office with your notebook, and you're wearing one of those prim little suits of yours, and your hair is tied up neatly, and you're wearing your stern glasses.'

'It doesn't sound much of a fantasy to me,' I said. 'That's just normal.'

'Ah, yes, but when you've finished taking notes you don't do what you normally do. You take off your glasses, the way you do, but instead of going back to your desk in my fantasy you come round until you're standing really close to me.'

His voice dropped. 'Then you shake out your hair and you

unbutton your jacket *ve-r-ry* slowly and you don't take your eyes off mine the whole time.'

My heart was beating uncomfortably at the picture, but I managed a very creditable roll of my eyes.

'It's a bit hackneyed, isn't it? I was expecting you to come up with something a little more exciting than that.'

The corner of Phin's mouth twitched. 'Well, I *could* make it more exciting, of course, but it wouldn't be fair, given that you're going to have to actually do this.'

'I don't think so,' I said, a combative glint in my own eyes. Still, there was no point in pushing it. 'So that's it? Take my hair down and unbutton my jacket if—and that's a very big *if*—I enjoy the next ten days?'

'Oh, you would have to kiss me as well,' said Phin. 'As to what happens after the kiss…well, that would be up to you. But it might depend on how many other people were around.'

'I'm sure that wouldn't be a problem,' I said with a confident toss of my head. 'So: hair, jacket, kiss for me if you win, and turning up on time for you if I do? I hope you've got a good alarm clock! This is one bet I'm deadly sure I'm going to win.'

CHAPTER NINE

BUT I lost.

The first night was really uncomfortable, yes, but in the days that followed I was so tired that my sleeping mat might as well have been a feather bed, I slept so soundly.

We spent the next ten days helping the villagers to finish the medical centre they had started a couple of years earlier but had had to abandon when they ran out of money to buy the materials. Somehow Phin had organised delivery of everything that was needed, and I didn't need to be there long to realise what an achievement that was.

It was an eye-opening time for me in more ways than one. For most of the time it was hard, physical labour. It was hot and incredibly humid, and the closest I got to a shower was a dip in the river, but I liked seeing the building take shape. Every day we could stand back and see the results of our labours, and we forgot that our hands were dirty, our nails broken, our hair tangled.

When I think back to that time what I remember most is the laughter. Children laughing, women laughing, everyone laughing together. I'd never met a community that found so much humour in their everyday lives. The people of Aduaba humbled me with their openness, their friendliness and their hospitality, and I cringed when I remembered how dismissive I had been of their huts when I first arrived. When I was invited inside, I found that the mud floors were swept and everything was scrupulously clean and neat.

'Why can't you keep your house like this?' I asked Phin.

The women particularly were hard-working and funny. A few of them had some words of English or French, and I learnt some words of their language. We managed to communicate well enough. I kept my hair tied back, as that was only practical, but I forgot about mascara and lipstick, and it wasn't long before I started to feel the tension that was so familiar to me I barely noticed it most of the time slowly unravelling.

I learnt to appreciate the smell of the rainforest, the way the darkness dropped like a blanket, the beauty of the early-morning mist on the river. I began to listen for the sounds which had seemed so alien at first: the screech of a monkey, the rasp of insects in the dark, the creak and rustle of vegetation, the crash of tropical rain on the tarpaulin and the slow, steady drip of the leaves afterwards.

But most of all my eyes were opened to Phin. It was a long time since I had been able to think of him as no more than a bland celebrity, but I hadn't realised how much more there was to him. He was in his element in Aduaba. He belonged there in a way he never would in the confines of the office.

Wherever there was laughter, I would find him. He spoke much more of the language, and had an extraordinary ability to defuse tension and get everyone working together, sorting out administrative muddles with endless patience. I suppose I hadn't realised how *competent* he was.

I remember watching him out of the corner of my eye as he hammered in a roof joist. His expression was focused, but when one of the other men on the roof shouted what sounded like a curse he glanced up and shouted something back that made them all laugh. I saw the familiar smile light up his face and felt something that wasn't familiar at all twist and unlock inside me.

At night I was desperately aware of him breathing nearby, and knew that he was the reason I wasn't afraid. He was the reason I was here at all.

He was the reason I was changing.

And I *was* changing. I could feel it. I felt like a butterfly struggling out of its chrysalis, hardly able to believe what was happening to me.

That I was enjoying it.

It wasn't all work. I played on the beach with the children, and helped the women cook. One of the men took us into the forest and showed us a bird spider on its web. I kid you not, that spider was as big as my hand. None of us thought of wandering off on our own after that.

Once Jonathan and I took a little boat with an outboard motor and puttered down the river. I felt quite comfortable with him by then. My mind was full of Aduaba and our life there, and I'd almost forgotten the desperate yearning I had once felt for him.

We drifted in companionable silence for a while. 'It's funny to think we'll be going home soon,' said Jonathan at last. 'I'll admit I was dreading this trip, but it's been one of the best things I've ever done.'

'I feel that, too.'

'It's made me realise that I never really knew you before, when we…you know…' He petered off awkwardly.

'I know,' I said, trailing my fingers in the water. 'But I think I've changed since I've been here. I wasn't like this before, or if I was I didn't know it. I thought I was going to hate it but I don't.' I remembered my bet with Phin and shivered a little.

'I know you and Phin are good together,' Jonathan blurted suddenly, 'but I just want you to know that I think you're wonderful, Summer, and if you ever change your mind about Phin I'd like another chance.'

I stilled for a moment. How many times had I dreamt of Jonathan saying those words? Now that he had, I didn't know what to say.

I pulled my hand out of the water. 'What about Lori?' I asked. It wasn't that long since he'd been mad about her.

'Lori's back with her ex. It was quite intense for a while, but I think I always knew she was on the rebound, and now that she's back with him I realise how close I came to making a big mistake.'

So I couldn't use Lori as an excuse to say no, I thought, and then caught myself up. Excuse? What do you need an excuse for, Summer?

'I know I didn't appreciate you when I had you, but I can see now that you were so much better for me than Lori,' Jonathan was saying. 'We've got so much more in common.'

'Yes, I suppose we have,' I said slowly.

He leant forward eagerly. 'We've got the same outlook, the same values.'

It was true. That was exactly what I had loved about him, but why did he have to wait until now to realise it? Frankly, his timing sucked.

'Jonathan, I—'

'It's OK,' he interrupted me. 'You don't need to say anything. I know how things are with you and Phin right now. I just wanted to tell you how I felt—to let you know that I'm always here for you.'

Why did he have to be so nice? I thought crossly as we made our way back. It would have been so much easier for me if he had turned out to be lazy, or a whinger, or even if he just hadn't liked Cameroon very much. Then I could have decided that I didn't love him after all. But in lots of ways I had never liked Jonathan as much as I did then.

Jonathan knew Phin's reputation as well as I did. He wouldn't have said anything if he hadn't thought there was a good chance that my supposed relationship with Phin would end sooner or later.

As it would.

Everything was working out just as Phin had said. It was just a pity I didn't know what I really wanted any more.

There was a party on our last night in Aduaba. We drank palm wine in the hot, tropical night and listened to the sounds of the forest for the last time. Then the music started. There's an irresistible rhythm to African music. I could feel it beating in my blood, and when the women pulled me to my feet I danced with them.

I must have looked ridiculous, stamping my feet and waggling my puny bottom, but I didn't care. The only time I faltered was when I caught Phin watching me, with such a blaze of expression in his eyes that I stumbled momentarily. But when I looked again he was laughing and allowing himself to be drawn into the dance and I decided I must have imagined it.

I ran my fingers over my keyboard as if I had never seen one before. It felt very strange to be back in the office. My head was still full of Africa, and I had found the tube stifling and oppressive on my way into work that morning.

Unsettled, I switched on my computer, and sat down to scroll through the hundreds of e-mails that had accumulated while we'd been away. It was hard to focus, though, and my mind kept drifting back to Aduaba and Phin.

Phin stripped to the waist like the other men, his muscles bulging with effort as they lifted the heavy timbers into place.

Phin laughing with the children in the river.

Phin looking utterly at ease in the heat and the humidity and the wildness.

He strolled in some time after ten, and all the air evaporated from my lungs at the sight of him. I was annoyed to see that he seemed just the same as always, while I felt completely different.

I looked at him over the top of my glasses. 'I see you didn't invest in that alarm clock,' I said crisply, to cover the fact that my heart was cantering around my chest in an alarmingly uncontrolled way.

'No, but then I don't need to turn up on time every day, do I?' said Phin, not at all put out by the sharpness of my greeting. '*I'm* not the one who lost the bet.'

The mention of the bet silenced me, and I bit my lip. Nothing more had been said about it, and I'd convinced myself that Phin hadn't really been serious. It had just been joke…hadn't it?

Much to my relief, Phin didn't say any more, but went into his office and threw himself into his chair. 'So, what's been happening?' he asked. 'Is there anything that needs to be dealt with right away?'

Grateful to him for behaving normally, I took in my notebook and ran through the most urgent issues. 'Shall I make some coffee?' I said, when I had finished scribbling notes.

'Not just yet,' said Phin. 'There's the small matter of the bet we made.' He smiled at me as I stared at him in consternation. 'I think you owe me.'

It was typical of him to let me relax and then catch me off guard. I should have known he'd do something like that.

I swallowed. 'Now?'

'I always think it's best to pay debts straight away, don't you? Do you remember the terms?'

Drawing a breath, I took off my glasses. 'I think so,' I said. Now that it had come to it, I felt a flicker of excitement. I met Phin's eyes and wondered if he was waiting for me to re-negotiate, and I knew suddenly that I didn't want to do that.

'You were right,' I said clearly. 'I loved it.'

Calmly, I got to my feet and went round the desk to where Phin sat in a high-backed executive chair. He was silent, watching me as I leant back against the desk and very deliberately pulled the clip from my hair, so that I could shake it loose and let it tumble around my face.

How embarrassing, my sensible side was saying. How unbelievably inappropriate. How *tacky*.

It was bad enough making a bet like that with your boss, without playing up to his patriarchal male fantasies. How had I got myself into a situation where I was feeling a bit naughty, a bit dirty, a bit sexy *in the office*?

How could I possibly be turned on by it?

But I was. I can hardly bear to remember it without cringing, but at the time…oh, yes, I certainly was.

I smiled slowly at Phin. 'How am I doing so far?'

'Perfect,' he said, but his voice was strained and I felt a spurt of triumph, even power that I could have that effect on him just by letting down my hair.

Levering myself away from the desk, I moved closer to him. One by one I undid the buttons of my jacket, even though I was having one of those out-of-body experiences again and screaming at myself, *What are you doing? Stop it right now!*

Phin said nothing, but his eyes were very dark as he watched me, and I could see him struggling to keep his breathing even. When my jacket was open to reveal the cream silk camisole I wore underneath, I leant down and pressed my mouth to the pulse that was beating frantically in his throat.

I heard Phin suck in his breath, and I smiled against his skin, slipping my arms around his neck and easing myself onto his lap so that I could kiss my way slowly, slowly, along his jaw to the edge of his mouth.

'Am I doing it right?' I whispered.

'God, yes,' he said raggedly, and his arms came up to fasten around me as I kissed him at last.

His lips parted beneath mine, drawing me in, and the chair spun round as his hand slid possessively under my skirt. It might have been tacky, it might have been deeply, deeply inappropriate, but it felt so good I didn't care.

I have a hazy memory that I thought I should be in control, but if I ever was I soon lost it. It wasn't as if Phin was in control either. That kiss was stronger than both of us. It ripped through our meagre defences, rampaging like wildfire in the blood, sucking us up like a twister to a place far from the office where there were only lips and tongues, only hands moving greedily, insistently, only the pounding of our hearts and the throb of our bodies and the sweet, dangerous intoxication of a kiss that went on and on and on.

Sadly, the office hadn't forgotten us. The sound of a throat being loudly cleared gradually penetrated. We paused, our mouths still pressed together, our tongues still entwined, and then our eyes opened at exactly the same time.

The throat was cleared again. As if at a trigger, we jerked apart, and I would have leapt off Phin's knee if he hadn't held me tightly in place as he swung his chair back to face the door.

Lex Gibson was standing there, looking bored.

'I did knock,' he said. 'Three times.'

I struggled to get up, but Phin held me tight. 'We're a bit busy here, Lex.'

'So I saw. Good to see that work ethic kicking in at last,' said Lex, who had his own line in sardonic humour when it suited him.

'Did you want something?' Phin countered. 'Or are you just here to ruin a perfect morning?'

'I wouldn't be here if it wasn't important,' said Lex dryly.

That hardly needed saying. Lex rarely left his office. Staff were summoned to see *him*, and could often be seen quailing in Monique's office while they waited their turn. It was unheard of for him to seek someone out himself.

Phin sighed as he released me. 'It had better be,' he said.

My cheeks were burning as I scrambled to my feet, desperately trying to smooth back my hair and rebutton my jacket as I went.

'Um…can I get you some coffee?' I asked Lex. I was mortified at having been caught in such a compromising position but, with that kiss still thrumming through me, probably not nearly as mortified as I should have been. 'Then I can leave you two together.'

'Actually, this concerns you,' he said.

Oh, God, he was going to sack me for unprofessional behaviour!

'Shall we sit down?' said Lex, gesturing at the sofas.

Biting my lip, I sat obediently, and Phin came to join me. We glanced at each other like naughty children, then looked at Lex.

'I believe Monique has already told you that she's expecting a baby?' he began, with a hint of disapproval.

I was so relieved that I wasn't getting fired that I started to smile—before it occurred to me that something might be wrong.

'Yes, she did. Is everything OK?' I asked in concern.

'No. At least, Monique is all right,' he amended. 'But she's been ordered to rest until the baby is born. Something to do with high blood pressure.'

I could tell Lex wasn't up on pregnancy talk. Not that I was much better.

'Oh, dear. Poor Monique. She'll have to be so careful.'

'It's very inconvenient,' said Lex austerely. 'It was bad enough that I was going to lose her in August, but she went home on Friday and now she's not coming in again until after her maternity leave.'

'So why are you here, Lex?' asked Phin with a hint of impatience. 'Or can we guess?'

'I would imagine you could, yes. Obviously I need a PA immediately—and preferably one who's familiar with my office.'

'Summer, in fact.' Phin's voice was flat.

Lex looked at me. 'Monique told me she'd mentioned the possibility of you replacing her during her maternity leave already. I'd like you to come and work for me now, even if it's only to help me through this immediate period.'

I was finding it difficult to concentrate. I'd been jerked so rudely out of that kiss, and every cell in my body was still screaming with frustration.

'Well…er…what about Phin? I mean…working for Phin,' I stumbled, realising that my concern for Phin might be misinterpreted in view of what Lex had just seen us doing.

'I'm here as a courtesy,' said Lex, looking at his brother. 'I appreciate that you've established a good working relationship with Summer—a little too good, some might say—but your office doesn't generate nearly the same amount of work as yet. It seems to me that you could quite easily manage with another secretary, or share assistance with one of the other directors.'

Phin's jaw tightened. 'I'm not going to get into a discussion about how much work I do or don't do here, Lex,' he said grittily. 'This is about Summer and where she wants to work. I'm sure she's happy to help you over this crisis period…' He looked at me for confirmation and I nodded.

'Of course.'

'But after that it's up to her.'

'That seems fair enough,' said Lex, getting to his feet. 'I'm grateful,' he said to me, and I got up, too.

'Er…would you like me to come now?'

'If you would.'

That was Lex—straight back to work. It clearly didn't occur to him that I might want to talk to Phin on my own.

I glanced at Phin, who was watching me with an unreadable expression. 'I'll…er…I'll speak to you later,' I said awkwardly.

'Sure. Don't let him work you too hard.'

So there I was, walking down the corridor with Lex to the best career opportunity of my life, and all I could think was that only minutes ago I had been in the middle of the best kiss of my life.

Lex behaved as if nothing whatsoever had happened, and I was grateful. I couldn't believe now that I had actually stood there in front of Phin, unbuttoning my jacket, that I had kissed him like that. But at the same time I couldn't believe that I had stopped.

I was torn: my body raging with the aftermath of that kiss, but my mind slowly beginning to clear. Where would it have ended if Lex hadn't interrupted us? Would we really have made love in the office with the door open? I went hot and cold at the thought. I could have jeopardised my whole career. It had been bad enough Lex finding us like that, without the whole office stopping by to gawp at Summer Curtis out of control with her boss.

Everything was getting out of hand, and I didn't like it.

It was a strange, disorientating day. I slipped back into place in Lex's office as if I had never been away. Monique was fantastically efficient, which helped. It meant I could pick up where she had left.

Lotty, the junior secretary who had replaced me, was hugely relieved when I appeared. 'I was terrified I was going to have to take over myself,' she confided. 'I like my job, but Lex Gibson reduces me to a gibbering wreck.'

I knew what that felt like. Phin could do the same to me, but for very different reasons.

Somehow I managed to keep up a calm, capable front all day, and I don't think anyone guessed that behind my cool façade I was reliving that kiss again and again.

The more I thought about it, the more glad I was that Lex had interrupted us when he had. I mean, that wasn't *me*, sliding seductively onto my boss's lap. I was cool, I was competent, I was *sensible*.

Although it would have been hard to guess that from the way I'd been carrying on recently. It wasn't sensible to get involved with your boss, to pretend a relationship you didn't have, to make stupid bets with him, to *kiss* him. What had I been thinking? I had put my career—everything I believed in, everything I'd always wanted—at risk. I'd done exactly what I had sworn I would never to do and got carried away by the moment.

How my mother would cheer if she knew.

At six o'clock I made my way back down to Phin's office. My desk looked empty and forlorn already. I knocked on his door.

Phin was on one of the sofas, reading a report. He dropped it onto the table when he saw me in the doorway and got to his feet, the first blaze of expression in his eyes quickly shielded. 'Hi.'

'Hi.'

There was an awkward pause.

'So how's it going?' he asked after a moment.

'Fine.'

Had we really kissed earlier? Suddenly we were talking to each other like strangers. I couldn't bear it.

Another silence. I stepped into the room and closed the door behind me.

Phin watched me warily. 'Somehow I get the feeling you're not about to pick up where we left off,' he said.

'No,' I agreed. 'I paid my debt.'

But my heart twisted as I said it. It had been so much more than a jokey kiss to close a bet, and we both knew it.

I went to sit on the other sofa. 'I've decided to take the job with Lex while Monique is away.'

'I thought you would,' said Phin, sitting opposite me.

'It's a fantastic career opportunity for me,' I ploughed on. 'And when I thought about it I could see that it would make it much easier for both of us. It would be awkward to carry on working together now.'

'Now?'

'I think it's time to call an end to our pretence,' I said. 'It's served its purpose.'

Phin sat back and regarded me steadily. 'Has Jonathan come through?'

'We had a talk in Aduaba,' I admitted. 'He said he wanted to try again.'

'And what did you say?'

'I said I'd think about it.'

'I see.'

I bit my lip. 'The *Glitz* article has come out. Even Jewel's given up on you.' I tried to joke. 'There's nothing in it for you any more. We should pretend that it's over now.'

'Is that what you want?'

'To be honest, Phin, I don't know *what* I want at the moment,' I said with a sigh. 'It's all been…'

I tried to think of a way to describe how it had felt, but couldn't do it. 'I'm confused,' I said instead. 'You, Jonathan, Africa, this new job…I don't know what I feel about any of it. I don't know what I'm *doing* any more.'

'You seemed to know exactly what you were doing earlier this morning,' said Phin.

I could feel the colour creeping up my throat. 'I got… carried away,' I said with difficulty. 'I'm sorry.'

'Don't apologise for it,' he said almost angrily. 'Getting carried away isn't always a bad thing, Summer.'

'It is for me.' Restlessly, I got to my feet. Hugging my arms together, I went over to the window and looked down at the commuters streaming towards Charing Cross.

'My mother's spent her whole life being carried away by one thing or another,' I told him. 'I was dragged along in her wake, and all I ever wanted was something to hold onto, somewhere I could stay, somewhere I could call home. That's why my job has always been so important to me. I know it's not a high-flying career, but I like it, and I do it well.'

I turned back to Phin, trying to make him understand. 'This morning…that was so unprofessional. When I saw Lex, I thought he was going to sack me. I wouldn't have blamed him, either.'

'He wouldn't have sacked you. I wouldn't have let him.' There was an edge of irritation in Phin's voice as he got up to join me at the window. 'It was only a kiss, Summer, not embezzlement or industrial espionage. You should keep it in perspective. It wasn't that big a deal.'

'For you, perhaps,' I said tautly. 'You don't care about this job. You don't really want to be here. I know you'd rather be off travelling, challenging yourself...there are so many things you want to do. It's different for me. My job is all I've got.'

There was a long silence. We stood side by side, looking out of the window.

'Perhaps it's just as well Lex interrupted us when he did,' said Phin at last.

'I'll find you a replacement PA as soon as I can.'

'There's no hurry,' he said, turning away, restless again. 'I was thinking of taking off for a while. One of the crew on the Collocom ocean race has been hospitalised in Rio, and they've asked me if I could fill in on the next leg to Boston. I just heard today. I said I'd ring tonight and let them know.'

Why was I even surprised? Had I really thought he would persuade me to change my mind? Phin would never be happy to stay in one place for long.

'What about things here?'

'There's nothing urgent. The projects we've set up will keep ticking over, and if not maybe you could keep an eye on them. Otherwise I was just due to do PR stuff, and I might as well do that on a yacht. Gibson & Grieve is one of the race's sponsors, so Lex can't complain—especially not when he's taken my PA away from me!'

It would always have been like this, I realised. Me clinging to the safety of my routine, Phin always in search of distraction. It could never have worked. We were too different. Better to decide that now. Phin was right. It was just as well Lex had come in when he had.

'So…what will we say about our relationship if anyone asks?'

'You could tell everyone you got fed up with me never being around,' he suggested. 'That would ring true. Everyone knows I'm not big on commitment.'

They did. So why had I let myself forget?

'Or you could say that I wasn't exciting enough for you,' I offered. 'Everyone would believe that.'

'Not if they'd seen you take down your hair this morning,' said Phin with a painful smile.

There seemed nothing more to say. We stood shoulder to shoulder at the window, not looking at each other, both facing the fact that it was all for the best. I wondered if Phin was feeling as bleak as I was.

'Well,' I said at last, 'it looks as if it's all change for both of us.'

'Yes,' said Phin. He turned to look at me, and for once there was no laughter in the blue eyes. 'Thank you for everything you've done, Summer. I hope Lex knows how lucky he is.'

'Thank you for all the doughnuts,' I said unevenly.

'They won't be the same without you.'

I wanted to tell him that I would think of him every time I had coffee. I wanted to tell him that I would miss him. I wanted to thank him for taking me to Africa, for making me *feel*, for refusing to let me give up on my dreams. But when I opened my mouth my throat was too tight to speak, and I knew that even if I could I would cry.

'I must go,' was all I muttered, backing away. 'I'll see you before you go, I expect.'

I don't know whether it made it easier or not, but I didn't see him. He sent me an e-mail saying that he had got a flight the next day and that he'd be out of contact for a while.

'*I know you're more than capable of making any decisions in my absence,*' he finished. '*Enjoy your promotion—you deserve it.*'

I tried to enjoy it. Honestly I did. I told myself endlessly that it was all for the best. I had the job I'd always wanted and a salary to match. I would be able to save in a way I never had before. If I was careful, I could think about putting down a deposit on a studio at the end of the year. What more did I want?

Whenever I asked myself that, Phin's image would appear in my mind. I could picture him in such detail it hurt. That lazy, lopsided grin. The blue, blue eyes. The warmth and humour and wonderful solidity of him. The longing to see him would clutch at my throat, making it hard to breathe, and I wanted to run down the stairs, back to his office, to throw myself onto his lap and spin and spin and spin on his chair as we kissed.

But his chair was empty. Phin wasn't there. He was out on the ocean, in the ozone, the wind in his hair and his eyes full of sunlight. He was where he wanted to be.

And I was where *I* wanted to be, I reminded myself, coming full circle again. I threw myself into work, and mostly people left me alone. There hadn't been any need for an announcement. With Phin gone, and me concentrating fiercely at work, I think most people assumed that we'd split up. They eyed me sympathetically and murmured that they were very sorry. I was just glad not to have to talk about it.

It was very different working for Lex. There were no coffee breaks, no doughnuts. Lex never sat on my desk or held my stapler like a microphone or pretended to make it bite me. It would never occur to Lex to call me anything but my name, and he wasn't interested in my life outside the office.

Not that I had much of one. Anne worried about me. 'You

went to all that trouble to get Jonathan back,' she pointed out. 'I don't understand why you won't go out with him now. It's not like he isn't trying. He's always asking you out, and this time he sounds serious. Look at all those hints he's dropped about getting married.'

'I don't want to marry Jonathan,' I said. 'It wouldn't be fair.'

'Because you're in love with Phin?'

I didn't even try to deny it, but there was no point in thinking about Phin. I had to be realistic.

'I do like Jonathan—I actually like him more now than I did when I was in love with him—but if I married him it would just be because he's got a steady job and is ready to settle down. That's not a good enough reason. I know that now. I've got my own steady job,' I told Anne. 'I don't want a relationship for the sake of it. I've realised that I don't need to rely on anybody else to make me feel safe. If security is what I want, I have to make it for myself. I'm earning a decent salary now, and I can think about putting down a deposit soon. I'm going to buy my own place, and then I'll be safe.'

Anne made a face. 'I know security's important to you, Summer, but don't you want more than that?'

I pushed Phin's image firmly away. 'Feeling safe will be enough,' I said.

CHAPTER TEN

OF COURSE, it wasn't that easy. It was all very well to resolve to make my own security and put Phin out of my mind, but how could I do that when he was stuck out in the wild Atlantic? I couldn't think about buying flats until I knew he was safe.

I followed the Collocom race on the internet. I knew six boats had set off from Rio, but they had run into appalling weather. One boat had lost its mast, a crew member on another had been swept overboard in gigantic waves, and I was in such a panic that I actually interrupted Lex in the middle of a board meeting to ask if he knew what boat Phin was on.

'It's not the one you think it is,' said Lex, sounding almost bored. 'Phin's on *Zephyr II*. They've gone to rescue the boat that's lost its mast.'

So he would still be out there in those waves. Offering a belated apology to the board members, who were staring at my desperate interruption, I went back to find out everything I could about the seaworthiness of *Zephyr II*. My heart was in my mouth for four more days, until I heard that the weather had eased and the battered boats were all limping towards land.

As if I didn't have enough to worry about with Phin, my mother announced that she wanted to throw up the precarious existence she had eked out with her shop in Taunton to—and I quote—'become a pilgrim along the sacred routes of our ancestors'.

How she would support herself while criss-crossing the country on ley lines wasn't clear. 'It's all part of the healing process,' she told me, brushing aside my questions about national insurance and rent and remaindered stock. 'This is important work, darling. The galactic core is in crisis. We must channel our light to restore its equilibrium.'

It seemed to me that it wasn't just the galactic core that was in crisis. Her financial affairs were in no better state, and sadly no amount of channelling was going to sort them out.

'Can you believe it?' my mother huffed incredulously when I tried to pin her down about what was happening with the shop. 'They've cut the electricity off!'

That's my mother for you. No problem at all in believing that she has a direct connection to the galactic core—whatever that is—but entirely baffled at the notion that a utility company might stop providing electricity if they're not paid on time.

Is it any wonder I couldn't concentrate on buying a flat?

And, as it turned out, it was just as well.

It became clear that I would have to go down to Somerset and sort things out for Mum. I had encouraged her to rent the shop a couple of years ago. It had seemed like something that would fix her in one place. I should have known that the enthusiasm would pass like all the others.

Things were so busy at work that there was no way I could take time off for the first few weeks, but as soon as I heard that Phin's boat had made it safely to port at the end of that leg of the race I nerved myself to ask Lex if I could have a couple of days the following week.

'Are you thinking of a holiday?'

'I'm afraid not.' I told him about my mother's shop. 'I'll probably need to talk to the bank and her landlord, otherwise I'd just try and do it all in a weekend,' I finished.

Lex looked at me thoughtfully. 'It's unfortunate for you that you're so good at sorting things out. Take whatever time you need,' he said, much to my surprise. I knew he hated it when his PA wasn't there, and he was only just adjusting to having me instead of Monique. 'Lotty will just have to steel herself to deal with me on her own.'

He turned back to his computer. 'I believe all the Collocom boats have made it to Boston,' he said. 'I imagine Phin will be on his way home soon.'

Phin. I felt the memory of his smile tingle through me. 'We're not…it was just…' I stammered, unsure how much Phin had told his brother about the agreement we had made.

Lex held up a hand, obviously to forestall any emotional confession. 'You don't need to explain,' he said. 'I'd rather not know. Have you heard Jonathan Pugh is leaving us? Parker & Parker PR have poached him. It's a good move for him,' Lex added grudgingly.

'I'll still be in London,' Jonathan said, when I congratulated him. 'This doesn't have to be goodbye.'

He insisted on taking me out for a drink to celebrate his new job, and, once fortified by a glass of champagne, he took my hand and asked me to marry him.

'We could be so good together, Summer,' he said.

I looked at him. He was clever, attractive, successful. I

had adored him once, and now…now all I could think was that he was a nice man. I remembered how much I'd loved being with him, how I'd loved feeling safe, but his touch had never thrilled me. I had never felt the dark churn of desire when I was with him. I don't think Jonathan had ever suspected I could feel desire at all until Phin had made him wonder.

I think it was then that I stopped trying to tell myself that I wasn't in love with Phin. I was, whether I wanted to be or not. I said no to Jonathan as gently as I could, and took the train to Taunton feeling as if I had let go of something I had been holding tight for too long.

I felt a strange mixture of lightness and loss—the relief of leaving something old and unwanted behind combined with the scariness of setting off on a new road all on my own again.

My mother was as vague and as charming as ever. She had got a lift into Taunton from the field where she and several others had pitched tepees in order to live closer to nature, and we had lunch together in an organic wholefoods café where tofu and carrots featured largely on the menu. I tried to get her to grasp the realities of giving up the shop, but it was hopeless.

'The material plane has so little meaning for me now,' she explained.

I sighed and gave up. I had been the one who had dealt with all the financial arrangements when she started the shop, and it looked as if I would be the one who would have to close it down.

Still, I was unprepared for quite what a muddle her affairs were in, and I had a depressing meeting with the bank manager and an even worse one with the owner of the shop, who was practically foaming at the mouth with frustration as he recalled his attempts to get my mother to pay her rent, let alone maintain the property.

'I want her out of there!' he shouted. 'And all that rubbish she's got in there, too! You clear it out and count yourself lucky I'm not taking her to court.'

Mum wafted back to her tepee, and I spent that night in a dreary B&B. I sat on the narrow bed and looked at the rain trickling down the window. I felt so lonely I could hardly breathe.

I had been so careful all my life. I had been sensible. I had been good. I had always said *no* instead of *yes*, and where had it got me? All alone and feeling sorry for myself, in a single room in a cheap B&B, with nothing to look forward to but another day spent clearing up more of my mother's mess.

I thought about ringing Anne, but she was out with Mark, and anyway she was so happy planning her wedding that I didn't want to be a misery. Besides, the only person I really wanted to talk to was Phin.

I missed him. I missed that slow, crooked smile, the warmth in the blue eyes. I missed the energy and humour that he brought with him into a room. I even missed him calling me cream puff, which just goes to show how low I was feeling.

I missed the way he made me feel alive.

Again and again I relived that last kiss. Why had I waited so long to kiss him like that? Why had I hung on so desperately to the thought of a commitment he could never give?

It seemed to me, sitting on that candlewick bedspread—a particularly unpleasant shade of pink, just to make matters worse—that I had been offered a chance at happiness and I had turned it down. I'd been afraid of being hurt, afraid of the pain of having to say goodbye, but I was hurting now, and I didn't even have the comfort of memories, of knowing that I'd made the most of the time I had with Phin.

If he ever came back to Gibson & Grieve, I resolved, I was going to go into his office, and this time I would lock the door. I would shake my hair loose and slide onto his lap again, and this time I wouldn't stop at a kiss. I wouldn't ask for love or for ever. I would live in the moment. I'd do whatever Phin wanted as long as I could touch him again, as long as he would hold me again.

I wrinkled my nose at the musty smell that met me as I opened the shop door the next morning. I had to push against the pile of junk mail and free newspapers that had accumulated since my mother had last been in.

Depressed, I picked it all up and carried it over to the counter. Straight away I could see that someone had broken into the cash register. The only consolation was that they wouldn't have found much money. The stock, unsurprisingly, was untouched. I didn't suppose there was much of a black market in dusty dreamcatchers or vegan cookbooks.

A manual on how to make contact with your personal guardian angel was propped on display next to a pile of weird and wonderful teas. I could have done with a guardian angel myself right then, I thought, riffling through the pages with my fingers as I looked around the shop and wondered where to begin.

Coffee, I decided, dropping the book back onto the counter. There was a kettle out at the back, where the back door had been broken down. I supposed I would have to do something about that, too.

The kettle didn't work. No electricity, of course. Sighing, I went back into the shop—and stopped dead as the whole world tilted and a fierce joy rushed through me with such force that I reeled.

Phin was standing at the counter, with a takeaway coffee in each hand and a bag under his arm.

'Oh, good,' he said. 'I've found the right place at last.'

'Phin…' I stammered. He looked so wonderful, lighting up the shop just by standing there. He was very brown, and his eyes looked bluer than ever. I was so glad to see him I almost cried.

'Hello, cream puff,' he said, carefully putting the coffees down.

I still couldn't take in the fact that he was actually there. I had wanted to see him so much I was afraid I might be imagining him. 'Phin, what are you doing here?'

'Lex told me you were down here trying to sort out your mother's finances,' he said conversationally. 'I thought you could do with a hand.'

'But how on earth did you find me?'

'There aren't that many New Age shops in Taunton, but I've been round them all. I only had one more to try after this one.'

My throat was so tight I couldn't speak.

'It's nearly eleven o'clock,' said Phin, lifting the paper bag. 'I knew you'd be craving some sugar.'

'You brought doughnuts?'

'I thought that was what you'd need.'

No one had ever thought about what I needed before. That was what I had wanted most of all. To my horror, my eyes filled with tears. I blinked them fiercely away.

'I always need a doughnut,' I said unevenly.

'Then let's have these, and we can talk about what needs to be done.'

We boosted ourselves onto the counter. I'll never forget the taste of that doughnut: the squirt of jam as I bit into it, the contrast of the squidgy dough and the gritty sugar. And, most of all, the incredible, glorious fact that Phin was there, right beside me, sipping lukewarm coffee and brushing sugar from his fingers.

Only last night I'd decided that if I ever saw him again I would seduce him into a wild affair, but now that he was here I felt ridiculously shy, and my heart was banging so frantically in my throat I could barely get any words out. Typical. I didn't even know how to begin being wild.

But right then I didn't care. I only cared that he was there.

'I thought you'd still be in the States,' I said as I sipped my coffee.

'No, I decided to come straight back once we got to Boston. I got home first thing on Friday morning.'

I did a quick calculation. It was Tuesday, so he had been back four days and I hadn't known.

'What have you been doing with yourself?'

'I had things to do,' he said vaguely. 'I didn't realise you were here until I talked to Lex last night.'

And he had come straight down to help me. My heart was slamming painfully against my ribs.

'It must be a bit of culture shock,' I said unsteadily. 'From glamorous ocean race to failed New Age shop in Taunton.'

Phin smiled. 'I like contrasts,' he said.

'Still, you must be exhausted.' Draining my coffee, I set the empty beaker on the counter beside me. 'It was so nice of you to come, but there was really no need.'

'I didn't like it when Lex said you were here alone.'

'I'm fine. Taunton's not exactly dangerous.'

'That's not the point. You don't have to do everything on your own.'

But that was exactly what I *did* have to do. 'I'm used to it,' I said.

'Where's Jonathan?' said Phin, frowning. 'If he cared about you at all, he would be here.'

'I'm sure Jonathan would have come down if I'd asked for his help, but it never occurred to me to tell him about my mother. Besides,' I went on carefully, 'it wouldn't have been fair of me to ask him when I'd just refused to marry him.'

I felt Phin still beside me. 'You refused?' he repeated, as if wanting to be sure.

'Yes, I... Yes,' I finished inadequately.

My eyes locked with his then, and silence reverberated around the shop. 'Anyway,' I said, 'you're here instead.'

'Yes,' said Phin. 'I'm here.'

Our eyes seemed to be having a much longer conversation—one that set hope thudding along my veins. I could feel a smile starting deep inside me, trembling out to my mouth, but I was torn. Part of me longed to throw myself into his arms, but my sensible self warned me to be careful.

If I was going to seduce him, I was going to do it properly. The scenario I had in mind demanded that I was dressed in silk and stockings. My hair would be loose and silky, my skin soft, my nails painted Vixen. I couldn't embark on the raunchy affair I had in mind wearing jeans and a faded sweatshirt, with my hair scraped back in a ponytail.

I wondered if Phin had also been having a chat with his sensible side, because he was the one who broke the moment. Draining his coffee, he set down the paper cup.

'So, what needs to be done?'

I didn't say that he had already done everything I needed just by being there. 'Really just cleaning up and getting rid of all this stuff somehow.' I told him what the landlord had said.

Phin's brows snapped together. 'He *shouted* at you?'

'He was just frustrated. I know how he feels.' I sighed. 'I'd spent the whole day trying to deal with Mum, too. I was ready to shout myself! It's OK now, though. I've paid the rent arrears and settled the outstanding bills so everyone's happy.'

'That must have added up to a bit.' Phin looked at me closely when I just shrugged. 'You used your savings, didn't you, CP?' he said.

I managed a crooked smile. 'It's just money, as Mum always says.'

'It was for your flat,' said Phin, looking grimmer than I had ever seen him. 'Your security. You worked for that money. You needed it.'

'Mum needed it more,' I said. 'It's OK, Phin. I'm fine about it—and Mum's very grateful. I've freed her up to get on with healing the galactic core, and the way things are going at the moment that might turn out to be quite a good investment!'

Phin's expression relaxed slightly, and I saw the familiar glimmer of a smile at the back of his eyes.

'Anyway,' I went on, 'I've decided to stop worrying so much about the future.' I smiled back at him as I jumped off the counter. 'You taught me that. I'm going to try living in the moment, the way you and Mum do.'

'Are you, now?' The smile had spread to his face, denting the corner of his mouth and twitching his lips.

'I am. You won't recognise me,' I told him. 'I'm going to

be selfish and irresponsible…just as soon as I've finished clearing up here.'

Phin got off the counter with alacrity, and tossed the paper cups into the bin. 'In that case, let's get on with it. I can't wait to see the new, selfish Summer.'

I can't tell you how easy everything seemed now that there were two of us. Phin sorted everything. He left me to start packing up and went off to find a man with a van.

He was back in an amazingly short time to help me. 'Somebody called Dave is coming in a couple of hours. He's agreed to take all the stock off our hands.'

'What on earth is he going to do with it?' I asked curiously.

'I didn't ask, and neither should you. Your problem is his trading opportunity.'

We were dusty and tired by the time we had finished. Dave had turned up, as promised, and to my huge relief had taken away all the stock—which wasn't all that much once I started to pack it away. Then we'd bought a couple of brushes and a mop and cleaned the shop thoroughly, and Phin had mended the back door where the thieves had broken in.

I straightened, pressing both hands into the small of my back. 'I think that's it,' I said, looking around the shop. It was as clean as I could make it.

Then I looked at Phin, sweeping up the debris from his repair. I thought about everything he had done for me and my throat closed.

'I don't know what I would have done without you,' I told him.

Phin propped his broom against the wall. 'You'd have coped—the way you always do,' he said. 'But I'm glad I could help.'

'You did. You helped more than you can ever know,' I said. 'You helped me just by being here. I'm only sorry to have dragged you all the way down to Somerset as soon as you got home.'

'You didn't drag me anywhere,' said Phin. 'I wanted to be here.'

I laughed. 'What? In a quiet side street of a pleasant provincial town? It's not really wild enough for you, is it? I can see you wanting to trek to the South Pole, or cross the Sahara or…or…' What *did* risk-takers like to do? 'Or bungee-jump in the Andes. But clear up an old shop in the suburbs? Admit it—it's not really your thing, is it?'

'You're not the only one who's changed,' said Phin. 'It's true that I used to be an adrenalin junkie, but it took that race from Rio to show me that I could push myself right to the edge, I could face everything the ocean could throw at me— and believe me that was a lot!—but hanging out on a trapeze over the waves in an Atlantic gale was still nothing like the rush I get when I'm with you.'

His tone was so conversational that it took me a moment to realise just what he'd said, and then I felt my heart start to crumble with a happiness so incredulous and so intense that it almost hurt.

Phin was still standing on the other side of the room, but it was as if an electric current connected us, fizzing and sparking in the musty air. I was held by it, by the look in his eyes and the warmth of his voice, and I couldn't move, couldn't speak. All I could do was stare back at him with a kind of dazed disbelief.

'I thought about you every day at sea,' he said, his voice so deep it reverberated through me. 'It was tough out there, tough and exhilarating, but as soon as we got into port all I wanted was to see you, Summer. I wanted to hear your voice. I wanted to touch you. I suddenly understood what people mean when they say they want to go home. It wasn't about being in my house, or in London. It was just being with you. And if that means spending a day clearing out an old shop, that's where I want to be.'

I opened my mouth, but no sound came out. The air had leaked out of my lungs without me noticing and I had to suck in an unsteady breath.

'I've missed you, Summer,' said Phin.

I felt my mouth wobble treacherously and had to press my lips firmly together. 'I've missed you, too,' I said, my voice cracking.

'Really?'

I made a valiant effort to pull myself together. It was that or dissolve into an puddle of tears and lust. And what a mess that would be.

'Well, apart from your fiddling, obviously.'

A smile started in his eyes and spread out over his face as he took a step towards me. 'I even missed your obsessive tidying.'

'I missed you being late the whole time.' It was my turn to take a step forward.

He came a little closer. 'I missed the way you scowl at me over your glasses.'

'I missed your silly nicknames.'

We were almost touching by now. 'I missed kissing you,' said Phin—just as I said, 'I missed kissing you.' Our words overlapped as we closed the last gap between us, and then we didn't have to miss it any more. I was locked in his arms, my fingers clutching his hair, and we were kissing—deep, hungry kisses that sent the world rocking around us.

'Wait, wait!' I broke breathlessly away at last. 'It's not supposed to be like this!'

'What do you mean?' said Phin, pulling me back. 'This is *exactly* how it's supposed to be.'

'But I want to seduce you,' I wailed. 'I had it all planned out. I was going to be your fantasy again—but this time I was going to lock the office door so that Lex couldn't interrupt us.'

Phin started to laugh. 'CP, you're my fantasy wherever you are.'

'Not dressed like this—all dirty and dusty!'

'Even now, without your little suit,' he insisted. 'You're all I want.'

Well, how was a girl to resist that? I melted into him and kissed him back. 'That's all very well, but *my* fantasy is to seduce you properly,' I said. 'And I can't do it here.'

'I agree,' said Phin, his eyes dancing. 'If I'm going to be seduced, I'd like it to be in comfort. Does it have to be the office? Let me take you home instead. There's something I want to show you, anyway.'

So we picked up my bag from the B&B, dropped the key to the shop through the landlord's door, and headed back to London. Phin's car was fast, and incredibly comfortable as it purred effortlessly up the motorway, but I was so happy by then that I could probably have floated all the way under my own steam.

I was shimmering with excitement at the thought of what was to come, and it was still incredibly easy being together. We talked all the way back. Phin told me about sailing up the coast of South America, about winds and waves and negotiating currents, and about their dramatic rescue mission. I told him about my mother's new plan, and Anne's wedding, and how I'd decided to rent a little place on my own and not tie myself down with a mortgage.

We caught up on office gossip, too. I told Phin about Jonathan's new job. 'It's a big promotion for him.'

'Lex won't be happy, but I can't say I'm sorry he's leaving,' said Phin. 'But then, I'm just jealous.'

It was so absurd I laughed. 'You can't possibly be jealous of Jonathan, Phin!'

'I am,' he insisted. 'I remember how you felt about him. I know how important steadiness and security has always been to you. When you told me you'd talked to Jonathan in Aduaba, it seemed to me that he was offering you everything you really wanted.'

'Is that why you left when I went to work for Lex?'

He nodded. 'I thought it would be easier for you to get together with Jonathan, but as soon as I agreed to go to Rio I knew I had made a terrible mistake. All the time on the boat I thought about you with him, and I hated it. I couldn't believe how stupid I'd been. What had I been thinking? Helping you to get Jonathan back when all along I'd been falling in love with you myself. *Duh.*'

Phin slapped his forehead to make the point. 'And who had I been trying to kid with all that stuff about wanting you to be happy with Jonathan if that was what you really wanted? I was way too selfish for that. I wanted to make you happy myself, and I knew that I could do it if only you'd give me a chance. I had my strategy all worked out.'

'What strategy?' I asked, turning in my seat to look at him.

'You'll see,' said Phin. 'I flew back to London as soon as we hit land, which gave me the weekend to put the first part of my plan into action. The next stage was to find you and separate you from Jonathan somehow. So I went into the office yesterday, but of course you weren't there—and nor was Lex. I couldn't get hold of him until later, and that's when he told me you were down here on your own. I was partly outraged that Jonathan wasn't here to help you, but I was pleased, too, that you were alone so I could tell you how I felt.'

He glanced at me with a smile. 'Then you told me that you weren't going to marry him after all. You'll never know how relieved I was to hear that, cream puff.'

I smiled back at him. 'It took you going for me to realise how much I loved you,' I told him. 'I knew then that I couldn't marry Jonathan. I thought I loved him, but I didn't really know him. You were right. I loved what he represented. But you knew more about me after that first time we had coffee than Jonathan ever did. He never made an effort to see what I was really like until you made it easy for him. You were the only one who's ever looked at me and understood me. You're the one who's made me realise I can be sensible some of the time, but I don't have to be like that all the time—and I won't be when I seduce you,' I promised.

'I love the fact that you're so sensible,' Phin told me. 'I love the contrast between that and your sexiness, that you wear sharp suits but silk lingerie. And most of all,' he said, 'I love the fact that I'm the only one who sees that about you. Everyone thinks you're wonderful—'

I goggled. 'They all think I'm nitpicking and irritable!'

'Maybe, but they also know you're kind and generous, and the person they can all turn to when they need help or something has to be done. But I'm the only one that sees the cream puff in you,' said Phin, and his smile made my heart turn over.

'Don't joke,' I said, laying my hand on his thigh. 'I'm

going to be channelling my inner cream puff from now on. I hope you're ready!'

Phin covered my hand with his own. 'Don't distract me while I'm driving,' he said, but his fingers tightened over mine and he lifted them to press a kiss on my knuckles.

'I've never been the kind of girl who has an affair with her boss,' I said with a happy sigh. 'I hope I'll be able to carry it off.'

'Perhaps it's just as well I'm not going to be your boss any more,' said Phin. 'We'd never get any work done. But who's going to keep me in order in the office? Have you found me a new PA yet?'

'No. Everyone I've considered has been too young or too pretty for you to share doughnuts with. I'm looking for someone who's ready to retire.'

Phin laughed. 'I won't eat doughnuts with anyone but you, I promise.'

'It's only until Monique comes back,' I said. 'I'm thinking we could get by if we look after you in Lex's office. Lotty could keep your diary.'

'Sounds good to me,' he said. 'As long as you come down to my office occasionally and lock the door before you take your hair down!'

We had been making our stop-start way along the King's Road, but now Phin turned off into his street. I looked at his house as we pulled up outside. 'There's something different… You've painted the door!' I suspect my eyes were shining as I turned to him. 'It's exactly the right shade of blue. How did you know?'

'Phew,' said Phin, grinning at my delight. 'I have to admit that was a lucky guess.'

I got out of the car, still staring. 'And window boxes!'

'I got a gardening company to do them. What do you think?'

My throat was constricted. 'It's just like my dream,' I said, wanting to cry. 'You remembered.'

'Wait till you see inside!'

I hardly recognised the house. It was immaculately clean, and all the clutter had been cleared away so that the rooms felt airy and light.

I stood in the middle of the living room and turned slowly around until my eye fell on the sofa.

Two cushions sat on it, plump and precisely angled.

I looked at them for a long, long moment, and then raised my eyes to look at Phin.

'They look all right, don't they?' he said.

Taking my hand, he drew me down onto the sofa, careless of the cushions. 'You know that studio you were thinking of renting? I was thinking you could move in here instead. I had cleaners blitz the house yesterday, so I can't promise that it will always be like this—but you could tidy up all you want.'

'Move in?' I looked around my dream house, then back to the dream man beside me, and for a moment I wondered if this really *was* just a dream. 'But aren't we going to have a passionate affair?'

'It depends what you mean by affair,' said Phin, picking his words with care.

'I mean sex with no strings,' I said adamantly. 'I don't want to tie you down. I've learnt my lesson. I want being with you to be about having fun, being reckless, not thinking about the future or commitment or anything.'

'Oh,' said Phin.

'That's what you want, isn't it?'

'The thing is, I'm not sure I do.'

I stared at him.

'I think,' he said, 'that I've changed my mind.'

My heart did a horrible flip-flop, leaving me feeling sick. 'Oh,' I said, drawing my hand out of his. 'Oh, I see. I understand.'

But I didn't. I didn't understand at all. I had just let myself believe that he wanted me as much as I wanted him. Why had he changed his mind?

Phin took my hand firmly back. 'I'm fairly sure you *don't* see, Summer. For someone so sharp, you can be very dense sometimes! I haven't changed my mind about you, you idiot. I've changed it about commitment. I've spent my whole life running away from the very idea of it,' he admitted, 'but that was because I had never found anyone or anything that was worth committing to. Now there's you, and it's all changed. It was all I could think about on the boat. It wasn't that I didn't enjoy the sailing, but this time I wanted you to come home to. I wanted to know that you would always be there.

'So I'm afraid,' he said, with a show of regret, 'that if you want to have an affair with me you're going to have to marry me. I know you're just interested in my body, but I'm so in love with you, Summer. Say you'll marry me and always be there for me.'

I looked back into those blue, blue eyes, and the expression I saw there squeezed my heart with a mixture of joy and relief so acute it was painful. I was perilously close to tears even as exhilarating, intoxicating happiness bubbled along my veins like champagne. It was like stumbling unexpectedly into paradise after a long, hard journey. It was too much, too wonderful. I could hardly take it in.

Unable to tell Phin how I felt, I reverted to joking instead.

'But what about my fantasy to seduce you?' I pretended to pout. 'I was so determined that I was going to live dangerously. You can't have an affair with your own fiancé!'

'If you want to be reckless, let's get married straight away,' said Phin.

'I don't think Lex would like that very much. He's running out of suitable PAs.'

'He'd be furious,' Phin agreed, and grinned wickedly at me. 'Let's do it anyway.'

I pretended to consider. 'I still don't get to have an affair,' I pointed out.

'How about we don't get engaged until tomorrow?' he suggested. 'Then you can have your wicked way with me tonight with no commitment at all. But I'm warning you— that's it,' he said with mock sternness as he pulled me down beneath him. 'One night is all you're going to get, and you won't even have that unless you say yes. So, just how badly do you want an affair, my little cream puff?'

'Very badly,' I said, a smile trembling on my lips.

'Badly enough to stick with me for ever after tonight?'

'Well, if I must…' I sighed contentedly.

Phin bent his head until his mouth was almost touching mine. 'So here's the deal. You seduce me to your heart's content tonight, and then we get married.'

'I get to do whatever I want with you?'

'It's your fantasy,' he agreed. 'I'm all yours. And tomorrow you're all mine.' He smiled. 'Do we have a deal?'

Well, it would have been rude to say no, wouldn't it?

I put my arms around his neck and pulled him into a long, sweet kiss. 'It's a deal,' I promised.

'Good,' said Phin, satisfied. 'Now, about this fantasy of yours…where are you going to start?'

I took hold of his T-shirt and pulled it over his head. 'I'll show you.'

THE SANTORINI MARRIAGE BARGAIN

BY
MARGARET MAYO

Margaret Mayo was reading Mills & Boon® romances long before she began to write them. In fact she never had any plans to become a writer. After an idea for a short story popped into her head she was thrilled when it turned into a full-scale novel. Now, over twenty-five years later, she is still happily writing and says she has no intention of stopping.

She lives with her husband Ken in a rural part of Staffordshire, England. She has two children: Adrian, who now lives in America, and Tina. Margaret's hobbies are reading, photography, and more recently watercolour painting—which she says has honed her observational skills and is a definite advantage when it comes to writing.

CHAPTER ONE

RHIANNE heard the screech of brakes before she saw the car. By then it was too late. Lost in her own world of misery she had not thought to look before she stepped off the pavement. Urged on by the front fender of the car, she spun across the road and for a few moments lay curled in blessed silence. It was as though everything in the whole world had stopped. No traffic noise, no voices, no birds singing. Nothing except a strange calm. She wasn't even hurting.

Then came the voice. A deep, gruff male voice. 'Why the hell didn't you look where you were going?'

Why the hell didn't she look? Rhianne struggled to turn her head and glare at the owner of the voice. He was clearly the man who had knocked her down. Beyond him was his car with the door still open, the engine still running. 'Why didn't I look?' Her tone matched his for hardness. And why shouldn't it when he was behaving as though she was the one at fault. 'Why the hell didn't *you* look? Call yourself a driver. This is a busy main road. You should have had your wits about you.'

'Are you hurt?'

The belated question angered her still further. She closed her eyes, needing to shut out the handsome face that had come a little too close. The man was on his haunches now, peering at her, making her feel like an insect under a microscope.

'Hello. Can you hear me?'

So he thought she'd passed out! Rhianne snapped her eyes open again and scrambled to her feet. She felt wobbly but nothing appeared to be broken. At least she didn't think so. Her legs still held her up and she could move her arms. Her hip felt a little sore and she guessed she'd be bruised tomorrow, but other than that she was okay.

No thanks to Mr Fast Car Driver.

When she looked about her she saw that a crowd had gathered, each face filled with concern and curiosity. But the only face she saw clearly was that of the man who'd given her his hand to help her up—the hand she had ignored. The man who was now looking at her with a frown digging deep into his forehead.

'It was my fault. I apologise.' Eyes that were neither grey nor brown but somewhere in between looked intently at her. Eyes that under other circumstances she might have found attractive. At this moment in time, however, she saw only the eyes of a man who was instrumental in her having made a silly fool of herself. It hadn't been entirely his fault but she wasn't going to admit it.

She could hear the murmur of voices as the crowd dispersed; they were happy that she hadn't been seriously injured and were now prepared to carry on their daily lives as though nothing had happened.

Rhianne wished that nothing had happened, that nothing had changed, that she was still in the job she loved and that she hadn't made that awful discovery about Angus.

'Apology accepted,' she answered, belatedly realising that the man was still looking closely at her.

'It was, of course, an error of judgement on my part. I apologise most profusely. If there is anything I can do to—'

Rhianne registered for the first time that the man wasn't English. He was olive-skinned and dark-haired—hair that could do with cutting, she noticed, hair that looked as though it wanted to curl, and he had a deep, attractive accent that she couldn't quite place. 'Not a thing. I'm not hurt; you can go, I—' Suddenly the world spun around her, and she put a hand to her head.

Immediately a pair of strong arms supported her, held her against a body that was strong and firm. Even in her woozy state she recognised that this man seriously looked after himself. She drew in a deep, shuddering breath and then wished she hadn't when the scent of his cologne filled her nostrils. She knew that whenever she smelled this same scent again it would forever remind her of this moment.

Smells did this to her. Lavender reminded her of a holiday she'd once had in Jersey, tobacco reminded her of her grandfather. When she was tiny he used to pick her up and swing her around with his pipe still in his mouth.

'You are hurt,' he insisted. 'Allow me to take you home; it is the least I can do. Or do you need a doctor, should I take you to—'

'No, it is nothing,' she exclaimed.

'Then home it is.'

'No!' declared Rhianne, more strongly this time. She had no home; she'd just walked out. She couldn't bear to go back there again.

'In that case I will take you home with me,' he declared imperatively. 'I cannot leave you in this condition.'

'What condition?' she queried, drawing back, widening her attractive blue eyes. 'I'm all right—just a few bruises, nothing more.'

'A good strong cup of tea is what you need, isn't that the English way of doing things? It is my fault that I knocked you down; it is up to me to ensure that you suffer no serious after-effects.'

Rhianne was given no chance to protest further. With her arm firmly held in his, the stranger led her to his car. Another smell, leather this time, she realised as he helped her inside: soft, luxurious leather. It was a big car, big like the man. And expensive.

Who was he? she wondered. She appreciated his concern even though it wasn't necessary. His suit was dark grey and elegantly tailored, his fine cotton shirt was white and his tie the colour of French mustard.

'I can manage,' she declared when he reached for her seat belt. But he ignored her, insisting on fastening it himself. In such close proximity the full impact of this dangerously attractive man hit her with as much force as when he had knocked her down.

Again his cologne filled the air around her. Musky and woody, not one that she had smelled before. It suited him; it suggested a strong male with firm opinions and a sense of what was right and wrong. It was strange how this thought popped into her head. He was making a big impact on her, that was for sure, but she sincerely hoped that she wasn't making a huge mistake letting him take her to wherever he lived.

What did she know about him? Nothing. Not even his

name. Clearly he felt at fault for knocking her down or she wouldn't be here now. But who was he? The effort of thinking proved too much, and she closed her eyes and kept them shut until the car stopped and he killed the engine.

She dared to look about her and saw a tall imposing building. But it wasn't a house, it was a hotel. Alarm bells rang in her head. What purpose did he use it for? Did he make a habit of picking up helpless females?

'You live in a hotel?' she questioned, unaware that nervousness sounded in her voice, or that her eyes had widened dramatically, their normal pale blue darkening to almost navy. She could feel her heart pitter-pattering in her chest and she felt strangely dizzy.

The man smiled. 'In the penthouse suite. Come—' he held out his hand '—let me take you up. I can assure you that you will be perfectly safe. My main aim is to make sure that you have suffered no ill effects. I hold myself completely responsible, of course.'

'It wasn't your fault,' declared Rhianne at once. 'I didn't look where I was going.'

One dark brow lifted, reminding her of her emphatic declaration that he was the one to blame. Nevertheless his voice remained perfectly calm. 'But I should have seen you and made allowances. Let us not talk about this now. Let us go inside and get you that cup of tea. Then you can tell me what it is that was troubling you to such an extent that you didn't see me.'

About to retort that there was nothing bothering her, Rhianne changed her mind. He was probably testing her, trying to find out what was wrong. She had no intention of sharing her problems with a stranger.

As they walked into the hotel, his hand on her elbow,

Rhianne couldn't help wondering whether she was doing the right thing. He hadn't a clue what was going on in her mind. She wasn't after tea and sympathy. In fact she ought not to be here at all. In a state of panic she pulled away from him and would have ran had he not grabbed her arm.

'You're in no fit state to be going anywhere on your own,' he insisted, his voice deep and gruff and very firm. 'If it's me you're afraid of I can arrange for a female member of staff to be in attendance. I can, however, assure you that it won't be necessary.'

His dark eyes looked deeply into hers, and all Rhianne saw was sincerity. She felt faintly foolish and drew in a deep, unsteady breath. 'That won't be necessary.' There were no other words she could find that wouldn't make her look more idiotic than she already felt.

Today had to be the worst day of her life, and receiving kindness from a total stranger when she'd been so badly let down made her feel both grateful and weepy at the same time. Which was not something she was accustomed to. She rarely cried; she'd had the sort of family life that needed strength of character, and she'd always prided herself that she could handle anything.

Now this man was seeing her at her lowest ebb. It did her pride no good at all, and she felt distinctly uneasy as the lift swept them up to his penthouse suite. She stood with her back to the mirrored walls, her hands pressed against it. She could see a dozen images of both herself and the handsome man, each one receding into the distance. She looked absolutely petrified, her auburn hair tousled, her eyes wide with aftershock and fear.

'Is this your permanent home?' she enquired in an effort to break the silence. She honestly couldn't see why anyone would choose to live in a hotel, but he had called it home—so? 'Or are you here on business?'

'It's both. Business is what's keeping me here, and this suite suits me very well. It has everything I could possibly need.'

He had an aura of great wealth—it was in the way he dressed, the way he held himself, his total control and confidence. But there was more than that. Even in her distraught state, Rhianne could see that he was a charmer. She guessed that he probably charmed the hide off every woman he met. He was handsome, suave, good-looking, with a twinkle in his brown eyes that, if she hadn't been in the state she was in, might have affected her senses.

At the moment she was immune to any man, good-looking or not. Rich and powerful or not. She wanted no man in her life for a very long time.

So what was she doing here? Why had she let him persuade her to accompany him? What could he do for her? She wasn't seriously injured, there had been no need for him to make such an offer. And she didn't even know his name. She was accompanying a complete stranger to his suite in a hotel. How foolish was that?

As though he had zoomed in on her thoughts, her companion held out his hand. 'I think it's about time we introduced ourselves. I'm Zarek Diakos. And you are—?'

Rhianne smiled weakly. Zarek Diakos! It sounded Greek, and she couldn't help wondering what business had brought him to England. 'I'm Rhianne Pickering,' she said quietly.

The lift stopped, and the doors silently opened. 'Well, Rhianne Pickering. Welcome to my humble abode.'

Nervously she stepped out on to a deep-piled carpet,

and he led the way through to a living room that was the size of the whole apartment she shared with her friend. She wasn't even aware that her mouth had fallen open. There were valuable paintings on the walls, Venetian mirrors, hand-cut crystal chandeliers. Luxury beyond compare.

'You're renting this?' she asked, unaware that her voice was no more than a breathy whisper.

Zarek shrugged. 'You think it's a little ostentatious perhaps? You get what you pay for in my experience. I can afford it, so why not surround myself with beautiful things? I work hard all day; it is a pleasure to come home.'

There it was again, the word *home*. Rhianne could never imagine calling a place like this home. How could he relax here? There was not a thing out of place. It was a showpiece. Supposedly that was what money did for you. You lost track of home comforts, bought into a life-style that suited your image.

She couldn't imagine living anywhere like this, not even for a holiday. How could anyone get comfortable on those overstuffed armchairs? You wouldn't even want to kick off your shoes and leave them lying around for fear of offending the room's intrinsic sense of order.

'Please, sit down,' invited Zarek. 'I'll ring for tea.'

Rhianne perched on the edge of a chair, and, when he had finished issuing his order, Zarek joined her. 'So, tell me how you're really feeling?'

'Bruised,' she answered on a reflective sigh. 'But other than that I'm OK. I don't really need to be here.'

'You were lucky I wasn't driving any faster. You might not have got away with such slight injury. Would you care to tell me what it was that made you walk out into the road like that?'

'I was deep in thought, that's all.'

'Some thoughts,' he said, his brows rising as though he didn't believe her simple explanation. 'Would it have anything to do with the fact that you didn't want me to take you home? Were you running away?'

'Running away?' echoed Rhianne indignantly. He was too astute for words. 'Why would I want to do that?'

'It's the impression you give.'

Rhianne dropped her head into her hands. 'I have a raging headache. Do you have any aspirin?'

Immediately he sprang to his feet.

It had the desired effect. It stopped him asking any more questions. But her reprieve was short-lived. A glass of water and the tablets appeared as if by magic. He handed them to her and stood over her until she had taken them. 'Would you like to lie down?' he enquired.

Lie down? On a bed? In his private suite? A worst-case scenario raced through Rhianne's head. 'No, I'll be all right,' she answered firmly.

'I could send for a physician.'

'I said I'll be all right,' she said even more emphatically, shooting sparks of fire from her brilliant blue eyes. 'But I would like to use your bathroom.'

'Of course, why did I not think of it?' He crossed the room and opened a door.

Inside Rhianne could see a bed, but nothing else. A four-poster bed! Her heart slammed against her ribcage. She was treading on dangerous territory here.

'The bathroom is to the right.'

It was as if he had read her thoughts, but there was nothing at all on his handsome face to suggest that he had anything other than her well-being in mind. In fact he was deadly serious. Serious or not, though, Zarek Diakos was a dangerous man.

He was as sexy as sin, and she wouldn't have been human if she hadn't felt some reaction to him. Thick dark brows hovered over brown eyes that were seriously striking. Long lashes guarded them. His nose was as straight as a die, very imperial-looking, and his lips were full and wide and mobile. At this very moment they were closed, but she knew that he had beautiful even white teeth.

His hair was thick and dark and touched his collar; his square jaw was darkly shadowed as though he already needed another shave. He was all man; even his body was beautiful. He had taken off his jacket and carefully hung it on a coat hanger in the entrance hall, and through the fine cotton of his shirt Rhianne observed a tangle of dark hair.

Angus had no chest hairs. His body was smooth and clear and—angrily Rhianne dashed all thoughts of him out of her mind. He no longer deserved a place in her memories. She ran through to the bathroom.

Zarek guessed that here was a woman who had more on her mind than the few bruises she had suffered. He went cold every time he thought about what the consequences of the accident could have been. Thank goodness he'd reacted quickly. She had walked out in front of him as though she had had a death wish, and he didn't know how he'd managed to stop without seriously injuring her.

He had a feeling that reaction hadn't yet set in. She didn't realise how dangerously close she had come to being killed. She was an attractive woman with rich auburn hair that curled and waved down over her shoulders, and fantastic blue eyes. It was a shame they were shadowed, and he didn't think it was all to do with the near miss. Something was clearly disturbing her, and he wanted to find out what it was.

Perhaps she would relax shortly and begin to talk. It would do her good. Not that he'd ever been in this position before, but he felt deep down in his gut that she seriously needed to get something off her chest. She had emphatically declared that she didn't want to go home, so it was something that had happened there that was troubling her. And who was he? Sherlock Holmes? He had no idea what was wrong. He was clutching at straws, trying to work something out that had nothing to do with him.

Except that it had. He had knocked Rhianne over and he felt responsible. He even wondered again whether he ought to take her to hospital, get her checked out. Perhaps he should.

Then the tea arrived, and Rhianne rejoined him. After she'd drunk two cups she looked a little perkier. The colour returned to her cheeks, and she even managed a faint smile. It was a lovely smile. It made her whole face lighten and brighten and she looked even more beautiful.

Zarek had had his fill of beautiful women, but Rhianne was—well, she was Rhianne. A good-looking woman with no interest in him whatsoever—which made a change—and a heap of trouble sitting heavily on her slender shoulders.

They drank even more tea, and finally he suggested that he take her home.

The shadows returned to her eyes. 'I can't go back there.' And they filled with tears.

Immediately, without even thinking what he was doing, or that his actions could be misinterpreted, he knelt down and pulled her against him. Rhianne buried her head in his shoulder and stayed there for several long seconds while he inhaled the freshness of her shampoo and felt her hair's thickness between his fingers as he cradled her head.

Whew! He didn't like this, not one little bit. He didn't like the feelings that were beginning to throb within him. This wasn't supposed to happen. He was being a good Samaritan here; sensations like this weren't allowed.

Gently he put her from him. 'Feeling better?'

She nodded, and he reached out a handkerchief, handing it to her so that she could pat her tear-stained face. 'Care to tell me what's troubling you?'

'It's private.'

'And I'm a stranger you're hardly likely to see again. You know what they say about a trouble shared. You never know, you might feel better. I promise not to tell anyone.'

Rhianne found herself giving an involuntary smile. Actually, she didn't feel like smiling, so why it happened she didn't know. Except that this man seemed to understand her needs. It was true, she wouldn't see him again after today. They were passing strangers—even though he had invited her into his house, and she had shared tea with him and buried her head into his shoulder when she had begun to cry.

But to tell him such personal things!

All of a sudden she wanted to. She was filled to bursting with unhappiness, and sharing it with a stranger wouldn't be as difficult as telling her mother for instance. Or a friend. They would ask questions. They knew Angus. They knew she had been planning to marry him. This man would listen and console.

'I don't know where to begin,' she said at length.

'The beginning's always a good place,' he responded,

but she remained silent for so long that he leaned forward and took her hands into his. 'Is it a man who has done this to you?' He asked the question quietly and patiently, not wanting to stir up too much anguish unless she was prepared to confide.

Rhianne nodded, and suddenly tears began to slide down her cheeks, gathering momentum until they were chasing each other in an incessant flow.

Zarek hated to see women cry; it made him uncomfortable; he never knew exactly how to treat them. Though, in all honesty, the women who had cried in front of him had done it for effect. Rhianne was different. She couldn't stop herself. Some man had hurt her like crazy, and she was beside herself with anguish. No wonder she had walked out in front of his car.

Silently he passed her his handkerchief and watched as she dried her tears. He had a strong urge to gather her in his arms and hold her until her sobs subsided. It was an urge he found hard to resist but somehow he managed it. He could imagine her reaction had he given in. She would hate a complete stranger holding and comforting her. Especially a man. She'd quite possibly slap his face.

She needed her mother. Mothers always knew what to say in these situations. He wondered where she lived, whether he ought to suggest he take her there. Even as he thought this, she drew in a deep, shuddering breath and, without looking at him, staring at the carpet instead, she said shakily, 'I lost my job this morning. The company has been taken over and half the workforce has been given their cards. I was secretary to the general manager but it made no difference. I was asked to clear my desk and go, just like that.'

'I see,' he said quietly. 'It's not a practice I condone,

but unfortunately it does happen. Where does your boyfriend fit into this?'

Rhianne shuddered, and once more he wanted to comfort her, but again he knew that it would be overstepping the mark.

'I went home. I was angry and upset. I'd lost a job I love. And what did I find? My boyfriend—the man I was going to marry—making love to my best friend.' And once more she burst into tears.

CHAPTER TWO

Zarek couldn't stop himself. Rhianne's disclosure had disturbed him, and he took her into his arms and held her close, so close that he felt her heart beating rapidly against his chest, felt the sobs racking her body.

What sort of a man would do such a thing? Not a true and faithful friend. Not a man who loved Rhianne as much as she evidently loved him.

It was none of his business; he'd only just met her and ought not to feel anything, but because he had been instrumental in the accident he felt somehow involved.

'The man's a swine,' he declared fiercely. 'How could he do this to you? He doesn't deserve your tears. He should be strung up to the highest tree. What did you say to him when you found him in such a predicament?'

'I said nothing,' admitted Rhianne, her mouth twisting into a wry grimace. 'I ran away. I couldn't believe my eyes. I felt sick. I just turned around and ran—and why am I telling you this? It's my problem, not yours. I'm sorry, I should be going.' She twisted out of his arms, feeling stupid now for having confessed. And he must think she was stupid for running away instead of facing up to Angus. The truth was she had been so deeply and utterly shocked, so overwhelmingly angry, that words could never have justified her feelings.

'You're going nowhere,' he declared, folding his arms across his chest, his eyes suddenly fierce. 'You're in serious shock, and I don't blame you. What you need to do is devise a plan of action.'

'Action?' queried Rhianne. 'What I'd like to do is march back there and strangle them both with my bare hands.'

'That is good.'

Rhianne dragged her brows together. 'Good? How can wanting to kill someone be good?'

'I mean anger is good. You need to get it out of your system. You need to release it and let it go. Take your anger out on me if you like. Then, when you are calmer, go back and confront these two people who have turned your life upside down.'

'That's easier said than done.' Rhianne's eyes flared a vivid blue, locking with Zarek's steady brown ones, seeing there an understanding that she would never have expected from a stranger. It was hard to believe that she was here in this grand apartment with a man she had met under exceptional circumstances, talking about her private life. She dropped on to her chair.

'May I be permitted to say that your friend cannot be much of a friend if she steals your future husband from you,' he pointed out, sitting again himself, but on the edge of his seat this time, his elbows resting on his knees, his body leaning towards her. 'Was this the first time, do you think? Or are you perhaps wondering how long it has been going on?'

Rhianne's thoughts hadn't even got this far. All she'd

been able to think about was the fact that she'd caught them making love on the living room floor, such mad passionate love that for a few seconds they had not even been aware of her presence, not until she had cried out in anguish.

Then Angus had jumped to his feet, his face a picture of guilt and regret. 'This isn't what you think,' he had said, snatching up his shirt and holding it in front of him.

Rhianne hadn't deigned to answer. How could it be anything different when she had seen it with her own eyes? She hadn't even looked at her flatmate, aware only that Annie had held a shocked hand over her mouth. She had spun on her heel instead and raced from the building, feeling sick with anger and disgust, knowing that the vivid picture of their naked bodies locked together would haunt her for a long time to come.

'I don't know and I don't really care,' declared Rhianne vehemently. 'All I know is that I don't want to see either of them again.' She was still finding it hard to believe that they had both let her down. Her best friend and the man she was going to marry. She put her hand to her mouth and raced for the bathroom again.

Rhianne waited until she had composed herself before rejoining Zarek. In her absence he had ordered a carafe of iced water and, as he filled two glasses, the sound of ice cubes clinking together sounded loud in the room. Rhianne concentrated on the sound, allowing it to take over, to shut out all other thoughts.

Taking her elbow, Zarek led her outside to an enormous terrace with magnificent views over the Thames and the far reaches of London. It was filled with potted palms and flowering shrubs, populated at this moment by brightly coloured butterflies. A haven of peace in the middle of an insane world, thought Rhianne as Zarek urged her in to a padded chair before sitting down himself.

'Are you feeling better?' He was worried about her; she looked desperately pale, still beautiful but with no colour in her skin. It gave her a kind of ethereal beauty, and this woman who had erupted so suddenly into his life intrigued him.

She was such a strikingly good-looking woman that it was difficult to believe that her boyfriend would turn to someone else. If she were his, he would never want to let her out of his sight. Already he felt a strong urge to hold her and kiss her, reassure her that everything would be all right, at the same time taking pleasure in the feel of those full breasts pressing against his chest, her hips against his hips, thighs against thighs.

The thought caused a tightening of his muscles. The worst part was that he wanted to take her to bed, to make her forget everything that had happened. And yet it was this very thing, this act of greedy self-indulgence, that had sent her running.

Disgusted by his thoughts, Zarek busied himself refilling Rhianne's glass. She hadn't answered his question, so he asked her again, 'How are you feeling?'

'Like hell, if you must know,' she declared fiercely, her hands clenching and unclenching on the arms of her chair. 'We've known each other for two years; we're in the middle of arranging our marriage. And now he does this. I hate him. And I hate my friend for being a part of it. I never want to see either of them again.'

'But don't you live with her?' he asked carefully.

'Not any more.' Her eyes flashed angrily and beautifully. 'I'm going to fetch my stuff and move out.'

'Where will you go?' Zarek suddenly realised that he didn't want to let her out of his life. He wanted to help her. It was ridiculous when he didn't know the first thing about her, but fate had brought them together, and he wanted to find out more: what made her tick, what she did for a living, about her family, her mother, her father, brothers and sisters—everything, in fact. 'There's room here.'

He tacked those last words on and then wished he hadn't when Rhianne's eyes opened wide with horror. 'Move in with you—a complete stranger? The man who nearly killed me. Are you insane?'

'It was just a thought,' he said as patiently and non-chalantly as he could. It was a fight to remain calm and impartial when he wanted to offer her the sun and the stars and the moon. 'Of course, you must do whatever you feel is right.'

'I have another friend who'll put me up,' she told him firmly, taking a further sip of water and looking anywhere but at him.

'No family?' It was one of those times when she needed her family around her.

'No!' she declared quickly and tersely, and he didn't follow it up because it was really none of his business.

In one respect he was glad she had turned him down because her big sad eyes overwhelmed him. On the other hand, surprisingly, he wanted her to depend on him. He wanted to tease her back to life, to see those blue eyes sparkling with happiness, to see colour in her cheeks and her mouth wide with laughter. She had incredible lips, full and wide and very, very sexy.

'I'll phone her now.' Rhianne plucked her mobile phone from her bag and walked away from him to the edge of the terrace, leaning on the ornate wall and looking out across the river where life was going on as normal; no one there had had their world turned upside down. She couldn't believe that this man, this stranger, had suggested she share his penthouse. What the hell was he thinking? Strangers didn't make offers like that without an ulterior motive.

He wanted her in his bed, that was what. He thought that because her boyfriend had cheated on her that she would be willing to get her own back by turning to someone else. And although he had to be the most strikingly handsome man she'd ever met, he was too, too gorgeous, in fact—she was definitely not in the market for a quick affair. Zarek Diakos was seriously out of his mind if he had thought she would agree.

Karen answered after only two rings. 'Rhianne, what's wrong?'

Taken aback by her friend's instant realization, she said, 'How did you know?'

'Because you never phone me when at I'm at work. Are you in trouble?'

'Actually, yes,' answered Rhianne, 'but it will wait. I'm sorry, I wasn't thinking straight.'

'Don't you dare end the call,' said Karen at once. 'What's up?'

'I need somewhere to stay for a day or two.'

'Then you've rung the right person. Have you fallen out with Annie?'

'It's worse than that.' Her voice broke.

'Don't say anything now,' urged her friend. 'Tell me tonight. Get your clothes and come round after I've finished work. Are you all right until then?'

'Yes,' agreed Rhianne faintly.

'I have to go,' whispered Karen. 'My boss is giving me the evil eye.'

'Is it sorted?' asked Zarek when she rejoined him.

He looked concerned, a faint frown creasing his brow, his eyes watchful on her face. She wished he wouldn't look at her like that—as though he cared! It was guilt, of course, but even so she would have preferred he kept everything on an impersonal level.

Rhianne nodded faintly. 'She'll be home soon. I'll return to my flat meantime and pack my bags.'

'I'll drive you,' he said immediately.

'That won't be necessary.'

'I think it is,' he stated firmly. 'You need someone with you in case your—er, friends are still there.'

Hot sparks flashed from Rhianne's beautiful eyes. 'I can handle them; I'm over it now.'

'Are you?' he asked darkly, his eyes burning into hers, seeming to see right into her soul.

He knew, she realised, that she hated the thought of returning, but it had to be done. Perhaps having him with her might help. At least she wouldn't have to trundle her cases through the streets; he could take her right to Karen's door. And if Angus should happen to be there then Zarek would be her back up. Even if it gave Angus the impression that she had run into the arms of another man, she didn't care. It would serve him right. He certainly hadn't thought of her feelings when he had made a play for her friend.

She still found it hard to believe that Annie would go behind her back like this. They'd gone through school together, university together. Her betrayal cut as deep as any surgeon's knife.

Unaware that tears were streaming down her face again, Rhianne was shocked when Zarek stood up and pulled her into his arms. Actually, she needed comfort. She needed someone to tell her that it wasn't the end of the world and that one day she would laugh at it.

'Life has a habit of testing us,' said Zarek in his deep, soft voice. 'There are those of us who go under and there are those who rise above it and turn tragedy into triumph. Which category do you belong to?'

His rich dark eyes bored into hers, never blinking, never moving, and Rhianne knew what he expected her answer to be. 'The latter,' she said firmly, resolutely squaring her shoulders.

'Then I have a suggestion which might help you in your hour of need, and it will certainly help me.' He stepped back a pace but kept his hands on her shoulders.

Rhianne looked at him suspiciously. Why did she think that she might not like what he had to say? If he was going to suggest moving in with him again then—

'My secretary is away on maternity leave,' he told her, cutting into her thoughts. 'I've had a series of temps, each one of them as hopeless as the last. The job's yours if you want it.'

Snatching away from him, she stared in total amazement, her blue eyes wide and disbelieving. Why would he offer her a job when he didn't even know her? It didn't make sense. She felt that he would be a devil to work for, and this was why none of the others had come up to his expectations—but to offer *her* the job! 'Is it to alleviate your guilt?' she asked, unable to hide the suspicion in her voice.

When he answered, his tone was clipped and tight. 'I

wasn't the guilty party—you stepped out in front of me, remember. You're lucky I managed to stop so quickly. But it was foolish to think that you'd want to work for me. I take back the offer. Let's go. The sooner you're out of my hair the better.'

Immediately Rhianne regretted her words. She was doing herself a disservice. Where else would she be made such a good offer? 'You took me by surprise,' she said quietly. 'I hadn't even got round to thinking about finding another job.' All she'd been able to think about was Angus's deception, the hurt she'd felt, still did feel. But she had to live; she needed money—why not take Zarek up on his offer?

His face was all hard angles, his eyes brilliantly cold. He stood in front of her like a Roman general, tall and imposing, back straight, chin high. There was no sign of the man who had held her close to his heart, who had caused tiny sensations to creep into her traumatised body.

'Can you reinstate the offer?' Rhianne's voice sounded tiny and hesitant when she had hoped it would be strong. She feigned a smile. 'I wasn't thinking straight.'

'Evidently, or you'd have snapped my hands off. I pay well, but I expect nothing less than perfection. Are you an efficient secretary?'

Don't you think you ought to have asked me this before making your offer? The question formed in Rhianne's mind but she didn't voice it. 'The best,' she answered firmly, taking her courage in both hands and sticking her nose up in the air.

'Then it's a deal. Come, let us go.'

Zarek realised that he had behaved entirely out of character. He didn't normally make offers without thinking them through—so what was different on this occasion? Rhianne Pickering was different, that was what. As well as feeling sorry for her, he was intrigued. He wanted to see more of her, find out more about her, and what better way than having her work for him?

Although he remained silent on the journey, he was conscious of her presence beside him. She was totally different to any other woman he knew, already getting beneath his skin in a way he'd never expected. He was looking forward to working with her, very much aware that it would give him the perfect opportunity to get to know her better.

The block of flats where Rhianne lived were plain and ordinary, and as they went up in the lift to the third floor, standing silently side by side, facing the graffiti-covered doors, he wondered how she could have lived here. She was a classy lady and ought to be spending her time in an equally classy apartment.

He tried not to imagine her living with him in the penthouse, or in his villa in Santorini, but somehow he couldn't help himself. He could imagine her swimming in his pool, all her cares forgotten, laughing and happy, her amazing blue eyes alight with mischief, her white teeth flashing as she smiled into his face.

Glancing at her, he saw the way her fingers were curled into her palms, the way her lips were clamped tightly together, a frown drawing her perfectly shaped brows down over her eyes.

Without even stopping to think what he was doing, Zarek took her hands into his and turned her to face him. 'Are you sure you're up to this?'

Rhianne stiffened, her eyes evading his. 'It has to be done.'

'Do you think he'll be gone?'

'I hope so.'

'I'll support you if necessary,' he said softly. Although everything that had happened was no fault of his, he felt a powerful urge to look after this woman who had had her world so swiftly turned upside down, who had experienced the worst day of her life, who was alone and vulnerable and needed a male figure to stand by her.

'There's really no need.' Rhianne's eyes flickered up towards his face, and there was a brief second when she held the contact, when something flowed between them, but he never found out what would have happened because the lift doors opened and she turned swiftly away.

He had briefly seen gratitude, but her back was to him now as she turned her key in the lock, hesitating for just a moment before pushing open the door, then, squaring her shoulders, moving inside. Zarek followed more slowly, glancing around the room with interest.

Rhianne had been dreading this moment, and her heart drummed loudly, echoing through her body in painful little bursts. All she could see in her mind's eye was Angus and Annie. Together!

To her relief the flat was empty—she hadn't checked the bedrooms, of course, but there was no sound save for the drum of her heart, and she glanced over her shoulder at Zarek, smiling faintly.

He gave a nod of understanding but remained near the door. He had closed it quietly behind him, not intruding, giving her space and time to do whatever she had to do. She was glad of his presence. In truth, she had been dreading coming back here for fear of what she might find.

But her sense of relief was short-lived when she saw

Angus's tie draped over the back of a chair. Angus was a rep for a pharmaceutical company and always wore suits and ties. Had he left in a hurry after she'd walked in on their lovemaking? Or was he still here?

Annie's bedroom door was closed, and there was no sound, but Rhianne's curiosity took her across the room. Without even stopping to think, she pushed open the door. The room was unoccupied, but as her eyes roved the space she saw further evidence that Angus had been here, perhaps even stayed. A pair of shoes in the corner, the sleeve of a shirt hanging out of the washing basket, and Rhianne knew instinctively that if she opened the wardrobe she would see one of his suits hanging there.

Actually, now that her initial anger and revulsion was over, Rhianne realised that she ought to have seen something like this coming. Angus had always had a reputation for being a womanizer, but she'd ignored that fact when he'd asked her to go out with him, believing him when he'd said she was special. And when he'd asked her to marry him, she had said yes immediately.

Only later, when their wedding arrangements were being made, had she begun to have doubts. There had been whispers that he was seeing other women; she'd actually tackled him about it, but he had convinced her that there was no truth in it, that he loved her and wanted to marry her, and, stupidly, she had believed him.

But to bed her best friend! Why, she asked herself, had she never seen the signs before? How had they managed to keep their liaison a secret?

She slammed the door shut, and immediately Zarek crossed the room and pulled her hard against him. He didn't speak; he seemed to know instinctively that no words would make her feel better.

Rhianne felt his strength seep into her. It was easy to forget that he was a stranger whom she'd met only a few hours ago. He was her saviour, holding her strongly when she felt like collapsing, stroking her hair, murmuring in his native language, finally, tilting her chin with a gentle finger, compelling her to look into his face.

And suddenly he was kissing her—and she was kissing him back! Hungrily and deeply, taking and savouring, her body flooding with alien passion. How could it be happening? How could she react like this when she was still upset by Angus's cavalier attitude? The truth was Zarek's kiss meant a whole lot more to her than Angus's ever had.

Angus had considered himself a lady's man, God's gift to women—which she had blindly ignored—but Zarek was in a whole different league. She sensed that immediately. He wasn't taking advantage of her weakness, he was comforting her. And how!

Her head began to spin, and when he put her from him she clung to the doorpost for support. Wow! A raging heat consumed her, and she was in such a daze that it was impossible to move.

Whether Zarek knew that it was because of his kiss, or whether he thought it was still a reaction to her fiancé's perfidy, she didn't know. But, whatever, he took command.

'Let me help you pack,' he said. 'Where are your suitcases?'

Rhianne ineffectively tried to clear her head. He must think her an idiot standing there with her mouth open and her eyes wide. She pointed across the room, and he dragged them from the cupboard.

'Right, I'll empty your wardrobe, you do the drawers.'

Never had she imagined that she would let a man, a stranger at that, fold her dresses and skirts and place them carefully into a case. She was mesmerised by the way he did it, by the way he stroked out the creases before putting the next garment on top. Until he looked at her, until his dark eyes smiled and teased. 'Do I have to do everything?'

Mentally shaking herself, Rhianne slid open drawers and threw her undies into the other case, going hot at the thought that if he hadn't urged her into action, it would have been his hands lifting her intimate garments. And then the next time she wore them she would have remembered that he had touched them, maybe even covertly examined them. It didn't bear thinking about.

How one comforting kiss could have sent her into such a tizz she didn't know. Because that was all it had been. He had meant nothing by it.

'You shouldn't have kissed me,' she said, and then wished she hadn't because it gave too much of herself away.

'You were hurting, I wanted to kiss you better.'

'I'm not a child,' she shot back, knowing she was over-reacting but unable to help herself. She had enjoyed the kiss! *Enjoyed it*, for heaven's sake, and that scared the hell out of her! She felt awful. How could this be happening? But worse still, she had promised to work for him. They would be in close proximity for several hours each day. She couldn't do it. Not with the memory of his kiss hanging between them like a tantalising fruit.

'I'm very much aware of that fact,' Zarek informed her, his voice suddenly terse. 'I am merely here to provide support. What happened was unfortunate. If you can put it behind you then the job is still yours, if you cannot forgive me then I will take you to your friend's house, and you will never see me again.'

He paused for a moment, his eyes connecting with hers, cool brown fighting hot blue, and Rhianne knew that she had a hard decision to make.

CHAPTER THREE

TURNING down Zarek's job offer would be both pointless and senseless, realised Rhianne. She needed a job, she needed something to take her mind off recent events, and work would be her salvation. Feeling vaguely guilty now for saying that he shouldn't have kissed her, she said quietly, 'I'd still like the job.'

'Then it's yours,' answered Zarek, his voice calm now, his eyes steady on hers, one eyebrow rising in a crooked arc. 'Although I must warn you that I'm a hard taskmaster. I shall work you long hours, probably longer than you've ever worked in your life, but the rewards more than make up for it.'

Rhianne's eyes widened. 'Rewards?' She needed to know exactly what those rewards were.

'I pay well for good work and loyalty.'

She breathed a sigh of relief, chastising herself for thinking that he might have meant rewarding her by taking her out to dinner, for instance. Or to the theatre. Or even suggest a weekend away. Her mind had run amok at the kind of rewards Zarek might offer her.

If he hadn't kissed her, she would probably never have thought along those lines, and even though she had explained away the kiss to her own satisfaction there was one tiny part of her that knew she must be on her guard at all times. Not from Zarek, but from the feelings that had amazingly risen inside her when their lips had touched.

It didn't take long to finish packing, to drop her toiletries into a holdall, and her shoes into carrier bags. When she was finished, she looked around the room. She had shared this flat with Annie for three years. It wasn't sadness she felt, though, but anger that her friend had cheated on her.

'I'm ready,' she announced crisply.

Zarek's eyes met hers, and he looked at her steadily, saying nothing, simply picking up her bags and carrying them down to his car. He wished that there was something he could say or do to make Rhianne feel better. Her face was deathly pale, and he was afraid she was going to pass out. But he knew that to even touch her again would be a mistake.

She was proudly beautiful in her unhappiness. Her long eyelashes shading her incredible blue eyes, her chin high and haughty, her mouth—well, he preferred not to think about her mouth because he wanted to kiss it again. He wanted to feel its softness; he wanted to encourage a response. Because he had felt a tiny one, even though she had told him off.

Give her a few days, a week or two at the most, and she might return his kisses. Not that this was his prime aim. He felt inordinately sorry for her; he didn't want to see her walking the streets looking for work.

But that earlier kiss had told him that she wasn't immune, and he liked the fact that she was fighting him. In fact, it had been a long time since he had met anyone who intrigued him as much as she did.

The journey to her friend's house was accomplished in silence. Rhianne did not seem disposed to talk, and Zarek respected that. Karen was already home from work, and as she welcomed Rhianne, she looked curiously at Zarek.

But Rhianne didn't introduce them. She simply turned to him and said, 'If you give me your business card, I'll see you at nine sharp in the morning.'

Zarek bowed his head, plucked a card from his wallet and silently handed it to her. 'Do not be late,' he warned.

'Who the hell was that?' asked Karen the moment he had driven off.

'My new employer.'

'You're changing your job?'

Rhianne nodded. 'I've been forced to. I was told this morning to clear my desk and get out.'

'Are they allowed to do that?' asked Karen curiously. 'How does that guy fit into the equation? How did you meet him?'

'It's a long story,' Rhianne answered. 'I need a drink before I tell you. Preferably something stronger than tea.'

'A G&T it is, then,' said her friend. 'And I'll join you. Why don't you put your stuff into my spare room while I'm mixing it?'

As soon as they'd sat down, Rhianne blurted out the events of the day, from discovering Angus and Annie to being hit by Zarek.

'Oh, Rhianne, I'm sorry.' Karen clapped a hand to her mouth, her eyes as wide as saucers. 'What a terrible day you've had!'

'Don't I know it. Luckily I escaped with a few bruises, and that guy who dropped me off was the one who knocked me down. Whether it's because he felt guilty I don't know, but he's giving me a job.'

Her friend's mouth fell open. 'Talk about landing on your feet.'

'It's only temporary, but it will do while I look around.'

'You don't sound impressed,' said Karen. 'He's truly gorgeous. Just the man to get you back on your feet.'

Tell me about it, thought Rhianne. Angus had been good-looking, but Zarek was doubly so. With added charisma. Which would be difficult to ignore. 'I couldn't care less what he looks like,' she told her friend fiercely. 'I'm seriously off men for the foreseeable future.'

'I don't blame you,' agreed Karen. 'I still find it hard to believe that Angus has cheated on you with Annie. Did he really think he could get away with it? I wonder how long it's been going on?'

'I don't think it's the first time he's done that sort of thing,' acknowledged Rhianne bitterly. 'Someone at work told me ages ago that she'd seen him with another woman. He denied it, of course, and I stupidly believed him. He's away such a lot with his job, how do I know what he gets up to? But to cheat with my best friend…I shall never forgive him. In fact, I shall never trust another man as long as I live.'

'They're not all the same.'

'No?' she queried, her eyes rising disdainfully. 'My father cheated on my mother, it's why they got divorced. I always swore it would never happen to me.'

It was late when they went to bed, and Rhianne slept fitfully, thoughts of both Angus's betrayal and Zarek's kiss whirling round and round in her mind. Contrarily, when it was time to get up, she was in her deepest sleep.

The alarm woke her, and she jumped out of bed, forgetting her injuries until she put her foot to the floor. It was stiff and painful, and in the full-length mirror on the wardrobe door she saw a huge bruise on her thigh, a vivid reminder of all that had happened yesterday.

And today she was starting a new job!

She actually felt fit for nothing. She wanted to stay in bed and wallow in her anguish. Both physical and mental. But jobs like the one Zarek had offered didn't come along very often. The salary he'd mentioned was virtually double what she'd been earning. She'd be a fool to throw it away.

Karen had already left, so Rhianne had the house to herself. She showered and dressed carefully in a charcoal-grey suit, teaming it with a white blouse and medium heels. She brushed her thick hair and fastened it up on top of her head, and, with a final glance in the mirror, she pronounced herself ready.

The address was in the centre of the city, and she caught the tube in. Living in London, or even its suburbs, there was no point in having a car—even if she could have afforded one. Limping the last few yards to Zarek's office, her heartbeat quickened.

This job offer had been so sudden, so unexpected, that she wasn't sure whether she was up to it. He was a hard taskmaster, he'd said. Which also meant that she wouldn't have time to dwell on what had happened. This had to be good. So why wasn't she feeling happy? Why was she feeling that she would regret taking on this job?

Diakos Holdings occupied the top two floors of an impressive building. She was shot upwards in a high-speed lift and was evidently expected because she was shown straight through to Zarek's office.

He stood up from his desk the moment she entered. 'Good, I'm glad you made it.' He wore a navy suit and a pale blue shirt and he looked the epitome of a successful businessman. His silk tie was navy also with pale blue polka dots. Everything about him screamed elegance and good taste.

'Did you have any doubts?' she enquired, looking curiously around her once her perusal of Zarek's attire was over. His office was state-of-the-art efficient, cool colours, sleek furniture. There were no paintings on the walls, nothing to take his mind off the job in hand. There was a view over the Thames, but the venetian blinds were angled so that they blotted it out.

'I wouldn't be human if I didn't,' he answered. 'We did meet under rather exceptional circumstances, and my offer of a job was not done in the normal way. I would have perfectly understood if—'

'Mr Diakos,' interrupted Rhianne. 'I gave my word.'

'Of course you did,' he said. 'I should never have doubted it. You're a woman of integrity, and I like that. How are you feeling this morning?'

'Stiff and painful,' she answered.

'Up to working?'

'Of course.'

'Then we'll begin.'

Her office was next to Zarek's with an interconnecting door. In business mode he was very different to the man she had met yesterday.

She discovered that this was the newest branch of Diakos Holdings, and that Zarek was here to oversee things. Their head office was in Athens, and they had other branches in Europe and the United States. It was a world of high finance, and the sort of figures that were tossed around caused Rhianne's head to spin.

He worked her hard, giving her no opportunity to think about her problems and when Zarek said they were finished for the day, she was amazed to see that it was nearly seven o'clock.

'You've done well,' he told her. 'I didn't expect you to keep up.'

'Do you always work this late?' she asked.

'Sometimes later. Is it a problem for you?'

Rhianne shook her head. 'It helps take my mind off…' She tailed away, but Zarek knew what she was talking about and nodded. 'I'd like to repay your hard work by taking you out to dinner. You must be starving.'

Almost immediately Rhianne recalled her suspicions. Her eyes blazed and, with a defiant lift of her chin, she declined his offer. 'My friend is expecting me. She'll have a meal cooked by now. In any case, Mr Diakos, I don't believe in mixing business with pleasure.'

'Of course,' he answered evenly. 'But bear it in mind for another occasion. Dining with me is part of the deal. It would certainly be business because I rarely switch off. You'd find yourself taking notes.'

Rhianne looked long and hard into his dark eyes and saw nothing other than complete honesty—or was there something more? The intensity she saw there made her heart leap and unwanted heat flood her skin. She felt raw vibes crossing the divide between them. With a shake of her head she turned away, picking up her bag and heading for the door. 'Goodnight, Mr Diakos.'

'Goodnight, Rhianne.'

The next few days followed a similar pattern. He

worked her hard, but Rhianne didn't mind, and then on Friday afternoon Zarek asked whether she would be prepared to work the next day.

'Is this what you mean by being a hard taskmaster?' Rhianne asked. 'Seven o'clock every night and then weekends.'

'So it's a no?' A wry smile curved his lips as though it was what he had expected.

'You push yourself too much,' she pointed out. 'Is it really necessary to work on a Saturday? I thought everything was up to date.' Heavens, he'd worked like there was no tomorrow every day, what else was there left to do?

'On this occasion, yes, because I have to go home to Santorini. My father's not well, and I want to be on top of things before I go.'

'Then of course I'll come in,' she answered quickly and quietly. 'I'm sorry to hear about your father. Is it serious?'

'I'm sure it's not, but my mother needs me. Will you be all right in my absence? I know you must still be hurting over your fiancé's indiscretions. Have you spoken to him yet?'

Rhianne shook her head, and the pins came out of her hair, causing it to tumble about her shoulders in a cloud of auburn waves. She had always been so careful to keep it neat and tidy for work that she felt embarrassed, putting her hands to it and trying to fix it back up.

'Don't,' said Zarek at once. 'Your hair is your crowning glory; leave it loose. I like it that way.'

He liked it! What was that supposed to mean? He wasn't supposed to like anything about her except her efficiency. Personal issues were not allowed. Hadn't they straightened that out after The Kiss?

'Don't you think you should speak to him?' he asked quietly. 'His defection was a turning point in your relationship. You need to tell him that; you need to make it perfectly clear that he has no part to play in your future—unless you're hoping that—'

'You think I haven't tried?' she cut in crossly. 'His mobile phone's always turned off. He never answers his house phone either. I've even tried going round, but there's never anyone at home.'

'So the whole thing is still an issue between you?'

'I suppose so.'

'How about your wedding plans?'

'I've cancelled them,' she announced firmly.

'And your friend, the one whose flat you shared,' he persisted. 'What does she have to say about the matter?'

Rhianne's eyes flashed a furious blue. 'She's uncontactable as well—if there is such a word. It's my guess they've run away together, gone into hiding somewhere. And if she can't be decent enough to speak to me and apologise, then I never want to see her again.' Her voice rose until she was speaking far more shrilly and loudly than she realised, verging on the hysterical.

Zarek immediately took her into his arms—and, foolishly, Rhianne didn't stop him. The whole issue had been building all week. Not being able to contact either of them was too frustrating for words. She could have thrown herself into the Thames for all they seemed to care.

'You are right, Rhianne,' he said gently. 'They are not worthy of you. Why don't you come to Santorini with me.'

Rhianne felt her heart stop beating. Everything around her stilled. The world grew silent. And then, just as suddenly, she felt a roar in her ears, and she clutched the back of her chair for support.

'I think you know what my answer will be,' she said coolly. 'I like working for you, Mr Diakos, and I like the job, but as for anything else, it's out of the question. I've learnt a huge lesson, and I am nobody's fool. I'm grateful for the job, but if you want more from me, then I'm afraid I will have to quit.'

She snatched up her bag and would have walked out of the door if he hadn't crossed the room in double-quick time and grabbed her arm.

'I have no ulterior motive.' His voice was icy-cold now, his eyes, more grey than brown at this moment, were like flint. 'How could you think like that? I didn't have to come to your rescue. I could have left you lying right there in the road. Your attitude sometimes makes me wish I had.'

'Then you shouldn't make improper suggestions,' she shot back, trying unsuccessfully to snatch away.

'Improper?' He turned her to face him, gripping both her arms, effectively making her his prisoner. 'You have no idea what you're talking about. And if this is all the thanks I get for helping you out then perhaps it would be as well if you did leave.'

He let her go, but he didn't move away, and Rhianne found that she couldn't move either. For some reason she was transfixed to the spot, her eyes locked into his, her wild heartbeat echoing in her ears.

'The offer to come to Santorini was because I thought you could do with a break. There won't be much work for you here in my absence, and I didn't want you to spend time worrying about your broken love life.'

Rhianne began to feel slightly foolish. 'I appreciate your concern, but I really will be all right.'

'Do you still want to quit?' he asked, his tone quieter now, but his eyes remained hard as they looked into hers.

She shook her head. 'I'd be a fool. Good jobs are hard to come by.'

'So I'll see you when I get back?'

She nodded.

He fetched a card out of his pocket and scribbled something on it. 'This is the number of my private cell phone. If you need me, just ring, even if it's only to talk.'

Rhianne's fine brows lifted, and her eyes widened. He sounded as though he really meant it. 'I don't think I'll be doing that.' Nevertheless she took the card and slipped it into her bag.

It was not until she got home that the full implication of what he had done hit her. He was, in fact, offering her a lifeline. He still thought she was cut up about Angus's defection—which she was but was bravely trying not to show it—and he wanted to act as her—counsellor. She could ring him and talk things through; that was what he was saying. He clearly felt involved after the accident. First he had taken her home, then he'd given her a job, and then offered her a holiday in Santorini.

She was sorry to hear his father was ill—it was not going to be a pleasant visit. And she'd done the right thing in refusing to join him. He'd need to spend time with his family, he wouldn't want or need her hanging around. It was not as if they were friends—they were nothing more than acquaintances, really. They'd met by accident, and now she worked for him. Full stop. That was it. Nothing more, nothing less.

When Rhianne went in to work on Saturday morning, she was half afraid that Zarek might ask her again to accompany him to Santorini, and she didn't know whether to be relieved or disappointed when he never mentioned it.

Instead, he was in full business mode, and she felt none of the electricity that had passed between them. It could have been in her imagination, of course, but somehow she doubted it. Zarek was too masculine, too gorgeous, not to let it intrude into his everyday life.

She imagined that most women would fall at his feet, and she probably intrigued him because she was different. It wasn't that she didn't see what a striking man he was—she saw everything—but she had no intention of getting involved with him or any man. She'd lost her trust in men. And Zarek was so incredibly sexy that it would be easy to fall for him—and she couldn't afford to do that. Not to be tossed to one side again when he had finished with her. Admittedly, some affairs lasted, some marriages were happy and lasted, but they were the exception rather than the rule. She had no intention of becoming another statistic. Once was enough.

They worked hard until almost two, and when he had signed the last of the letters, when he had read the last of the reports, he sat back in his chair, ran his fingers through his thick dark hair, and announced that he was finished.

'I don't know about you, but I'm starving,' he declared. 'And as a reward for today you're going to join me for lunch.'

'But—'

'I refuse to take no for an answer.' Brown eyes met and held hers. 'You're a hard worker, Rhianne, efficient, almost second-guessing me. I cannot let it pass. You're having lunch with me.' He pushed his chair back and stood up. 'Let's go.'

Although dining with Zarek was the last thing she wanted, Rhianne knew she was being given no choice. She *had* worked hard, she *did* deserve a treat. When was the last time she'd been wined and dined in style? Not with Angus, that was for sure. He'd worked long hours and they'd usually had either a cooked meal at home or a meal in the local pub.

A public house certainly wouldn't be Zarek's choice. It would be a high-class restaurant where they would get the best treatment and the finest food. It would be nice to be indulged for a change. In truth, she hadn't been eating properly all week, but today she felt that she could do a meal justice.

'You win,' she said quietly.

But her comfort zone was shattered when she discovered that they were going back to his penthouse. 'What's going on?' she asked when his chauffeured car stopped in front of the hotel.

'Why, lunch, of course.' His eyes were full of innocence. 'They do a very good meal here. Simply choose what you like, and it will be sent up. Can you imagine Saturday lunchtime in London? Everywhere will be crowded. It's by far the best solution.'

There was a twinkle in his eyes as he spoke, and they were more grey than brown. Rhianne was fast beginning to realise that brown seemed to be his business mode, or his serious mode, but when he was being light-hearted they were actually grey. And she couldn't help wondering what colour they would be when he was making love.

As soon as the thought entered her mind, she dashed

it away. She even felt a warmth in her cheeks. How could she even entertain such a notion? Easy, said her conscience. Zarek Diakos is not a man who can be ignored. He's a very sexy individual, and you'll need to be careful if you don't want to get caught in his trap.

So how easy would it be when she was already being led into his lair?

CHAPTER FOUR

RHIANNE was relieved when Zarek suggested they eat outside, and she thanked her lucky stars that it was a hot sunny day. London was stifling, but up here, high above the streets, a light breeze cooled the air around them. And she needed it!

She hadn't felt comfortable with the thought of dining in Zarek's suite. It was far too intimate, especially as the memory of his kiss kept rearing its head. Should he decide to kiss her again, there would be nothing or no one to save her except her own conscience, her own dignity. And would she want to stop him?

Brief though his kiss had been, it had triggered an unexpected and overwhelming reaction, and she wouldn't have been human if she hadn't wondered what it would feel like to be really kissed by him. To feel those strong arms about her, to feel his passion, and, above all—to feel herself responding. She had been shocked to realise how enjoyable this Greek male's kiss had been. Despite its brevity. In fact, it had made such a lasting impression that she had actually dreamt about Zarek making love to her.

In the stark light of day she had despised herself, but here, on this secluded terrace, sipping pre-lunch drinks while the table was set and they waited for their food, Rhianne couldn't stop the loud thud of her heart. Working with Zarek was totally different to socialising with him. In the office she was able to shut out everything except the work in hand. He kept her so busy that she had no choice.

But here, now, when he was acting as though she were a friend rather than an employee, how could she ignore the racing of her pulses, or the heat of her skin which had nothing to do with the heat of the day?

It was a crazy situation; nevertheless, she ensured that her outer image was cool, that not by the merest blink of an eyelid, the flutter of an eyelash, did she let him know how much he affected her. He was her saviour, and that was all. He had given her a job in her neediest hour. And she was grateful to him. But gratitude did not equate to a need to be kissed again. Thoroughly. And satisfyingly. She was ashamed to admit that that one taste had whetted her appetite, and she wanted more.

'You look nervous.'

Zarek's voice intruded into her thoughts, and she looked at him guiltily. 'Not at all. I was actually thinking how fortunate I am.'

'To be dining here with me?' he asked, his eyes twinkling as he deliberately misunderstood.

Rhianne shook her head, unaware that her own eyes were an intense blue, that her rich auburn hair shone like spun silk in the sunlight, and that Zarek found it difficult to take his eyes off her. 'To have been offered another job so soon. If it hadn't been for you, I would be traipsing the streets still looking for work.'

'A lady of your talent? I think not,' he said lightly. 'You've exceeded my expectations, and all I can say is that your previous company's loss is my gain. I was fortunate to have found you.'

'But did you have to knock me down in the process?' Humour was the only way she could deal with the situation. It scared her to think how easily she was being sucked into Zarek's world. Who would have thought that one day she'd be dining in the penthouse suite of one of London's top hotels? Or that her host would be one of the world's wealthiest men? It was like winning the lottery, as though all her birthdays had come together.

'I couldn't have chosen anyone nicer to run over,' he said, and there was a gruff inflection in his voice that hadn't been there before. 'I'm glad you weren't seriously hurt, Rhianne. And I'm even happier that you've stepped into the breach. What would I do without you?'

Expressive dark eyes locked into hers, and Rhianne wondered whether he expected an answer. If he did, there was nothing she could say. She felt faintly breathless. She hadn't expected compliments like this. Or was it because she was on the rebound and read things that weren't there?

It had to be. Zarek wasn't interested in the likes of her. He was simply making her feel good because she'd worked overtime. He'd needed her and she'd helped out. This was his way of saying thank you. He appreciated how hard she worked, how dedicated she was to her job, and how quickly she had picked up the reins. This lunch was her reward before he went away to Santorini and gave her time to catch her breath.

Her mobile rang, and Rhianne felt a surge of anger when she saw Angus's number. 'I need to answer this. Do you mind, Zarek?'

'Not at all,' he said at once. 'I'll go and see what's happening to our food.'

Rhianne waited until he was out of earshot before she spoke. Even then, all she managed was a clipped, 'Angus?'

'We need to talk.'

'Do we?' she asked coldly. 'As far as I'm concerned there's nothing to be said. You took me for a fool. You thought I was so besotted that I wouldn't mind if you bedded my best friend.'

'That's not true, Rhianne. I love you, I really do.'

'So why did you make love to Annie?'

'Annie came on to me. I told her I was—'

'Don't lie!' Rhianne found it difficult to keep her voice low. 'This isn't the first time you've cheated on me. I was a fool to ever believe your lies. I'm well rid of you, and I pity any other girl who thinks you'll be true to her.'

Angus's tone became suddenly nasty. 'Do you want to know why I looked elsewhere? Because you're frigid, Rhianne. Do you hear me? Frigid! I reckon I've had a close call, and if you're not careful you'll end up an old maid.'

Rhianne heard the click as the line went dead, but she stood there for several more seconds before she found the strength to move. Maybe she was frigid, maybe that was what was wrong with her. Though her own interpretation was that she valued her virginity and wanted to save it for whomever she married.

Was that too much to ask?

She'd told Angus this in the very beginning, she had thought he understood and respected her wishes. It wasn't as though she had never let him touch her. They'd made love in lots of different ways, and he'd said that he found it exciting that he would be making love to a virgin on his wedding night. So what had gone wrong? Why had he felt the need to sow his oats behind her back?

When Zarek returned, he found her sitting with her head in her hands. She looked up at his approach, and her face was pale. 'Whatever is wrong?' he asked at once. 'Have you had bad news?'

'That was Angus,' she said faintly.

'Does he want you back?'

'No.'

'Was he apologising?'

'No.'

'Then the man's a moron and not worth wasting another word on, not even a breath. Are you hungry? Lunch is coming.' Zarek would have liked to say more but it was none of his business. Perhaps, when she'd had time to come to terms with whatever this man had said, she would talk to him.

'I couldn't eat a thing,' she declared.

She had such beautiful eyes; he couldn't bear to see them hurt like this. 'You must eat,' he insisted. 'You need to keep up your strength.' He felt like throttling the man who had done this to Rhianne. First he'd cheated on her, and now he'd said something so awful that she looked as though she was ready to pass out.

Their lunch was brought to them by a succession of waiters and laid carefully on the table. Chairs were pulled out, and they both sat down. At his bidding the young men drifted silently away.

'So what's it to be?' he asked, injecting cheerfulness into his voice. 'A little consommé, perhaps, to start?'

Rhianne shook her head. 'I'd like some wine, thank you.'

To drown her sorrows? He didn't blame her, but they'd

been working since eight thirty that morning; she needed food before drink. 'A bread roll, perhaps,' he suggested. 'Wine on an empty stomach is not good for you.'

He split a roll into two and buttered it before placing it in front of her. 'Now, eat,' he ordered. He kept his eye on her while she nibbled, but not until he was satisfied that she had lined her stomach did he pour her a glass of wine.

As he expected, she drank it quickly and held her glass out for more.

'Is it that bad?' he asked quietly.

'You don't know the half.'

Zarek closed his eyes briefly. He wanted to give her a good shake, tell her to forget what had happened and get on with her life. But he knew it wasn't that easy. 'It's not good to bottle things up, Rhianne, surely you know that?' he said softly. 'But if you don't wish to discuss it, I'll bow to your request. However, I have no intention of leaving you here in this state while I visit my parents. You're coming with me.'

She looked at him as though he had gone out of his mind. 'To Santorini?'

'That is correct.' And once she was out there she would, hopefully, relax. She would forget all about this guy who had carelessly hurt her and turn to him, come to depend on him.

Already his body ached for her. He wanted to kiss her again and again, he wanted her in his bed, he wanted to lose himself in her body. There was no way he could do that while her ex-fiancé still haunted her thoughts, but in Santorini she would become his. He would take it slowly and carefully, his seduction all the more satisfying because of it.

'I can't.' Plaintive eyes looked into his. 'It wouldn't be proper. I—we—oh, Zarek, please don't ask me.'

'Because you know you can't refuse?' She wanted to come, he was sure of it; it was the propriety thing that bothered her. But to hell with that. She needed to get away, and he wanted to find out more about her.

Rhianne was in a different league to other women he'd dated. His wealth did not impress her, nor did she care what she said to him. To her he was just a man. A man who had nearly run over her. A man who was now her employer. But even that gave him no hold over her. She wasn't afraid of hard work; in fact, she seemed to revel in it, but she didn't see him as a potential lover.

Not yet, at least!

It would be his pleasure to persuade her differently.

'My mind's all over the place, Zarek; I need time to myself. I'd be no company.'

'But you do agree that a change of scenery would do you a world of good?'

'I guess so.'

'Then at least let me do that for you. You don't have to spend all your time with me. You can do whatever you like; there'll be no boundaries, no pressure.'

'Would we be staying with your parents?'

'Not at all. My villa is large enough for you to not feel inhibited. You'll have your own rooms and your freedom. You'll be able to recharge your batteries and push all thoughts of your failed relationship out of your mind.'

What he didn't tell her was that he wouldn't be patient for ever. He wanted Rhianne in his bed. Seeing her like this was doing him no good at all. He wanted to crush her to him, he wanted to make love to her for hours on end so that she'd have nothing else left to think about but him.

He watched as Rhianne fought a battle with her inner self, and when at last she spoke, there was nothing on her face to hint at what decision she'd reached. 'I'll come, Zarek,' she said softly. 'But don't expect too much.'

His heart soared. 'All I want is for you to be happy.'

Rhianne frowned. 'Why are you doing this? Why do you care so much?'

Because I fancy you like hell and I want you in my bed. Of course, he didn't say this, he simply gave a gentle smile. 'Because you deserve a break. Because you've worked hard for me this last week, and I want to reward you. Because—well—you look as though you need a holiday. Do I need to go on?'

'You're too kind.' And at last Rhianne smiled.

Zarek felt his heart soar. Rhianne's smiles were heart-stoppingly lovely. She had the most beautifully shaped mouth he had ever seen: soft lips that simply begged to be kissed, and teeth that were white and even. He looked forward to the day when he kissed her again. A proper kiss. One that would shatter his senses—and, hopefully, Rhianne's too.

Rhianne couldn't believe that she had agreed to go to Santorini with Zarek. She felt sure that the only reason he had made the offer was because he felt sorry for her. She oughtn't to have taken the phone call, she ought not to have let Angus upset her. Except that it wasn't nice being called frigid. Her feelings were hurt. She really wanted to be on her own, not here with Zarek, who was being too nice.

But what was done was done. She had a new life to look forward to and a gorgeous man to share it with. At least for the duration of their visit. She suddenly realised that she had no idea how long he intended staying on Santorini. His father was ill he'd said, so possibly there was no time limit. It could be days, weeks, months even. Would he want her with him for that long? Would she want to stay for that length of time?

'I really think you should eat something.' Zarek's rich deep voice cut into her thoughts.

'Maybe I will have a little soup,' agreed Rhianne. Her heavy mood was beginning to lighten. Although the phone call had hurt her, it had also had the effect of bringing to an end one part of her life. And, conversely, a new one was beginning. A life where she made new friends, went to new places, where she could become a completely different person.

'In fact,' she said, 'I'll have a large bowl. I'm suddenly hungry.'

She enjoyed the rest of the meal; a light chicken salad followed the soup, with fresh strawberries for dessert. It was all very light and healthy, and she drank two more glasses of wine, then sat back replete.

Zarek had watched her eating with an amused smile on his face. But he wasn't mocking her, he was pleased to see her enjoying her food. Nor had he done too badly himself. Between them they had managed to finish everything that had been spread out before them.

'You did well,' he said, 'considering you weren't hungry. Did I tell you that my plane flies out first thing in the morning?'

Rhianne's eyes widened. 'Then I need to go home and sort myself out.'

'How long will it take you to pack?'

She shrugged. 'An hour.'

'Then there's no hurry,' he said. 'Stay a while. Relax. Keep me company.'

'Isn't there something you should be doing?' Rhianne wished that she knew why Zarek kept insisting she spend time with him. It was as though he didn't want to let her out of his sight. Perhaps he thought that if he let her go, she'd change her mind about going with him. And perhaps she ought to. There was something dangerous about going with this man to visit his family.

Zarek shook his head. 'Thanks to you we're up to date at the office. I don't even need to pack; it will all be done for me.'

How the other half live, she thought, though she wasn't bitter. Zarek had no airs or graces. He was a man comfortable in his own skin, who had shown considerable concern for her following the accident. She guessed he would help anyone in distress but wasn't he going a little bit over the top suggesting she holiday with him? It was difficult not to wonder whether he had an ulterior motive. And if he had, was she in danger of making a fool of herself, because he was without a doubt the most seriously sexy man she had ever met.

'Come, let us make ourselves more comfortable.'

He pulled back her chair and led her over to the softly cushioned cane seats they had vacated earlier. 'Can I get you anything else? More coffee, perhaps?'

He rested his hand on her shoulder, and Rhianne felt a *frisson* of awareness ride through her, starting in her throat before weaving its way into every part of her body. And it scared her. There were feelings here that she'd felt with no one else. Perilous feelings.

She ought to back out of this situation right now, this very minute. She was treading on dangerous ground, and before she knew it she could be in well over her head.

'No coffee, thanks,' answered Rhianne, and she watched him as he settled himself in one of the other chairs. Not beside her but facing her, which was even more disconcerting.

His dark brown eyes watched her closely, and Rhianne searched for something to say that would ease the situation. Because if he continued to look at her like this, she would end up a wreck. No man had ever managed to disturb her senses to such an extent.

'What's wrong with your father?' she asked, trying to steer the conversation into an impersonal direction. Impersonal for her, at least. Zarek must be very concerned about his parent, otherwise he wouldn't be making the journey.

'He has a recurring heart problem; he's had it for years. I'm not unduly worried but my mother's panicking, so I need to visit.' He spoke casually but his eyes, those eloquent golden-brown eyes, suggested that he would rather be talking about her.

She felt something alien slither down her spine; it was unnerving the way he kept looking at her, and she was surprised when her voice sounded normal. 'I hope she won't mind you dragging me along.'

'Dragging?' Dark brows rose. 'Is that what I'm doing?'

Rhianne gave a light shrug and a grimace. 'I find it hard to believe that I've agreed to go to Santorini with you. It's crazy. We hardly know each other.'

'Then we're going to have fun finding out, aren't we?'

Fun? It was one way of describing it, though it wasn't

exactly the word she would have used. 'But why? Why are you insisting I join you?' she asked. 'It's a family visit not something you should take your secretary to.'

'You're not going to be my secretary while we're away. Oh, no, Rhianne!'

His voice lowered until it became deep and sexy, and what she saw when she looked into his eyes troubled her deeply. 'If you have something else in mind, Zarek, then we can forget the whole thing. I'm not coming with you if—' Her voice tailed. How could she put into words what she was thinking? It would be far too embarrassing, especially if she'd got it wrong.

But Zarek was not letting her get away with it. 'If what?' His tone was serious, his face stern, and Rhianne couldn't be sure whether he was calling her bluff or whether she had actually annoyed him.

'I've just finished with one relationship, I have no intention of starting another.'

'And you think that's what I'm after?' There was indignation in his voice but a twinkle in his eyes. 'Really, Rhianne, you do me an injustice. I have a heart of gold, didn't you know that? All I'm doing is giving you the break you deserve.'

Zarek watched Rhianne's face closely, wondering whether she would believe him. God, this woman intrigued him like no one else ever had. He wanted to take her into his arms and kiss her senseless right here and now. And somehow he knew that she wouldn't stop him.

But afterwards, when the kiss ended, she would come to her senses and refuse point blank to accompany him.

He wanted her, yes—badly. But he'd never taken a woman against her will. And he wasn't about to start now. His seduction of her needed to be slow and sure.

CHAPTER FIVE

RHIANNE knew that she ought not to have been surprised that Zarek had his own private jet, but, nevertheless, she had been. After her initial shock, though, she had got used to the luxury. Zarek had busied himself with some paperwork, so she'd been able to relax and enjoy. An army of staff had pampered her and fed her, making her feel as though she was someone special, and now they had arrived on Santorini.

The heat greeted them. The sky was a hot blue, the waters of the Aegean translucent and inviting, and the white glare of the buildings made her wish that her sunglasses weren't packed in her case. Alighting from the plane felt like stepping into an oven. But in no time at all they were ushered into an air-conditioned car and whisked away from the busy little airport.

'We must go to see my mother first,' Zarek told her. 'She is expecting us.'

'Us?' queried Rhianne. 'You've told her about me?'

'I phoned her last night. She's looking forward to meeting you.'

'So she's used to your staff accompanying you?' Zarek

was such a busy man that she wouldn't put it past him to take a retinue of employees wherever he went.

'Actually, no. I've never brought any of my work-force here.'

A frown dragged Rhianne's fine brows together. If this was the case, why was he taking her to meet his mother? Why couldn't he have dropped her off at his villa and gone to see his parent alone? Surely they wouldn't want a stranger in their midst at such a critical time.

When they reached his family home—an impressive white villa near the beautiful village of Oia, overlooking a water-filled crater left by a volcanic eruption many years earlier—his mother came rushing out to greet them.

'Zarek.' She held out her arms and folded him in them. She was shorter than her son, very slender and elegantly dressed, and her dark hair bore no sign of grey. She looked like one very determined lady, thought Rhianne as she held back while mother and son embraced.

Zarek hugged her tightly and kissed the top of her head. 'You look well, Mother,' he said in English, which Rhianne guessed was for her benefit.

'Someone has to be,' she said lightly, pulling out of his embrace. 'And this is Rhianne, I presume?' Her English was good but heavily accented. 'You are very welcome here, Rhianne. Come inside both of you and I will fix you a cool drink. What was your flight like? And how is England? Is this your first visit to Santorini?'

She spoke non-stop, each sentence falling over the previous one, giving Rhianne no chance to say anything. She glanced at Zarek, watched the way his eyebrows rose and his lips turned down comically at the corners as if to say, this is my mother, this is what she's like. You'll never get a word in.

'How is your husband?' Rhianne managed to ask when the woman finally paused for breath.

'Ah, Georgios, he is not well. But he is looking forward to Zarek's visit. You too, of course, must go to see him. He was very, very happy when I told him Zarek was bringing a lady friend. Our son, he has no time for romance, you understand? He is always busy, busy, busy. I trust you will get him to change his ways. You are beautiful, Rhianne, just the sort of girl I envisaged for him.'

Swift alarm filled Rhianne's body, sparking its way through every inch of it, and she flashed a pointed glance at Zarek, suddenly guessing that he had known all along that his mother would assume they were in a relationship. It might even have been what he'd wanted her to think, though why was a mystery. Why would he want to pretend that she was his girlfriend when they'd only known each other for five minutes?

He looked completely unperturbed by the deception; in fact, he was grinning. And this infuriated Rhianne even more. How dare he put her in this position! What sort of game did he think he was playing? If it hadn't been for his father's illness, she would have lashed out there and then and told him exactly what she thought of him.

She could feel her blood boiling and her brain cells working overtime. She wouldn't mention it in front of his mother as she didn't want to upset her. She would bide her time. But if he thought she would sit back and take it all in her stride, then he was very much mistaken.

'Come and get your drinks.' His mother's voice broke into her thoughts. 'And then you must both go to see

Georgios. He is waiting impatiently. Leave your cases, Zarek. Yannis will take them up to your room.'

'We are not staying here, Mother,' he informed her quickly. 'Rhianne and I will be staying at my villa.'

His mother smiled knowingly. 'But, of course. What was I thinking? You two lovebirds will want to be on your own. And I do not blame you. But you will come to see me every day? You will visit your father?'

'Naturally,' answered Zarek. 'But I also want to show Rhianne around the island.'

It was but a short journey to the hospital. Rhianne sat quietly fuming, well aware that Zarek knew what was going on in her mind. Whether he was grateful that she was holding her tongue she didn't know, but he sure as hell needn't think that he'd got away with it. If it wasn't for the chauffeur, he'd be feeling the sharp edge of her anger right now.

Zarek was very much like his father, decided Rhianne, as they sat beside the older man's hospital bed a few minutes later. Georgios's face was pale, with lines of strain, but the similarities were strong. The shape of the face, the well-marked brows, even the same eyes. He was a gentle man who welcomed Rhianne warmly.

'I am sorry you have to see me like this,' he said. 'But it is better this way than not to see you at all. My son doesn't come home often enough; you are obviously a good influence on him.' He turned to Zarek. 'Why have you never told us about Rhianne? She is very beautiful. I have never seen hair such a rich colour. May I touch?' he asked with a faint smile.

'Of course.' Self-consciously Rhianne leaned forward. She had pinned it on top of her head for the flight, but after freshening up at Zarek's mother's house she had left it loose about her shoulders. Zarek had once said that he preferred it this way but she'd done it for quickness, most definitely not for him.

Georgios stroked her hair slowly, letting its luxurious length slide through his weak fingers. Rhianne glanced at Zarek and saw the narrowing of his eyes and a muscle pulsing in his jaw, and she knew instinctively that he wished that he was the one touching.

But she also knew that he wouldn't be content to just stroke; he'd want more from her. He'd want something she wasn't prepared to give. And if these were the sort of plans he'd had when he persuaded her to join him, then he was in for a very big surprise.

Eventually Georgios's eyes closed, and Zarek indicated that they should leave. This time the car took them towards his villa. The streets of Oia were on many different levels, running like mazes between whitewashed cottages with sunny verandas; the blue domes of the churches provided a startling contrast.

Zarek's villa was on the opposite side of the village to his parents' house, for which Rhianne was grateful because she had envisaged his mother calling often to see them. Again, it was high on the cliff-side with spectacular views over the caldera and the tip of the volcano, which now formed an island.

The views were magnificent but the villa even more so. Far too big not to be used on a regular basis. Biding her time, still waiting for the right moment before she said anything, Rhianne allowed Zarek to give her a tour of the house.

On the ground floor was the kitchen, plus several dining and living areas, with doors leading out to a shady courtyard. Beyond that was an impressive swimming pool. Each room was minimally furnished with dark furniture and wall hangings but everything was of the highest quality. It took Rhianne's breath away.

Upstairs was a stunning master bedroom with a high-domed ceiling and an en-suite bathroom with its own jacuzzi as well as a separate shower. Her jaw dropped when she saw it. 'If I had a place like this, I'd want to live here all the time.'

'I used to,' he answered with a wry smile, 'until we opened the UK branch. And I fully intend coming back.'

Along the corridor were several smaller bedrooms, each with their own en suite shower room, and Rhianne wondered which one would be hers—until they reached the last one, which again took her breath away. It was oversized and magnificently furnished, with an archway leading through to a dressing room. Beyond that was the bathroom where again only the highest quality fittings had been used.

Another door led through to a large terrace where trailing bougainvillea offered something restful to feast her eyes on. She took a deep breath. 'This is lovely. And just look at the views.'

But when she turned, Zarek was studying her instead. Was that hunger she saw? The brown of his irises were flecked with gold, something she had never noticed before, and the awful thing was that she couldn't drag her eyes away.

She stood there for a full thirty seconds, tingles of fear rippling through her veins, and it was Zarek himself who finally spoke. 'So which room is it to be?' he asked quietly.

Rhianne came to her senses, shaking her head, squashing her unbidden thoughts. 'I don't care which room I sleep in,' she retorted, her eyes flashing suppressed anger. 'What I want to know is why you didn't correct your mother? Why did you let her think that we were—lovers.' The last word choked from her throat like a splinter being drawn from a festering wound.

'How could I disillusion her?' he asked innocently.

'You could have told her the truth in the first place.' Rhianne's eyes blazed a brilliant blue. 'You must have known what conclusion she would draw. You've made my position untenable. What is it that you're expecting me to do? Pretend to be the girl you're in love with? I'm sorry, but if that's the case then I might as well head home straight away because I'm not going along with that lie. Not at all. Never. Not under any circumstances.'

She stood her ground, glaring into Zarek's dark eyes which had narrowed dangerously.

'And if your father wasn't so ill, I'd insist that you tell them exactly what the position is between us.'

'And that is?' asked Zarek slowly.

Rhianne shook her head. 'You're unbelievable. You really think you can get away with this, don't you?'

'And you think a little mild deceit is worth all this rage?' he enquired.

The fact that he wasn't raising his voice, that he was treating the whole issue as if it meant nothing, caused Rhianne to heighten her defences.

'Mild?' she echoed loudly. 'I don't call being lied about mild. It's an unforgivable offence.'

'I didn't lie.'

'Of course not.' Sarcasm dripped from her voice like venom from a snake. 'But neither did you put your mother right.'

'You haven't told me which bedroom you're taking.'

Rhianne could have slapped him. Didn't he care what he was putting her through? Did he think it was funny? Did he think she'd be able to walk away unscathed? She drew in a deep, unsteady breath and glared at him with as much ice in her eyes as she could manage. 'You tell me. I simply couldn't care less. All I want to do is get back home to England.'

'Then you shall have this one,' he said. 'And when you've finished unpacking, you'll find me downstairs.'

Zarek smiled to himself as he left her. Rhianne's anger was healthy, and expected. And she would, hopefully, get over his little deception.

There had been times recently when her eyes had given her away. They had alternated between fear and desire. Not fear of him, but of her own feelings. And the desire— well, he knew that there were times when she had wondered what it would be like to be kissed by him.

Not the sort of kiss he had given her the day she'd collected her belongings, though even then he'd been aware that she'd felt something, but a real kiss. A lover's kiss. Otherwise why would she have reacted so wildly? It was a defence mechanism that had kicked in. Fear of the unknown. Fear of letting go again after she'd been so badly hurt.

Hopefully, it wouldn't be long before he got her to change her mind. This place was conducive to romance. He could almost imagine the seduction scene in his mind. One of Santorini's soft scented nights, a faint breeze stirring her amazing hair as they sat outside with after-dinner drinks. Rhianne relaxed and beautiful, heady with the new sights and sounds all around them.

It would take but a soft touch, a gentle word, eyes full of promise, to have her falling into his arms. He would feather kisses across her face—her eyes, her nose, her lips. He would become more daring with each second that passed until finally she gave in and kissed him back, when a whole frenzy of emotions would be released.

When Rhianne eventually came back downstairs, having changed into a short white skirt and a black camisole top, his heart gunned at an alarming rate. She looked younger and dangerously beautiful. Her magnificent hair was tied up on the top of her head, the resulting ponytail swinging as she walked.

It was silly, but he'd been jealous of his father when he'd asked to touch Rhianne's hair. The times he'd wanted to do it himself but hadn't dared ask for fear of offending her! What a sly old man his father was. Zarek had never really considered it before, it wasn't the sort of thing you thought about your parent, but he must have been a real ladies' man in his time. Perhaps the feelings never went away!

Actually, he'd like to think that when he was an older man himself, when he was married with children, maybe even grandchildren, that his feelings for his wife would never lessen. That to touch her, or even look at her, would still result in the same leaping of his senses.

'All done?' he asked, forcing himself to sound casual, when in fact he wanted to implement the seduction scene he had been planning in his mind.

Rhianne nodded.

'Then let's sit outside. It's shady in the courtyard under the old olive tree. It's one of my favourite spots. I'll get Spiros to bring us a bottle of wine. I could do with a drink before dinner, as I'm sure you can too.'

And then who knew what might happen? Maybe his dreams would come true…

Rhianne hadn't wanted to join him; she had wanted to stay in her room, her anger and resentment simmering. But she had realised how immature this would make her seem. She had hung away her clothes as slowly as she dared, putting off the moment when she had to face him again.

The real truth was that Zarek excited her like no other man ever had. And it scared her to death. She wanted to remain angry with him, and yet one look into those brown eyes, which seemed to have turned golden beneath the heat of the sun, made everything inside her melt.

After her disastrous relationship with Angus she had told herself she was done with men—for all time. Why, then, had she let Zarek slip beneath her guard? And how could she build it up again?

Every time she glanced at him his eyes were on her, and even though she tried to ignore the way her senses leapt, even though she attempted to hang on to the shreds of her anger, even though she endeavoured not to look at him, it was impossible. It was as though an invisible string kept pulling her gaze in his direction.

Their wine arrived, and Zarek waved Spiros away, filling her glass himself. 'I'd forgotten how magical this place is,' he said softly, his fingers touching hers as he handed her the drink.

Magical? Wasn't that a strange word for him to be using? It was magnificent, yes, but magical? Was he implying that this place could cast a spell over her? Was he hoping for more from her than she was prepared to give? Did he want to turn their *faux* relationship into reality?

She faced a big dilemma and needed to not only guard against Zarek—but her own feelings too.

Thankfully, over dinner Zarek defused the situation by talking non-stop about his childhood, about his younger brother, Christos, who, he declared, was nothing like himself. 'He has no get up and go,' he claimed derisively. 'Christos relies too heavily on other people.'

'Does he live here? Will I meet him?' asked Rhianne.

Zarek's eyes flashed. 'I doubt it. He married a girl from the mainland and lives there now. But he's not averse to sponging off my parents. I'm not even sure what he does for a living any more, if anything. He's work-shy I'm afraid.'

'How can two brothers be so different?' she mused. 'I used to long to have a sister. I imagined that we'd be very close and very alike in our tastes. But it wasn't to be.'

'Do you want children of your own?' There was an odd inflection in his voice that made Rhianne look at him sharply.

'Do you?'

For a moment there was silence between them. Rhianne took a sip of her wine and waited for his answer. A light breeze rustled the leaves on the olive tree. She didn't know why, but she felt that his answer to her casual question was important.

Finally, he spoke. 'As I've never considered marriage an option, I guess I've never thought about it.'

'But now that you have—thought about it, I mean?' Heaven forbid that he should think she was asking him about the marriage option.

'If they turned out like Christos, definitely no, I wouldn't want any. But if I had a daughter who looked like you—well, I'd want to lock up every eligible young man in the neighbourhood. Has anyone ever told you how beautiful you are, Rhianne?'

How had the conversation got round to her? Rhianne felt herself blushing furiously, something she hadn't done since she was a young girl. 'You flatter me,' she said, trying her hardest to keep her tone light and inconsequential. 'Do you say that to all the girls?'

An eyebrow lifted, and he appeared to be considering her question. Then he smiled, a wicked smile that suggested he might be teasing; on the other hand he could be deadly serious.

'You know what it is that I find attractive about you, Rhianne? Your hair. Sometimes it glows red like in a Titian painting. At other times it's so dark as to be almost sable. Do you know I was jealous of my father touching it? The times I've wanted to do exactly the same thing but been too scared.'

Zarek scared? She didn't believe that for one second. What she did believe was that if he dared to run his fingers through her hair, it would be the beginning of something more. She was well aware how thick and luxurious it was, and she'd always been complimented on it. Not that she ever consciously thought about it herself, but if Zarek touched it, if he let its silky length fall through his fingers like a curtain, if he took it in his hands and pulled her face close to his, then she would be lost.

Here in this place that he had declared magical, a spell would be woven over her, and every inhibition she'd ever had would be lifted by the breeze and floated away over the sea.

And she was being fanciful!

'I can't believe that you'd be scared of anything,

Zarek.' Bravely she steadied her eyes on his face, daring him to refute it.

'You'd be surprised, Rhianne. Some things are too good to spoil.'

CHAPTER SIX

ZAREK watched Rhianne over the breakfast table. He hadn't enjoyed sleeping in separate rooms at different ends of the villa. He'd lain awake half the night trying to imagine what it would be like to have her lying beside him, to feel her soft body against his, to inhale the seductive womanly smell of her. Even thinking about it now tightened his muscles, made him clamp down on urges that would give him away.

Last night they'd sat and talked long into the night, and he had felt an impulse to bed her like none he had ever felt before. But Rhianne had remained highly defensive, still unhappy about the way he had deceived his parents, and he hadn't dared force the issue so early in their relationship.

This morning she wore a blue strappy dress that reflected the colour of her eyes. It was made of some thin fabric that clung slavishly to her breasts, and the second she'd joined him for breakfast his breath had caught in his throat.

It didn't look as though she was wearing a bra underneath, and he'd looked forward to spending the whole day with her, visualising her gently rounded breasts free of any restrictions. His fingers ached to touch, to feel her delectable shape, and he'd had problems stopping his mouth from going dry.

But when he suggested she accompany him to the hospital, Rhianne shook her head vigorously. 'I told you yesterday I'd be happy here on my own. I need time to unwind.'

He knew it was an excuse. She was still angry with him. And, in reality, he couldn't blame her, but, hell, pretending that she was his girlfriend had seemed a good idea at the time. 'Are you positive you won't come? I don't like the thought of leaving you here on your own,' he suggested, lowering his voice persuasively.

Rhianne's blue eyes boldly met his. 'You really think I'd be comfortable facing your parents again under the circumstances? This is *your* mercy visit, not mine.'

'They will think it strange if you don't accompany me.' He wasn't afraid to use emotional blackmail.

But still Rhianne shook her head. She did not want to see Zarek's parents; she did not want his mother to gush over her in the opinion that she was her son's chosen one. It was wrong. He should have put her right straight away. 'Go visit your father, talk to your mother, I will stay here,' she said resolutely. 'And then, if you still want to, we will go out together.'

'Do you promise?' he enquired, his dark eyes filled with doubt.

In the distance Rhianne could hear the faint jingle of bells from the mules ferrying goods from the docks up to the villages, and she heard gulls mewing as they circled far below, looking for fish. She tried to concentrate on these sounds instead of answering Zarek, but soon realised that she could remain silent no longer.

'I promise,' she said huskily.

Zarek tried again. 'My parents will be disappointed.'

'Tell them I insisted. Tell them that I thought you should spend time on your own with them. Better still, tell them the truth, Zarek,' she finished firmly.

He closed his eyes, and she knew that he wouldn't. He preferred the misunderstanding. Perhaps his mother was keen for him to settle down. Perhaps it was for his own peace of mind that he allowed the illusion.

The villa felt empty when he had gone. Rhianne had thought she would enjoy being here by herself, but in fact she felt isolated and lonely. It was filled with Zarek's personality. Even though he'd lived in London for a long time his presence here was dominant.

She wandered from room to room, running her fingers over the dark pieces of furniture, peering at paintings of local scenes, wondering who had painted them. She even ventured into his bedroom, with its unusual domed ceiling, feasting her eyes on his bed.

The maid had straightened the covers, and there was nothing to suggest that Zarek had spent the night here. Alone! Her heart did a little wobble. What would it be like, she wondered, to share the bed with him? To feel his body against her? To be kissed by him, to be touched, to be teased, to be brought to vibrant life?

God, where had those thoughts come from? It was so unlike her. In all her years she had never had such thoughts. Shaking her head, Rhianne wandered through to the magnificent en suite.

Here were Zarek's toiletries, lined up on a glass shelf in soldierly fashion. The musky smell of his cologne lingered in the air, the same one that he'd used in London, she realised. She guessed it was a subconscious thing, and she couldn't help wondering whether there was anything else she had unknowingly noticed about him.

He was getting through to her in a way she had never envisaged. She ought to be in the depths of despair having been let down so badly by Angus, she ought to still be angry with Zarek for misleading his parents, and yet her thoughts constantly turned to him.

Why, was the question she kept asking herself.

'I don't believe you're telling me this.' Zarek stared at his father in disbelief, his dark eyes passionately angry. 'You're saying that if I'm not married when you—' he choked on the words '—when you die, that the business will go to Christos?'

'That is correct, my son. It is an unfortunate state of affairs, but that is how it is.'

'But Christos would run it into the ground,' declared Zarek fiercely, his voice filling the hospital room. 'He has no business sense. He will spend, spend, spend. You know what he is like.'

'I do indeed,' answered his father sadly. 'But there is not a thing I can do about it. My great grandfather put the condition into his will because he felt that marriage made a man more stable. Failing that, it would pass to his second son, and so on down the line. Each generation has honoured his wish. It is now my turn to do the same. Do not think I am taking this lightly; I have consulted lawyers many times, and it is always the same. It is an airtight condition; there is no getting out of it.'

'There must be a way,' declared Zarek heatedly. 'I'll look into it. There has to be a loophole. It's ridiculous.'

'Exactly what I thought, but believe me I have tried.'

Not hard enough, thought Zarek. The very thought of Christos inheriting made his head spin. He'd spent years running the business, increasing it in value, opening new offices. He couldn't let it go. *He couldn't!*

'Why didn't you tell me sooner?' he demanded, getting to his feet and pacing the room.

'Because, my son, I didn't want you getting wedded solely for the sake of the business. It would be disastrous. I want you to be as happily married as I am.'

'So you thought you'd wait until…near the end—and then drop the bombshell on me?' Zarek questioned loudly and angrily, sinking back into his chair.

'Nothing of the sort,' declared the older man, sitting up much straighter, his weary eyes suddenly fierce. 'I'm not going yet, don't worry about that. But surely you must guess the reason I've told you now. Your beautiful friend, Rhianne. It did my heart good to see that you've finally found a woman to love.'

'But—Father, I—'

'Don't say anything. Don't tell me it's too soon, that you haven't been going out long. I know love when I see it. Why else would you have brought her to see us? She is perfect for you, Zarek. Your mother and I, we are very happy.'

Zarek wanted to hotly deny feeling anything but lust for the beautiful Rhianne, but his father's hand was on his, his eyes trusting now, and an idea began to form.

When Zarek returned home, he found Rhianne sitting reading in the shady courtyard. While she was still unaware of his presence, he was able to quietly observe her. She still wore the blue sundress, a matching band holding her hair back from her face. Thick dark lashes fringed her stunning eyes, and a faint smile played about her infinitely kissable lips.

Her eyes swivelled in his direction, and she smiled. A faintly guarded smile; nevertheless, it did treacherous things to his body. 'I didn't expect you back this soon,' she said softly. 'How's your father?'

'Much the same. No worse, no better.' He walked over to her and looked down. 'He asked why you didn't accompany me.'

Whether it was because Rhianne was here, in his home country, looking for all the world as though she belonged, he didn't know, but he had the strongest urge yet to haul her to her feet and kiss her soundly. He didn't, of course. He fought the feeling with every ounce of strength he could muster. There was no sense in frightening her away before he'd put his plan into action.

'What did you tell him?'

'That you thought it was a son's duty to visit his father alone.'

Rhianne's lovely eyes widened in denial.

'Actually, no, I didn't,' he responded with a grin, 'but he did ask where you were. And he enquired after your well-being. He likes you, Rhianne.'

'He hardly knows me.'

'I didn't know you when I offered the job. It was a good choice, though. You proved yourself to be a good worker.'

'And now you're rewarding me with a holiday. I know. I've heard it all before,' she said with exaggerated boredom.

'And I'll carry on saying it. But it's my reward too. It's rare I take holidays these days, and I intend, if you will allow me, to enjoy it. Come—' he held out his hand '—let me show you my beautiful island.'

Rhianne felt her heart lurch as she let Zarek pull her to her feet, and the whole day flew by in a blur of new sights and sounds. He took her to secret coves, and a tiny hidden restaurant. It was like being in a world of their own, a world where fun and relaxation was the order of the day.

They were laughing at some silly joke he'd made when they got back to his villa, and when Rhianne stumbled down one of the steps he was quick to catch her. The smiles were wiped off their faces as their eyes made contact, and, in less time than it took to draw breath, Zarek's mouth claimed hers.

Rhianne didn't stop him. She couldn't. She had known all day long that it would happen. There had been a rapport between them, an extra awareness, a special sensitivity, and something deep down inside her had cried out for his kisses.

In fact, it was a relief when he did kiss her because it released the tension and she was able to breathe more easily. Sliding her hands behind his neck, she returned his kiss with a passion that shocked her. Never had she kissed a man so deeply before, never had she felt electrical impulses zizz through her veins. It was as though she'd touched a live wire.

'Oh, Zarek!' The words were dragged from her lips as they paused for breath.

'Oh, Zarek, what?' he asked softly, his mouth still against hers.

She could taste his clean breath, feel the tautness in his limbs, and even more telling was the extent of his arousal. 'What are you doing to me?'

His smile was slow and sensual. 'The same as you are doing to me.' He punctuated each word with more tiny kisses at the corners of her mouth.

'But I didn't ask for any of this, we're not supposed to be—'

'Kissing? Exciting each other? Having fun? Life's too short, Rhianne, not to take advantage of every situation.'

'You mean that you're taking advantage of me?' she asked with mock indignation. She knew that he wasn't; she was a willing participant—amazingly so. She was shocking even herself by her openness.

'What do you think?'

'I think it's time we went indoors and showered off the dust of the day.'

'Good idea, Rhianne. And after the shower, the jacuzzi. It's simply begging to be used.'

There was no escape, not that she wanted any. She liked the feelings he generated. So long as he didn't expect too much of her then she was prepared to go along with his game. He was actually making her feel good about herself again, and for that she was grateful.

But as she pulled on a swimsuit following her shower, Rhianne began to feel nervous. Perhaps it wasn't such a good idea sharing the jacuzzi. It would be far more intimate than sitting in his car, or exploring the island. It might even lead to something that she wasn't ready for. Even as the thought occurred to her, Zarek came to find out what was taking her so long.

All he wore was a pair of black close-fitting shorts, and she couldn't help sucking in a breath at the sight of his hard-muscled body. It was long and lean with a scattering of dark hairs on his chest. His hips were slim and his legs powerful.

'I thought you'd changed your mind,' he said easily, 'but I see that you're ready.'

Rhianne nodded, unable to speak. The breath had been whisked from her throat at the sight of him. He was more male than she had imagined, and deeply, darkly dangerous.

She followed him along the corridor, unable to take her eyes off him. There was not an ounce of superfluous fat anywhere. His olive skin was smooth and toned, his limbs powerful, and she couldn't help but wonder what it would be like to be held against that naked body, to feel the power for herself.

They reached his bedroom, and it felt faintly indecent to be walking through it—even though she'd taken that inquisitive look this morning—and when they reached his bathroom she stood for a few seconds before climbing into the hot tub.

Actually, it was heaven. The jets of water soon relaxed her tense muscles, and Zarek's non-stop conversation had her in fits of laughter. But then, without warning, his face became serious. 'My father told me the terms of his will this morning.'

And he was telling her for what reason? Rhianne couldn't help feeling puzzled. 'Judging by your expression, you're not impressed. But you shouldn't discuss it with me. This should be private between you and your family.'

'One would think so,' he agreed. 'But it's not that simple.' He rubbed his fingers over his brow as he spoke, and Rhianne itched to take them, to touch her lips to them, to still his movement.

'I don't see how I can help. Really, Zarek, I'd feel embarrassed if you disclosed any details.'

'But that's the point. You can help.' There was raw pain

in his eyes now, something Rhianne had never seen before. He was such a big, capable man that she couldn't imagine anything hurting him.

'How?' Her question was little more than a whisper. Did she want to do this? Did she want to get involved in something concerning his family when she was only just beginning to get over the trauma of her own problems?

'By marrying me.'

Whatever Rhianne had expected Zarek to say it had been nothing like this. For a few seconds she stopped breathing, did nothing except stare at him, her blue eyes wide and fixed. Outside a pair of birds squabbled. In the room her pulses threatened to jump clear through her skin. 'Did I hear you correctly?' And was that her speaking, was that strangled, tiny voice really her own?

Zarek merely nodded, as though he too found it difficult to voice his thoughts. Beneath his tan he was pale, and his hands, spread out on either side of him, clutched the side of the tub as though he was afraid of being dragged under.

'But why?' Her faint whisper barely reached above the sound of the throbbing water.

'It's complicated.'

'It sure sounds it.' Complicated didn't even begin to describe her fear.

'It goes back to an iron-clad condition my great grandfather—the one who started the family business— put in his will.'

'He said you had to marry Rhianne Pickering?' Rhianne tried to make light of the situation, but her words merely sounded stupid.

'Each eldest son has to be married before he can inherit.'

'So?' she questioned, still not sure that she understood what he was saying.

'If he's not, it's the second eldest and so on.'

'Then there isn't a problem, surely, not with Christos being married?'

Zarek's eyes flashed angrily. 'Christos couldn't run the business if his life depended on it. He'd spend the profit rather than earn it.'

'So you're telling me that if you're not married when your father dies, then everything goes to him. And you think that would be the end of the business?'

He nodded. 'I'm sure of it.'

'And you've only just been told this?' Her brows rose dramatically. 'Why?'

'Because my parents didn't want me to marry purely for the sake of the business. They want me to marry for love.'

The full import of what he was saying began to sink in.

'And they think that you and I—are…'

Zarek nodded.

CHAPTER SEVEN

RHIANNE couldn't believe that Zarek was actually asking her
to marry him. Surely he must know what her answer would
be? Heavens, she was still getting over Angus's betrayal.
Marriage was out of the question for many years to come.
If ever!

He had an incredible nerve. Did he really think she
would agree? How could she marry a man she hardly
knew? And Zarek certainly wasn't the type to enjoy a
marriage without sex—even if it was to save the company.
He would want more from her, far more than she was
prepared to give. He would want a proper relationship,
and even though her feelings had stirred when he had
kissed her—dangerous feelings—she had no intention
whatsoever of committing herself to him.

How long she sat in the bubbling waters of the Jacuzzi,
tossing Zarek's question round and round in her mind,
Rhianne did not know. It felt like hours, though in all pro-
bability it was only minutes, maybe even seconds.

Did he really know what he was asking? How impossible it would be for her? Maybe when he'd had time for
everything to sink in he would think differently. He'd

realise that it was an unfair proposition. He would know that she couldn't possibly do it.

His voice cut into her thoughts, caused her eyes to swiftly turn in his direction. Every muscle in his face was set and hard; even his eyes looked as though they had turned to stone. 'It's my life we're talking about. If you refuse, you'll be crumbling everything to ashes beneath my feet.'

Rhianne drew in a long, slow breath through her nose; there was a tangible silence between them. The very air had stilled as though it too was waiting to hear what her answer would be.

'I'll think about it,' she said softly, not wanting to hurt him any more at this moment, but confident that her answer would be no. She couldn't marry a man she hardly knew. For whatever reason. It would be disastrous. Heavens, she'd known Angus for years before she'd agreed to become his wife. And even then events had proved that she hadn't known him as well as she'd thought!

She was well aware of the fact that the business meant everything to Zarek, and his fear that he might lose it was very real. But was his brother really as bad as he made out? Would the business really go down? It could be that the rivalry between them had nothing to do with the company. It could be some private feud of which she knew nothing.

'I'd like to meet Christos before I make a decision,' she said firmly, daring to meet his eyes, shocked by the dullness in them. Zarek truly believed that she was his only hope. He was certain that Christos would ruin everything he'd worked for. But she couldn't take his word for it, she needed to find out for herself.

'I assure you there's no point,' he declared. 'Christos

is a wastrel. He always has been and always will be. Ask
my father.'

'I don't want to ask your father,' declared Rhianne
fiercely, her blue eyes blazing into his now. 'I want to find
out for myself.'

'You do realise that you're my only hope?'

Zarek wanted to take her into his arms and kiss her
senseless, he wanted to make her his in every sense of the
word so that she wouldn't even think about refusing him.
Rhianne was undoubtedly struggling with her conscience.
She'd only just escaped one unwise marriage, why should
she even think about entering another?

Somehow he had to persuade her. It wasn't as if there
was no spark between them. There was. Most definitely.
Even if she denied it. Marriage to Rhianne would be no
hardship. In fact, it would be a pleasure. Whether it would
work out long term was another question, but not one he
intended to think about now.

There was nothing in the will to say that a divorce
somewhere down the line would affect his inheritance.
And he would make certain that she didn't lose out. Was
this why she was hesitating, wondering what would
become of her at the end of it all?

'I wouldn't tie you to a loveless marriage for the rest of
your life, Rhianne,' he said carefully. 'And I'd definitely
make it worth your while. You'd end up a very rich woman.'

'You make it sound so simple,' she said, her eyes wide
and shadowed. And very, very beautiful. He had never
seen them look so luminous or so large. He cursed himself
for making the suggestion so quickly. He should have
forewarned her, he should have explained the situation
first so that she knew the predicament he was in. If she'd

felt sorry for him, she might have been more amenable to his suggestion.

Now she clearly felt that he was exaggerating. She wanted to meet his brother, for goodness' sake, find out for herself what he was like. It would all take time, and time wasn't something he had a lot of. He had never seen his father look so ill as he had this morning. He'd put on a pretence, but his sallow face and dull eyes had given him away.

Zarek didn't want to wait for her decision. He didn't want to give her time to think about it in case she turned and ran. He needed an answer now. A commitment now. Otherwise, all the hard work he'd put into building up the business had been for nothing.

And he knew who'd jump in at the kill if Christos decided to sell the business rather than go to the trouble of trying to run it. Their bitterest competitor and enemy, Theron Papadakis.

Zarek had gone to school with Theron; they'd been rivals even then. And over the years Theron had done all he could to poach Zarek's customers. Fortunately, they had remained loyal to Zarek, and the company had gone from strength to strength. It would be the deepest humiliation if it fell into his enemy's hands now.

Somehow he had to persuade Rhianne to say yes.

'I realise this is all very sudden,' he said, smiling softly, keeping his voice soft too, though he had no idea how he managed it when inside he was burning with despair, 'but it's a matter of the utmost urgency. My father doesn't have long to live.' He hadn't actually been told this, but his parent had deteriorated rapidly since his last visit, and he knew now why his mother had asked him to come.

'Then you'd better fix a meeting with your brother as soon as you can,' she declared. The more he pushed her the more determined she was to dig her heels in. Without another word, she climbed out of the hot tub and headed back to her room.

With the door firmly closed behind her, Rhianne drew in several deep steadying breaths. Zarek's proposal had come out of the blue, and she felt disturbed by it. He'd never been more serious in his life, she could tell that. He was deeply worried about the business and saw her as his only saviour.

Didn't he realise how much he was asking of her, though? He'd made it sound as though he was asking her for a date. Not a lifelong commitment. Why he ever thought she would agree Rhianne had no idea. And she hoped against hope that his brother would turn out to be a decent guy.

Family feuds always dragged up deep resentment. If Zarek's hostility towards Christos was caused by something else, then it would be up to him to resolve it. Not drag her into the mire. He was being most unfair, and she wished, not for the first time, that she had never come out here with him.

After another shower Rhianne threw herself down on the bed. It was almost time for bed anyway, and she had no wish to talk to Zarek again. She'd said all she wanted to say; it was up to him now.

She half expected him to come tapping on the door, but it grew dark and she fell asleep, not waking again until the early hours of the morning.

When she went down for breakfast, Zarek was missing. Spiros informed her that he'd gone out early, and he had no idea when he would be back.

So Rhianne ate breakfast alone, not really hungry, merely nibbling on the fresh bread that had appeared on the table. Drinking cup after cup of black coffee instead. Her thoughts were deep. She had dreamt about being married to Zarek, resenting him for forcing her into it and totally refusing to share his bed. Which angered him because he couldn't see the point of marriage without sex.

When he came back he didn't look in the best of moods, and Rhianne was almost afraid to ask him what was wrong. 'Is it your father?' she suggested tentatively. 'Is he worse?' Oh, God, what if he died and Zarek's worst fears were realised? It would be her fault.

'I've been in touch with Christos,' he told her tersely.

'You've said I want to see him?'

'Of course not. I told him how ill Father is. I've said he should get over here.'

'And is he coming?'

Zarek lifted his broad shoulders, letting them drop again slowly. 'Time will tell.'

Nevertheless, Rhianne couldn't get it out of her head that Zarek might be exaggerating. Surely his brother wasn't quite such the cold callous man he was painting? He could be a perfect gentleman. Their enmity could be nothing more than a conflict of opinion. It wasn't unknown for two brothers to hate each other's guts, but it didn't mean that one of them wasn't capable of running a business.

'Tell me more about him,' she said. I always wanted a brother, someone older, someone I could look up to.'

'Christos would most definitely not have fitted that bill.' Zarek gave a derogatory snort, a flash of fire in his eyes. 'He never looked up to me. He was a mummy's boy.

I think he objected to having an older brother; he wanted all of her attention. Admittedly, he was a sickly child and needed extra care, but did he play on it!'

'I'm sorry,' said Rhianne softly. 'That's not how it should be.'

'In a perfect world,' he snorted.

'It's a shame you two don't get on,' she said softly, reaching out to touch his hand across the table.

'Tell me about it,' he answered crisply. 'If Christos was a different man, and we ran the company together, there'd be no stopping us.'

'It seems to me that you've done pretty well by yourself.'

He nodded. 'I'm satisfied.'

'But if Christos takes over…'

Zarek's nostrils flared. 'It doesn't bear thinking about.'

Rhianne shivered at the dark tones in his voice. Nevertheless, she still felt the need to meet Christos herself.

It happened sooner than she expected. A few hours later Zarek took a phone call from his brother to say that he was at the hospital. 'We're meeting up at my mother's house,' he told Rhianne tersely. 'Come, we'll go now.'

'I'd rather meet him here,' she prevaricated. The very thought of facing Zarek's mother again, of seeing the happiness in her eyes that her eldest son had found the woman he wanted to marry, made her uneasy.

'It can't be done. I would not allow him into my house. It might sound hard to you, Rhianne, but you don't know him.'

How could anyone be that awful, she thought. How could you hate your own brother so much? But when she met Christos two hours later she saw for herself why.

Christos looked nothing like Zarek. He was tall, yes,

but his body carried a lot of excess weight—as though he enjoyed the high life without too much thought about what it was doing to him. Nor did he attempt to hide how much he despised his older brother.

'Who is this?' he asked sneeringly when he saw Rhianne. 'Don't tell me you've finally found someone to put up with all the long hours that you work? Does she know what she's letting herself in for?'

And, without waiting for Zarek to answer, he turned to Rhianne. 'There'll be no fun for you with my brother,' he declared. 'No life for you. He's in love with his job. You'll come a poor second best.'

'I think I should be the judge of that,' she said, lifting her chin as her hackles rose.

From the moment the two men met she had seen antagonism flare. They didn't even try to hide it from their mother. And later, when Rhianne heard Christos asking his mother for money, she knew that everything Zarek had said was true.

She felt deeply sorry for him and could see now why he feared for the business if it ever fell into Christos's hands.

It was a very uncomfortable two hours before Zarek finally announced that they were leaving.

'So soon?' asked his mother.

'Rhianne and I have things to do,' he answered. 'I'll see you tomorrow.' He kissed her fondly but he didn't even look at his brother.

Neither of them spoke until they were in the car and on their way back to his villa. She could see from the way Zarek's knuckles gleamed white as he gripped the wheel how angry he was, how much he had hated forcing Christos to come over and prove his point.

'I hope now you believe me,' he growled fiercely, flashing her a swift, brutal glance.

'I'm sorry,' replied Rhianne, feeling as if he had kicked her. 'I should have believed you; it would have saved all this embarrassment.'

'I think Christos did a very good job of proving to you what a bastard he is?'

Rhianne nodded uncomfortably.

'Perhaps now you'll be prepared to consider my offer? It's my only hope—you are aware of that?'

How could she not be? It had been on her mind since he had mentioned it yesterday.

Perhaps if they agreed to a marriage on paper only then it wouldn't be so bad. She enjoyed Zarek's company, and it would certainly give her security. It might even be the only way she ever found happiness with a man, because how could she trust anyone after the way Angus had behaved, after the way her father had treated her mother? She had even begun to wonder whether there was any man in the world who remained true to one woman for the whole of his life.

Zarek's parents excluded. Though they were the exception rather than the norm. She sensed that if Zarek gave his word that would be it. She wouldn't need to fear that he would renege on their deal. She could settle down without fear that he would try to persuade her into a more personal relationship.

Couldn't she?

An element of doubt still lay in her mind. Zarek was a healthy male with a healthy male appetite, and she didn't want him to make promises that he couldn't keep. Dared she trust him?

What she had to do, if she agreed to his suggestion, was make sure that he understood the rules of the game. Otherwise it was a definite no. Rhianne was giving her body to no man—not unless she loved him truly and deeply and he returned those very same feelings.

This marriage was not about love, it was about saving a very successful company. It was a business proposition—and she was going to get well paid for it at the end of the day. If they made rules and stuck by them then she would be foolish to turn down what could prove to be a very lucrative agreement.

Rhianne didn't answer Zarek's question. The rest of the journey was accomplished in silence, each deep in their own thoughts. Not until they had reached his villa, and he had garaged the car, did he speak of it again.

Spiros brought wine to them outside where they sat silently in the courtyard, and after they had taken a few sips Zarek once more asked the inevitable question. 'You've had time to think about it, you've seen for yourself that I was speaking the truth about my brother, do you want the downfall of Diakos Holdings to be on your conscience?'

'That's not fair,' she retorted immediately, her eyes sparking blue flashes. 'That's blackmail.'

'I don't know how else to ask you.'

'Persuasion usually works.'

Zarek's eyes narrowed. And after a few seconds he leaned closer towards her. Rhianne felt his soft, clean breath on her face and realised what sort of persuasion he thought she had meant. Instantly she fended him off with her hands, not exactly touching him, but making sure that he knew her defences were up.

'I'll tell you the decision I've reached,' she said quietly, trying to ignore the way her body had reacted to his nearness. She really would have to make the rules very clear if she wanted any peace of mind.

Zarek immediately sat back in his chair and folded his arms. His dark eyes never left her face, scrutinising every tiny movement: the way she nervously sank her teeth into her lower lip, the way she tried to avert her eyes from his gaze, how her breathing grew that little bit quicker.

'I'll agree to marry you, but with certain conditions.'

His well-shaped brows rose, and Rhianne knew that he was already wondering whether he would like what she had to say. She knew in her own mind that he wouldn't. Zarek would expect nothing less than a normal marriage, with her in bed beside him every night.

It couldn't be done. All her life she'd been waiting for Mr Right. Zarek wasn't that person. She hardly knew him. He'd almost run her over and then made amends by offering her a job. But if he thought it gave him some prior claim on her body then he was deeply mistaken.

'Our marriage would be in name only,' she said quietly. 'A pure business deal. Nothing more, nothing less.' She kept her eyes steady on his, trying to judge his reaction, but not by the flicker of an eyelash did he give anything away. He remained still and silent, waiting for her to continue.

'We would sleep in separate rooms, and you would not even attempt to kiss me. Whether we remain here or in England it makes no difference. And at the end of it all, when I get my freedom, I shall expect you to let me go and not bother me again.'

Even as she said these words Rhianne knew that she sounded hard and callous. But she had to safeguard herself;

she couldn't go through with the marriage otherwise. She hadn't remained a virgin for all these years to lose it to some man who wanted to save his family business.

No matter that he was stunningly handsome with eyes that should never be allowed to look at a woman as though he wanted to ravish her right there and then. It was going to be hard to ignore his sexuality, she was well aware of that, but it was what she had to do.

It would be cruel of her not to help. Having got to know Zarek, discovering for herself that he was a kind, fair man, it was the least she could do.

So long as he understood the rules!

'You drive a hard bargain, Rhianne. Have you any idea how utterly gorgeous you are?'

Rhianne shrugged. 'I've never looked at myself in that light.'

'Do you know how hard you're making this for me?'

'It depends how badly you want my help. As I see it, you have no choice.'

Zarek drew in a deep, unsteady breath, closing his eyes for a few seconds, and when he looked at her again she saw that relief had taken the place of fear. He held out his hand. 'We have a deal.'

But when she took it he pulled her hard against him, sealing their deal with a kiss. A full on kiss that went against everything she'd just said. And yet before she could fight him, before she could drag her mouth away and protest, he let her go.

But not before she had felt the full impact of his kiss.

It had ripped through her body with lightning speed, it had set off a chain reaction, each pulse in turn stammering to make itself felt. He had fed new life into her veins, and for one crazy second she had wanted the kiss to continue. Just for one second, that was all, and now she was left staring in horror into his face.

'You shouldn't have done that.'

'I was sealing our bargain.'

'We could have shaken hands.' The moment the words left her lips she realised how ludicrous they sounded. Admittedly, it was a business deal, but shaking hands would surely have been better when emotions were running high!

'It's a pity you don't want me to kiss you any more, Rhianne, because you're a very kissable person.'

'I hope you're not going to renege on our deal?' Rhianne's heart continued to hammer and she began to fear that she could be letting herself in for something more than she could handle.

Zarek had a way of persuading her to do things against her will. Which meant that their marriage... She dared not let her thoughts go any further. She needed to remain cool and calm. She was the one doing the favour. She had the upper hand. Hadn't she just made everything clear?

The trouble was, Zarek was used to being in control. He could manage any situation—including a marriage of convenience! Her life as she knew it was unravelling. Two weeks ago she'd been happy and carefree. Two weeks ago she'd had a marriage to look forward to. Now she was still getting married—but to a different man! And for a very different reason.

It was the stuff of novels. Such things didn't happen in real life, not to someone like her. She looked at Zarek and then wished she hadn't when she saw the expression on his face. It was not the answer to her question that she wanted. 'I need to be alone,' she said.

'You have much to think about,' he agreed. 'But, Rhianne—' his eyes narrowed warningly '—don't think about changing your mind.'

She lifted her chin. 'I've given my word. You needn't fear that I'll go back on it.'

'Then I'll see you at dinner.' His voice followed her as she walked away. 'We can thrash out the wedding details then.'

The wedding was going to be one big rush, thought Rhianne as she threw herself down on the bed. A Greek wedding! She'd never attended one but she knew what they were like. Unless of course he was talking about some simple civil ceremony.

Actually, she couldn't see his parents settling for that. It would be an all-or-nothing affair.

Rhianne lay on the bed for a long time, staring at the whitewashed ceiling. The room was cool and a merciful relief from the heat outside, but her body was sizzling. Her emotions chaotic. What she ought to do was get up and run, and not stop running until she had reached some safe place in the world where she could relax and be herself. Where she could start a new life, alone and independent.

Except that she had given her word. She could not let Zarek down. She would honour him in front of his parents; they would never know that it was a loveless marriage.

But behind closed doors…

Rhianne did not let her thoughts go any further because she knew how persuasive Zarek could be. How he could set her pulses on a race through her veins, how he could make her heart feel as though it wanted to leap out of her chest, how he could send an impossible heat through every inch of her body.

Such disturbing thoughts had her leaping off the bed and straight under the shower. But even cold water did not calm her nerves. She was shivering by the time she had finished, but her mind was on a completely different tack.

A marriage ceremony!

A wedding night!

A honeymoon!

Would he expect this? She knew the answer. He would want his parents to believe that they were deeply in love, and he would do everything that normal, very-much-in-love couples did. And she would be expected to go along with it, to act like she had never acted before.

The more she thought about it, the more nervous she became, the more she wished that she had never come out here in the first place.

By the time Zarek came in search of her, she had slipped into a red silk strapless dress that should have clashed with her auburn hair but for some reason didn't. It was a dress she always felt good in, and she most definitely needed the armour now. 'I was just about to come down,' she said, unaware there was defensiveness in her tone.

'You look beautiful. Stunning, in fact.' His voice was a deep growl somewhere low in his throat. 'It will be an honour to marry you, Rhianne Pickering.'

'You're not forgetting that this won't be a real marriage?' Alarm filled her and, in contrast, Rhianne's voice rose sharply. She was right to be worried. He made it sound as though there was no way in the world he was going to honour her request.

'Of course not,' he answered swiftly.

'It doesn't sound like it.'

'I appreciate what you're doing more than you'll ever know.'

Rhianne wasn't so sure. The gleam in his eyes told her that he wanted her in his bed—and one way or another he intended doing precisely that. And unhappily she couldn't help wondering whether this whole marriage thing had just been an excuse.

Except that something told her she was being silly. She had never seen Zarek more sincere than when he had told her that there was a strong possibility the business could fall into his brother's hands. And after she'd met Christos she knew exactly why he was worried. The two men couldn't have been more opposite if they'd tried.

Over dinner, when she had expected him to talk more about his business fears, he spoke about their wedding instead. 'My mother will expect a full traditional wedding. A big family affair—uncles and aunts and cousins. Every relative you can imagine will be invited. Christos denied her that pleasure. He married Eugenia on the spur of the moment. I can't let my parents down.'

So the onus really was being put on her!

The future of Diakos Holdings was in her hands; that was what he was saying. And, on top of that, the wedding was going to be one very big sham. It didn't bear thinking about.

'Tomorrow you must get in touch with your parents and other family members. They must all come.'

'Are you telling me that you've already set a date for our marriage?' Her heart hammered in her breast, trying its hardest to escape. She felt as though she could hardly breathe.

'It will of necessity be very soon,' he told her. 'Probably within the next two weeks.'

Rhianne's eyes widened. 'And you think everyone can take time off at such short notice? If you must do things in such a hurry then I suggest a quickie wedding of some sort with just your parents present.' What was the point of such an extravaganza?

'So you don't intend telling your own parents? Is that what you're saying?' Harsh criticism entered his voice now, and his eyes lost their soft persuasiveness, became as hard as diamonds instead.

Rhianne shrugged. 'My mother lives in Seattle with her third husband. She's no recipe for a happy marriage. Why should I ask her? Why should she come all this way when it's a loveless marriage anyway? And my father, well, I have no idea where he is. He's a musician in a band and he travels the country.'

The harshness went, to be replaced by disbelief. 'That is the saddest thing I've ever heard. So in effect you're alone in the world?' He looked as though he wanted to take her into his arms, but he thought better of it, smiling faintly instead. 'More reason to make the most of our wedding. I'd like your parents to be present, but I can understand you not wanting to invite them.'

'I hadn't even got round to telling them I was marrying Angus,' she told him ruefully. 'I guess I would have done nearer the time but…'

'I can see how awkward it is for you,' he said. 'And I'm wondering how to tell my own mother about your predicament. Their marriage has been as strong as a rock. She truly believes in the sanctity of it, she would never have done anything to hurt my father.'

'Tell her the truth,' said Rhianne. 'I've never hidden the fact that my father cheated on my mother. So did her second husband. This last marriage has surprised me by its longevity. Though, actually, who knows what's happening. It could be on the rocks already. It's why I've always sworn that I'd only marry once I was very, very sure what I was doing.'

'And Angus let you down,' he said quietly.

Rhianne nodded, painful memories pushing to the surface.

'I would never do that.'

'It's hard,' said Rhianne, ignoring the way he was looking at her, 'finding your true soul mate. There's a whole world of men out there. How do you know which one you can trust?'

'I guess it's gut instinct,' said Zarek quietly, his dark eyes reaching out to hers.

Not wanting to read anything into them, Rhianne deliberately turned away. All this talk of weddings and families was getting to her. It seemed that the longer they talked, the deeper the hole she was digging for herself.

'My mother will smother you with love if I do tell her your story—which might not be a bad thing,' he added with a wry twist to his lips. 'Your life hasn't been happy. I'd suggest doing the loving myself but—'

He laughed when he saw indignation flare in her eyes. 'But I know my place. Not that I promise not to kiss you on our wedding day. We need to keep up appearances.'

It was a warning, thought Rhianne. She must be on her guard. Zarek was not a man to be easily ignored. If she wasn't careful, she would find herself swept off her feet, entering into the spirit of their marriage as though it was the real thing.

Dinner was a silent affair after that, each deep in their

own thoughts, Rhianne drinking far more Riesling than she was accustomed to. Zarek finally refused to pour her any more. 'Drowning your sorrows is not the answer.'

'Is that what you think I'm doing?' asked Rhianne, trying to look offended but fearing that she failed. She did feel inebriated, not that she wanted to admit it, but at least it allowed her to forget that she'd just agreed to marry a man she did not love.

'I think it's time you went to bed,' said Zarek.

Rhianne nodded. 'Good idea.' And she stood up, sitting again quickly when she discovered that her legs felt as though they were made of rubber.

Zarek's face didn't change. He simply got to his feet and offered his arm. 'May I escort my future wife to her room?'

Fearing he was mocking her, Rhianne glared into his eyes. She saw nothing but politeness. And she knew why he was pretending not to notice that she was drunk— because he didn't want to offend her! From now until the minute he married her he would bend over backwards to be nice.

What would happen after that was anyone's guess. She would be safe, though, tonight. He would take her up to her room and then leave her. He wouldn't dare try to take advantage. Even if he wanted to!

And Rhianne knew that he did. The kiss earlier had told her that he was hot for her. As she had been for him! Amazingly so! But hot sex did not constitute a good reason for marriage. And if she relaxed her code of ethics then she would never forgive herself.

They climbed the stairs together, his arm about her waist, and Rhianne held on to her thoughts with every shred of dignity that she could dredge up. It was hard when their bodies touched, when the heat of him filtered into her, making her hot too, when some little demon inside her head announced that she would be foolish not to let him kiss her again.

But she knew where a kiss could lead. Zarek had a way of making her forget her own set of rules.

It was with strength born of desperation that she said a firm, 'Goodnight,' and closed the bedroom door in his face.

But even though he wasn't with her in person, he remained with her in spirit. When she shrugged off her clothes and lay down on the big comfortable bed she couldn't stop herself thinking about him. And the fact that she'd agreed to marry him!

It was going to be the hardest thing she'd ever done. Zarek wasn't a man to live with a woman and not bed her. Even though he had promised, she was still fearful that he might not keep his word. Or that she might not want him to keep it!

She lay awake for a long time, listening to the faint call of a night bird, watching an almost full moon creep slowly across an inky sky, but then tiredness claimed her and her eyelids closed and soon she knew no more.

When morning came, she wondered whether all that had happened yesterday had been a dream. Surely she hadn't promised to marry Zarek? A man she hardly knew and certainly didn't love. It didn't make sense. She would never do such a thing; she was too sensible and level-headed.

At least, that was what she'd always thought.

But as soon as she saw him at the breakfast table, Rhianne knew that she was in dire trouble. Feelings came running back fast and furious. Feelings she had tried desperately to deny, to tell herself she didn't want.

He was dressed in a white T-shirt and a pair of denim jeans, which moulded to the shape of his body like a second skin. He was a lean, lithe man, with tight, hard muscles and not an ounce of superfluous fat. His London hotel had its own private gym, so she guessed that he must have used it on a daily basis to look so good. He'd possibly worked out all of his working life, and she remembered what it had felt like yesterday to be held against that hard muscular chest.

Her breath caught in her throat at the memory, and she had to forcibly tell herself that she must not let it happen again—or their convenient marriage would turn into a proper one. And that was the last thing she wanted because how could she possibly extricate herself from it if she had given herself totally to Zarek Diakos?

'Rhianne, good morning. You slept well, I hope? You certainly look refreshed.'

So did he! But she didn't tell him so. She was too busy fighting the demons within. Every time she looked at Zarek she was reminded that any day soon she would become his wife. The thought filled her with both fear and excitement.

'I slept very well, thank you.'

'That is good; I need you to be at your best this morning. We're going to see my mother and tell her about our wedding plans.'

CHAPTER EIGHT

'RHIANNE, Zarek, this is the best news I could ever have hoped for.'

Zarek's mother opened her arms wide and enveloped Rhianne, hugging her so tightly that she had to fight for breath.

'I knew you two were made for each other the moment I set eyes on you. This is a dream come true; you've made me so happy. We must go to the hospital straight away and tell Georgios. He'll be as excited as I am.'

Finally, she let Rhianne go and folded her son into her arms instead. 'Zarek, my darling son—I've waited so long for this day. Oh, I can't wait to start making arrangements. It's—'

'Mother,' protested Zarek, gently extricating himself, 'it's early days yet. I've only just proposed to Rhianne; please—'

But his mother was having none of it. She continued to talk excitedly, and Zarek looked at Rhianne and raised an eyebrow.

Rhianne had been nervous to begin with and she was even more so now. Even though Zarek had warned her about his mother, she hadn't been prepared for her over-the-top enthusiasm.

'Oh, my goodness,' the older woman kept saying, 'this is the best day of my life.'

The whole day was one big round of congratulations. Zarek's father was quietly happy for them, but his mother phoned every one of her family and told them the good news. And each time Zarek suggested they leave she persuaded him to stay a while longer.

'You cannot leave your poor mother now,' she kept saying. 'Not when you have just made me the happiest woman alive.'

Eventually, though, they managed to get away. 'My mother excelled herself,' declared Zarek, rolling his eyes as he glanced across at Rhianne. 'May I say how well you handled everything. I fully expected you to tell her it was all a sham and then run as fast as you could. And in truth, I wouldn't have blamed you. You were magnificent.'

Rhianne was glad that he was driving because she had the feeling that he wanted to thank her with kisses. The whole affair was escalating at an alarming rate, and she wasn't sure that she could handle it. She needed some time alone.

But Zarek had other ideas. As soon as they reached the villa he insisted she join him on the terrace where he opened a bottle of champagne. 'To my beautiful wife to be,' he said, raising his glass.

There was just the right amount of irony in his voice to remind Rhianne that it was all a game and yet, when he looked at her, his amazing dark eyes registered something more. And that something scared her. They had made a pact. Their marriage was to be in name only.

Nevertheless, she sensed a burning passion inside him and knew that she was in danger, not only from Zarek, but from a similar fever within herself. It was creeping up on her whether she liked it or not.

'I'm not sure I can go through with this.' She spoke the words without thinking, intending to say them to herself and not Zarek, and was startled when he slammed his glass down on the table with so much force that it was a wonder it didn't shatter into a thousand tiny pieces.

Rhianne watched as the champagne spilled over, fizzing onto the table top, each tiny drop spreading until they all merged into one. She knew that she dared not take her eyes from it; she did not want to look at Zarek, see his anger; know that she was creating a storm which could have severe repercussions.

But somehow he pulled himself together, and his voice was calm when he spoke to her. 'Every bride has nerves when she's about to get married. Every bride worries and wonders. Believe me, Rhianne, you'll be the most beautiful bride in the world, and it will be an honour to marry you.'

She raised her head, thinking he was mocking her, but saw nothing but sincerity in his eyes.

'My mother's enthusiasm has alarmed you, hasn't it?'

Rhianne nodded.

'I apologise on her behalf. I fear, though, that you'll have to get used to her exuberance. It's not every day her favourite son gets married.'

'It scares me,' she admitted.

'Perhaps this will help.'

Before Rhianne could sense his intention, Zarek got up from the table and pulled her to her feet. The next moment his lips were on hers, and there was nothing gentle or persuasive about his kisses this time.

Rhianne struggled with her conscience but couldn't fight the sensations that ricocheted through her body. Against her will she felt herself relaxing, her lips parting of their own volition, a whole volley of feelings exploding. It was both hell and heaven at the same time. She didn't want the kiss to stop but she knew the danger of letting it continue.

It seemed like forever before he finally set her mouth free. 'Does that allay your fears?'

Allay her fears? It scared her to death. She had felt an unexpected lightning response. He had awoken something primitive inside her that no other man had touched. In some strange way he had made her his.

'Rhianne?'

Realising that she hadn't answered him, Rhianne gave her head a tiny shake, struggling now to free herself. Not that it did her any good. Zarek's arms were like bands of steel, and she knew that he wouldn't let her go until she'd given him the answer he wanted.

'I'm all right,' she whispered, but she hated the fact that she had let herself be consoled by a kiss. The whole event was going to be one big roller-coaster ride of terror. She ought to have escaped while she had the chance.

There was no chance now. He had bound her to him with a kiss that had stirred senses she didn't know she possessed. They must have lain there dormant for years waiting for the right man to come along and discover them. She curled her fingers into her palms as she tried to make sense of the situation.

The right man wasn't Zarek; she wasn't ready for any

man. She didn't trust men. He was an expert seducer, that was all. He knew exactly what to do to get her onside. And, silly fool that she was, she had fallen for it.

She was committed now to the biggest marriage of the century, and she had to go through it with her head held high and a smile on her face.

'Good,' he growled. 'You're talking sense at last.'

And before she could stop him he kissed her again. Another mind-blowing kiss that had her straining against him, that sent her whole body into spasm, and there was a pleased smile on his face when he finally let her go.

For the rest of the day Zarek talked wedding plans, insisting that she contact her mother even though Rhianne swore she would not come. She was wrong. When her mother answered the telephone and heard the news she screamed her excitement.

'I thought you and Angus would never set the day.'

'It's not Angus, Mother. He and I are finished.'

There was a long silence while her mother assimilated this piece of information. Then she said more quietly, 'So who is he?'

'His name's Zarek Diakos and I'm here on the island of Santorini with him. We're having a Greek wedding, Mother. Next week, as a matter of fact. I hope you can come.'

Another scream from her mother. 'Next week? What's the rush? Are you pregnant?'

Rhianne almost laughed. 'Certainly not. But Zarek's father's ill, and if we wait too long he might not—'

Zarek gently took the telephone from her. 'Allow me.' And by the time he had finished talking to her, Rhianne's mother was won over.

'Of course I will come,' she said to Rhianne when Zarek

handed the phone back to her. 'My only daughter getting married, how could I not? Have you asked your father?'

'How can I when I don't know where he lives?' asked Rhianne sharply. 'I've not had a birthday or Christmas card from him in all the years he's been gone. It's his loss, not mine.'

Rhianne was glad when it was time for bed. So much had happened today that her head was spinning, and she longed for the solitude of her room. She needed to be alone with her thoughts.

Even then, when she found relative seclusion, she didn't feel any easier. It was hard to believe that she had allowed herself to be talked into marriage and on top of that Zarek had managed to awaken something inside her body that she had never discovered before.

It was the most frightening thing that had ever happened, and she even found herself wondering what it would be like to have Zarek make love to her.

Sleep was a long time in coming, and when she finally dropped off it was to dream about her forthcoming marriage. She dreamt that she wore the most outrageous wedding dress, Zarek only a pair of swimming briefs, and all the other guests were in fancy dress. It was bizarre and worrying, and when they went away on their honeymoon the whole family came with them.

She woke in a sweat and took a long, cooling shower. But she felt no better when, over breakfast the following morning, Zarek said that he was taking her shopping. 'You need to choose your wedding dress, otherwise my mother will insist on accompanying you. Her choice won't be yours, and I'm afraid she might force her decision on you.'

'I wouldn't let her,' declared Rhianne. 'But neither will I let you take me. It's bad luck for the groom to see his bride in her wedding dress before the day.'

'So who would you like with you?' He folded his arms across his broad chest and looked at her with a hint of amusement in his eyes. 'There is no one, is there?'

'I can wait until my mother gets here.'

Zarek shook his head. 'Too risky.'

'Then your driver can take me.'

Several long seconds passed. Their eyes met, and Rhianne felt a reincarnation of the desire she'd experienced last night. An aching need burned through her as she remembered his kiss, a kiss that had awoken new senses and told her how dangerous it was to tangle with this man.

She was right to insist that she shopped alone. Imagine what it would be like to parade before him in breathtaking wedding dresses. It wasn't the protocol thing she was worried about, it was Zarek's eyes feasting on her, taking in every curve of her body. Her insides tightened as she pictured the moment. Zarek sitting in a chair, his long legs stretched out in front of him, his eyes hooded as he scrutinized every tiny detail of each dress—and her body beneath it. Simply thinking about it whipped her emotions into overdrive.

'I'll meet you half way,' Zarek said finally. 'I'll drive you but I won't come into the shop. And after you've finished we'll find somewhere for lunch.'

'And would you really be content sitting outside while I pretend to be a happy bride to be?' She couldn't see it happening; she could imagine him sneaking into the shop and taking a crafty look.

His lips thinned dangerously. 'I don't want you to

pretend, Rhianne. I know it's unconventional but I want you to feel good about it too. You're at a hiatus in your life, why not treat this as a big adventure? You're in a win-win situation.'

He was right, though she was damned if she would admit it. They were playing games here, an exciting game, and she ought to grab it with both hands and make the most of it.

'Lunch it is then,' she agreed, and then almost wished she hadn't when she saw the gleam in Zarek's eyes.

Rhianne chose the plainest wedding dress she could find, unaware that its very simplicity was a stunning combination with her slender figure and glossy auburn hair. She had fixed it on top of her head this morning, but by the time she had tried on several dresses, long strands had escaped and curled flatteringly either side of her face.

Her colour was heightened too, and the service she received couldn't be faulted.

With one final look in the mirror before she took the dress off, Rhianne almost couldn't recognise herself. She was radiant, like a real bride. And she'd only had to mention Zarek's name and the sales women had fallen over themselves to be helpful.

Rhianne almost wished that she had let him come in with her. It didn't feel right to be trying on wedding dresses alone. She ought to have had a friend with her at least, but they were home in England and everything was so rushed.

True to his word, Zarek was waiting for her. 'All done?'

Rhianne nodded.

'You've chosen wisely?'

'Of course. And I've arranged to have the dress delivered. I didn't want it getting creased in the car while we have lunch. And thank you, Zarek, I didn't expect you to pay for it.' She hadn't been entirely surprised when she was told that he was settling the bill, and she'd had half a mind to insist that she pay herself. Until she saw how much the dress cost and realised it would practically empty her bank account.

'It is my pleasure,' he said, dark eyes hot and smouldering.

Rhianne fastened her seat belt and tried not to look at him. The whole experience had heightened her senses and she was more aware of him now than ever before.

The restaurant he took her to was hidden in a back street. They were early and had the room to themselves, and the proprietor looked after them personally. Rhianne hadn't felt hungry and she'd let Zarek order for her, but once the *kleftiko* lamb was placed in front of her, the fine smell alone had her taste buds salivating.

'Tell me about you as a little girl,' Zarek said, pausing between mouthfuls. 'Have you always had long hair, for instance? It's amazingly beautiful, do you realise that? My fingers are always itching to touch it.'

Heat invaded Rhianne's cheeks. It was not so much what he said but the way his eyes almost caressed her. She might even say they were making love, and it sent goose bumps across her skin and her senses skittering. 'For as long as I can remember,' she answered quietly and was horrified to hear a tell-tale tremble in her voice. 'Before my father deserted us I used to sit between his legs and he'd brush it and brush it until it shone.'

'How old were you when he left?'

'Ten, I think. Yes, I'd just had my tenth birthday. He wasn't there for it. I sensed there was something wrong, but didn't know until I was much older that he was having an affair.'

'It must have hurt you?'

Rhianne nodded. 'I adored him. I couldn't understand why he went away. For a long time I thought it was my fault.'

'And so you remained an only child?'

'Yes,' she answered sadly. 'My mother eventually married again, but they didn't have any children. Which is as well because he cheated on her the same as my father had, and she threw him out.'

'It would appear she doesn't have a very good taste in men. Either that or she's been extremely unlucky. How about husband number three?'

Rhianne wondered why he was asking all these questions. On the other hand, his relatives would be asking him about her at the wedding, and he'd need to be prepared. They hadn't even told his mother that they hardly knew each other.

'They're still married and, as far as I know very happy.'

'Do you have aunts and uncles? People we should invite to the wedding?'

'Both of my parents were only children,' she told him with a rueful smile. 'And to save you asking, no, I don't have any friends I want to invite either. I do have friends, naturally, but I have no wish to put myself up for all sorts of awkward questions.'

'You're ashamed of me?' A frown flitted across Zarek's forehead, pulling his dark brows into a formidable straight line.

'That would be impossible,' she answered with a tiny nervous laugh. 'You're any woman's dream.'

'Except yours?' he asked, the frown fading to be replaced by a wry smile.

Rhianne shrugged. 'I'm not ready for a serious relationship. I doubt I ever will be. And you can surely see why?'

Zarek nodded. 'I can, but not all men are the same. You and your mother have both had incredibly bad luck. But bad luck does not last. I would never hurt you, Rhianne. Whatever happens in our relationship, I promise you that.'

His eyes darkened with an emotion Rhianne could not read, and she felt a quiver sweep through her. When Zarek reached out across the table and took both her hands into his, the quiver deepened and became a rush of sensation. It careered through her veins setting off electric sparks at every vital point.

Unable to draw her eyes away from his, Rhianne allowed the feelings to run out of control, and it was not until she discovered that her lips were parted and were being moistened by the tip of her tongue, that her breathing had deepened and Zarek's eyes had dropped to the swell of her breasts, that she realised what was happening and immediately brought herself back to the present.

'I'm sorry,' she said, snatching her hands away from his.

'For what?' he asked softly. 'For allowing yourself a little pleasure?'

'I was not—I didn't—'

'Do not lie to me, Rhianne *mou*.'

'You're mistaken.'

'I think not. I think, Rhianne, that you're in denial. You do not think it right that you should feel something for me so soon after your tragic affair. But let me tell you something. The fact that you do feel—what shall I say—

an awareness, means that you never truly loved the man you were going to marry. You had a lucky escape.'

'And you're an expert in that sort of thing?' By this time Rhianne had come to her senses and sought anger to hide her embarrassment.

'I know a bit about women.'

'Not this woman.' Rhianne lifted her chin and fixed stony eyes on him.

A smile lifted the corners of his mouth. 'Then it will be my pleasure to find out.'

They were silent after that, and it annoyed Rhianne that Zarek's smile still lingered. She was glad when their dessert arrived: a sensational nut pie with a chocolate and orange sauce.

'That was truly delicious,' she acknowledged after she had eaten every last crumb, and when she looked around her she was startled to see that all the tables were now occupied. Zarek had been the sole focus of her attention, he had filled her every thought, her every breath, actually. Even here in this room, with the aroma of food wafting in from the kitchen, she was aware of Zarek's individual smell: clean and fresh and faintly musky. And she felt deeply shocked that he had managed to get through to her in this way.

Zarek ordered coffee and while they were waiting his cell phone rang. 'I'm sorry, do you mind?' he asked.

Rhianne shook her head, watching Zarek's face, realising that she was beginning to learn by his various expressions what sort of a mood he was in. When he was in a playful mood his eyes lightened to almost gold, his mouth softening; when he was serious his eyes narrowed and his mouth straightened. When he was angry his nostrils flared and his eyes became almost black. When he wanted to kiss her—Rhianne stopped herself there, not wanting to let her thoughts go down that channel.

Even as she watched him now she saw an entirely different expression. First the widening of his eyes then an instant narrowing as his brows drew together. His mouth grew tight and grim. 'I'll be right there,' he announced before shutting off his phone.

'We have to go.' He was already on his feet. 'My father's had another heart attack. It's touch-and-go whether he lives.'

CHAPTER NINE

ZAREK feared for his father's health. He had looked so pale and lifeless yesterday that he had expected the worst.

His mother too was desperately worried and had clung to Zarek. Her son was her lifeline and she had asked him to stay with her. He had phoned Rhianne, not even thinking to ask whether she wanted to join them, simply telling her that he wouldn't be home.

But now he was on his way back to her, his father having improved during the night. He was still far from well but his colour had returned and he had been reasonably cheerful during Zarek's visit.

Rhianne came to greet him as he entered the villa, real concern on her face, and Zarek's heart lifted. Rhianne had no idea how beautiful she was, what simply looking into her eyes did to a man, or how very glad he was that he had met her.

'How is your father?' she asked at once.

'Much better this morning, thank you.' But Zarek was conscious of having neglected her, and Rhianne's well-being was his concern now. 'Did you sleep well? You weren't afraid in this house on your own?' His cook and cleaner came in on a daily basis, but it hadn't occurred to him that she might be uneasy sleeping here alone.

'I was fine,' she said with a smile that made his heart leap. She looked genuinely pleased to see him, which must surely bode well for their future?

There was something deep down inside him that suggested he would not want to let her go when the time came. He wasn't sure that he wanted to ever let her go, and it scared the hell out of him. A lifetime's commitment to one woman was something he had never entertained. Not once. Business had always came first; it was his main priority. It was his life!

If he'd thought at all about marriage, it was how could anyone possibly know whether they'd met the right person? How would you know it would last for the rest of your life? How did you know you would never grow tired of them?

Marriage was a risky business. Admittedly, his own parents were still very much in love after almost forty years, but that wasn't the norm. Rhianne's parents were a case in point. He didn't know what the statistics were these days, but he guessed that more marriages failed than lasted. Certainly most of his friends were divorced.

'I was worried about you,' he said. 'What have you been doing?'

Rhianne shrugged. 'I explored the neighbourhood, I swam in your pool, I read a little. I picked some flowers for the house.'

Zarek realised that before Rhianne, his villa had been like a heart without a soul. Empty. Spiritless. Now it had suddenly become alive.

Nothing had changed except Rhianne's presence, but

what a difference she had made. It hadn't happened straight away, not until she had sensed he wasn't a threat and relaxed, and yesterday she had even seemed to enjoy his company.

And this didn't take into account the response she'd made to his kisses! Every time he thought about it he felt knots in his stomach. Whether she knew it or not Rhianne was a dream to kiss. Totally different to other women.

Rhianne was special. Most females gave themselves to him easily, some even tried to force themselves on him. But not Rhianne. She had held back until she felt ready to let him kiss her.

And who was he trying to kid? Rhianne was suffering a broken heart. How could he forget that? Kissing him meant nothing. Certainly she wasn't ready to enter into a serious relationship. He was lucky she'd agreed to marry him.

'Are you a keen swimmer?' he asked.

'I enjoy it,' she replied, 'but I haven't done any in ages. It's usually when I go on holiday.'

The thought of Rhianne in her swimsuit sent a series of vivid pictures through his mind. He dashed them away before they did things to him that should never be allowed.

Her hair swung in an attractive ribbon of waves as she shook her head. 'You look as though you need to rest,' she said softly. 'Have you been at the hospital all night?'

'Most of it; I managed an hour or two at my mother's. I couldn't leave her, she was in such a state. I'm sorry I had to neglect you.' He opened his arms, half expecting her to ignore the gesture, feeling a rush of adrenalin when she stepped into them.

Rhianne didn't know what had prompted her to move so close to Zarek. Perhaps because she'd felt lonely without him. She had lied when she'd said that she hadn't felt fearful last night. Every little sound had had her pricking her ears; she'd almost been afraid to go to sleep.

It wasn't like being at home in England where everything was familiar. Here there were different sounds and smells. At night came the occasional soft bray of a donkey, the call of an unfamiliar bird, the faint sound of voices. And far, far below was the whisper of the ocean, calling, calling.

If Zarek's hug was supposed to be comforting it turned into something more. It started in her toes, the warmth spreading higher and higher, triggering each sensitive spot on its way until the whole of her body was infused with sensation.

It was almost impossible to keep still. She had the strongest urge yet to press herself against him. His arousal was hard and alarmingly evident, and whether it was the discovery that he too felt an echoing need, or whether it was her own feelings that terrified her, Rhianne wasn't sure, but she placed her hands flat against his chest ready to push herself away.

Before she could do any more than think about it, Zarek's arms tightened and his mouth made a move on hers. 'Mmm, you taste good.' He slid his hands down to her bottom and urged her even closer towards him.

Rhianne's mouth fell open in a shocked, 'Oh!' as she felt the force of his desire against her. 'We shouldn't be doing this.'

'Give me a good reason why not and I'll stop.' A wicked smile accompanied his words.

Rhianne knew that she ought to say that he was breaking his promise. But how could she when every inch of her was on fire, when need was growing greater than common sense?

'See,' he claimed triumphantly. 'You're simply denying yourself pleasure. Nevertheless, it will wait.'

And to her disappointment he let her go. She was shocked by her feelings and couldn't help wondering whether she was in danger of actually falling for Zarek. Admittedly, she thought of Angus less and less often, but that didn't mean she was ready for another relationship. Did it?

The thought that she could be trapped in a loveless marriage filled her with dread. It had been okay when she had no feelings for him, when it was a business transaction and nothing more, when she knew that she could walk away at the end of it all with her heart whole and a healthy bank balance into the bargain.

But something was happening to her, something totally unexpected, and—

'Come,' he said, cutting into her thoughts. 'I know a beautiful little cove where we can swim to our hearts content. Have you had breakfast?'

'Not yet.'

'Then we'll eat out as well.'

'Do you really think we ought to leave the villa?' she asked tentatively. 'What if your father takes another turn for the worse? How will anyone get in touch with you if we're out?' Even as she spoke Rhianne wondered whether she was using this as an excuse not to go swimming with Zarek.

Visions of his fabulous naked torso flashed in front of her eyes. He was perfectly tanned and toned. He was every woman's dream. Not an inch of anything superfluous. So amazingly gorgeous that even thinking about him sent a bevy of butterflies through her stomach. It was a hot day, but she felt even hotter and dashed away her disquieting thoughts before they became reflected in her eyes.

'I'm always contactable, Rhianne. It's part of the job.' One eyebrow lifted, and his mouth quirked. 'Does that satisfy you?'

'I guess so,' she said quietly.

'Good. Go and get ready and we'll be on our way.'

The cliffs were high, the walk down to the cove steeply zigzagged, and the thought of climbing back up afterwards made Rhianne wish that she had suggested the pool. Except that the sea hadn't seemed quite so intimate.

As they walked she was faintly fearful of what the outcome of the day would be. Zarek merely hummed to himself. He was undoubtedly happy with the situation, and, knowing how hard he worked normally, and how worried he must be about his father, she was glad to see him relaxing and letting his hair down.

Even if it was to her disadvantage!

She felt that she was getting into a situation too big to handle. That one day she would regret every second of it. The attraction she felt for him, the fact that she feared she might be falling in love with him, made her fearful of every moment that they spent together.

He shouldn't be so damn sexy. He wasn't safe to be around. He aroused feelings inside her that were alien, that made a mockery of her virginal vows.

By the time they reached the cove Rhianne's thoughts were in chaos, but it wasn't until she shrugged off the wrap she had tied over her swimsuit that she realised to her horror that the clasp on her halter neck had broken. Her breasts were swinging bare!

Did she make an issue of it, declare that she wasn't going to swim after all, or take off the rest of her swimsuit and dart into the water as quickly as possible, hoping against hope that Zarek would not notice?

She chose the latter option, not even glancing at Zarek, running as if her life depended on it until the azure water of the Aegean swallowed her up. She swam and swam, intent only on getting as far away as possible.

Although she was a strong swimmer Zarek's long arms and powerful strokes soon brought him to her side. 'I didn't realise we were in a race.'

He had been surprised when he saw Rhianne run into the water stark naked. More than surprised. Faintly shocked if the truth were known. But excited too. If it was good enough for her then…

'It's not a race,' she said. 'I happen to enjoy swimming. Anyway, I knew you'd catch me up.'

'I'm enjoying the skinny-dipping experience,' he said with a grin, treading water at her side.

Rhianne looked down at him and her face went a fiery red. The water was too clear for her to be mistaken.

Zarek laughed. 'Don't be embarrassed. It's the best feeling in the world. We should do it more often.'

'The fastener on my swimsuit broke,' she told him defensively, looking somewhere over his shoulder instead of into his face.

'I'm glad. Anything to free you of your inhibitions, Rhianne. Have you ever swum naked before?'

She shook her head. No one had ever seen her without her clothes on, only her parents when she was a child. She had always thought that it was a mystique to be shared in marriage. It was ironic under the circumstances.

For several long minutes they swam and played in the water, Zarek gently brushing his body against hers, nothing to alarm her; she couldn't even be sure that it was deliberate. She was actually enjoying herself, relaxing in a way she had never thought possible.

Zarek was making it easy for her. Even though she knew he must be worried about his father he was relaxed and fun, and when he finally suggested that they head back to shore she didn't want the pleasure to stop.

And, amazingly, when they reached the shoreline and strode up to where they had left their clothes, she still did not feel embarrassed. Something had happened out there, something that had brought them closer together. It was not a physical intimacy but a mental one; they had crossed a line, and, as she wrapped her caftan around her, and Zarek pulled on his shorts and T-shirt, she felt that it was almost a shame that they must dress.

She had become a free spirit out there in the clear waters, she had let the love she was beginning to feel for this man shed her inhibitions, but now, with her body covered, Zarek's too, it was almost like a step back. This was the man she was marrying purely to protect his inheritance.

Reality set in once again.

The dark cliffs that enclosed the beach seemed to have moved in on them, making Rhianne feel trapped. There was not another soul about, and she knew they had a long climb back up. The turquoise sea, which had been so inviting earlier, was now her enemy. Trapping her in this tiny space with the one man who had managed to turn her blood to water so that it raced through her body at lightning speed.

'Let's go,' he said softly, almost as though he had read

her thoughts, was aware of her sudden fear, and he began to lead the way back up the hillside.

Their strenuous climb took them to a tiny café where he was on good terms with the owner.

'And this is your—er—girlfriend?' the man questioned Zarek.

'My future wife,' he claimed proudly. 'Rhianne, this is Nikos, we grew up together.'

'Congratulations,' said Nikos. 'This is a good man; you have made a wise choice.'

As soon as he had gone Rhianne glared. 'I wish you hadn't told him we were getting married. It's not as if it's for real.'

'No one knows that,' he answered solemnly, reaching out for her hands and touching his lips to the back of them.

Light though the kisses were, they sent electrical impulses sizzling through her veins, making her clamp her thighs and buttocks tightly together, terribly conscious that she wore nothing beneath her caftan. She was growing more aware of him with each hour that passed, and it troubled her deeply.

'We need to keep up the pretence of our relationship being the real thing,' he explained, 'because once word gets around that we're married everyone will want to know who you are. Why not tell them now?'

'It just doesn't feel right,' she said quietly, sadly.

'I thought we'd reached a turning point out there.'

Rhianne felt her cheeks grow warm as his eyes rested questioningly on her face, but she didn't answer his question. How could she admit that she too had felt— something? A whole lot of something! Something that scared her half to death.

A few moments later their breakfast arrived. Greek yoghurt beaten with honey, fresh figs with goat's cheese and bread still warm from the oven. It was a simple breakfast but one of the nicest Rhianne had ever eaten.

'That was truly delicious,' she said, sitting back.

'Simple is often the best.'

'So why can't we have a simple wedding instead of the massive extravaganza you're planning?' she retorted.

'You think my mother would allow it?'

Rhianne giggled; she couldn't help herself. Here was a man right at the top of his profession, in control of goodness knows how many companies, and he was worried about what his mother might think.

'Why are you laughing?'

'Because I can't imagine you being frightened of your mother.'

'If you knew her as well as I do then you'd be frightened too,' he said, his brows rising comically. 'When Christos and I were little we were frequently in trouble. My father rarely scolded us; it was always my mother.'

'At least you had both your parents.'

'That's true. It must have been hard for you when your father left.'

'It was at first,' she admitted, 'but I got tough. I had to. I became my mother's little helper.'

'I'm looking forward to meeting her. Do you look like your mother?'

Rhianne laughed. 'Not at all. I have some of my father's features. I have his eyes and forehead.'

'And your hair?' His voice, which had gone deeper as he spoke, tailed off as he reached out and knotted a lock through his fingers each side of her face.

His eyes held hers.

Rhianne stopped breathing.

Then he pulled gently until her face was very close to his, until she could see every pore, smell the freshness of him, feel his heat. See the gold flecks in his eyes. He was going to kiss her, without a doubt he was going to kiss her, and considering how high her emotions were running she wouldn't be able to stop him.

The situation was getting out of control. He was playing unfairly.

'Don't do this, Zarek,' she said quietly.

'Nikos is watching us,' he returned equally as quietly. 'We need to act as though we're very much in love.'

She didn't believe him for one second. He was doing this because he wanted to. And, heaven help her, she wanted it too.

Why she felt like this when only two weeks ago her life had been destroyed, when she had felt she would never trust a man in her whole life again, she didn't know. She was getting carried away by this beautiful place and Zarek's persistent attention. He was such a charmer that no woman in her right mind could possibly resist him.

But it was all a game as far as he was concerned. He'd just admitted that he needed to keep up appearances. She wished he would stop to think what it was doing to her. He was exciting sexual emotions that she didn't want, had never felt before, at least not to this extent. No one had ever set her body on fire like this, not with just a look. Zarek's eyes were seriously disturbing, sending out silent signals that triggered a deep and unexpected response. Heaven help her when they were married if he carried on like this.

'I don't care who's watching,' she said, still speaking

quietly. 'I don't feel comfortable.' And if he didn't stop right now she would get up and leave. Let Nikos think what he liked.

For a long moment he didn't speak. He simply continued to look deeply into her eyes. Then with a mysterious little smile he relaxed his fingers. Her hair swung back and brushed her cheeks. A feather-light touch, almost as though it was Zarek's hand caressing her.

Rhianne swallowed hard and sat back, closing her eyes momentarily, trying to bring her emotions under control.

'It's time we went.' Zarek's voice ruptured the silence. 'I'll take you to my mother's; you can help her with the wedding preparations.'

It was a good idea; Rhianne knew she ought to be doing something. In fact, she ought to be the one doing everything. The trouble was she feared that his mother would ask so many personal questions that she wouldn't be able to carry on lying.

'Won't she be at the hospital?' she asked, mentally crossing her fingers.

'We'll check there first,' he answered. 'And, Rhianne,' he warned, 'don't let me down.'

CHAPTER TEN

THE next few days passed quickly. Rhianne duly helped Zarek's mother with the arrangements, and even though she was ridiculously nervous in case she gave the game away she managed to give a creditable performance of being the happy bride to be.

Georgios's health improved as well, and it looked likely that he would be able to attend the wedding.

Zarek remained the pure gentleman. Polite and kind but nothing more. Which should have pleased her but instead dismayed her, and she couldn't help wondering whether it was because she had said that she didn't like him touching her in public. She had meant it at the time—she'd felt embarrassed by his attention—but now she began to wish that she had never spoken.

On the day before the wedding, her own mother arrived. 'Darling,' her parent enthused, 'you're looking wonderful, positively radiant, in fact.'

Rhianne didn't feel radiant, she felt distinctly uneasy. Conversely, her mother was more elegant than she had ever seen her, in a smart Chanel suit with her auburn hair cut fashionably short.

'So this is where you're living?' she asked, looking around her with interest. 'Zarek must be extremely wealthy to own a place like this. Where is this magnificent man? I'm dying to meet him.'

'Mother, I hope you don't talk to Zarek like that. He—'

'Your mother, dearest Rhianne, can talk however she likes.'

Zarek walked into the room, having clearly heard and liked the 'magnificent' bit.

He kissed her mother's hand in a gallant gesture. 'Now I can see from where Rhianne gets her good looks. I trust you had a good flight? Your room is ready; I'll arrange to have your luggage sent up while you talk to your daughter. Drinks on the terrace, perhaps?'

Her mother was instantly won over. 'What a charming man,' she said to Rhianne once he had disappeared. 'Do tell me how you two met. And what happened to Angus? What did you fall out over?'

Rhianne gave a brief version of events, avoiding any questions she didn't want to answer, and was glad when Zarek rejoined them.

For the next hour he entertained her mother, and Rhianne was able to sit back and listen to their conversation. Then jet lag caught up and her parent announced that she would like to take a rest before dinner.

Rhianne was relieved. Her mother had watched the two of them keenly, and Rhianne had been forced to act as she had never acted before. She had flirted with Zarek, she had even sat on his lap at one stage and linked her arms around his neck.

In response he had tilted her chin and kissed her, an amazing kiss that had sent Rhianne's hormones running frantically. There was hard evidence that it had affected Zarek too!

'If I didn't know you better,' said Zarek once they were alone, 'I would think that you were beginning to feel something for me. That was quite a little performance you put on.'

Rhianne said nothing. It had been no act. She had only to look at him these days for her body to hunger for him. But she had no idea what Zarek's true feelings were. And now that the wedding was less than twenty-four hours away, she was scared to death that he would want her in his bed. And how could she deny him, feeling as she did?

'If you carry on like that tomorrow,' he said now, his voice low and husky, 'you'll make everything so much easier. Can you imagine what it would be like trying to convince everyone that we're deeply in love if we felt nothing for each other?'

'You're saying that you feel something for me?' Rhianne's heart began to race.

Zarek guarded his eyes. 'I'm saying, Rhianne, that we've made a connection. So much so that we'll be able to fool everyone that we're in love. I'm deeply grateful to you.'

Rhianne swallowed hard. Grateful! He had no idea what was really going on inside her head.

'And think what you'll be getting out of it,' he continued. 'A home here and in London. An allowance that will let you buy anything you want—a trip to America to see your mother, for instance. And by the way, is your father coming?'

His quick change of subject took Rhianne by surprise. 'Heavens, no!' Her whole face filled with scorn. 'He's ignored me all these years, so as far as I'm concerned he's no longer my father.'

Zarek groaned and gathered her against his hard chest. 'I'm sorry. I find it hard to believe that any man could abandon his family.'

'My mother's agreed to step into his shoes,' she told him as mixed signals shot through her brain.

It felt like a game she had played as a child when she was thinking about the best-looking boy in her class. One by one she had pulled the petals off a daisy and chanted, he loves me, he loves me not, he loves me, he loves me not.

She really did not know how to take Zarek. Was he simply using her or was he not? Was he beginning to feel something for her or was he not? Sometimes she thought he was, but at other times she was convinced that it was nothing but a game to him. A serious game because his future success depended on it, but a game all the same.

It, oddly, hurt to think this, especially as her feelings towards him were changing. As far as he was concerned he was buying a wife. And she must remember that. A wife in name only!

She was the one doing the favour, so she could call the shots.

Easier said than done. Especially when everything around her faded into insignificance, when she was aware only of Zarek's throbbing body next to hers. Was it his heart pounding or her own? Perhaps both in unison.

'I'm relying on you, Rhianne, to get through tomorrow without letting me down. The future of Diakos Holdings is in your hands.'

Why did he feel the need to keep reminding her? It

was the only reason she was still here. Except that when she had agreed to the contract she hadn't expected to experience these strong feelings. They terrified her.

'And by the way, I'm going to sleep at my parents' house tonight. Your mother reaffirmed that it was bad luck to see my bride before the ceremony.'

Rhianne's eyes opened wide. 'You cannot leave me, Zarek. How will I know where to go, what to do?' Now that the big moment was almost upon them a swift ribbon of fear flowed through her veins.

'I will never leave you, Rhianne.'

There was a deepness to his voice that she hadn't heard before. It came from low in his throat, and it sent a shiver over her skin.

Zarek came to his senses just in time. Holding Rhianne against him and feeling the exciting warmth of her body, inhaling the floral shampoo she'd used on her hair, was leading him into temptation. For just a moment he had been lulled into believing that their marriage was real. It was time to take a step back and reassess himself.

'I will never leave you in the lurch,' he amended, relaxing his arms and letting her back out of them. 'As far as the actual wedding is concerned, tomorrow my whole family, including the priest, will walk over here. Christos is best man, did I tell you that? He will then lead the party from here to the church.'

'Why Christos?' asked Rhianne fiercely. 'Don't you have a friend who could do it?'

'My parents would never forgive me. Don't worry, he'll behave himself. He wanted to know why I'd decided to get married so suddenly. I told him it was love at first sight and we saw no reason to wait. You're quite something,

Rhianne, do you know that? Not many people would give up their life to help someone they hardly know.'

His feelings for this beautiful woman were growing deeper by the day. He wasn't sure whether it was actually love he felt, or a very, very deep desire to possess her. She was certainly the only woman ever to make him feel like this.

'We're foregoing some of the traditions because of my father's health; it would be too much for him.'

'Thank you,' said Rhianne quietly, turning to look out of the window towards Oia, picking out the blue-domed roof of the church where she would soon become Zarek's wife. It was a daunting thought, and she was really glad that her mother was here. She felt so alone, so vulnerable. Zarek wasn't forcing her into this; she could have said no anywhere along the way. But even so…

They finished their drinks, and Rhianne stood up. 'I don't think I'll sleep tonight.'

'Me neither,' he said, unfolding himself too. 'It will be a big day. And, Rhianne, I really do appreciate what you're doing for me. I know it's a lot, and I know you'll be putting your life on hold, but words cannot express my gratitude.'

Rhianne wasn't sure whether he reached out to her or whether it was the other way round, but she found herself in his arms. His mesmerising eyes looked deep into hers, one hand rising to caress the side of her face, and Rhianne found herself pressing her cheek into his palm. It was pure instinct that drove her, especially when she lifted her own hand and placed it on top of his.

She expected a kiss to follow, wanted it even, but Zarek did no more than touch his lips to her brow. 'Goodnight, *agapi mou.*'

'Goodnight, Zarek.'

Neither of them moved.

Their eyes locked, and Rhianne felt as though all the breath was being sucked out of her body. Zarek was the first to break the invisible bond. He pressed a kiss to his first and second fingers and touched them to her lips. 'Go get your beauty sleep. I'll see you tomorrow.'

The morning of their wedding day dawned bright and clear. Rhianne was understandably nervous, her mother even more so. 'I feel that I should have done more towards this wedding of yours. Zarek's family will judge me.'

'How could you do anything from so far away?' questioned Rhianne. 'They understand. Zarek's father's been ill—it was touch and go whether he lived at one time—and Zarek wanted to ensure that he saw us happily married. In any case, Zarek's mother enjoyed making all the arrangements. I didn't do very much myself, to be honest.'

'You're lucky, my darling, to have found someone like Zarek.'

'And you, Mum, how is your marriage?' Rhianne didn't want to keep on talking about Zarek as though he was the love of her life.

Her mother's eyes shadowed. 'We're going through a tricky patch. David's been playing away. What is it with me and men, Rhianne?'

'Perhaps it's all men,' she said sadly.

'I'm sure Zarek won't let you down. I've seen the way he looks at you; he loves you dearly, and I know I'm not a very good judge of character where my own affairs are concerned, but I feel that his values are all in the right place. Have a happy day, my darling, and a lifetime of happiness to follow.'

Her mother wasn't usually this sentimental. For one tiny moment Rhianne thought about telling her the true story, but Zarek's face flashed in front of her eyes, and she knew that she couldn't do this to him. Instead, tears begin to well. 'Will you come and help me get ready?'

Zarek had sent in a hairdresser to fix her hair and a beautician to do her makeup and nails, but when a dresser turned up as well Rhianne politely but firmly sent her away. She wanted no one but her mother.

When they had finished, Rhianne hardly recognised herself. She looked more beautiful than ever in her life. Taller too in the body-skimming dress. Then her mother handed her a white satin box. 'Zarek asked me to give you this.'

When Rhianne opened it she gasped. A diamond necklace with matching drop earrings that must have cost the earth. He really had gone to town, while she had bought him nothing. It hadn't seemed appropriate under the circumstances. She had a wedding ring for him, but that was all, and they'd chosen that together when he had bought her ring.

Her mother too was open-mouthed in disbelief.

By the time the wedding procession arrived Rhianne was ready. Her eyes met Zarek's and everything inside her went on to high alert. He looked devastatingly handsome in an ivory dress suit, and she felt a momentary stab of pain that this wasn't going to be a permanent marriage.

Christos led the procession to the church; Rhianne followed behind with her mother escorting her. She presumed Zarek was close behind but she didn't look around. She couldn't. She felt stiff with fear now. This was a big thing she was doing and it was too late to back out. Then she heard his voice in her ear, felt his warm breath on the back of her neck. 'You're doing well, Rhianne. I'm proud of you.'

It was enough to make her stand that little bit straighter and hold her head high. She fixed a smile on her lips and walked into the church.

It was filled to overflowing, and Rhianne was glad when the long ceremony was over. She had felt her whole body tremble as she'd made her vows. It was the most difficult thing she'd ever had to do. Zarek, on the other hand, had acted as though he were really in love; it had shone from his eyes as he looked at her.

On the way to the hotel for the champagne reception he squeezed her hand. 'Thank you, Rhianne,' he said quietly. 'I don't think I've told you how stunning you look. Truly the radiant bride. I've had so many compliments on my choice of wife. You've done me proud.'

'It's all part of the service.' God, she hated herself for saying this, but she had to keep up the act or else she would begin to doubt whether this marriage was a fake one or for real. 'And thank you for the jewellery. It's dazzling, but I won't be able to keep it. I trust you had it on sale or return?'

She heard the whoosh as he took a sudden harsh intake of breath. 'Rhianne, they are yours. To keep or do with as you like.'

At the hotel she was overwhelmed by the welcome she was given by the various members of his family. The impression she got was that they had all thought Zarek would never get married. Some of them spoke a little English, most none at all, but they all shook her hand or gave her a hug and let her know that she was now one of them.

After their meal there was lots of traditional dancing that Rhianne had to fake her way through. Every man in the room claimed a dance with her, and when it was Christos's turn he wanted to know how they had met. 'My brother always said he was married to his work and would never take himself a wife. You must have something special.'

'I guess we have,' answered Rhianne with a sweet smile. 'Zarek is a very special man.'

'A very wealthy man as well.'

A frown quickly furrowed her brow, and her heart did a double beat. 'Are you suggesting that I'm marrying your brother for his money? You insult me. I—'

Before she could say any more Zarek took her elbow, his dark eyes narrowed and hard. 'Do not talk to my wife like that, brother, or you'll regret it. There is only one reason Rhianne and I have married and that's because we're both very much in love. Any more of that sort of talk and I won't be accountable for my actions.'

He dragged Rhianne away. 'I'm sorry about that. Christos was out of order. He's jealous, that's his trouble. You've met his wife, have you? She's a sourpuss. I think he's regretting marrying her. But I thank you for your support.' He pulled her into his arms and kissed her. Nothing deep, a thank you kiss, a mere touching of his lips to hers. But it awoke a treacherous desire, and she clung to him, her mouth softening and opening. She heard his faint groan, but before he could enter they were surrounded by laughing, clapping people.

'It's what they've been waiting for,' he said against her lips. 'They want to see a show of our love. We must not disappoint them.' Nor did he. His kiss was spectacularly passionate. Rhianne forgot for the moment that they were being watched and gave herself up to the mind-blowing pleasure he was giving her, linking her arms around his neck, gyrating her body against him, very much aware of an arousal that both thrilled and shocked her.

His tongue explored and teased in a kiss far deeper than any other he had given her—and all in front of an audience! Whether it was an act on Zarek's part, she wasn't sure, but, whatever, she was most definitely having trouble hiding the fact that her most basic instincts were surfacing.

When he finally set her free, when the floor show was over, a further bout of spontaneous clapping took place.

Then the money dance began. Zarek had warned her about this. Everyone pinned money to their clothes as they danced their way around the floor, and Rhianne thought the evening was never going to end.

But finally they managed to make their exit. A car was waiting to take them home, and it was then that Rhianne's real fears began.

Her heart beat loudly when Zarek led her straight upstairs. The door to his bedroom had been left tantalisingly open, and the first thing she saw was a diaphanous nightie laid out on his bed.

'What is this?' she asked, her throbbing heart feeling heavy in her chest.

'What does it look like?'

'But ours isn't a real—'

'Shh!' Zarek placed a gentle finger on her lips. 'Rhianne, *agapi mou*, you've shown me in a thousand different ways how you feel about me. Your lips might lie but your body doesn't. Do not be afraid.'

CHAPTER ELEVEN

DO NOT be afraid!

The words echoed inside Rhianne's head, going round and round until she felt dizzy. But it wasn't Zarek she was afraid of, it was her own feelings. Each day she had spent in this man's company they had spiralled and grown until she knew that she couldn't last much longer without letting him make love to her. Her moral innocence, that she had treasured so much, was a thing of the past. Zarek had whipped her body into a frenzy of need and desire from which there was no escape.

But even though she desperately wanted him to make love to her, she also knew in her own mind that if he did, there would be no going back. He would expect her in his bed every night.

For the duration of their marriage.

Big warning bells rang in her head. Not so much rang as clanged—loudly! She clapped her hands to her ears to stop the distressing sound.

'Rhianne, what's wrong?' Zarek took her face between his palms, deep concern in his eyes. 'Do you have a headache? The day has been too much for you. Come, come and sit down, I'll get you some aspirin and—'

'No, Zarek. I don't have a headache, I'm in a state of shock. Can't you see that?' She pulled away from him, burning from his touch but still feeling a need to protect herself. 'What's happened to your promises?'

'Naturally, they still hold,' he said with a faint quizzical frown. 'I won't do anything you don't want me to do.'

'But all this.' She indicated the bed, the rose petals scattered over the pillows, the chocolates, the bottle of champagne waiting on ice.

'It can go. I thought you might—'

'You thought wrong, Zarek,' she interrupted him sharply. 'You know how I feel. I don't want to sleep with you.' Even as she spoke Rhianne's body ached with a need that scared her to death.

Walking back to the door, he held it open. 'Feel free to go to your own room,' he said, his lips tightening, and something she didn't want to see locked into his eyes.

He knew, she thought, he knew she wouldn't go in there and sleep by herself. How could she after today? That kiss on the dance floor—it had knocked her sideways. She had given herself away. And he was aware of it. He was calling her bluff.

She heaved a sigh and sat down. 'I'd like some champagne. I was too afraid to drink much today in case I got drunk and made a fool of myself.'

Zarek looked at her, his expression softening. 'I don't imagine you've ever got drunk in your life, nor made a fool of yourself—except perhaps when you walked in front of my car. And that was my gain.'

Yes, it was his gain, and in some indefinable way it was also hers. She smiled weakly, watching as he opened the bottle and poured the sparkling liquid into elegant crystal flutes. But when he passed her drink and their fingers touched she no longer felt weakness. Fire ignited and raced out of control through her body.

'My sweet Rhianne,' said Zarek, briefly touching his hand to her face. 'Maybe it's time you got out of that dress and into something you can relax in. But before you do, in case I didn't tell you earlier, you look stunning. I didn't expect such a simple dress—I thought something frothy and extravagant—but it is perfection. No other words can describe it. You are beautiful.'

Rhianne caught a glimpse of herself in the mirror across the room. Her cheeks were flushed and her hair was awry, but her eyes were bright and, yes, she did look beautiful, more beautiful than she'd ever looked in her life. On the other hand, she'd never before worn a dress that had cost as much as this. It would make any woman look good. She almost didn't recognise herself.

She looked like a woman in love!

Her fingers reached up to touch the beautiful diamond necklace at her throat, and she wondered when she would wear such a striking piece of jewellery again. And the earrings, long droppers that sparkled magnificently in the light, what sort of an event would she need to attend to wear them?

She hadn't even realised that Zarek had moved to stand behind her until she saw his face reflected above hers. He laid his hands on her shoulders and more flames of fire licked their way through her entire sensory system, growing in intensity with each passing second.

Without even realising what she was doing Rhianne lifted her hands to touch his, causing a further whirlpool of rich emotion, and when she caught her reflection she was shocked to discover that her feelings were echoed clearly for Zarek to see.

Her eyes had gone from bright to overbright, the colour in her cheeks had heightened, and her lips were parted and moist. Strange, she couldn't remember passing her tongue across them, though she must have done. Her heart was pounding so erratically that she thought it might leap out of her chest.

Without a word Zarek hauled her into his arms, and when he kissed her Rhianne was surprised to feel how gentle his lips were. She had known this was going to happen and that she wouldn't be able to stop him, but she had expected blazing passion.

All day she had been aware of his hunger. It had flared in his eyes whenever he'd looked at her. And each time she had felt a dizzying response. It was not something that could be ignored, try as she might.

The tenderness of his kisses, however, made no difference to the sensations swirling in her head. She clung to him for support and realised that somewhere along the way he had discarded his jacket and bow tie, and that the first few buttons of his shirt were undone, revealing his dark chest hair.

She had the urge to touch, to find out what it was like to feel those whorls of springy hair beneath her fingertips. These were alien feelings and yet, conversely, they felt right. Everything felt right tonight.

It had been a day without parallel, a day she would remember for the rest of her life—regardless of what happened in the future.

Unconsciously she pressed her body closer to his, feeling some of his heat spread into her, feeling her bones begin to melt. And it alarmed her to discover that she wanted still more. More of this man, more of everything he had to offer.

She threaded her fingers into the thickness of his hair, pulling his head closer so that their kisses grew harder and wilder, their lips parting hungrily. His tongue tasted and sensitised the inside of her mouth, creating new pleasures, inviting more, expertly seducing her. Rhianne's fingers trailed down to his nape, feeling the faint rasp where he'd had his hair cut short for their wedding, and then on to his shoulders where muscles were bunched.

She didn't realise that Zarek had been gradually undoing the long line of buttons at the back of her dress until she felt his fingers on her naked skin. A ripple of sensation ran through her, and she wanted to be free of the dress's encumbrance, free to feel Zarek's hands on every part of her body. Her head fell back and her eyes closed, her lips were parted and moist, and she shrugged her shoulders to allow the dress to slip to the floor.

Zarek groaned. All day long he had waited for the moment when Rhianne became his. He'd not been sure that it would happen, but the kiss on the dance floor had given him hope. His hopes had been dashed when Rhianne declared she wanted separate rooms, and he'd almost thundered that he would allow no such thing. How he'd held back those words he did not know, but now he was glad that he had. Rhianne was responding to him of her own free will. There had been cracks in the composure she had tried her hardest to retain, but now they were wide open, and it looked as though tonight she would be sharing his bed after all.

He dared not let himself go down the road of what

would happen in the future. His main aim had been to safeguard the business, and he'd achieved that. Now his aim was to keep Rhianne happy—and, hopefully, in his bed. He couldn't possibly sustain the marriage if Rhianne didn't allow him to touch her—not when he was in grave danger of falling in love with her. A thought that filled him with both pleasure and fear at the same time!

As she stepped out of the dress he took her hand, feeling her tremble, seeing the uncertainty in her eyes. All she wore now was the briefest of white bras and a G-string, and sheer stockings that looked as though they were held up by willpower. Her body was long and slender and faintly tanned, and his whole being went onto high alert simply looking at her.

With a groan he pulled her against him, making her aware of the hard force of his erection. In response, a quiver ran through Rhianne's entire body, and a strangled sound escaped her throat as her head fell back. He pressed his lips to the tantalising arch, tasting the sweet fragrance of her skin, touching his tongue to the rapid beat of her pulse, and slowly but surely moving lower and lower, one hand against her back now, the other cupping one softly rounded breast.

When it became clear that Rhianne was not going to stop him, that she appeared to need this as much he did, he snapped the fastening on her strapless bra and watched in total fascination as it slowly dropped away to reveal breasts that were firm and beautifully formed, with tight dark pink nipples already on high alert.

He felt her sway backwards as he lowered his head to take one of her nipples into his mouth, delighting in the soft helpless little sounds she made deep in her throat.

'Not only do you look beautiful, *agapi mou*,' he groaned, 'you taste beautiful too.'

Rhianne was unaware of Zarek manoeuvring her across the room; she was conscious only of the flood of sensation streaking through her body like a jet across the sky. It was not until he sat down on the edge of the bed, urging her towards him so that her legs were wide as they straddled his knees, that she realised what he was doing.

From this vulnerable position he continued his assault on her breasts, and as he sucked each nipple in turn into his mouth, as he teased them with his tongue and teeth, Rhianne grew almost faint. This was an experience too far. Zarek was turning this marriage into a proper one.

He was claiming her as his bride in every way!

So why didn't she stop him?

The answer was simple. She couldn't. Zarek was an expert in the pleasure stakes. He must have known that once he began she wouldn't want him to stop. Her fingers threaded through his short springy hair, clutching the fine shape of his head. In contrast, her own head was thrust back, her eyes closed as she lapped up the attention he was paying her.

When his mouth moved lower, trailing hot kisses over her stomach, pausing for a moment while his tongue explored her belly button, where she discovered a high state of sensitivity that she had never known existed, she couldn't find the strength to stop him, and when she heard the snap of material as he tore off her G-string, she knew that she had gone too far now to back out.

Zarek was drawing her into his web like a spider did a fly. Irrevocably. She had become his to do with as he liked.

Somewhere, deep, deep down inside her, she still did have a mind of her own, but she didn't want to listen to it.

With one swift, deft movement Zarek reversed their positions. She was the one on the edge of the bed now and he was kneeling. Almost reverently his tongue touched and stroked the most intimate part of her, and the pleasure was so alien and so exquisite that she thought she was going to faint.

She lay back, reeling as wave after wave of electrifying sensations flooded the lower part of her stomach, reaching out long, intense fingers to excite other parts of her body.

Zarek lifted her legs over his shoulders and continued to taste and tease her with his hot, eager tongue, and Rhianne became lost in a world of feelings that made her feel as though her body no longer belonged to her.

It seemed an age before he finally stopped, a whole lifetime, and when he slowly drew her to her feet Rhianne was unable to stand. Every bone in her body had melted and she was compelled to cling to Zarek for support.

She wore nothing but her stockings and high heels, whereas he was still fully clothed. His face, though, mirrored her own. His lips were soft and moist, his eyes as black as night. 'I think,' he said gruffly, 'that that's enough for now.'

Rhianne couldn't believe the disappointment she felt. Instead of feeling relieved that he was going to take it no further, she contrarily wanted more. He had shown her pleasure on a scale she had never felt. He couldn't end it here, she wouldn't let him.

'Oh, no,' she said, looking him straight in the eye, 'it's not over yet.' With great daring she began to unbutton his shirt, and as each inch of flesh was exposed she layered kisses on to his burning skin, not stopping until she had his shirt fully open. With impatient fingers she tugged it out of his waistband and off his shoulders and threw it to the floor.

Then she began rubbing herself against him, her hips against the part of him that throbbed and pulsed and needed urgent attention, her aching breasts against his chest, enjoying the roughness of his body hair on her tender skin. She had never done anything like this before—it was as though Zarek had woken a siren inside her.

His groans were deep, his eyes dark and glazed. With unsteady hands he twisted a length of hair through his fingers, using it to pull her head close to his so that he could take and taste her lips in a hard kiss that ground her lips back against her teeth until she tasted blood.

Rhianne began to undo his belt buckle. Her fingers felt shaky and awkward, but somehow she managed it, then the clip on his trousers, followed swiftly by the zip. The sound it made was heightened by the atmosphere in the room. The air around them had thickened and was full of tension, but there was no stopping Rhianne now.

Zarek hopped obligingly out of his trousers, kicking off his shoes and socks as he did so. But it was left to Rhianne to take off his black briefs. She did wonder for a few seconds whether she could rip them off, as he had done to hers, but then decided that if it didn't work it would ruin everything that had built up between them.

Instead, she began a line of kisses from his chest to his navel, following the pattern he had set, feeling a smile of triumph when he groaned and squirmed. 'What are you doing to me?' he asked gruffly.

Rhianne didn't answer. His hands were on her head, threading once again through the thickness of her hair so that he could hold her hard against him. Inching his briefs down, she nibbled each area of skin as it was exposed. The roughness of his hair tickled her nose, and when she found her goal Rhianne almost began to wish that she hadn't started this. It was a totally new experience, and it was instinct alone that drove her.

Zarek felt as though he'd died and gone to heaven, but he also knew the danger of allowing the situation to get out of hand. He'd urged Rhianne into it, and if she was enjoying herself too much then it was his fault. But he didn't want her throwing everything back in his face afterwards.

He used a few choice Greek phrases. There was only so much a man could stand, and he was reaching the end of his limit. 'Rhianne, please stop.'

She turned her eyes up towards his face. 'You do not like what I am doing?' She looked hurt and vulnerable, and he crushed her head against him. But he hadn't stopped to think, and her lips encountered again the part of him that throbbed like hell and was ready to leap out of control.

Immediately he let her go, and when she looked at him this time her eyes were so luminous he thought they must be awash with tears. Hell, why had he stopped her? She so clearly wasn't averse to kissing him in this manner, and he hated the thought that she'd done it to some other man. But she must have done because otherwise how would she have known what to do? She had touched and kissed him in exactly the right spots to send his testosterone levels shooting sky high.

This wasn't the way he had intended the evening to go. He had wanted to take it slowly, much more slowly, probably lasting the whole night through. Instead,

Rhianne was drawing him so close to the edge that it could all be over in a matter of minutes.

'It's not that I don't like it, *agapi mou*, but I wanted us to take things more slowly; I wanted to—oh, God, what am I saying? I want you now, desperately.' Without another word he lifted her up and dropped her on the bed, sweeping chocolates aside with one swift movement of his hand.

His breathing was deep and out of control as he kicked off his briefs that Rhianne had so tantalizingly entered. Free of all restrictions, he lowered himself on the bed beside her. Her shoes had fallen off but she still wore the sheer stockings with the delicate lacy tops, and just the sight of them on her amazingly long legs was like receiving a kick in the gut.

He found it hard to breathe now, and for the moment he wanted to feast his eyes on her. She looked incredibly beautiful: her eyes dreamy, her fantastic auburn hair fanned out over the pillow, her lips parted expectantly, just the tip of her tongue showing as she moistened them.

His own mouth was dry; he knew exactly how she felt. This was a significant moment for both of them. He trailed a finger from the pulse at the base of her throat, encircling her breasts, watching as her nipples seemed to spring into even more vibrant life, but he didn't touch them, much as he wanted to, much as he knew Rhianne wanted him to do. No, his fingers were on a different journey. They traced a path over her belly button, pausing a moment to explore its creases, then moved ever lower, entwining now in the softness of her hair which excited him by being the same shade as the hair on her head.

When he reached his goal, Rhianne bucked and tightened beneath his touch. She was so ready for him that all his thoughts about exciting her some more flew out of the window. Time for that another day. Nothing was needed now except the uniting of their bodies. Waiting would be agony for both of them.

But he had one last question. 'You are all right with this?' he asked as he turned his back on her for a moment to pull on a condom.

Rhianne gave the faintest of nods. Her throat was so tight that she couldn't have spoken had she wanted to. She was more than ready. Her whole body ached to be possessed. Nothing else existed in the whole world except the two of them, here, now, in this beautiful room. She didn't know what Zarek had done to her, but she wanted him with something approaching desperation. If this was what making love was all about then why had she waited so long?

Zarek entered her carefully and slowly, even though she knew he probably wanted to take her fiercely and sensationally. She appreciated his thoughtfulness but she too was hungry, and she raised her hips in instinctive invitation.

With a deep-throated groan he slid his hands beneath her bottom and urged her even closer. He hesitated only briefly when his entry was restricted, too far gone then to stop, and besides Rhianne didn't want him to. The pain was gone in an instant, and it seemed like only seconds before her whole world exploded, sensations such as she had never felt before chasing through every inch of her in wave after wave. Moments later Zarek reached his own climax. His body jerked and throbbed on top of her, and it was a lifetime before he found the strength to roll away.

Rhianne had never felt like this in her whole life. Euphoric was a word that came to mind. Stunned, as well, that such magic could take place. And in that moment came the realisation that she had fallen deeply and irrevocably in love with Zarek.

But her euphoria didn't last long. Not allowing himself the pleasure of glorying in the feelings that must have filled him too, Zarek jumped off the bed and glared down at her.

'Why the hell didn't you tell me that you were a virgin?'

CHAPTER TWELVE

RHIANNE'S eyes dimmed with tears. What did it matter that this had been the first time for her? Hadn't he enjoyed it? Wasn't she good enough? Had he expected more? She turned her face away from him, feeling as though her heart was about to break. For the very first time in her life she had given herself to a man, freely and joyfully, and now he was throwing accusations at her.

'I didn't think it was important.'

'Not important?' he asked angrily. 'The first time is special for every woman.'

'And you think that wasn't special for me?' she asked sharply, her head jerking back so that her eyes could glare into his. She wished that she knew what he was saying. He was ruining what had been the most beautiful experience of her life.

'I'd like to think it was, but...' He shook his head again as though trying to rid it of unholy thoughts. 'You should have told me. I thought that you and—'

'No!' Rhianne cut in swiftly, adding without thinking, 'I always swore I'd remain a virgin until I married.'

Zarek dropped his head into his hands. 'What have I done?'

'It's not your fault,' insisted Rhianne swiftly. 'I wanted it as much as you.'

'But—'

'But nothing,' she cut in fiercely. She wasn't going to let him ruin this exquisite moment. 'I wanted it too, Zarek. I was ready.'

'I don't understand.' His dark eyes bored into hers, trying to read the reasoning behind her change of mind.

'I don't understand either,' she answered. 'All I know is that I've never felt like this in my whole life. I've discovered that I didn't know what I was missing.'

Zarek snorted, and after one further glare in her direction he marched across the room.

Rhianne felt like crying. Her fantastic experience was turning into a nightmare. She had wanted this night to go on and on. She had even forgotten for a while that their marriage was only make-believe, something Zarek had dreamt up to save the future of his company.

If that was the case then he shouldn't have encouraged her. He should have left her alone. She hadn't asked for any of it.

Anger began to pulse through her veins now, and she went after him. 'Don't think you can walk away and make me feel the guilty party,' she yelled.

He turned and looked at her with eyes so bleak that they scared her. 'You should have told me,' was all he said before leaving the room and closing the door resolutely in her face.

Zarek felt sick to the very core of him. He had done the unforgivable. He knew that some women didn't think twice about losing their virginity, but Rhianne was different. Rhianne had been saving herself for the one man she fell deeply in love with and ultimately married, and he applauded her for that.

Now he had ruined everything.

Whichever way he looked at it their marriage wasn't real. He had forced her into it. He'd like to think that he had persuaded her but, no, he had taken advantage when her defences were low.

He would never forgive himself.

Downstairs he poured himself another glass of champagne before setting the bottle down on the table so loudly that he didn't hear the door open or Rhianne step inside. The first he knew of her presence was when her hand touched his shoulder.

'If you're feeling as bad as I am then I'm glad,' she said briskly, her blue eyes filled with fighting spirit.

He turned to look at her, and his heart lurched agonisingly. Oh, Lord, he wanted to take her again, and knowing that it was now forbidden was like someone hammering a nail into his head.

'But the fact remains that I knew exactly what I was doing when I allowed you to—' her voice faltered for a second '—make love to me. And I don't regret it. If you do, that's your prerogative, but your anger is badly misplaced.'

Zarek turned away from her, moving to look out the window. The courtyard was in darkness, and it suited his mood. A few stars winked in the sky, but he could see nothing else except Rhianne's reflection in the glass. He tapped his fingertips together. She looked so hauntingly sad. He wanted to apologise profusely, but at the same time he wanted her in his arms and in his bed again.

Desire fought with honour.

Conscience fought with craving.

He watched in fascination as she moved slowly towards him, each footstep silent and wary, totally oblivious to the fact that he could see her in the glass. His heart hammered at an alarming rate, so loud that it echoed in his ears, so loud that he felt sure Rhianne must hear it too.

It seemed to fill the room, and he knew that he was in danger of forgetting his good intentions. Once he touched her again he would not be able to let her go, and they would end up sharing his bed for the rest of the night.

When she was almost upon him, when he couldn't bear to watch her any longer, he spun around. Immediately she grew as still as a statue—nothing moved except her eyes. They had turned almost navy, and deep down inside them he saw his own pain mirrored, his own need mirrored. She didn't speak, she didn't do anything except look at him.

'You know what I want from you?' he asked, his voice harsher than he'd intended.

Rhianne nodded, the movement so slight that he almost missed it.

'You also know I'm not offering you anything permanent? Once the business is safe you'll be free to go your own way. To find yourself a man to love. To settle down and have children.' Why did these words hurt when Rhianne meant nothing to him?

Except that she did. She meant more to him than he dared admit. But she was doing him a favour, that was all. She would be well rewarded.

She had also been a virgin, prompted his conscience.

Zarek cringed. He needed no reminding of what he had done. But what was done couldn't be undone, and if Rhianne was willing to share his bed for the duration of their marriage then he would be a fool to deny himself the pleasure.

'I knew what I was taking on when I agreed to marry you,' said Rhianne quietly.

'You didn't know that I expected you to be my lover.'

'Well, no,' she agreed, 'but having done so once it would be cruel of me to deny you the pleasure again.'

'Even though I've taken what has to be a woman's most important virtue?'

Rhianne nodded. 'I guess the right man never came along.'

Zarek frowned, alarm bells ringing. 'And you're saying that I'm the right man?'

'You touched the right button, Zarek, that is all.' Rhianne knew that she dared not let him see how she truly felt. Not when it was the last thing in the world that he wanted. He was a normal, healthy male who needed a woman in his bed. Not a woman to love, to keep by his side for the rest of his life, but someone to feed his natural hunger.

'You set me alive,' she said now. 'No other man's ever done that. You've shown me how much pleasure there is in making love. I don't regret saving myself all these years, but neither do I regret letting you take my virginity.'

Throwing caution to the wind, Rhianne flung herself at him. 'I want to make love again, Zarek, and again and again.' She lifted her mouth up to his, and with a groan he gathered her to him.

The rest of the night passed in a blur of lovemaking and sleeping, one became entwined with the other, and when Rhianne finally opened her eyes to bright blue skies and an empty bed beside her all she did was smile satisfyingly and curl up again.

But not for long. Wide awake now, she flung back the covers and walked out to the terrace, stretching her arms up high and appreciating the warmth of the sun on her naked body. It felt good to be alive.

She didn't hear Zarek return; she knew nothing until she felt his arms around her slender waist, holding her against his hard body which was again burning with need. His hands moved to cup her breasts, and she sank her head back on his shoulder.

'How are you this morning, Rhianne *mou*?'

His voice was thickly accented, the Greek in him coming to the fore. It was also incredibly sexy, and she twisted in his arms and raised her lips up to his. 'I feel wonderful,' she said. 'I'd go so far as to say that I've never felt like this in my whole life.'

Zarek groaned and kissed her hard and long. 'Breakfast is ready if you're hungry.'

'I'm hungry for you,' she murmured, gyrating her hips against him, exulting when she felt his immediate arousal. Heaven help her, but she wanted him again, now, urgently. As if she hadn't had enough of him during the night! It was as though once she'd discovered the potential in lovemaking she couldn't get enough of it.

'*Agapi mou*,' he said softly, 'there isn't time for this. Breakfast awaits us in the courtyard and you need to shower. I'll see you there.' He disentangled himself from her embrace, and Rhianne pulled a sad face.

'We could shower together.'

'Don't tempt me,' he groaned. 'I've already showered and I need to phone the hospital.'

'I thought your father looked remarkably well yesterday,' said Rhianne. So well, in fact, that she feared he would surprise them all and live for ever. And the longer their marriage lasted the harder it was going to be to walk away when he had no further use for her. Just one night spent in Zarek's bed had taught her that she never wanted to let him go.

'That is the trouble; he can look a picture of health when indeed he is suffering. And you'll be wanting to see your mother again this morning, of course.'

In consideration that it had been their first night as man and wife, her mother had stayed at Zarek's family home. His mother, of course, had been pleased to have company because Christos and his wife had declined her invitation, declaring that they needed to get back home.

'How long is she staying?'

Rhianne had no idea. 'I don't think she's in any particular rush. But won't your parents expect us to go away on honeymoon?' she asked hesitantly, her stomach churning at the very thought of them going off somewhere on their own. Not that they weren't alone here, but there was always his family to be considered.

'Not with my father so ill. I've told my mother that we're putting it on hold; she understands. Are you disappointed, Rhianne?'

His voice was deep and gruff, and he looked so deeply into her eyes, as if trying to see right into her mind, that Rhianne shook her head quickly. 'Of course not. Like you said last night, ours isn't a proper marriage. A honeymoon would be farcical.'

'Precisely,' he said, his voice taking on an odd inflection as he swung quickly away and left the room.

He wanted her body but he didn't want her, thought Rhianne as she hurried along to her own room to shower and dress. It was a disturbing thought, but there was nothing she could do except make the most of the situation. Zarek was unashamedly using her—and she was unashamedly letting him! That was all there was to it.

Breakfast consisted of coffee and *koulouraki*—delicious biscuits, some studded with nuts and raisins, others flavored with cinnamon, cloves and nutmeg. Zarek didn't seem hungry, and neither was she if the truth were known, delicious though the biscuits were.

He seemed to be brooding over something. 'Is your father worse?' she asked softly, that being the only reason she could think of for his mood. 'Was yesterday too much for him?'

He looked at her as if she were a stranger before shaking his head. 'I'm sorry. What did you say?'

'I was asking about your father.'

'Oh, yes. He's very tired this morning, but according to the nurse he's in good spirits.'

Because he knew that the company was now going to fall into the right hands, thought Rhianne. His father had told her time and time again yesterday how happy he was that Zarek was finally getting married, unaware that it was a plot they'd conceived to save the business. If he ever found out that his son felt no love for her, and that their marriage would be dissolved as soon as he died, it would be enough to kill him off far earlier than anyone anticipated.

'So what's on your mind?' she asked. 'Are you still beating yourself up for taking my—'

'No!' He said it with such vehemence that Rhianne knew he was lying. But she also knew that it would be fatal to question him further. If Zarek had demons he had to deal with them himself.

From her own personal point of view she wasn't at all sorry for what they had done. Zarek had taught her so much about her body and the way it could react that she wanted to skip and sing and tell the whole world about it.

'I'd like to go and see my mother,' she said. 'Find out what her plans are.'

'Naturally. I will drop you off there on my way to the hospital.'

In the end there was no need. They had just finished breakfast when a taxi arrived. Her mother looked radiant. 'I've just had a phone call from David. He's apologised profusely for letting me down. He's promised it won't happen again. He says it was the biggest mistake of his life. I'm flying home today; I hope you don't mind.'

Rhianne hugged her tightly. Her mother's happiness meant a lot to her. 'Not at all. I've always thought he was the right man for you.'

After her mother left, saying she already had a flight booked, Rhianne went in search of Zarek, only to discover that he had already left for the hospital.

She sat down, feeling deflated. He could have told her. Why hadn't he? Why had he slipped away so silently? His mood this morning was an enigma. Whereas she had been full of the joys of life, he had retreated into himself.

Now she was bored. There was nothing for her to do. She was stuck here without a car or companionship. Even his housekeeper had disappeared. She resented this place now. It was undeniably beautiful, but it was not somewhere to be alone. Especially the day after her wedding!

On an impulse she decided to jump into Zarek's Jacuzzi. Would their night of passion be a one-off, she asked herself as she switched on the tub and climbed into the pulsing water. Or would he want her to share his bed every night from now on?

Her eyes were closed when she heard the sound, and when she snapped them open it was to see Zarek standing in front of her, stark naked, his clothes on the floor at his feet.

'Were you waiting for me?' he asked, stepping into the hot tub as casually as if he was sharing a car with her.

'I had nothing else to do,' she claimed, determined not to give him the privilege of seeing how her heart leapt at the sight of him, how it thudded in her breast as though it wanted to escape and hook up with his.

'Where is your mother?'

'She left shortly after you.'

'In that case, I'm sorry for leaving you. I thought she would want to spend time with you.'

'She's going back to David. They're making up. I hope it lasts this time. Your parents are a good example of true love; I admire them. I would like to think that—' Rhianne stopped, suddenly realising what she'd been going to say.

Zarek nodded slowly. 'Let us hope that one day you too will meet the right man.'

But I already have, don't you know that? she questioned silently. She wanted no one else. She was truly convinced that no one in the whole world could make her feel the way that Zarek did. She was consumed by an unbelievable passion whenever he was near.

Like now!

She wanted to inch closer to him, she wanted his arms around her; she wanted his kisses; more than anything, she wanted to taste his mouth, his skin. Even thinking about it drew a response deep down in her stomach, and she was glad he could not see her wriggling on the narrow seat. The force of the jets hid the tremors that ran through her, but as well as hiding they intensified her feelings.

Zarek, on the other hand, sat there looking as cool as if they were sitting in church. He gave nothing away. He'd got her now, thought Rhianne miserably. He'd married and bedded her and had her where he wanted her. He didn't have to try any more; he knew that she would remain loyal until such time as the business fell into his hands.

Quite how it happened Rhianne didn't know, but when Zarek's thigh unexpectedly touched hers she pulled back sharply. She dared not let him touch her because there was no way she could hold back on the hunger that filled every pulsing inch of her.

Zarek knew that his fears were confirmed. Rhianne had done her duty by him, but now that she'd had time to think about it she didn't want him to even touch her any more. It was hard to believe this after last night. Had it all been an act? Had she forced herself to respond to him?

No, it had been real, he was sure of that. But in the time they'd been apart she'd come to her senses and realised that giving herself to him so wildly and innocently could have far-reaching consequences.

He could understand her feelings because hadn't he been cross with himself this morning? Yet she had been the one who had come begging for more, and he'd have had to be a very strong man indeed to turn her away. Their lovemaking had been wild and exciting, in fact he would dare go so far as to say that he'd never met a woman who reacted so wonderfully, who seemed to know instinctively what he wanted her to do. For a virgin she'd been dynamite.

But he most certainly couldn't sit here and not touch her. 'It's time I took you on another tour of the island,' he said decisively, getting to his feet. 'You've seen very little of it so far.'

Rhianne gulped at the sight of his nakedness so near to her face. Her awareness trebled in microseconds, shooting tremors through every cell and causing her whole body to set on fire. She didn't want a tour, she wanted to stay here and make love.

But Zarek's face was stern; she really had no option.

She waited until he had moved through to his bedroom before she stepped out of the tub, then realised that she didn't have a towel or a robe. All she could do was pretend that it did not bother her. She stood tall and proud, her chin high, her eyes straight ahead as she walked past him. It was not until she reached the door that he called her name. Rhianne halted but did not turn.

'Rhianne,' he said again softly.

She turned her head.

'Where are you going?'

'To get dressed.'

'You look stunning as you are.'

'If we're to go out, then—' She got no further.

With a deep guttural growl Zarek closed the space between them. 'You tempt me too hard. I told myself I wouldn't take advantage of you again. But then you parade in front of me as naked as the day you were born. What is a man supposed to do?'

'Close his eyes,' said Rhianne, feeling her breath begin to come in short bursts. Zarek had pulled on a pair of boxers and therefore had the advantage. Heat spread through her with amazing speed, starting at the very core of her before reaching its long tentacles to reach every cell in her body.

'Impossible,' he declared. 'And since you're my wife I think I have every right to feast my eyes on you. Turn around, Rhianne.'

Slowly she did as he asked, trying to ignore the butterflies in her stomach, trying to keep still as he took in the way her nipples stood proud and erect—and ready. The way little goose bumps rose all over her skin despite the heat. The way she kept her chin high and her eyes on his.

Not by the merest flinch was she going to let him see that she was seriously aroused. There were some things she could do nothing about, but what was happening inside her—blood racing madly through her veins, pulses working overtime, her mouth drying up—these things she could hide.

But not for long!

Enough was enough. The way his sensational golden-brown eyes appraised every inch of her body sent her senses spinning into space, and with her eyes now locked into his, she sashayed her way towards him. She couldn't help herself; everything seemed to be happening of its own accord.

Zarek's groan was deeper than she'd ever heard it. Their ride out was forgotten. They tumbled onto the bed, and where Zarek's eyes had roved, kisses now peppered her skin. Kissing and sucking, nipping and grazing. Her whole world felt as though it had fallen off its orbit. Where his mouth touched, her skin burned, her head rocking from side to side in an attempt to deny herself such pleasure. It was impossible.

'Zarek…'

'Rhianne?' For a fraction of a second his eyes met hers, seeing her torment, delighting in it. He covered her mouth with his, his tongue urgent, seeking, touching, tormenting, creating a fresh stream of emotions that were almost too much to bear. Then it was off again on another exploration. There was not one inch of her body that he did not investigate, did not taste, did not set on fire, but when Rhianne attempted to turn the tables, when she wanted to touch and explore and kiss him he was having none of it.

Instead, he spread her legs and lowered himself over her, his eyes never leaving hers. The only sound that could be heard was their heavy breathing—and the telephone!

Rhianne wanted him to ignore it. She was fast approaching the point of no return. He couldn't leave her like this.

Zarek swore loudly, but he nevertheless reached out for his phone where it sat on the bedside table. In seconds he was on his feet.

'I'm needed at the hospital,' he said bluntly.

CHAPTER THIRTEEN

ZAREK'S heart and mind were in turmoil as he drove to the hospital. Rhianne had begged to come with him, but she'd already driven him half crazy; he needed time alone to clear his head.

And the news wasn't good when he got there. His mother was in tears, and his father was critical. He telephoned Rhianne to tell her that he was staying for as long as his mother needed him—and then during the night his father passed away.

Although they had known it was coming, his mother was inconsolable. Zarek took her home and sent a car to fetch Rhianne. His brother arrived as well, and Zarek was annoyed that he hadn't even made it to the hospital. He kept the peace, though, for his mother's sake, and in the days that followed there was nothing but sadness in the Diakos villa.

Rhianne helped wherever she could and was invited to stay in the room when the lawyer came to the house to read the will. As Zarek had told her, the business would now fall into his hands.

'So what do I get out of it?' asked a very cross Christos. 'This is ridiculous; it should be shared between us.'

'Have you ever had anything to do with it?' asked Zarek coldly.

'Well, no, but—'

'Your father's left you a considerable sum of money,' said the lawyer.

'And you'll get this house when I die,' explained his mother.

But Christos still felt that the biggest share of his father's estate was going to Zarek, and he didn't bother to hide his jealous anger.

A few days later, when his mother announced that she was going to stay with her sister for a while, Rhianne and Zarek returned to the villa.

By this time Rhianne was absolutely convinced that she had now served her purpose. Not once during the time they'd spent at his parents' house had Zarek made love to her. He'd not even kissed her. He'd lain by her side in bed, and although she knew that sometimes he wasn't asleep, he hadn't spoken, or touched her even.

He was upset that his father was gone, and she would have liked to comfort him, but unless he turned to her she did not feel it was something she could do. He was locked in his own world of grief in which she had no part to play. If it had been a real marriage he might have turned to her for comfort, but as things were…

Sadness enveloped her. She had made the mistake of falling in love with Zarek. She hadn't realised quite how deeply until this moment, and it broke her heart to think that any day soon he would tell her that she was no longer needed.

'What are your plans now?' she asked, as they sat outside after dinner. The air was heavy with the scent of honeysuckle, a dog barked and another answered, there was the usual distant bray of a donkey, but there was total silence between them.

'I'm going back to England,' he announced. 'For a while, at least. There's no point in me staying here while my mother's away.'

And how about me, she wanted to ask. Will I be returning to your apartment with you, or will you give me a lump sum of money and tell me that I'm on my own now? It was what he had promised her. He had no other obligations. As far as he was concerned she had done what he'd asked. Otherwise why was he leaving her severely alone?

A tear trickled down her cheek, and Rhianne jumped up, intending to go to her room, surprised when Zarek reached out and grabbed her arm. 'Stay with me. I want— Rhianne, you're crying! What is wrong?'

'A weak moment,' she answered, with a wry twist to her lips. 'It's been a sad few days.'

Zarek nodded. 'My father was my best friend; I shall miss him.'

'Of course you will,' she said softly. 'At least you made him a happy man towards the end.'

'But I married you for mercenary reasons. I wasn't being fair on you, Rhianne. Naturally, I will—'

'Pay me for my services?' She lifted her chin and smiled. No way was she going to let him see how upset she was. 'Thank me for a job well done? It was my pleasure, Zarek, but I'm looking forward now to a new life of my own. I might even move away from London. Make a start somewhere else.'

Zarek's grip on her arm tightened, and he drew her

towards him. 'You don't have to do this, Rhianne. We can work something out. I don't want you to—'

'It's not a matter of what you want any longer, Zarek, it's what I want.' She kept her voice terse and allowed herself to look straight into his eyes, then wished she hadn't when she felt the familiar lurching of her senses.

But she was no longer his, not in the true sense of the word, and she wished now that she had never let him make love to her because the end of their marriage could have come so much more quickly with an annulment.

'And what do you want, Rhianne?' he asked quietly.

'Didn't you hear me, Zarek? I want a life of my own.'

A shield came down in front of his eyes. They were impassive now, and there was no expression in his voice when he spoke. 'So be it. I shall be sorry to let you go, but…'

Sorry to let her go! Because she was good in bed? Because she was an excellent secretary? But not because he loved her! Which was what she wanted most.

He enjoyed making love to her, but he was not in love with her. It was a bittersweet thought. With Zarek at her side for the rest of her life she could have climbed mountains. He was a strong, capable man, caring as well as mercenary, and he would have always been there for her.

Now she had a future to face on her own because it was doubtful she would ever find anyone else to fill his shoes. He had taken her heart and made it his own, and when she walked away from him she would be leaving it behind.

She suddenly realised that he had let go of her arm. She was simply standing there, looking at him, imprinting every tiny detail of his face into her memory so that she could take it out occasionally and think about what might have been.

'But what?' she enquired, suddenly remembering that he had tailed off mid-sentence.

'The ultimate decision is yours; that's what I was going to say. It's a woman's prerogative to change her mind.'

'I shan't,' she declared firmly.

'Then we'll fly home tomorrow. You'll stay with me, of course, until you find a place of your own, which I shall buy for you, naturally. I'll also see to it that there are sufficient funds in your bank account to—'

'*Stop!*' Rhianne held up hand. 'I don't want all of this, just enough to tide me over until I find another job and somewhere to rent.'

'A promise is a promise, Rhianne.'

'And promises are made to be broken.'

'Not by me. You gave up your life for me, Rhianne. You'll never know how much I appreciate it. And although it was for a shorter time than I expected, I shall honour my word. And that is final.'

So let him, she thought, Let him waste his money on her. It would actually be a small price to pay when she had given him something that she had prized for so long.

She would never feel the same again as far as making love was concerned. No other man would ever make her fly with the stars or ride on the moon. She had discovered secrets about herself that she could have never guessed. Precious secrets. Precious memories.

'If that is your wish, Zarek. I'm going to bed now. Goodnight.'

'Goodnight, Rhianne. Sleep well.'

Zarek found it hard to believe that Rhianne wanted to leave him so soon. He had thought, mistakenly it would appear, that Rhianne had begun to feel something for him. Would she have given herself to him so willingly otherwise?

How could he have got it so wrong?

He had even begun to think that she was falling in love with him. How stupid was that? All she'd felt was the excitement of making love. He had taught her how to appreciate her body, and she had used it to full advantage.

He had always known that their deal would end one day; what he hadn't counted on was that he would actually fall in love with Rhianne in the process. He didn't want to let her go—*ever*. But he was faced with the fact that Rhianne didn't return his love.

It was with an aching heart that he let her go. What he really wanted to do was follow her up to her room and throw caution to the winds. He wanted to make love to her so fiercely that it would drown out all his unhappy thoughts. He wanted to lose himself in her body and—

Zarek suddenly realised that he was thinking of himself again. His needs, his unhappiness. He wasn't thinking about Rhianne. She had every right to want to walk free. It was part of their contract. And if he didn't do the right thing and let her go, he would have to live with it for the rest of his life.

Rhianne had made it very clear that she didn't love him. She had discovered the thrill of lovemaking, but it would now be the turn of some other man to win her heart and enjoy everything that he had taught her.

Anger filled Zarek now. Had taking over the family business really been worth forcing Rhianne to marry him? What had he been thinking? How brainless was he? His fingers curled and uncurled, and every breath he took filled him with even more fury.

In the end he tore off his clothes and dived into the pool, swimming length after length after length until he could physically do no more. He collapsed onto one of the canvas loungers and remained there until the first fingers of dawn appeared in the sky, when he forced himself up to his room to shower and dress.

By this time his mind had cleared. He knew exactly what he had to do.

During the flight home Rhianne buried her head in a book, though she didn't read a single word. The letters danced before her eyes like gnats on a hot summer night. Zarek had rescued her out of a desperate situation, but now she was on her own. She had to find somewhere to live and a job to pay for it. Although Zarek had insisted that he would provide her with a home, she was not counting on it.

This morning he had barely spoken. His lips were tight and grim, and he looked as though he hadn't been to sleep. Which could be because of his father, or it might be because he was now faced with the problem of house-hunting on her behalf. Not that he would do it personally; any one of his minions could take on the job. It was something he might ask his secretary to do—except that she was his temporary secretary. In all the excitement she had forgotten. Would he expect her to continue working for him? And if so how difficult would that be?

Endless thoughts chased through her mind, and she was glad when the plane touched down. They were met by his chauffeur and taken straight to Zarek's penthouse.

There was no escape here either. The big blue skies of Greece were replaced by leaden grey ones. And although the apartment was sumptuous, with plenty of space and its own terrace garden, it felt like a prison. There was no aquamarine sea to look out over. No outdoor pool to laze away the days by. Whereas once she had felt intoxicated by it all, now she was anxious to get away.

'I'm going to the office,' Zarek told her, still with no smile on his face. Nothing but a frown tugging his brows together and no expression at all in his handsome dark eyes.

'Do you need me?' she asked quickly.

His brows rose questioningly. 'If you feel up to it, you can start work again tomorrow,' he answered, with a quick shake of his head. 'For now I want you to relax. The last few days can't have been easy for you either.'

You'll never know how hard they've been, Rhianne thought. Hiding the love she felt for this man was the hardest thing she'd ever had to do.

But once he'd gone, and the apartment was empty, Rhianne began to wish that she'd insisted on joining him. There was nothing to do. She could go window shopping. Or a walk in Hyde Park. But neither of these options appealed.

She sat down with the same book that she'd tried to read on the plane, but ten minutes later she still hadn't turned a page. She watched a butterfly dancing in the breeze. She heard the drone of a plane high overhead. Then her cell phone rang.

Her first thought was that it was Zarek—until she realised that he would use the house phone if he needed to speak to her. Then she recognised Annie's number. The first time her so-called friend had called since the day Rhianne had found her in the arms of her fiancé. For a few seconds she was tempted not to answer. Annie was the cause of everything that had happened to her. But there were things that needed to be said.

'Rhianne,' said Annie at once. 'Where have you been? I've been trying to get in touch with you for ages.'

'So that you can apologise? Tell me that it was a mistake? That you'll never do it again? Forgive me, Annie, for not wanting to listen. I thought you were my best friend. I thought—'

'Rhianne,' interrupted Annie. 'I admit I made the biggest mistake of my life. But it wasn't all my fault. Angus practically forced himself on me. And I've always fancied him, as you know. He told me that you two had fallen out and—'

'He was lying,' cut in Rhianne fiercely. 'I don't really wish to continue this conversation, Annie. I have a new life now—and you're not a part of it.'

Her thumb hovered, preparing to cut the call short, and as though Annie knew what was happening she cried, 'No, wait! You have to accept my apology. I didn't set out to hurt you. I had to go away, and when I got back you'd disappeared off the face of the earth. Your phone was never switched on and no one knew where you were.'

'Actually,' said Rhianne, 'I was getting married, to the most amazing man. So if you see Angus again you can tell him that.' And this time she did end the call. She also switched off her phone.

Zarek arrived home in the middle of the afternoon. Rhianne wasn't expecting him until much later, and her heart went into spasm at the sight of him. In his dark, exquisitely tailored suit and white shirt he looked very much the businessman again—a complete contrast to the casually dressed man who had won her heart in Santorini.

Whatever he wore, though, whether it was swimming trunks or his wedding suit, he was just as incredibly sexy. It oozed from his pores, and simply looking at him made her want to share his bed again.

'Has everything run smoothly in your absence?' she enquired, hoping her voice didn't give away her inner turmoil.

'Actually, yes,' he answered. 'Which proves I have good staff running my office. I've also heard that my secretary has decided not to return to work. Motherhood suits her, apparently.'

'So you'll be looking for someone else?' Rhianne wondered why the thought of no longer working for Zarek felt like a knot tightening in her belly. She had known the day would come when their paths took them different ways; indeed, she had intended it so, but she had thought there might be a winding down process.

'As a matter of fact,' he said, his eyes watchful on her face, causing further *frissons* of awareness to rush through her veins as though they were in a race all by themselves, 'I'm offering you the job. I know you were talking about moving away, but you'll never find another position as well paid. You've told me that you enjoy the work; therefore, it makes sound economical sense.'

His eyes were more gold than brown as they locked into hers, and Rhianne felt a further tortuous spiral of awareness, which she swiftly slammed back down.

'And as promised I'll find you somewhere to live— though it has to be a decent house—not a poky little apartment like the one you used to live in. In the meantime your home is here.'

Rhianne swallowed hard. 'You're more than generous,

Zarek, but it really isn't necessary.' How could she go on working and living with him while loving him at the same time? It might make economical sense, but not common sense. Not where her heart was concerned. Or her sanity. Or her feelings. It would be fatal.

'I think it is,' he said. 'There is no way that I can throw you out now and leave you to fend for yourself.'

'You make me sound like a cat,' she said, trying to make a joke of it, but aware that she failed miserably.

'I happen to love cats,' he answered, a quick, whimsical smile playing about his lips. 'But the fact remains, Rhianne, that I can never repay you enough for what you've done. The least I can do is ensure that you're both comfortable and financially sound. But it all takes time.'

'You could pay me off and I'll find my own job and somewhere to live,' she ventured, though it wasn't really what she wanted to do. But staying here with him, loving him, knowing it wasn't reciprocated, was going to be the hardest thing she had ever done.

'Rhianne, I feel totally responsible for you, and until…' his voice tailed off, a closed look crossing his face '…until such time as you have somewhere else to live, until I've seen to it that you have no money worries—or any other worries for that matter—then I insist you remain here.'

Rhianne felt sure that he had been going to say something else, but she knew better than to ask. She lifted her shoulders instead. 'You're the boss.'

Zarek wanted to be more than her boss. He wanted to be her lover, her husband and her best friend all rolled into one. He wanted to be the father of her children. He wanted to spend the rest of his life with her.

He had never felt like this about any other woman. He'd gone to work today not for the reason he'd told Rhianne, but because he'd needed to get away so that he could think. When she'd said that she wanted to move out and begin again without him, he had felt distraught.

If he didn't want to spend the rest of his life regretting letting her slip away, he had to do something about it *now*. He fought battles all the time in the boardroom. This was no different. His plan had been to take things slowly, but he was not sure there was time. Give Rhianne an excuse and she would be off.

'I thought we'd eat out this evening,' he said to her now. 'I've booked a table at—'

'If I'm working tomorrow I'd like an early night,' she said quickly, her chin jutting in that determined way he was beginning to recognise.

'We don't have to be late, Rhianne.'

'I'd still prefer to stay in,' she declared, her blue eyes challenging his now.

If they did, he wouldn't be responsible for what happened. It was safe to go out, but eating here, having a few drinks, sitting so close to her that he could smell the tempting fragrance of her body, he wasn't sure that he could handle it.

She was far too dangerous.

'You drive a hard bargain, Rhianne.'

'I don't see why you should continue to spend money on me when my job is over.'

Zarek was aghast. She was clearly determined that they had reached the end of their agreement. From now on it was pure business as far as she was concerned.

'Maybe our business deal has come to an end,' he

agreed, 'but it doesn't mean to say that we can't still be— friends.' It was not a word he wanted to use. She was his lover and his wife, and he was determined that she would stay that way. 'Tell me, Rhianne, the true reason you seem anxious to see as little of me as possible. Why you want to walk away so quickly.'

He waited a long time for her answer. In fact he thought she wasn't going to answer at all. First of all she avoided looking at him, staring out the window instead. Then she drew in a deep breath and faced him, her eyes filled with such sorrow that he couldn't help himself.

In less than a second he closed the space between them, took her into his arms and held her tightly against his chest. 'Rhianne, what is wrong?'

Her whole body trembled, and he was fearful that she was perhaps ill and hadn't told him about it. He stroked her hair, he felt the racing pulse in her temple, and he crushed her against him even harder.

Suddenly she tilted her head to look up at him, and when he saw the vulnerability in her eyes he couldn't stop himself. He lowered his head and kissed her, a long, hard kiss from which she had no escape. He didn't want her to escape. He wanted to show her how much he cared.

Rhianne returned his kiss with a passion that excited him, but when he pulled away so that he could look into her face and wonder what was happening, he saw tears. He asked her again, 'What is wrong, Rhianne?'

Rhianne knew that she had no choice but to tell Zarek the truth. If she didn't, she would go on wondering for the rest of her life whether she had made a huge mistake. It was a case of humiliation now because he didn't return her love. Or the chance of a lifetime's happiness.

She had sensed a change in Zarek since he'd returned from the office. Prior to that she'd felt there was no point in hanging around. But now he was making it clear that he didn't want her to go. Dared she hope that he'd fallen in love with her too?

Closing her eyes, not wanting to see his reaction, she said faintly, 'I'm sorry, Zarek, but I've fallen in love with you. I know you didn't want it but—'

He gave her no chance to say any more. With a deep groan Zarek's mouth crushed hers yet again in a kiss that ended with them both gasping for breath.

'Rhianne, *agapi mou*, you have no idea how happy you've just made me. I was dreading the thought of losing you.'

'You—you love me too?' she asked breathlessly, her eyes turning wide and almost navy in their surprise.

He nodded. 'With all of my heart.'

'You're not just saying that?'

'Rhianne,' he said softly, cupping her face with both hands and looking deep into her eyes. 'I've never said it to any other woman in my life. I guess I didn't believe in true love. I loved my work more. But you have given me something so rich and so beautiful that I never want to lose it. I adore you, my gorgeous wife. You're the best thing that's ever happened to me. I want to make babies with you, I want to live into my old age with you, I want to—'

'Stop!' Rhianne placed her finger over his lips. 'I need to ask you a question.'

Zarek smiled, a slow, warm smile that softened his entire face. 'Whatever you like, my darling.'

'Would you have let me go if I hadn't declared my love?' Rhianne held her breath as she waited for his answer. It was something she needed to know because if he said yes it would mean that he didn't love her as much as she loved him.

'It was my initial intention,' he admitted, with a wry twist to his lips. 'But then I realised that I couldn't do it. I could never let you go. I love you too deeply. I would have found some way of persuading you to fall in love with me—no matter how long it took.'

Rhianne gave a sigh of happy relief. 'Maybe I spoke too soon. I think I might have enjoyed the persuasion. Would it have gone something like this?' She draped her arms around his neck and pressed her soft lips against his in a kiss that took them both into a world where only happiness existed, a world where their future lay together—through thick and through thin—for ever more.

HIRED:
SASSY ASSISTANT

BY
NINA HARRINGTON

Nina Harrington grew up in rural Northumberland, England, and decided at the age of eleven that she was going to be a librarian—because then she could read *all* of the books in the public library whenever she wanted! Since then she has been a shop assistant, community pharmacist, technical writer, university lecturer, volcano walker and industrial scientist, before taking a career break to realise her dream of being a fiction writer. When she is not creating stories which make her readers smile, her hobbies are cooking, eating, enjoying good wine—and talking, for which she has had specialist training.

To Stephen. For everything.

CHAPTER ONE

IT WASN'T every day of the week that you saw a librarian carrying a package on her head that looked bigger than she was, struggling to get off a London tube train at eleven o'clock in the morning.

Especially when that librarian had sun-streaked blond corkscrew hair that fell around her shoulders in long, wavy tendrils.

As he stepped out onto the platform, Kyle Munroe glanced back to the next carriage just in time to see the librarian stretch up on tiptoes, lift the wide bag over the heads of her fellow passengers, then thrust it forward to use as a wedge through the crush of travellers rushing past her to board the train. They had little regard for anyone who might dare to get in their way.

Seconds before the train door beeped closed behind her, the blonde had to practically jump onto the platform, before snatching the package out of the jaws of the sliding doors with such force that she almost fell backwards as the tube sped away.

The librarian tried to restore her dignity by tugging the jacket of her dove-grey skirt suit a little lower, and lifting her cute, small nose a little higher, before hoisting the straps of what looked like an artist's portfolio case over her neck and shoulder. Only the bag was still dragging on the floor, so she forgot the straps and went for Plan B. This involved holding the edges of the case with her fingertips, arms at full stretch, while trying to hitch the wide strap around her neck with one shoulderblade and her chin.

After two trial steps in amazingly rickety-looking heels, she strode forward, the portfolio flapping against her chest, head high, eyes set on her goal—the escalator. Only Plan B let her down, and she was reduced to sliding, dragging and cajoling her oversized package towards the escalator.

Perhaps she was actually a schoolteacher, and any second now she would tell the unruly portfolio to go and sit in the naughty corner?

Nope—she was definitely a librarian. The only woman he had ever seen wearing that kind of dull grey skirt suit by choice had been the technical librarian at his medical school. That particular lady could dance a mean mambo, and was a world expert on parasitic diseases, but she still chose those hideous suits!

Then again, she had never, ever worn dove-grey mules below legs like the ones trying to walk ahead of him at that minute—the kind of legs that forced the first smile of the day from his lips.

So what if he was a leg man and proud of it?

This was turning out to be the high point of a journey that had started in squalor and sunshine a long way from London. Three hours across the mountains in a bone-shaking Jeep with bald tyres had been followed by a very long flight in economy class, surrounded by wonderful but exhausted screaming kids. Coming up with games and toys to amuse them had been fun—for the first couple of hours.

It had been a long day, and his body clock was starting to kick in. Perhaps it was time to show his appreciation for the lady who had finally given him something to smile about?

With his long athletic legs, and her shorter, high-heeled ones, it only took Kyle a few steps to catch up with her.

'Do you need any help with that?' he asked, trying to sound casual and non-threatening.

The librarian didn't break stride as she took a sideways glance at his six feet one of athletic hunkiness—or at least that was how the TV company liked to describe him. From the stunned look in her pale blue eyes, she had decided that he was clearly not to be trusted.

He tried to act casual by running a few fingers through his shaggy, dark brown, now mostly dust encrusted hair. Hmm. Not his best look. Perhaps he should have made the time to take a shower and change his clothes at the airport?

'I'm fine, but thank you for offering.'

Except the words were barely out of her mouth before the portfolio slid off her shoulder and Kyle had to reach forward to stop it from being trampled underfoot by the crush of passengers trying to cram onto the escalator.

As they were swept along in the rush, the librarian took a sharp intake of breath and clutched onto the handrail. Her other hand was pressed to her throat, where a red welt showed that the weight of the bag was very far from being fine.

'It's okay—I've got it,' Kyle reassured her. 'Maybe I could carry it as far as the barrier? How about that?'

'Okay, just to the barrier.'

She half turned around to face him, and he was struck by her closed-mouth smile. His medical head noticed immediately that her right eye was flecked with deeper shades of blue than the other. Whatever she saw in his face he could only guess, but the half-smile creased the corner of a wide, plump mouth set in creamy skin sprinkled with freckles over her nose and cheeks. Like cinnamon powder on whipped cream.

Freckles. Why did she have to have freckles? He almost groaned. *Doomed.*

'I see that you've flown from Delhi. That's a long flight. Been there on holiday?' she asked, her dainty head tipped slightly in the cutest, loveliest, most freckly pose.

Drat! The airline tags were still attached to his old rucksack!

'Just passing through,' he replied, trying to sound flippant, before nodding over her shoulder. 'Here we go.'

The librarian suddenly realised that they were at the top of the escalator, and whipped around so that she could step to one side and stay within touching distance of her precious package.

He took a firmer grip on what felt like a thin wooden frame—not heavy, but an awkward size and shape—and casually swept the handles over one shoulder.

'What sort of picture is this?' he asked as he fumbled for his ticket, half expecting to hear that it was some Old Master bound for restoration by learned scholars in an ancient London guild.

'Orchids. Yellow orchids, to be exact.' She paused and nodded. 'I'm sure I can manage from here. It's only a short bus ride to the South Bank. Sorry to have been such a nuisance.'

'No apology necessary.' Kyle was just about to pass the portfolio over when he paused. 'Did you say the South

Bank? That's where I'm headed. Why don't we share a cab?' He hoisted the bag a little higher. 'The bus could be a problem.'

Even though she had been the first to mention her destination, she hesitated, clearly weighing up the benefits of getting there in one piece against the danger from a scruffy potential stalker and orchid-picture thief. Kyle stared at her silence as she bit her lower lip before going for it.

'Um, okay. Yes, that would be great. Thank you. Normally I would walk along the Embankment—but not in these shoes, carrying that. And I am rather late.'

'Me too. Shall we risk it?'

That seemed to stun her for a few seconds, but with a gentle nod, the blonde climbed the steps out of the station. The crush of other pedestrians and the awkward shape of the portfolio conspired together to thwart most of Kyle's view of the spectacular legs in action on the stairs, but the little he did see was well worth the effort.

It took only minutes to clamber out into the noise and chaos of the city street. After eighteen months in the mountains he had forgotten what a physical assault on the senses it all was, and the girl in the grey suit had hailed a black cab before he'd pulled himself together.

Kyle made a point of swinging the package onto the backseat, then holding open the door for her before jumping in himself with his rucksack.

While he knew as much about London art galleries as she probably did about yaks, the name the librarian gave to their driver sounded familiar enough for him to be impressed.

As their cab took off into the traffic she collapsed back against her seat and slowly exhaled, her arm wrapped protectively around the edge of the portfolio.

'Are there a lot of career opportunities for art couriers these days?'

She looked across at him as though she had almost forgotten that he was there.

'Oh, this is only a sideline,' she replied in a matter-of-fact voice. 'My real job is in art forgery. That's where the real money is.' She leant closer and whispered, 'But I'm relying on you to keep my secret to yourself.'

'My lips are sealed. Best of luck in prison.'

The blue eyes crinkled up into a smile as she took in his filthy jacket, two-day stubble and the trousers that had last seen water two weeks earlier after an emergency Caesarean section on a riverbank.

'Passing through Delhi? That sounds like a lot of fun. Is it still warm and sunny there?' she asked in a light-hearted voice.

'Very,' he replied with a sigh. 'At this time of year they're getting ready for Diwali—the festival of lights. I'm sorry I'm missing that! It's a fantastic city. Do you know it?'

'Not personally,' she replied, then gave him a wistful smile. 'But people have told me about the wonderful colours and the atmosphere. I've always wanted to go there. Maybe one day,' she added, shrugging her shoulders. Then the blonde gestured towards his jacket with her head. 'I can see that you've spent time in the mountains. Let me guess. Have you been climbing or hiking?'

Wow. She really was observant. It was a pity that the truth was far too complicated, because ideally he would have loved to find the time to do precisely those things. But he had never got the chance.

'Not even close. What makes you think that I've been in the mountains?'

She grinned back before replying. 'I noticed that you're wearing a white Buddhist scarf, and you have Hindi graffiti scribbled on your arm.'

Kyle stared down at the plaster cast encasing his left wrist, which was completely covered with colourful messages. Um. Perhaps some of them were a bit crude.

'You can read Nepali?' he asked, with genuine admiration in his voice.

'No, but I do recognise the Hindi characters,' she held up one hand, palm forward. 'And I don't need a translation, if it's all the same to you.'

'Probably just as well. I'm Kyle, by the way.'

He reached forward with his right hand, and she glanced at it for a second before giving it a firm, quick shake with small, thin, cool fingers. His rough fingertips rasped in contact with her delicate skin. Perhaps that was why she pulled back immediately, as the cab slowed for some lights, and started scrabbling about in her messenger bag?

'I could give you my name,' she replied, 'but I am on a very important mission where secrecy is vital. That sort of personal information is strictly on a need-to-know basis. This should cover my share of the cab fare.'

Kyle looked at the pile of coins she had passed him in bewilderment, and wondered if cab fares had increased at the same rate as female sass since he had been away.

'A mission at the art gallery? Ah. Of course. The old forgery trade.' He tapped his nose twice. 'Your secret is safe. What are you running late for?'

'I have to drop this off and then make a twelve-o'clock appointment. I'm cutting it fine.' She glanced at her watch, and noticed that he was not wearing one. 'How about you,

Kyle? What are you late for? Oh, sorry—another time. This is the gallery.'

She flashed a beaming smile in his direction as the cab slowed in front of an elegant glass-fronted building. 'It's been a pleasure, and thanks again. I hope I haven't delayed you too much.'

'Wait,' Kyle replied, pushing the bag towards her. 'One question. Please? I have to know. Are you a librarian, by any chance?'

She stopped trying to drag the portfolio over her shoulder and looked at him wide-eyed for a second, before breaking into the kind of warm smile that stopped traffic and turned curly haired, blond librarians into supermodels.

'Not even close.' And with that she closed the cab door and gave him a regal wave, before striding away without looking back.

Twenty minutes later Lulu Hamilton sauntered down the wide South Bank pavement as best as she could in her godmother Emma's dove-grey mules, and revelled in the sights and smells of the crisp, late-October day.

As a beam of bright sunshine broke through the clouds she dropped her head back and closed her eyes to enjoy the moment.

Not bad, girl. Not bad at all. She had reached the gallery right on time. The job was done. It had meant sharing a taxi with a cheeky tourist with a killer smile, but for once her risky decision had paid off and she had delivered her painting in one piece.

The yellow orchid acrylic was destined for a luxury boutique in the city. The gallery was delighted, the client was thrilled, and best of all, she had been paid a bonus for delivering the piece in time for their grand opening. If she kept to a tight budget, the cheque in her pocket would see her through the first few months of art college. Her dream had just come one step closer.

She inhaled deeply, soaking in the sights and smells of the city. Ten years ago she had been a student here, before she'd left university to take care of her father after her mother was killed. She rarely came back. It was too painful to think about what could have been.

Not any longer. That was then and this was now.

For the first time in many years she was finally moving forward with her life and putting the past behind her. So what if it was a baby step, and she had a few steep hills head? Mountains, even? She was moving forward and she was doing it through her own hard work.

One thing was certain. She had forgotten how crowded the city was—and how noisy. The traffic din was worse than ever. The cacophony of mixed fragments of sound from buses, taxicabs, cars and people seemed to collide inside her brain.

Well, that was something she could control!

In one smooth, well-practised motion, her fingertips smoothed her shoulder-length hair down over her left ear and, oblivious to anyone else, she turned off the small digital hearing aid fitted behind it.

That was better. Much better.

Brightly coloured leaves in amazing shades of scarlet and russet, from the maples and London plane trees which lined the Embankment, blew against her legs in the fresh breeze from the Thames.

She loved autumn—it had always been her favourite season.

She couldn't imagine living in a tropical climate. Not

when nature put on this glorious free display for people to enjoy.

The last few months had been tough, but the painting had been finished on time and it was as good as anything she had ever done. Perhaps her friends back home in Kingsmede were right, and she should take some time out to enjoy herself for a change and smell the rosebuds?

A half-smile creased her face as she glanced at her fellow pedestrians, crowding the pavement. Most of them either had their noses pressed into the pages of a tourist guidebook, or were chatting away on cellphone headsets while keying something desperately important into a personal organiser.

With a brisk shake of her head, Lulu twirled around a cluster of teenage tourists, then swallowed down hard as her gaze fixed straight ahead on the impressive entrance to the stylish media company offices, where the book launch event was being held.

It was still a total mystery why Mike Baxter had invited her to this book launch at all. Of course she had been thrilled to hear that he had been promoted to Clinical Director at the medical foundation where her mother had worked for the last eight years of her life, but his letter had certainly been intriguing.

They had kept in contact, but this was the first time that Mike had invited her to a press conference—so that he could talk to her about an 'exciting opportunity' over lunch. Mike was one of the few people who knew about her partial hearing, and that crowded public events were not her favourite places.

After almost twenty-nine years on the planet, the words *exciting* combined with *opportunity* usually meant a lot of work for her with all the kudos going to other people. Except that Mike had made it clear that this was going to be a great way to raise money for her local hospice, where her father had spent the last few weeks of his life.

And for that she was willing to face a crowded room full of chattering people, most of whom she would not be able to hear, and questions about a woman who had been dead ten years and yet still managed to control her life.

Ruth Taylor Hamilton. Her celebrity mother. The famous pioneering surgeon.

The very last person she wanted to talk about. Ever.

Kyle Monroe stared out of the office window at the overcast sky of central London in October. It was hard to believe that only eighteen hours earlier he had been trekking through sunlit forests in the foothills of Nepal.

His eyes felt heavy, gritty, ready to close, but just as Kyle's head fell back onto the sofa cushion, Mike Baxter finished the call on his mobile phone.

'They're ready and waiting for us. Did you get any sleep at all on the flight? Eight hours, wasn't it? Nine?'

'More like twelve—and, no, not much. The flight was packed.' Kyle yawned. 'You forget what airport crowds are like. The noise. The stress. The smell.' He raised his right arm and sniffed. 'Speaking of which, is there any chance I can get a shave and a shower? I think I startled a pretty girl on the tube this morning.'

'Nope,' Mike replied. 'We're already late. Besides, you have the perfect image—the media company have been working on it. "Dedicated medic flies in straight from the clinic, still in his working clothes." Natural grunge. The press will love it.'

Then he looked more closely at something on Kyle's clothes and recoiled back. 'Are those bloodstains on your trousers?'

Kyle reached down and casually pulled up one leg of his cargo trousers, revealing a surprisingly white, muscular hairy leg. 'Ketchup. Or chilli sauce.' He nodded. 'Probably chilli sauce. The blood is on my jacket. Sorry about that, but we had to use the last of the soap powder to clean the sheets. TB clinics wash a lot of laundry.'

Mike gave a quick nod. 'No problem. Now, what's the story with your wrist?'

Kyle waggled the crusty filthy plaster cast which encased his lower left arm.

'Clean break. My own fault for sticking my arm out when I fell off a rope ladder. It was the only way across the ravine. I tried to do some sort of judo break-fall. And it worked. It broke. No problem.' He shrugged. 'The cast is coming off next week.'

'Any photographs from this ravine?' Mike asked, suddenly interested. 'They could always come in useful for the next book!'

'Next one?' Kyle laughed. 'I barely had time to write this one, Mike! Keep an online diary of your climbing and your medical life, you said. Take a few photos every now and then and post them on your blog, you said. Now look where it's got me!'

Mike lifted up his laptop computer and waved it in Kyle's direction. 'Over ten thousand hits a day. Online diaries are big business now. The income from your first book will pay for the entire Nepalese mission for the next few years. It's the best investment the foundation has ever seen!'

Mike came around to perch on the end of his desk.

'Look, Kyle, I need to talk business for a minute—so you can start groaning now. The way I see it, you're going to be out of action for at least another month. Am I right? Your wrist has not healed properly, and you need to get what's left of that chest infection out of your body.' Mike paused long enough to rub his hands along the edge of his desk in a nervous gesture. 'And then there is the real reason that I pulled you back from the mission. I know you don't want to talk about it, but from what your half-brother told me your family problems might take longer to resolve than you think.'

He was met with a shrug. 'That's not why I'm here,' Kyle replied. 'The rabies programme is behind schedule. That has to come before my personal issues. We need those vaccines, and we need them today. My job is to raise the money to make that happen.'

Mike looked hard into Kyle's face. 'Which is why I've been working with the TV company to pull together an amazing deal for your rabies project.'

Kyle sat up, his brows pulled together in concentration. 'What kind of deal? I don't know what else I can say about Nepal.'

Mike nodded. 'You're right. The film crew has already been to Nepal, and they have everything they need.' He paused and sat back. 'You might not have realised it, but you talked a lot over the past year about your very first mission. You went straight out of medical school into a war zone in Africa. I think you actually came out and stated on camera that it was a life-changing experience.'

There were a few seconds of silence before Kyle responded in a low voice, 'It *was* life-changing. For all of us.'

'That's why the producer wants to make a documentary about your first mission to Uganda. The problems you faced. How it inspired you. The film will probably be shown around March next year. If you could write a book about your diary from those days, and if it can be ready at the same time, it could be a top-seller.'

'Uganda?' Kyle breathed. 'That was ten long years ago, Mike, and I'm not sure I want to go back there. Even on paper.'

'They've offered to double your last advance to make it happen.'

There was another silence before Kyle coughed. 'Did you say double?'

Mike simply nodded. 'If you can force yourself to sit in one place long enough to finish this second book, you can be back in Nepal before the winter sets in—with enough cash to pay the drugs bill for at least the next five years, including all of the vaccines you've asked for.'

Kyle sat back and blew out hard, before shaking his head in resignation.

'You know me too well. When do they need the finished book?'

'The first draft is due in a month. But I know you like challenges,' Mike replied casually as he shrugged into his jacket.

'A month? You know what I'm like with paperwork! I haven't typed anything longer than a few paragraphs for my blog since university!'

Mike didn't even try to argue. 'We have a few suggestions on how we can help you with that—but later. Ready to rock and roll? All you have to do is enjoy the free beer, eat the snacks—and smile. Big smile. Use your charm.

Think of the vaccines your book is going to bring into that clinic of yours. Leave me to make sure the press go away happy.'

Kyle grinned back. 'Free beer? What kind of beer?'

CHAPTER TWO

'DR BAXTER should be arriving with Dr Munroe any time now, Miss Hamilton,' the excited little secretary said, almost rocking in her seat behind the wide curved reception desk.

Lulu locked her smile firmly into place before replying in a sweet voice, 'You did say the same thing forty minutes ago, Marta. Are you sure this time?'

'Dr Munroe's flight was delayed, but they are on their way.' The young girl swallowed, smoothed down her mini skirt and gazed in wonder at the stack of books on the desk. 'Isn't Dr Munroe the dreamiest? Perhaps I could persuade him to sign my book for me?'

Each chair in the stylish reception area carried a copy of a paperback book with the words *Medicine Man* in large dark letters.

But it was the stunning cover that was designed to captivate and enthral.

It was an amateur photograph of a bearded young man, in brightly coloured clothing and large dark goggles, standing in deep white snow, with high mountain peaks behind him, reflecting bright sunshine. Buddhist prayer flags fluttered in the breeze above his head against a cobalt-blue sky.

He was grinning widely for the camera, clearly full of life.

According to the press release tucked into each book, K. B. Munroe was a British doctor doing pioneering work on disease control in the High Himalaya of Nepal.

From what Lulu could see, the photograph might just as well have been from a fashion shoot for an adventure sports magazine. Only there was something extra-special in the single image that shone from the man himself. She could not see his face behind the beard and the goggles, yet his energy leapt from the photograph. A life-force so powerful it was practically hypnotic.

The photograph was clearly of some sort of strange mythical creature—because this medic was one broad-shouldered, tanned, handsome and unshaven hunk. All in all, a tousle-haired, square-jawed dream of an emergency doctor and mountaineer. Beyond rugged. Relaxed. In total control. Captured for ever in a moment. Frozen in time.

The creature in that photo could have been a film actor playing the part. Maybe that was it? Maybe the real Dr Munroe was a wizened and cynical hard nut, still tramping through the ice and snow in Nepal, and the publisher had taken the easy way out with a gorgeous action-hero actor to play the role?

She smiled to herself. Doctors like K. B. Munroe did wonderful work in hard conditions. They deserved every scrap of praise and recognition. But she knew better than most people that the reality of that life was anything but attractive. Nobody should have to make those kinds of sacrifices.

As she picked up the book and looked more closely at the heroic figure on the cover, she could not help but wonder if this man had a wife and children back home. How did *they* feel when he left them for the mountains? Not knowing if they would ever see him again?

A cold shiver ran down her spine and she almost dropped the book back onto the chair. Too many memories. Too many ghosts.

Suddenly aware that Marta was still waiting for some kind of response from her, Lulu held back on her honest opinion and managed a polite, 'Oh, yes, he certainly is something. Do you think there is time for another tea before they get here?'

'Tea? Right, sure. Rush job. Don't want to miss him,' the receptionist blurted out, and scurried off in the direction from where the previous two cups of tea had come in the forty minutes Lulu had been waiting, at about twice the speed she had before.

Lulu stood up and slipped the glossy style magazine back onto the flimsy black-and-red Japanese lacquer table beside a massive scarlet leather sofa.

Everything in the reception area shouted expensive, stylish—and in Lulu's eyes would be as long-lasting as the display of tall living white orchids which had been placed in the best position to catch the October blast from the Thames that blew in every time the doors slid open on the London street. Disaster!

She sauntered over as gracefully as she could in her borrowed shoes and fitted skirt, and checked the blossoms and leaves of the stunning blooms. If only the orchids in her conservatory back in Kingsmede were as lovely as these. They would look wonderful painted in a blue-and-white Delft porcelain bowl. Or perhaps against a backdrop of delicate foliage and lavender?

Lulu was so engrossed that she jumped back in surprise as she was suddenly jolted into the real world when the main street door was flung wide-open, sending it crashing against a chair. She turned back just in time to see a tall, gangly bundle of momentum and a flash of filthy stained khaki stride away from her towards the reception desk.

He had come 'In' through the 'Out' door.

A dark green, stained and heavy-looking military rucksack missed a stunned media company executive in a suit by inches as it swung out from one shoulder to the other. Judging from his back view, Lulu guessed this was a journalist who had just been involved in a street fight.

His stride was confident, powerful and energetic. Strong. Someone who knew exactly what he was doing and where he was going in life.

He had probably not even noticed her existence. Typical. Nothing new there.

She was glad when he pushed his way past the red sofa and dropped his heavy bag before the desk.

After looking from side to side a couple of times, he half turned, caught sight of her, and turned on a killer smile.

She had seen his back view a few minutes earlier.

Now Lulu got the full glory. And her mouth dropped open in surprise.

This man smiling across at her was the same tourist who had helped to carry her picture and shared her black cab not two hours earlier.

No doubt about it.

It was the crown prince of grunge.

As he strolled towards her, slowly this time, the confident swagger of his hips completing his hypnotic charm, Lulu could not look away from his face. In an instant she made the connection with the cover image on the book next to her.

He was *Medicine Man*.

K. B. Munroe. Kyle Munroe.

In one smooth movement she lifted her head, straightened her back and inhaled a fortifying breath. So what if she had always been attracted to the athletic type of man? She could handle this.

The adrenaline junkie sidled up to her with his best charm offensive. Lulu decided to take the initiative this time and stretched out her right hand. 'Hello, again. This is a pleasant surprise.'

Kyle stepped closer, but instead of releasing her fingers he raised the back of her hand to his lips, trying to avoid his sharp stubbly chin.

'The pleasure is all mine. It would seem that fate has had the good taste to put us in the same place at the same time. I had no idea that TV companies needed librarians.'

He slowly turned his head from side to side, looking around the echoing reception area before whispering, 'Or specialist art dealers...' And he gave her the kind of twinkly-eyed smile guaranteed to make any girl's heart beat a little faster.

And it was certainly effective! Lulu dragged her eyes away from his face as she slowly retrieved her fingers and casually picked up one of the books from the coffee table before waving it in his direction. 'Well, I wouldn't know about that. Seeing as I'm not a librarian. Dr Munroe, I presume?'

He shrugged. 'That's me. Did you make it to the gallery in time?' Then he leant closer. 'I don't know how undercover art forgers work, but if you have any influence around here at all, I shall have to throw myself on your mercy. If you can point me in the direction of a cold beer, I shall be your slave for a week.'

'Only a week?' Then her smile widened. 'I was right on time, so thanks for your help. You'll find the buffet and an open bar just through there—although...' She glanced down at her watch. 'You are running a little late. The presentation was due to start ten minutes ago.'

'No problem at all. You would be amazed at what I can achieve in ten minutes. Now, please allow me to do something to show my gratitude.'

He moved closer and leant his head towards her, and for a horrible, exciting, heart-thumping moment she thought he might kiss her. But as she leant back he simply laughed and gestured to the paperback with his photo on the cover, which she was still clutching to her side.

'Would you like me to sign your book for you?'

Lulu grinned back in relief, and possibly a touch of regret. He was good at this.

'Yes, please. If you could address it to my friend, Marta, that would be great.'

'No problem at all. I hope your *friend* likes it. Marta.'

Kyle squiggled a signature, then raised his eyebrows a few times before giving her another very saucy wink and a dazzling flash of white teeth, sweeping up his rucksack and striding over to the side entrance—just as Marta practically jogged up to the reception desk, splattering tea on the glossy black floor tiles before turning around to glare at Lulu in disgust.

Lulu was just about to explain when Marta stepped away to one side. 'Dr Baxter. You are running terribly late. Miss Hamilton has been waiting for ages!'

The next thing Lulu knew she was being crushed into a hug by a huge bear of a man with grey hair and wearing a smart business suit.

'Lulu—I am so sorry. But the Delhi flight was almost two hours late and the PR crew have tried to drink the bar dry. Let's get the launch out of the way so we can talk properly. Oh. Is that for me? Thanks, Marta. You're a star.'

And in one action Mike swallowed down what was left of Lulu's cup of tea, grabbed her arm, and almost dragged her towards the conference room, talking fast enough to stop her getting a word in edgeways. 'You look amazing, by the way. How have you been keeping?'

Five minutes of blurred, frantic activity later, Lulu was sitting in the second row in the conference room, watching Mike Baxter arrange his notes on the lectern. She was not entirely sure how she had come to be sitting there, in a crush of photographers, media company executives and journalists who all seemed to be talking non-stop.

She was starting to regret turning her hearing aid back on.

Mike waited patiently for the chatter and clatter to subside, before speaking into the microphone.

'Ladies and gentlemen. If you could take your seats? Thank you. My name is Mike Baxter, and it is my pleasure to welcome you all here today in my capacity as Medical Director of the Medical Foundation for Humanitarian Aid.'

He paused as the press settled into their chairs. 'As some of you will know, twelve months ago the foundation was asked by one of the largest television and multimedia companies in the western world to nominate three unique medical professionals working in hazardous conditions around the world who would be willing to be filmed as part of a TV series. Each mission would receive a charitable donation worth fifty thousand pounds. When that film was broadcast, earlier in the year, it soon became clear that one doctor in particular had touched the hearts of the viewers. Dr Kyle Munroe.'

Mike paused and looked around the room, making sure that he had the full attention of the audience before making his announcement.

'Ladies and gentlemen. What happened next has surprised us all. The programme made a bestseller of *Medicine Man* by Kyle Munroe. This book began as an online diary created during his first year spent working in the high Himalaya of Nepal. The diary is absolutely gripping from beginning to end, and has never been out of the top-ten list. I am pleased to announce that today marks publication of the paperback edition of the book, with a new introduction by the author.'

Mike Baxter glanced to someone at the back of the hall and nodded.

'I am delighted to tell you that the man himself has literally just got off a plane from Delhi, after travelling by foot, Jeep, and two international flights to be with us today. Ladies and gentlemen—Dr Kyle Balfour Munroe!'

The sandwich-chomping journo sitting in front of her, and everyone else around her, stood up to applaud, blocking Lulu's view and forcing her to step out into the side aisle just as Kyle stepped onto the podium from her side of the room. He was holding a pint glass of beer in his right hand, while trying to salute Mike with his plaster cast.

Only now he was wearing spectacles with thin metal rims, which instantly turned him into a younger and jaw-droppingly handsome version of Indiana Jones.

It might be sneaky, but it certainly was effective, and Lulu could not take her eyes from Kyle's face as he casually passed the beer glass to Mike Baxter so that he could raise up a copy of the paperback with his good right hand.

Turning to the microphone, Kyle cracked a beaming smile, displaying brilliant white teeth against his deeply tanned skin. She could see the corners of his mouth wrinkle up with the grin, the tiny pale lines radiating out from his full lips. The thin spectacles seemed to highlight his deep chocolate caramel hair and hazel green eyes. The kind of caramel a girl could savour and linger over for as long as possible, desperate to prolong the delicious pleasure.

Every eye in the room was focused on him long before he spoke.

'I am delighted to be here today to launch the new edition of *Medicine Man*. Every single person who bought the book has already made a huge difference to the lives of the people I work with on a daily basis. People who depend on you for the health of themselves and their families. On their behalf, I thank you all.'

And then he did it. He used the knuckle of his forefinger to just touch the end of his nose and push his spectacles higher. As though to conceal a glistening tear.

As the audience took a breath, Lulu stretched her head up over the reporter's heads as the scruffy Adonis stuffed the book casually into the front pocket of his cargo pants, retrieved his beer with a nod of thanks, and raised the glass to salute the rows of press and photographers, his face barely visible behind the flashguns and microphones.

Then he was swallowed up in the crush.

Mike paused for a few minutes for photographs, before

valiantly making his way through the rugby scrum of press already six deep around the podium, each desperate to capture the human interest cover story for the next day. A few seconds later he came to stand next to Lulu. He didn't even try to lower his voice as they stood watching the scene.

'I know he's a bit rough around the edges, but that boy has raised more money for the foundation in the last twelve months than in the previous five years put together. We want Kyle to write a second book, about the time he spent with your mother in Uganda, and the foundation needs *you* to help him do that. What do you say?'

'Mike Baxter, you have an awful lot of explaining to do. And I think you had better start right now. You *know* how I feel about that subject. Please tell me why I shouldn't get the next train back to Kingsmede right now?'

'Well, I might do if you stopped pacing for five minutes. Did you read the dedication in Kyle's book?'

Lulu turned to face her mother's old friend and planted her hands on her hips before giving him a disbelieving look. 'That would be difficult, since I had never even heard of Kyle Munroe until today.'

Mike sighed and flicked to a specific page before passing the paperback over to her.

'Perhaps you should finally get around to buying a television some time soon? Anyhow, you might want to see this before we go any further.'

Lulu breathed out in exasperation and glared at him before accepting the open book and glancing down at the page.

This diary is humbly dedicated to Dr Ruth Taylor Hamilton, who started me on this crazy journey in the

first place. The sacrifice and untimely death of this
remarkable surgeon taught me what it means to be
an emergency medic. Maybe one day I can come
close to being that good. Thank you, Stitch. I owe you
one.

Her balloon of annoyance popped into ragged shreds of
flimsy plastic. Lulu sat down on the hard chair in the now-
empty conference room and read it again. 'Oh.'

As she passed the book back to Mike, she felt sure that
the thundering of her heart was loud enough for him to
hear.

When she did force the air back into her frozen lungs,
she saw that his eyes were still looking into her face. Intense.

Unlike the squeaky voice that emerged when she did try
to speak through a bone-dry throat. 'Did they work together?'

'Uganda.'

She closed her eyes and tried to block out the horror of
what that experience must have been like. 'Her last mission.'

'There's more. Kyle needs every penny we can raise to
fund the infectious disease campaign. The TV company
want to film a documentary about the Uganda mission and
publish Kyle's diaries from that time. He needs help to
make that happen.'

Lulu stood up and paced across to the podium in silence,
before turning back to face her mother's friend. 'You don't
need me! You need a professional editor.'

He nodded. 'Yes, I could hire someone. But they
couldn't help Kyle like you can.'

There was something in his voice which caught Lulu's attention. 'What do you mean, like I can?'

'Do you remember the last time I came to Kingsmede? When Tom was still at home?'

'Of course.' She smiled back. 'Dad loved seeing you.'

'Tom made a point of showing me the work you had both done to organise the boxes of your mother's personal items we shipped back from Africa. You did a great job with sorting that lot out. I know he was proud of you for sticking with it and seeing it through. It must have been hard.'

Lulu swallowed down hard. 'Very. Where are you going with this, Mike?'

He lifted his head and looked her straight in the eyes.

'Kyle needs the letters and diaries your mother wrote from Uganda to help him write his book.'

Her face paled, and she had opened her mouth to tell him precisely what he could do with that idea when he raised one hand, palm up.

'Before you say no, please let me explain.'

Mike dropped his hands to his knees and spoke in a low voice.

'Kyle has already mentioned in interviews that Ruth Taylor Hamilton was the reason he got into emergency medicine. The media company have been inundated with requests for more information about this mysterious person, and they came to me.'

He waved his arms dramatically in the air while shrugging his shoulders. 'Things took off from there. I mentioned that your dad had collected together Ruth's letters and diaries from her time in Uganda, and the next thing I knew the publishing director wanted to know how soon they could have Kyle's manuscript about the time he spent in Africa! It's crazy, but they are serious. They want him to talk about Ruth and her work and how it inspired him.'

Lulu sucked in a breath and swallowed down the wave of nausea that swept through her. 'What? Not now!'

'Why not now? This is the perfect time! Kyle has already done the promotion work in advance! You couldn't ask for better publicity.'

'I think you might be forgetting something. My father and I didn't finish the work, and it would take months to pull everything together even if I wanted to do it. Which I don't.'

Mike held out a piece of paper with numbers written on it, and stretched it out in front of her eyes with a thumb and forefinger at each end.

Lulu inhaled sharply. Her eyes refused to take in the figure with several zeros at the end of it, and her brain stopped working as she blinked several times in rapid succession.

'They want this to be a very personal record. That was what made Kyle's first book so special. This would be one single payment. A consultancy fee, if you like.'

Lulu sat back in the chair and looked at the numbers again. 'You're serious about this, aren't you? '

'Very. The foundation gets a generous charitable donation, plus income from the film and the book, and this money is yours to do with as you will. And don't tell me that you couldn't put it to good use.'

Her brain went into overdrive.

Art college? Paid for by profits from her mother's sweat and ultimate self-sacrifice? No. She could never do that. However…

Lulu groaned out loud. 'Dad would want any money from the book to go to the hospice. It desperately needs a respite centre.'

'The hospice where Tom died?'

She nodded. 'They were brilliant. This money would probably pay for most of the work. I certainly don't have any spare cash to give them.'

Then the true impact of what he was talking about hit home.

'Wait a moment, Mike. This is going too fast. I need to think about this a lot more before agreeing to anything. You know that she wrote a letter home almost every week? I would have to read through all of her papers before Kyle could look at them. That could take weeks.' She sat back and shook her head. 'I'm not sure this could work. I'm only a bookkeeper and part-time artist from Kingsmede.'

'You're Ruth and Tom's daughter. They were two of the most extraordinary people I have ever met. And so are you. You can handle it. Besides, I have an idea about how I can help you pull it off.'

'I don't like the sound of that, but go on.'

Mike smiled and picked up Kyle's book. 'Kyle is a wonderful doctor and a good man, but he'd be the first to admit that paperwork is not one of his priorities. I paid two temporary secretaries to pull together his blog and the background material for this book, and they struggled with the technical details. The second book is going to be harder. He has already told me that his notes and diaries are scrappy at best. He needs help from someone who has done this before and can work with a field medic—otherwise he won't stand a chance of doing justice to the amazing work they did ten years ago.'

Lulu inhaled sharply. 'You can't be serious.'

'It's not as bad as it sounds. Kyle was only in Uganda for nine months. What he needs is help to put his boxes of personal notes into some sort of order so he can turn around the second book before he goes back to Nepal.'

'Just putting everything in order from those nine months? That's it? Simple admin and typing?'

'That's it. Kyle's notes will form the core of the book. Your mum's records covering those nine months will add the next level of detail.'

'And what does Boy Wonder think of this plan?'

'He doesn't know a thing. I thought I had better discuss it with you first. Why don't we go and break the happy news over lunch?'

'So he *could* say no?'

Mike looked at her over the top of his spectacles in disbelief. 'He could. But then he would miss the chance of spending time with a lovely young lady such as yourself. Most unlikely.' He smiled as she groaned in horror, and linked her arm over his. 'Can I tempt you with food and wine, madam?'

'Lead the way. I feel like I'm going to need it.'

CHAPTER THREE

LULU sat alone in the far corner of the bar and watched as the media executives circled around Kyle like vultures flying above a prime piece of food.

Mike Baxter had been instantly snatched away by medical journalists, all desperate for an exclusive interview with the bestselling author and media star who was currently holding court from his bar stool. Kyle had made a joke of gobbling up most of the bacon and the prawn sandwiches from the luxurious buffet table, much to everyone's amusement.

He was so handsome it was unfair. When he turned that killer smile on a woman it was as though he could see her secrets and make her feel like the most stunning person in the room.

But he had not even noticed that she was there.

Kyle was so totally natural in these surroundings, while she…she could just about hear the person next to her against the furious hum of chatter—if she leant close enough…

Suddenly she needed air, and a chance to think away from the barrage of broken sounds.

By squeezing past the elegantly dressed media executives by the door, who looked at her as if she was a creature from another much less stylish planet, where couture did not exist, Lulu made her way onto the sheltered decking outside the bar. The view was amazing. She leant on the edge of a metalwork table and looked out across the cold width of the Thames to hotels and the financial heart of the City of London. So many people—and they all seemed to know where they were going and what they wanted in life.

What was she doing here?

Mike was way too good at sweeping her along with his ideas. Of course she could do the basic admin on a non-fiction book. That was not a problem. She sorted out other people's financial records to pay her bills. But her mother's diaries and letters? That was a different matter.

How could she read those letters her mother had sent from Uganda in the last few months before she was killed? There had been a time when she'd used to run home from school to see if there was an envelope covered in brightly coloured stamps in the post. Not at the end. In those cold, bleak winter days she'd simply left them unopened in her father's studio, where he could have the private joy of reading them first.

She would find them later on the kitchen table. Treasured words to be savoured in a safe and warm place, far away from fighting and danger and disease.

Everything had changed on that last mission. Ruth had changed. Her mother had made a choice. And left her for the final time.

Going back to revisit that pain was not just a step into her past—it was bigger than one of the mountains Kyle Munroe was used to.

She was not ready to climb that mountain. She hadn't even reached base camp.

A gust of cold wind eddied around the wall and she shivered inside her suit. The weather had changed. Grey skies. Grey river.

She had her own life now. And more than enough work to do back home in Kingsmede. It was madness to even think of accepting Mike's offer. That connection to her past life had died with her father, and she had to move forward.

Time to go in and tell Mike that the answer was no. Kyle would have to write his book as best he could without her help. Perhaps there was another way? Was it possible for Kyle to use the diaries without her involvement and pay the hospice a fee? That might work.

Encouraged by having an alternative suggestion, she had just slipped in through the side entrance to the bar when she heard a loud, 'Marta?'

Lulu whirled around in surprise at the man's voice, and stepped back so quickly that the heel of one of her mules got stuck in a gap between the wide strips of wooden decking. As she tried to slip it back onto her foot the mule flipped up and landed on a table, happily unoccupied, clattering against the crockery. Lulu hopped over to the table to rescue her shoe before it could be held to ransom—only to find that Kyle Munroe had saved the day and got there before her.

Responding to the yelps from the waiters, Kyle gave a sudden whoop and snatched up the shoe before it could do any more damage. He shook his head when he saw who the shoe belonged to. 'I thought I recognised this rampaging item of footwear. This is starting to become a habit, Marta. Are you a secret stalker? I am honoured, of course, but should I be worried?'

'Sorry to disappoint you, but I'm here with Mike Baxter.'

He gave her a slight bow from the waist. 'How intriguing. In that case, I believe this is your glass slipper, madam. May I have the honour?'

Before Lulu knew what was happening, Kyle had dropped to his knees and her shoe was on the decking. A rough skinned hand gently wrapped around her left ankle and as though by magic Lulu found herself holding her leg in position so that Kyle could slide her backless shoe onto her foot.

As she tried to pull away, his fingers brushed the back of her calf through her thin black stockings, sending the most delicious shivers up her leg. Lulu instantly tried to move backwards to pull away from his grasp.

With the predictable result.

She overbalanced and found herself having to jerk forward to support her weight by pressing one hand onto each of Kyle's shoulders.

'Whoa! Steady there.'

Kyle was still on his knees as he looked up into her face. Their eyes locked.

And Lulu's world turned over. It was as though time had stopped and they were the only people on the riverbank. No sound except her own rapid breathing and Kyle's heartbeat. A beat she could sense through the gentle rise and fall of the muscular shoulders under her fingers.

Something at the bottom of her stomach clenched so hard she inhaled deeply.

He opened his mouth to say something, and then closed it again before giving her a half-smile with his eyes and mouth. A knowing smile.

Idiot, Lulu thought. *He knows exactly what he is doing and I fell for it.* So why did her stomach flip again when she looked at him?

It hit her with a very heavy thud that working close to this man every day could be *seriously* bad news. Yet another factor against the whole idea.

'Thank you. Again,' she managed to get out as Kyle stretched to his full height.

To her horror, Lulu realised that the whole sordid and humiliating scene had been acted out in full view of all the journalists and media company people, who were clearly sniggering behind their glasses of fizzy bottled water. And Mike Baxter. Whose lower lip was quivering so fast he had to be biting the inside of his cheek as he guided her inside, to a quiet table at the far end of the room.

Lulu narrowed her eyes, daring him to comment, but instead he pulled out her chair and waited until she was comfortable before going on.

'I'm sorry to have left you like that, Lulu, but the editors are pressing me for an answer about Ruth's diaries. This seems like as good time as any to get two of my favourite people together.'

'Then perhaps you ought to rescue your star?'

Lulu looked towards the bar, where Kyle was surrounded by a gaggle of tall leggy girls dressed in black and clearly revelling in the moment. As she turned away a beam of sunlight broke through the floor-to-ceiling glass windows, bringing his cheekbones and dark eye sockets into sharp focus. A little too sharply into focus.

'Has Kyle been ill, Mike?'

Mike nodded. 'Mmm. Not much misses you, does it?' He leant closer. 'The boy has lost weight. Chest infections are an occupational hazard, but this one is proving hard to treat. Oh, don't worry. He's responded well to the antibiotics, but it's going to take a while. Providing, of course…'

he paused for a second and looked up as Kyle sauntered in with two large steaming beakers of what smelt like tea '…I can hold him down long enough to take some rest.'

'Rest? Are you talking about me?' Kyle responded with a chuckle, before placing one of the teas in front of Lulu. 'You should know better than that by now, Mike.' He glanced across at Lulu before sitting next to Mike. 'Thought you looked a bit chilly out there, Marta. This should warm you up.'

'That's very thoughtful, Kyle.'

Mike looked from Kyle back to Lulu in surprise. 'I didn't know that you two had met before? How did that happen?'

'Oh, Marta and I are old friends. I think I should warn you to watch your back, Mike. This lady is on a secret mission of her own! I hope you don't have any precious artwork lying around the place.'

Mike shook his head. 'Whatever you have been drinking, stop now. And why are you calling her Marta? Do you have the faintest idea what this idiot is talking about, Lulu?'

'Lulu?' Kyle burst out laughing. 'Now, please—I expected a more convincing alias cover name than that!'

While Mike stared, open-mouthed, the lady in question decided to take control and casually tried her tea. 'Oh, it's all quite simple, really. Kyle and I have not been properly introduced.'

She lifted the beaker towards Kyle before taking another sip. 'Congratulations on the book launch, Dr Munroe—it seems to have been a terrific success. And also thanks for the dedication. You see, my real name is Lulu Hamilton, and Ruth Taylor Hamilton was my mother. Apparently Lulu is an African word for *pearl*. Don't you think that's pretty?'

* * *

Kyle stared in mute horror at the extremely pretty blonde woman sitting across from him and was shocked into silence.

Never in his wildest dreams—and some of them could be pretty wild, even by his standards—had he imagined for one second that the inspirational surgeon he had worked with in Uganda could have another life as a wife and a mother.

Ruth Taylor Hamilton had been capable of it. He had no doubt about that. Except that she had never once ever mentioned she had a family back home. Not one word.

Other medics had had letters and photographs clipped to the walls of their tent, and he had envied them that many times, but not Ruth.

He glanced sideways at Mike Baxter, who simply nodded, and then dared to speak.

'I had no idea.'

'Ruth left her husband and daughter back in England, and that was the way she liked it. Two separate parts of her life. She never talked about Tom or Lulu when she was on a mission. That was her way of coping.'

Kyle took a couple of breaths before looking into the face of the girl who was apparently the daughter of the most amazing woman he had ever met.

He scanned her features. The lovely full bow of her upper lip, the high cheekbones sprinkled with freckles and the stunning blue eyes below fair eyebrows. And that hair!

But he couldn't see one single thing in her face that reminded him of Ruth.

'Kyle, mate. You're staring.'

Mike's voice startled him. He was right. He had been

staring—and she knew it. His embarrassment was saved only by Lulu herself.

'It's okay, Kyle. I'm used to being compared to the famous Ruth Taylor Hamilton. It goes with the territory. I gave up on being upset about the disappointment in other people's eyes a long time ago. I know that I have my dad's colouring—and I'm definitely not the heroic type. In fact, didn't you think I was a librarian?'

Mike groaned and dropped his head into his hands.

'I'm very sorry for your loss, Miss Hamilton. Your mother was a remarkable woman. I apologise if I offended you, and… Is that your phone?'

Lulu dived into her messenger bag, where her cellphone was flashing away, and quickly checked the caller ID. *Drat.*

'Sorry, Mike, I have to take this. Why don't you tell Kyle about your crazy idea? I shouldn't be long.' She went outside again.

She'd lied. The text message was from an estate agent in the town closest to her home village of Kingsmede.

A month ago, after a hard look at her finances, she had taken the tough decision to tell the local agencies that she might be interested in renting out the huge family house she had lived in all of her life.

Big mistake. Since then she had been inundated with calls on a weekly basis. Now, apparently, a family with four small children were interested in renting the house for the next twelve months. Only there was a catch. They needed to move in six weeks. They were willing to pay the full rental rate and a cash deposit. Could she be out by then?

Her fingers hesitated on the keypad. She desperately

needed that rental income if she had any chance of going to art college, but six weeks was not long to finish clearing the huge house. And it would mean leaving her home just before Christmas.

Lulu pressed her thumb and third finger hard against her eyebrows.

She wasn't ready. This was what she had planned—only she had not expected it to happen so quickly.

Before she changed her mind, she quickly created a message expressing her apologies and pressed the 'send' button. A few seconds later she received a text of thanks from the agent.

Next year. That was it. She would make a start in January. In the meantime she would have to sell more paintings and work longer hours as a bookkeeper. She could do it.

Someone came up alongside her and leant on the metal railing a few feet away.

It was Kyle.

She half turned, and was about to explain that she could not possibly work on his project when he started talking in the same voice he had used at the table when he'd discovered who she was. Serious. Sincere. Intense. Adorable. A voice she could not interrupt.

'Two months ago I lost a very special patient. A little girl. Lakshmi was the daughter of my friends who run the field clinic. Most of the community are Buddhists. They refuse to kill any living creature, including the packs of wild dogs that roam the villages looking for food. Lakshmi was a typical five-year-old—bright, always laughing, and she loved puppies.'

Kyle looked out across the river as he talked.

'We don't know when she was bitten by a rabid dog, but by the time the first symptoms appeared it was too late to save her. If she had been vaccinated she might have stood a small chance of lasting out long enough to survive the treatment. She hadn't.'

He turned sideways and looked at her directly. 'I have the job of choosing who gets the vaccines and who doesn't. There simply isn't enough for everyone.' He glanced back to the bar and all of the busy, healthy people going about their lives. 'That's why I'm here today. That's why I agreed to write this book. It's not about me; it's about the patients and what they need. Every penny goes to the foundation.'

Lulu lifted her head before replying. 'And this second book will pay for the vaccines you need?'

He nodded. 'The first book paid to build and equip a complete clinic, and the paperback should pay the wages for the next few years. I have Mike and the TV company to thank for that. I'm just a jobbing medic. I like to keep things simple.'

She was not ready for the feel of his cold, long rough-skinned working fingers that meshed with hers as she clasped hold of the railing.

'Mike thinks that you are the best person to help me. My patients need those drugs. If I have to get down on my knees and beg you to help, I will. Because I cannot go back to that clinic and tell them that other children could suffer like that little girl.'

He moved closer to her, face to face, and his fingers locked onto hers, leaving his thumb to move seductively across her wrist.

'I have the feeling that you might like to see a man beg. Am I right?'

She locked onto those hazel-green eyes with their

tiny creases and her heart melted. She smiled when she didn't want to.

'That rather depends on what he's begging for.'

'Quite a lot, actually. Apparently I have three weeks to produce this book if I want to have it ready for March publication. I need all the help I can get! Ruth's diaries would make a huge difference. Ten years is a long time ago. And did I mention that I am a two-finger typist?'

That knocked the wind out of her sails for a few moments, and he could almost see the cogs in her brain working overtime before she nodded. 'Before I agree to anything, I do have a couple of conditions.'

He tilted his head slightly to one side, his heavy brows coming together in concentration. 'Fire away.'

'First, I would prefer that the diaries did not leave my home. So if you want to read them, then you'll have to come to see *me* in Kingsmede. Not the other way around.'

'Done. Next?' His eyes had not broken focus.

She faltered slightly and fought to regain control of her voice. 'I work best on my own, so it would make sense if Mike could send me everything you have from that time, plus any official records. If you can give me a week to sort it all out the best I can, then you can decide whether there is enough material to write the book. Or not. How does that sound?'

Kyle pursed his lips tight together before replying. 'A week? That might work. I'll need to dig out what I have from Africa, and I have this book tour to take care of. There is also some…well, personal stuff— But, yes.' He nodded. 'A week could work out very well.'

Her eyes locked onto his eyes, and she kept them there until he sighed and nodded.

'Okay. It makes sense to sort through the bulk of the work in one session. I'll soon find out what I am missing.' His head lifted. 'I'll do my best.'

Lulu stared him down. 'Does that mean you'll do it? You'll come to Kingsmede and work with me—starting next Sunday for two weeks?'

'Absolutely. You help me with my book, and I'll make it the tribute that Ruth Taylor Hamilton deserves. I'll be happy to shout about it from the rooftops when the time is right. So, Miss Hamilton…' He paused and squeezed her right hand a little tighter. 'Do we have a deal?'

Lulu inhaled deeply, took in the unshaven upper lip and the solid square stubbly jawline of the smiling face in front of her, and closed her eyes for a second before nodding.

'I'm not sure if I can do this, and it is one huge risk, but, yes, Dr Munroe, we have a deal.'

He brought her fingers to his lips for a fleeting second before releasing her.

'In that case—' he shuffled his jacket closed '—it's time to get down to the really important business of the day.'

Lulu held her breath, hardly daring to imagine what he had in mind.

'I have been dreaming about a huge British fry-up for the last six months. Care to join me?'

CHAPTER FOUR

LULU popped her pins and threads back inside her sewing kit and smoothed down the seam of the printed floor-length curtain so that the repair was invisible from inside the room.

Even in the faint autumn sunlight Lulu knew every pleat of the fabric where the sunshine had faded the pattern of bright yellow overblown roses to a dark cream. Her parents had never been able to afford to replace the curtains her grandmother had bought years earlier. Not with so many windows. Not in a house this size. Even her godmother Emma Carmichael had mentioned that surely it was time to change them before the winter.

A cool draft swirled the curtains, and Lulu suppressed a shiver that ran across her shoulders and down her back.

The unused dining room had been the obvious place to spread out the boxes of documents that Mike Baxter had sent over, but it was a cold, north-facing room and she had not lit the open fire in years. Time to change that.

Kyle might be used to the snows of Nepal, but she wasn't.

Lulu plumped up the cushions on the chesterfield sofa next to the fireplace, then turned to face the long, narrow antique dining table that ran the length of the room. The polished surface was hidden below neat parallel rows of folders.

One individual folder for each of the nine months that Kyle Munroe had spent in Uganda ten years earlier.

Mike had apologised in advance for the fact that the storage crates of records and files were 'a tad unorganised', but she had been unprepared for just how much of a mess they truly were.

It was only when the boxes of jumbled papers had arrived on the Tuesday morning following the book launch that the enormity of the task she was facing had begun to truly hit home.

It had taken her every spare minute for the last week, but she had done the best she could.

In a world and culture where computers had been a distant dream, the original records from Uganda were a jumble of single pages of handwritten notes, record cards with patient information, copies of invoices… In fact anything and everything that the foundation had saved from the Uganda mission for the last year or so before Kyle had been flown home.

Somehow all these simple pieces of paper seemed more intimate than an anonymous computer record or database. The hand that had created these marks on paper belonged to a living human being, and each piece seemed to have picked up some of the personality of the person who had created it.

Almost like the style of an artist, there was no mistaking who had written, or in many cases scribbled, the information. She had scanned through hundreds of separate pages over the last few days to check for dates, and some personalities shone through.

Kyle Munroe, for example.

Lulu picked up an undated but signed medical report from a crate of bits and pieces labelled *'Undated'* that only Kyle would be able to place. The handwriting was strong, direct and fervent, in long straight strokes and clear, concise language. Always in black ink. The man might have looked more than a little scruffy at the tube station, but the Kyle who had created these records was focused and organised. Professional.

Mike had already told her that Kyle would be bringing his personal diary with him in person, and yet there was so much of his personality in the box she was looking at now she felt that the diary would be almost too much.

She slipped the report back into the crate and her foot connected with a dilapidated old holdall with the letters KBM stencilled onto the cover.

It did not look too different from the rucksack she had seen Kyle carrying on the underground in London. And yet she had held back from opening up this bag.

It felt too private and too personal for anyone but Kyle to open.

Of course Emma had laughed at her, and accused her of simply being scared of what she might find inside. Frightened of the unknown. Right, as always.

Kyle Munroe remained an unknown entity.

She certainly did not recall hearing the name Kyle Munroe until Mike had told her about him. Perhaps her father had known about the new medics who had been re-cruited in that last year when she'd been away at univer-sity? It certainly wasn't something he would have talked to her about. Those last few months were a complete mystery. Just as much as Kyle himself.

Perhaps that was why she had taken the time to read *Medicine Man* and find out more about the work in Nepal. She had even visited his website.

The man in the book looked like the same man that she had met in London. There was no mistaking that.

Except that Kyle probably did not recognise how much of his personality came through the short posts he created every week on his blog. The humour. The dedication. The charm. She could well understand why the book and the TV documentary had become so popular. He was beguiling, and yet completely true to himself.

The thought of an emergency medic like Kyle sitting next to her at this table sent unfamiliar tremors of excitement direct to her cheeks, and instantly she felt the blood rush to skin. She had felt the fluttering sensation bubble up over the past few days, until the thought of actually seeing him again face to face was starting to make her nervous.

Skittery.

And she did not do skittery.

Not normally. Not ever. There was just something about this man. She actually *wanted* to see him again. Or was it the man in the book she wanted to meet? There was only one way to find out.

And he was due to arrive in—oh, a couple of hours.

A sudden flash of colour on the other side of the glass broke her thoughts, and Lulu looked up to see a young red setter running around the lawn to the trees.

Belle—the red setter puppy that her godmother Emma had given her for a Christmas present. Belle was totally adorable, and her constant companion, but a boisterous dog and official paperwork were not a good combination, and

Lulu was happy for her pet to exhaust herself in the huge garden instead of indoors.

Lulu smiled to herself and shook her head as she watched the madcap antics of the silly animal as Belle scampered and jumped around.

She was being an idiot. Mike Baxter had asked her to sort the files and paperwork into date order and she had done the best she could. Kyle should have no problem connecting his own diary pages with the records to create the background history for his book. And the sooner that was done, the sooner he would be out of Kingsmede and she could get back to her ordinary life.

This was simply a few days of work for both of them. Nothing more. And then the hospice would have the new respite unit they needed.

Tomorrow she would start reading through her mother's diaries. Tomorrow or the next day.

As for the personal letters? Well, that was a different matter.

Lulu turned her head away from the window and caught sight of her reflection in the silvered Venetian mirror above the fireplace. She stroked back her hair behind her left ear, so that her hearing aid was in full view.

She didn't need archived records to remind herself of what had happened in Africa. She saw the direct evidence every morning when she looked in the bathroom mirror, and every evening when she removed her hearing aid and reconciled herself to the fact that she would never hear again the things she'd once loved.

She lived with the memory every single day of her life.

The doctors had told her many times that she was very lucky to have survived the mysterious tropical infection that had robbed her of her hearing in that one ear. She still had her brain, and enough hearing in the other ear to enjoy life to the full.

Her father had brought her home and sat with her for days, only leaving her side when Emma had come over. It was probably the longest period of time that they had ever spent in the same room together.

Except of course he'd known that he was not the parent she wanted to see. Lulu remembered how she'd kept asking the same question of her father, the doctors—in fact, anyone who came into her room. Where was her mother? Why wasn't her mother there? She had repeated the question over and over again. Which only showed how ill she must have been. Because her mother had been in Uganda, and that had meant she might as well have been on another planet. Out of reach.

Lulu slowly uncurled her hair back over her ear.

No. She didn't need a diary to remind her of where her mother had worked and what she had been doing all those years ago. It was staring her in the face every day.

A series of playful barks on the other side of the patio door made her smile.

Poor Belle had been neglected. Time to make amends.

This was her life now. And it was up to her to make the best of it.

Kyle Munroe swung the Range Rover slowly around the bend from the narrow lane, his eyes scanning from side to side until he spotted a small hand-painted sign attached to a stone pillar. Taylor House. This was it. He had come to the right place.

Thanks to the satellite navigation system on Mike's car, and a very helpful lady walking a dog, he had found it.

The four-wheel-drive car slowed, and he pulled up on the wide gravel drive which circled around the front entrance of an imposing Georgian stone house, complete with narrow, square windows and a fine collection of chimneys. A decorative stone porch was lit up with bright pots of pink cyclamens and a pair of bay trees, either side of a very solid-looking wooden door painted in an elegant shade of dark navy.

His smart boots crunched into the gravel as he swung down from the leather seat and slowly uncurled his body into something like a standing position.

The drive from his father's flat in London had taken a lot longer than he had expected, and his body was paying the price. He raised his right arm above his head to release the tension in his neck.

Fractured vertebrae and strained ligaments and tendons did not heal overnight. Or at least they didn't in his case.

Maybe Mike was right. Perhaps he should cut back on his treks to remote clinics this year and focus on getting back into shape? His arm was only the latest of many little accidents he had laughed off over the years.

It was so frustrating. He wanted to be doing *more* aerobic exercise, building his lung capacity. Not less. He could not let this infection beat him. Not this time—not ever. He would carry on taking the antibiotics. He would clear his lungs. Persistent chest infections were a risk in his work. An occupational hazard. But it had certainly put a damper on his plans to extend the vaccine programme.

Kyle pushed his spine out, and looked up through the wide-open branches of the copper beech and oak trees above his head. Blackbirds and robins hopped from dripping branch to dripping branch.

So what if he did miss the English seasons? He sniffed and wrapped his father's scarf tighter around his neck. The people here had never seen the wild rhododendron forests in the Himalayas. Smelt the soil after the summer monsoon.

A grey squirrel scampered across the wet grass at the side of the house to scrabble among the fallen leaves. Kyle smiled. He had forgotten how much he missed such familiar things.

He looked up at the house, with its imposing neat front gardens. Open farmland spread out in all directions, broken by copses of woodland and a distant line of trees where black rooks were calling out to one another.

It was hard to believe that Ruth Taylor Hamilton had grown up and lived here, on the edge of a small country village in the South of England. Suddenly he was struck with a vivid memory of the last time he'd seen Ruth. Jumping into an ambulance just like on any other hot African morning. A quick wave to the local children and she'd been gone, in a cloud of red dust on the dirt road, before he'd even had a chance to speak to her.

And in that moment his life had changed. Yes, they had been working close to a war zone, but nobody could have predicted that only two hours later her ambulance would drive over a land mine on the way to the village clinic.

He shivered, and sniffed once more before crunching his way to the porch.

That had been ten years ago, and a world away from where he was standing now.

He had come to do a job, and part of that job was honouring Ruth—and that was what he intended to do. Her daughter need never know the terrible secret about what had truly happened that morning.

That thought made him stop and pull his hand away from the doorbell. Why had Ruth never told anyone that she had a daughter and a husband back in England? Living in this very house? He could have done something when he'd got back to London. Visited? Tried to appease his guilt in some way?

Of course he had never thought to ask Mike Baxter about Ruth's family, and he had not kept in contact with the other medical workers when they'd been disbanded to various missions around the world.

Well, it was not too late. And now Lulu was on her own he owed it to Ruth to make sure that her only daughter had everything she needed. It was the least he could do, seeing as he owed Ruth Taylor Hamilton his life.

Just as Kyle stretched out to press the brass doorbell there was a commotion in the direction of the squirrel he had just been looking at, and he turned just in time to see a red setter hurtling through the grass. The playful dog pounced, and pounced again, but her target was already halfway up the oak tree.

Kyle chuckled to himself as he strolled around the side of the house and called out to the dog.

'Hello, there! Not much luck with that one.'

The dog froze for all of two seconds, before bounding towards him and launching herself onto his trousers, yapping and trying to lick him so furiously that Kyle could not resist any longer. He swept the dog up into his arms. Her gangly red limbs and sharp nails scrabbled for purchase, but the muddy dog's muzzle, fur and paws had already done enough damage.

A sharp whistle echoed around the drive, and the red setter turned into a frantic bag of bones and fur that Kyle struggled to lower to the ground. This bundle of fun was in too much of a hurry, and soon squirmed her way out of his arm-lock to race away around the corner of the house.

With a shake of his head, Kyle shrugged up the collar of his coat and followed her. Perhaps the lady of the house was outside? The gravel crunched under his feet as he turned the corner, hands in his pockets. Then he stopped. Frozen into position by the scene being acted out in front of him.

On the other side of the flowerbeds and neat lawn, the woman he now knew was Lulu Hamilton was leaping from one foot to the other as she held a piece of twig high in the air, playing and pretending to fight off the loving and energetic attentions of the floppy red setter, who was jumping just as high and clearly having just as much fun as the blonde.

Suddenly content to simply watch in silence, Kyle leant on the corner of the house as Lulu threw the stick far across to the tall trees and turned back to an open bonfire.

With a single smooth and practised motion, Lulu lifted a small handsaw and cut through a branch of dry wood. Then again. Small twigs were thrown into a metal fire basket which glowed red and orange as the flames licked upwards, hotter and higher.

But it was Lulu herself who held him spellbound.

Her arms moved smoothly back and forth, collecting large logs into a crate. The glow from the burning embers shone back from her face in the fading light, and her blond corkscrew curls were scrunched back into a rough ponytail held away from her forehead with a striped bandana.

Her fine high cheekbones glowed pink with spontaneous energy and a sense of natural warmth and fun as she vigorously rubbed the dog's head before throwing another twig. The dull grey suit was gone. Replaced with faded jeans and a padded jacket over what looked like a man's check shirt.

She looked confident, self-sufficient, and totally in control in this space.

The Lulu Hamilton he had met in London had been pretty and intelligent, but also guarded and ill at ease with the grandiose plans that Mike had come up with.

This version of Lulu Hamilton was mesmerising.

She had such a sense of smiling joy in her simple task. She looked like a woman who was accustomed to chopping her own wood, content with the company of a mad dog and a burning fire.

One thing was certain. He had been expecting to meet a pretty blonde in a suit. What he saw instead was a stunningly beautiful woman with a style and body that no man could ignore. Which probably meant trouble.

This was Ruth's daughter, and he had a responsibility—perhaps even an obligation—to make sure that she was cared for.

He could have looked at her all day and not regretted it for one moment. Except the dog had other ideas, spotted him, and decided that it was time for Kyle to join in their game.

Lulu threw the last of the parchment-dry ancient newspapers her father had hoarded onto the fire, brushed down her gloves, and stood back to watch the white-hot flames flare up into the damp air.

This part of her garden looked out over the farmland leading down to Kingsmede, and she could just see the lights from the thatched cottages that were scattered around the old church with its familiar steeple. It was a dreamy scene of soft lights and faint misty air.

She loved this view. This was the only home she had ever known and the only one she ever wanted. Even if it meant renting the house out for a while when she was at art college, it would be here for her to return to.

That truly did make her smile and, picking up one final branch, she turned to see what new garden creature Belle had found to torment.

And stepped back in startled shock and surprise.

The most handsome man she had ever seen in her life was leaning against the wall of her house, only a few feet away from where she was standing. Watching her in silence.

Was she dreaming?

It was Kyle Munroe. The same man whose paperwork she has just been reading. Only this version of Kyle bore no relationship whatsoever to the skinny young medical student in a pop group T-shirt in the colour photos from his book. Her stomach decided to behave like a tumble drier. Skittery did not even come close.

She might have thought that Kyle was attractive that Friday afternoon in London, but this man was from another planet.

The dirty long hair had been expertly cut. Clean shiny brown layers lay flat around his ears, swept away from his cleanshaven face so that the prominent square jawline and the long, straight nose were the first things she saw.

Without his beard the square jaw was so angled it might have been sculpted. But it was his mouth that knocked the air out of her lungs and had her clinging onto the log pile for support. It was a mouth made for smiling, with slight dimples either side.

The corners of those amazing eyes crinkled slightly, and Lulu realised that he had been watching her as his smile widened. Despite the real fire close at hand, the warmth of that smile seemed to heat the air between them. It was so full of genuine charm and delight that she knew, no matter what, that this was the smile that would stay with her whenever she thought of Kyle.

Only now, at this moment, the smile was for *her*. Her heart leapt. More than a little. And just enough for her to recognise that the blush of heat racing through her neck and face were not only due to the flames warming her back.

At this distance in the fading light, his eyes were dark, scrunched up by the deep crease of his smile as he strolled across the grass towards her, Belle scampering around his legs. She knew that those eyes were mostly hazel brown, with flakes of forest-green, but for now all she could see were a pair of heavy dark eyebrows.

If she had ever imagined that Kyle Munroe could not possibly be more attractive than the photo on the cover of his book, then she had been wrong. The top two buttons of his pale blue shirt stretched open as the fabric strained to cover a broad chest, revealing a hit of deeply tanned skin and more than a few dark chest hairs.

He was stunning.

Oh, no. Do not stare at his chest. Just don't.

The pounding of her heart was simply because she had been taken by surprise—that was all. Trying desperately to regain some kind of control over feelings that were new and raw, Lulu was suddenly aware that she was standing there with a tree branch still in her hand, and casually she moved forward to throw it onto the fire before returning his smile and turning to meet him.

Luckily he spoke first, his voice low and husky in the quiet garden as he smiled and reached out his hand. Lulu shucked off her glove and felt long, cold fingers clasp hers for only a few seconds before she released him. The callused surfaces of his fingers rasped against the skin on the back of her hand. Gentle, but firm. And surprisingly very different from the handshake they had shared in the London taxi cab only a week earlier. Now his fingers seemed to linger and slide over hers, as though they wanted to maintain contact for as long as possible.

No complaints from her end on that point.

'Miss Hamilton. Sorry if I startled you. I tried the front door, but your burglar alarm found me first.' He nodded towards Belle, who was snuffling around their feet. 'Apologies for being so late. Not used to the traffic. But it's great to be here at last. Do you mind if I make use of your fire?'

In the fraction of a second it took Kyle to stroll over to the fire and stretch out his hands towards the flames, inappropriate and totally crazy thoughts about the effect those same fingers could have on other parts of her body flitted through Lulu's mind.

No need for flames on this side of the fire. *Oh, dear.*

Lulu inhaled deeply, straightened her back, and managed to find her voice at last as she smiled back at him. 'Please do. It *is* feeling chilly. Mike warned me that your timing was flexible, so no problem. And please call me Lulu.'

Belle sidled up to Kyle and tried to push her nose into the side pocket of his trousers.

Lulu laughed out loud. 'You'll have to excuse Belle. She

is totally spoiled and has already worked out that pockets are designed to hold treats.' To prove the point, she reached into her own jacket pocket and pulled out a dog biscuit, which Belle pounced on. 'Let's get inside before she notices we're gone. How does hot coffee sound?'

'It sounds wonderful. I've left something in the car. Back in a moment.'

Kyle jogged back to the Range Rover, scooped up the bakery bag and got back just in time to follow Lulu onto a wide stone patio with garden furniture which led to a dark green door at the back of the house.

Lulu turned the handle and swung the door wide as she shucked off her boots in the long porch. 'Please go through. Welcome to Taylor House.'

CHAPTER FIVE

KYLE walked past Lulu into what would have passed for an art gallery rather than a kitchen.

The riot of bright colours was so totally unexpected he almost recoiled at the sensory overload. The contrast between the cold grey garden and the exotic chaos of colour was shocking, and he turned back to his hostess with an expression of awe.

'Wow! This is like no other kitchen I've ever been in. Are you the artist?'

Lulu smiled across at him as she unbuttoned her jacket. 'Not guilty. My father spent a lot of time working on abstracts. He loved colour and hated change.' She shrugged her shoulders before filling the kettle, determined to settle her jangled nerves with the familiar world of her kitchen. 'I could have painted over it, I suppose, but it is distinctive.'

Lulu watched Kyle step slowly around the kitchen, grinning and peering closer at the images on the walls, before picking up a purple pottery pig dotted with bright splodges of yellow and red. Long, delicate surgeon's fingers moved over the model, lovingly caressing the little pig, and Lulu gulped down something very close to jealousy.

When he finally looked up at her his face was alive with

delight, and an energy so totally unexpected that she almost dropped the cups she was holding when he spoke.

'Please don't paint over it. It reminds me of Nepal. Brilliant! I love it.' He stepped away to loll against the wall, so that he faced Lulu as she busied herself with cups and coffee. 'I can see now how you came to the art world. No orchids, though. Do you have a special room for those? I had been wondering if you forge them yourself or have someone else do it for you?'

'Orchids?' Thank heavens for a change in the subject. 'Oh, of course—the gallery! Yes, I confess, I forge them myself. I'm surprised you remembered that.'

'Yellow orchids. How could I forget? Please—let me help you with that.'

Kyle took the tray from Lulu's hands before she could protest, and carried it over to the old pine kitchen table where she had been sorting through family photographs.

'Are you sure you can manage? I see the plaster cast is missing. How is your wrist?'

A rapid shake and flex of his strapped-up arm was his answer. 'It still needs work. Luckily Mike has an automatic car I can borrow for the week, so I am mobile—but thank you for the thought.'

He flashed her a half-smile, his wide mouth creaking into a lady-killer grin, practised over the years to ensure any female within his target radius would melt into radioactive decay in seconds.

Something strange happened to Lulu's stomach and her legs felt a little wobbly. No lunch. That was it. And the warmth spreading from her neck to her face was just the natural result of being taken by surprise. She tried to hide it by gathering together the photographs as Kyle continued.

'Speaking of Mike—I come bearing gifts from a certain patisserie which apparently you are fond of.'

'Gifts?' she asked, trying not to sound too keen, despite the bag of hares that had started kickboxing inside her stomach.

'Chocolate cake. As some form of compensation for the terrible mess my paperwork must be in.'

He held the bag out towards her, and a scrumptious smell wafted into the kitchen.

'I can assure you that your paperwork cannot be any worse than Mike's—but he does know my weaknesses.'

Lulu pursed her lips and gracefully accepted the bag from Kyle's fingers before bowing slightly in his direction. She could take a bribe now and again. And it gave her something to do with her hands, which were starting to crease the photographs with their pressure.

'That was very thoughtful. Won't you sit?'

She stepped back and flicked on lights as Kyle followed her to the table.

'Thank you,' he replied with a shrug, 'but my old bones need to stretch. Not used to sitting in one place for very long. This really is a lovely room. Oh, I'm sorry. I'm obviously disturbing your paperwork.'

Still spread out across the pine table was the rest of the jumble of old photographs, mostly black and white, and several storage boxes.

Lulu glanced back towards him from under her eyelashes as she unwrapped the deep, dense dark chocolate ganache cake. 'I was looking for a few family photographs you could use in the book. I always intended to put them into albums, but somehow never got around to it.'

'Well, I know that feeling. My dad has crates of my stuff

stashed in his apartment. It took me the best part of an hour to find what I had saved from Uganda.'

Aware that Kyle was leaning one handed against the dresser, she gestured towards the kitchen table.

'Some cake, perhaps, to go with your coffee?'

'Thanks, but the cake is for you. I'm not used to rich food.'

She watched as he perched on the edge of the table, only a few feet away from her, so that his long legs inside smart jeans could stretch out in front of him. He looked so at home. Casual. Relaxed. And clearly oblivious to the fact that his taut thigh muscles were straining against the fabric of the trousers.

Lulu felt herself blushing, the heat starting around her neck as she turned away to pour the coffee. It was certainly time to deflect this conversation. By moving back to her chair at the table, she was able to cradle her mug of coffee and divert his attention.

'How do you feel about being back here in Britain, Kyle? Away from the clinic in Nepal?'

He turned so that he could see her side view.

'You must miss them enormously.' Lulu replied. 'Your patients, I mean.' And kicked herself for being so tongue-tied.

How did he do it?

She was not normally so clumsy. She had never, ever felt so awkward and tongue tied and adolescent around a man in her life. And this was *her* kitchen! How was she going to survive two weeks of having Kyle Munroe in her life?

If Kyle had noticed her awkwardness he did not show it as he smiled across at her, raised his coffee with one hand

and waved his injured wrist in the air a couple of times. 'Ten weeks ago I was making my way through ice and snow down to the treeline when our ambulance was caught in a rockfall. We all slid out more or less in one piece. Now I'm sitting in this delightful kitchen in warmth and comfort. I consider myself very fortunate to be here. My patients are in excellent hands—but, yes, I do miss the people. Very much.'

Kyle reached forward and picked up one of the photographs from the table. A slim, handsome blond man in brightly coloured clothing was standing next to a large abstract painting, his arms wrapped around the shoulders of two other young men.

All three were laughing into the camera through bearded faces.

'Is this one of your relatives? He certainly has your colouring.'

Lulu casually accepted the photo from Kyle's hand, as though she had not seen it before. 'Oh, that's my father—Tom Hamilton. There were a couple of exhibitions of his work when he was at art school. Those lads with him in the crazy hippy gear are some of his mates from university. Apparently it was a wild time—and, no, I don't know what they got up to.'

There was a knowing chuckle from across the table.

'Mike told me that he had passed away. I'm very sorry. He must have been fun to live with. Was he a forger, as well?'

Lulu flashed a glance into Kyle's face, anxious to see if there was a hint of irony. Finding a genuine smile in place, she was totally disarmed by it. Of course there was no way that he could possibly know how hard living with Tom Hamilton had been.

'Not at all. Only the genuine article.' She smiled.

She was horrified to see her hand tremble just a little as Kyle focused the full heat of his attention on her. If only he was not dominating this small space! And so close to her. She had to regain control. Time to get down to business. The dining room. She could make sure that there was plenty of space between them in that room.

She lowered her beaker and scooped up the prints back into the box. 'Do you want to start work tonight?' she asked casually, trying to sound as though it was something she did every day. 'I've tried to collate everything Mike sent me from the official records into some sort of date order, but there are quite a few things where I have no clue. It's all laid out in the next room, any time you are ready.'

He leant his head slightly to one side. 'Absolutely. Although I do need to ask a favour of you before I see exactly what I have got myself into.'

'A favour?' Lulu frowned and half closed her eyes in pretend seriousness. She sat back in her chair. So he had an agenda after all. 'You are welcome to ask. After all, you did bring cake. Please go ahead.'

He turned his body so that he was directly across the table from her now, the full strength and force of his energy and personality focused on her small face. Burning into her skin. Demanding her total attention.

'I admired your mother very much. I meant what I said in my dedication. Stitch was an inspiration to me. Which is why I want this second book to be as much her story as it is mine. And I need your help to do that.'

Kyle gazed across at her and smiled as he stared into pale blue eyes the colour of a winter sky.

'When Mike introduced us last week I don't think I was very polite. For that I apologise. I could try and blame jet lag, but I always have been a bull in a china shop. I truly had no idea that Ruth had a daughter. So…' He clasped the back of the wooden chair, the knuckles of both hands white with the pressure. 'Here is my problem. I want to be back in Nepal in two weeks. Is there any way I could persuade you to spend more time with me so we can turn this book around in less than ten days? Please? Just tell me what I need to do to convince you, and I'm all yours.'

Lulu sat back in her kitchen chair and stared open mouthed at Kyle, who simply slid his delicious bottom onto the seat of the chair. She had certainly not intended to give this book one hundred percent of her time for the next two weeks. On the other hand, the sooner they finished the work, the sooner Kyle would be out of her life and she could get back to her normal quiet existence again. Which was what she wanted, wasn't it?

Drat this man for making her poor brain spin. Ten days? It might be possible, but there was a lot of material to work through.

'Do you know what you're asking?' she finally managed to blurt out.

Kyle waved one hand and shook his head. 'No clue. Like I said, I am a two-finger typist and proud. I can just about manage e-mails, and a few paragraphs a week, but everything else is handwritten. Pathetic, I know, but that is the truth. Which is why I need your help.'

And then he played his winning card. He turned on his best smouldering smile. Full beam. Maximum strength.

That was it. She couldn't hold it in any longer.

Lulu burst out laughing. 'Do you actually get results with

that type of pathetic pleading about being a two-finger typist?'

'Well…yes. I don't find many girls who turn me down.' His face twisted in mock horror. 'Was it truly that bad? I haven't had complaints before.'

She nodded.

'You really thought that I was pathetic?'

She nodded.

Kyle collapsed back against the kitchen chair. 'Crashed and burned. Maybe I *have* been out of this country too long.'

He shrugged and smiled at her apologetically. Suddenly his bravado disappeared in a puff of smoke, along with his playful attitude. The shadows under his eyes and his prominent cheekbones seemed to be even more pronounced without the permanent smile. Or perhaps that was the low-energy lightbulbs that Lulu had fitted to save on the electricity bill?

The change in him was so sudden it was as though someone had turned a light off inside his body. He looked exhausted. And probably was.

She decided to take pity on him and bring that smile back. The room seemed a lot darker without it.

'Don't worry; you haven't lost your touch. Your male ego is still intact, but there are two very good reasons why your plea was doomed from the start.'

Leaning her arms on the table, Lulu leant forward and looked into that beautiful strong and masculine face. His hazel eyes were totally focused on her, and for a second she resisted the urge to look away from the intensity of that gaze. The long dark eyelashes fluttered slightly. She was only inches away from him, and in that small space there was so much unspoken feeling that she almost sensed he knew what she was going to say before the words formed.

'First, I enjoy sorting out other people's paperwork so much that people actually pay me to be their bookkeeper. I like it and I'm good at it. You don't, and apparently you aren't. Fact. You are going to find it hard to keep up with me.'

She let that sink in, and for a moment—just a moment—saw something change in Kyle's face. Perhaps a glimpse of a suppressed smile? As though he was unaccustomed to having someone agree that he did not excel in all areas of his life?

Suddenly she needed an excuse so that she did not have to look at him, and she busied her hands with a completely unnecessary rearrangement of the beakers on the tray as she topped up his coffee. 'Secondly, I already know that you are only doing this book so that your patients can get the vaccines they need. Not for some personal ego trip or to fund your new yacht.' She flicked her eyes up to his. 'You don't have a yacht already, do you?'

Kyle bit his lower lip and shook his head emphatically in reply.

She paused, aware that she had his full attention. 'That's why I had already decided that *if* there is time—' she held up one hand for emphasis '—I *might* be able to help you with any typing you need to finish the book. It has nothing to do with you,' she added quickly. 'Just a sound business decision. The hospice needs those funds as soon as possible.'

He gazed into her face, slack-jawed, and smiled with a sincere warmth she had only glimpsed before. A real smile of genuine feeling that simply took her breath away.

He meant it. For that fraction of a second it was as though she had been given the key to look inside him and see the real Kyle beneath the façade. Outward bravado disguised a man capable of very deep feeling. And it surprised and intrigued her.

This was not the media star she had seen in London. This was more the man whose personality had shone through in his first book. She had misjudged him.

He truly was amazing.

Kyle raised both hands in submission, leant across the table, and with a grin as wide as the kitchen door said, 'Thank you.'

'You are most welcome. But don't thank me quite yet,' Lulu replied as she stood up and tugged down on the hem of her shirt to straighten it. 'You do still have to do the work. Even if it is one paragraph at a time. Using two fingers.' She looked across at him and gestured with her head towards the corridor. 'So, Dr Munroe, since you are in such a hurry to get back to the ice and snow, are you ready to get started?'

'After you. I'll bring my coffee and… Wow!'

Kyle stood at the door to the dining room, his beaker of coffee in one hand and his mouth open as he looked in shock and awe at the boxes and folders spread out across the long table.

'Perhaps we should start this tomorrow,' he whispered, and pretended to slink off back down the corridor on tiptoe to the kitchen.

Lulu shook her head and, throwing caution to the wind, hooked her hand around an elbow and drew him into the narrow room.

'It's okay. Don't panic just yet. Let me show you what I have been working on this last week.'

Lulu pointed towards the first set of folders as Kyle stood next to her, their arms still linked.

'Nine folders. One for each month that you were in Africa.'

Carefully sliding her arm out, with all of the casual *this sort of thing happens every day* nonchalance she could muster, Lulu was free of him. She licked her dry lips and picked up the first dossier.

'Mike Baxter sent over crates of official records. Most of it was a jumble of single pages, but I tried to focus on anything and everything which links to a specific month. I hope that's okay?'

She watched as Kyle flipped open the file and started scanning down the top page before chuckling out loud. 'Okay? It's amazing. You know, I actually remember that.' He looked up into Lulu's face and hit her with that heart-stopping smile. 'We were expecting a delivery of dried mango. Only there was a mix up at the warehouse and we were all eating macaroni for three months. It was wonderful—that pasta probably saved more lives than I did.' With a shrug, and a self-deprecating wistful grin, he looked down the full length of the table before giving a low whistle. 'Did you really do all of this on your own?'

'It wasn't too bad. But I haven't opened your personal rucksack. You will want to do that on your own.'

He winced in reply. 'Do I get any special dispensation at all for the fact that I had just left medical training and was totally green? Did you make *any* sense of it at all?'

'Some. Although there is also a box of memorabilia which you need to sort out. Did you bring your diary with you?'

Kyle patted his jacket pocket. 'I've been reading it on the book tour and trying to join the dots. Not easy. Ruth's diary is going to have to fill in a lot of gaps.'

Lulu stood at head of the table and watched him move down the line, smiling and then more sombre as he picked up one file and then another, before pressing both palms flat against the table and sighing out loud.

'Well, this seemed like a good idea a week ago. I now have ten days to relive all these memories of people and places and create something meaningful. Seeing it all spread out like this makes me realise just what I have got myself into.'

He turned to one side and gave Lulu a short bow. 'You've done a fantastic job. Truly. I would never have been able to do this in the time. The scope is the problem.'

'May I make a suggestion?'

There was a chuckle from the tall man as he ran both hands back from his forehead through his hair in a totally natural and spontaneous gesture, clearly oblivious to how charming he looked. 'Anything. Please. I'm begging you.'

'It might make sense for you to work through one month at a time. Perhaps take one month a day and write up everything you can think of, based on your notes and the background material. That way you can trigger your own memories about each month you were there.'

Lulu picked up an old airline boarding card and waved it around. 'How did you travel there, for example? Mum took a flight, then drove a truck from the city. Could you use that as a way into the diary? How you felt when you arrived at the camp? What the journey was like? Why you chose to go there in the first place? That's what I would be interested in.'

Kyle looked at her in silence for a few seconds, his brow creased with concentration.

'That…is a brilliant idea. Thank you. It would be an excellent place to start. As to why I went there in the first place…' He started to shake his head with a sigh. 'Well, that is a story in itself. Do you really think the readers would be interested? I had my reasons, but they are personal.'

'Of course,' Lulu replied in a gentle voice. 'And that would be your decision. I did get the impression from Mike that they were looking for that personal touch, but if it is painful…and some of it is bound to be painful…then they have to understand that there are boundaries. I know I couldn't write about—well, how my mother died, for example. I just couldn't.'

Her eyes were so fixed on the rug that she hardly noticed that Kyle had come over to her, until he reached out and took her hand, startling her with the gentleness of his touch.

'And I am an idiot for talking about my pathetic problems when you and your family paid a much greater price. I am sorry for being so insensitive.'

The sincerity and affection in his voice was so overpowering that for once Lulu felt like giving in and confessing everything about her confused emotions.

'No need to apologise. I know how this book ends, remember? But I don't know how it begins.' She smiled back at him now, and broke the tension between them as she slid her hands from between his. 'Are you really a two-finger typist?'

He grinned and wiggled his long, slender fingers in the air. 'I lied. Two fingers each hand. If I take my time and use the delete key a lot. Fear not—I won't be disturbing you or your family with ferocious hammering of the keyboard. Speaking of which—' he looked around the room '—when I do I meet the other Hamiltons? Are they out for the evening, or gone into hiding in fear of the wild man from Nepal?'

'The other Hamiltons?' Lulu asked, confused for a second before she realised what he was saying. 'Oh, you mean the rest of the Hamilton family? Well, you have just met them. Belle is a complete flirt, of course, but she doesn't hog the bathroom or leave her laundry on the floor. We get on very well.'

There was silence for a moment before Kyle replied in a low voice. 'You and Belle? That's it? You live in this big house all on your own?'

There was so much concern in his voice that Lulu frowned before replying. 'Yes, that's right. The Taylor family have lived here for generations. And I have no plans to change that.'

A chiming clock on the mantelpiece sounded out the hour, and Lulu turned to it in disbelief. 'Have you seen the time? I am so rude. You must be exhausted. Shall we meet back here at, say, nine tomorrow? That gives you time to get settled in and decide on how you want to work.'

'Nine would be great. Of course I don't want to disturb the rest of your evening.' He hesitated, then drew a piece of paper and a pen from his pocket. 'I shall need directions to the nearest hotel. Can you recommend some place fairly quiet?' He tapped his pen twice on the pad before frowning, which only seemed to increase the depth of the creases around his eyes. 'The media company have been fantastic, but it would be great to have some time to catch up with my sleep and not worry about waking everyone with my coughing in the night.'

Lulu brought her eyebrows together and stepped closer. 'Coughing? I thought you were taking antibiotics?'

He nodded before replying with a sigh. 'This infection likes me too much. The new drugs are helping, but it's going to take a while. Probably about ten days, actually. Strange coincidence that, isn't it?'

'Um…very,' she replied, with a nod of understanding. 'And who said doctors make the worst patients?'

'Anyway, I thought you would be staying up with the media execs at Lanston Manor.' Lulu raised her nose high in the air and wagged her fingers in the direction of the front door. 'It's about ten miles closer to London and quali-fies as our local stately home hotel. Much more suitable for you celebrity authors.'

Kyle snorted, and replied with a belly laugh that echoed around the quiet high-ceilinged room and was immediately followed by some serious coughing. A dry cough. Rasping, and so alarming that Lulu leant forward in concern as Kyle bent over from the waist for a few seconds before he recovered and pressed one hand to his chest, which he rubbed furiously before shaking his head at her.

'No more jokes like that, please. A stately home? I don't think so. The foundation is paying my hotel bill, not the media people. Every penny I spend on fine dining and fancy beds will be coming out of the Nepal budget. A room above a country pub will be fine.'

Lulu hissed in air between her teeth. 'I see. In that case turn right at the end of the lane and the Feathers is at the end of the village, next to the river. My godmother runs the place and the meals are excellent. But quiet? On a weekend? That could be a problem.'

Kyle nodded and sighed out loud. 'I'm used to late shifts, and it is within walking distance. The Feathers is the place.'

And then he looked straight at her and smiled *that smile*. The kind of smile that bored deep into her body like a laser beam of heat and combustion.

In that life-changing instant her deep frozen heart melted into a pool of warm smooth honey that flowed throughout her body, filling it with the most delicious kind of longing and delight. Fuelled by the presence of this man standing in front of her, her treacherous heart leapt in her chest, yearning, simply yearning for him to touch her and stay with her as long as possible. The sensation felt so sweet and startling that it had to belong to another woman. Not her. Not plain old country girl Lulu Hamilton.

Which was probably why the next words that came out of her mouth were so startling that someone else must have said them.

'There is one other alternative. Would you like to stay here with me? I have plenty of room.'

CHAPTER SIX

KYLE'S eyes widened and his jaw dropped.

That's incredibly generous of you,' he replied, with a touch of disbelief in his voice, 'but I couldn't possibly stay here. What would your boyfriend say? And then there are the neighbours. Kingsmede strikes me as a very small village. Thank you for the offer, but I think I've already caused enough problems for you.'

And that really did make Lulu stare at him.

The idea was not *so* very ridiculous. They could work more effectively, and the house was large enough that they would not be crowding each other. He was the one who wanted the book completed as fast as possible so he could get back to his life.

And he was worried about *her* reputation?

'Well, someone has a very high opinion of themselves! Prepare yourself for a shock. You are not as irresistible as you seem to think you are. Yes. You.' She pointed with one finger as the totally gorgeous man in front of her dramatically reeled back and pretended to be horrified at the revelation. 'And, just to make it clear, I may not have a boyfriend at the moment, but I do have a self-contained ground-floor studio.' Lulu busied herself with knocking the edges of some paperwork into straight lines so that she would not have to look at Kyle. 'My father had a bathroom installed there when he was ill, and I spend most of my time working in the studio anyway.'

Satisfied that the edges of the folders were aligned in parallel rows, she raised one hand towards the ceiling. 'You would have the whole of the first floor and the family bathroom to yourself. And as for the neighbours…'

She looked up and returned Kyle's gentle smile.

'Fifteen years ago there used to be a stream of medics arriving at all times of the day and night for free board and lodging. Plus, you are helping to build a new unit at the hospice. That gives you quite a few bonus points on the respectability scale; so don't worry about my friends in the village. Unless, of course…'

Her voice faltered, and she tilted her head before giving Kyle a cheeky smile.

'Unless? Please continue. I am finding these revelations so informative.'

'I was just going to say…unless you don't think that you will be able to resist my feminine charms for a whole ten days, Dr Munroe. Is that what you are worried about? Or should I expect your girlfriend to arrive any time soon?'

The smirk on his lips told her everything she needed to know.

'No girlfriend. Or wife. Only the press—who have been following me around like bloodhounds for the last week. *They* might find our arrangement a little too cosy to ignore. I can just imagine the headlines.'

'Good point,' she acknowledged. 'Leave that to the Kingsmede Neighbourhood Watch team. They can be a little over-protective. The press won't know what's hit them.'

A giggle escaped from Lulu at the thought of what would happen if city photographers started digging for saucy gossip about her from the lunchtime drinkers in the Feathers. Her godmother had been known to twirl a wicked rolling pin when she had to. Now, *that* would almost be worth seeing.

Kyle still looked uncomfortable, his knuckles white as they pressed against the back of a hard dining chair.

'What do you say, Kyle? Do you want to spend the foundation's budget on tiny bottles of fancy shampoo and a gargantuan buffet breakfast? Or would you like to stay here, where you can enjoy the peace and quiet you need and risk your saintly reputation being ruined for ever? I'll even ask Belle to let you pet her now and again, as part of your relaxation therapy.'

She paused.

'Unless there is another reason why you don't want to stay here? I don't like this quiet thing you do. It worries me. So out with it. I've started to come around to the idea. What's holding you back?'

What was holding him back?

The question echoed around the room and reverberated inside Kyle's mind.

For the last ten years of his life he had pushed himself hard. Very hard. Accepting every mission that Mike Baxter could find, regardless of danger or distance.

Jungle. Desert. High mountain ranges.

Driving himself day after day in a relentless search for something—anything that would prove that he could make a difference to the lives of people whose only hope for healthcare was the foundation.

And he *had* made a difference. He knew that. Time and time again.

So why was it not enough?

In all of those long, exhausting years he had failed to prove to the only person who truly mattered that Ruth Taylor Hamilton had not died that day in vain.

Himself.

He should have been in the ambulance that morning when Ruth had diverted onto a road set with landmines to avoid an army convoy.

He should have died that day. Not Ruth. Not this amazing woman's mother.

And he had been working every hour of every day since to convince himself that fate had not made a terrible mistake.

Except that fate in the form of a publishing contract had decided to play a cruel trick and bring him here. To the last place on the planet that he had ever expected to see. The house and family that Ruth had left behind. So that he could write about the worst—and the best—nine months of his life.

Suddenly aware that he had been staring at his hands, he looked up and locked eyes with this woman he barely knew and who was so full of surprises that he could hardly keep up.

What would she say if she knew the truth?

Would she still be inviting him to stay in her family home?

Or did destiny have another trick up its sleeve?

Was Lulu Hamilton the final piece in the puzzle of how he could finally put the past behind him?

He had never walked away from a challenge in his life.

And yet standing now in this quiet room, looking at the thick woollen socks of a girl who had lost her family, he felt as though he was standing on the edge of a precipice looking out over an unknown land.

A land where his heart was in control of his head.

He lifted his head to gaze in silence at the blonde only a few feet away. Both of her hands were pushed hard down onto slim hips. Several corkscrew curls had escaped from her bandana to create an aura of softness against her pink-flushed cheeks and gleaming eyes.

Blue the colour of a winter sky. Fire and ice.

She looked absolutely mesmerising.

He was going to need a guide before he could hope to venture into territory this dangerous and hope to make it through to the other side.

Her eyebrows came together in fierce concentration when he lifted his head to speak, as though she was willing him to reply with some profound and very logical explanation.

'I do have one question before I make my final decision. What are you planning for dinner this evening at Taylor House?'

'This evening?' Lulu replied casually. 'Oh, the usual. Home-made Shepherd's pie and green beans, followed by local cheese and crackers. All washed down with supermarket red wine.'

His eyes fluttered closed, his chest lifted, and his right hand pressed fervently over the place where his heart should lie as his mouth puckered into a contented smile.

'My private fantasy has come true,' he whispered. 'Miss Hamilton, I would he honoured to be your house guest.'

And then he spoilt the enchanting illusion by stepping

back, shrugging the tension from his shoulders and rubbing both hands together briskly.

'How soon can we eat?'

Lulu punched her pillow and turned over in the narrow bed. Then turned over again, twisting her duvet around her body, trying to find a comfy spot. And failing. Tugging the pillow over her head in disgust, she was forced to finally admit defeat and throw off the overheated covers.

Even her normally faithful Belle had tired of the constant tossing and turning and headed off to find a quieter spot at some point during the night.

She had slept in the studio many times and never had any trouble getting off to sleep before. What was the matter with her? Or should that be *who* was the matter?

The very idea that a man like Kyle Munroe was sleeping in her spare bedroom only a few yards above her head was enough to keep her head spinning.

How did he do it?

Was this normal?

Did he create chaos and upset wherever he went, like some smiling and benevolent tornado? Because he had certainly worked his magic in this house.

Had she been secretly sending out some kind of subtle message that said, *Please come into my home, which I have been guarding against intruders for the past ten years, and why not bring my pain from the past along with you? And if you wouldn't mind paying me some attention while you are, that would be nice too.*

What had she been thinking?

Sitting at the dinner table the previous evening he had been the perfect house guest, filling her kitchen with laughter and funny stories about his life in Nepal while he relished every mouthful of her food. It had been a pleasure to share his plans for the clinic, fired by his passion for his work and for people he lived with.

Perhaps that was why her dreams had been filled with soft-focus images of the cover photograph of Kyle from his first book blended with the real-live Kyle who had sat on her kitchen floor to play with Belle while she washed the plates?

Of course he was fascinating.

Of course he was handsome and charming and totally worthy of any schoolgirl crush.

Of course she wanted to get to know him better.

And of course her foolish heart should listen to her head. In ten days the cough that had interrupted their meal more than once would be gone, Kyle would be on a flight back to Kathmandu, and the tornado would have moved on, leaving her to clear up the devastation left in its wake.

Throwing her pillow onto the floor in disgust, Lulu slid her legs off the bed and opened her eyes a crack. Early-morning daylight filled the open-plan studio through a gap in the fabric blinds covering the floor-to-ceiling windows.

She sauntered down the hallway to the kitchen, stretching her arms above her head. And stopped, frozen. The kitchen light was on. Lulu swallowed down a fleeting thought of burglars before sighing out loud.

Her house guest. Of course. Kyle must be an early riser.

Groaning inwardly, because she was not prepared to speak to the live version of the man from her dreams, Lulu lifted her chin, inhaled deeply, and strolled into her kitchen as casually as she could.

It was empty, but the back door was slightly ajar, and

she stepped outside. Kyle was standing on her patio in bare feet, stretching his right arm high above his head, then his left arm, turning his neck from side as a gentle cough racked his ribcage. He was oblivious to the fact that as he did so the crumpled T-shirt he was wearing had risen up above the waistband of a pair of bottom-hugging jeans, exposing a healthy expanse of tight abdominal muscles.

Lulu had never appreciated the full meaning of the term 'six pack' before that moment, and it was going to be a long time before she forgot it.

Bells, whistles and several years' worth of unused female hormones sounded off inside her body, and she would have been quite happy standing there for a lot longer with a smirk on her face. The damp, cold morning was a blessing for her burning neck and cheeks. He was edible. Top to toe.

Except that out of the corner of her eyes she saw a red setter come hurtling around the corner of the house, and within seconds her delicious treat was ruined as the dog jumped up into Kyle's arms and was twirled up into the air, barking and barking in delight as he scrubbed her fur with his hands.

Lulu's heart melted.

He liked Belle. And Belle adored him. She was doomed.

Then Kyle turned around and saw her.

She could only gawp at the tousle-haired man as his eyes widened and shifted a little lower, before he twisted his mouth as though he was biting the inside of his cheek.

Lulu glanced down at what she was wearing and raced back inside the kitchen, her face burning again—now with embarrassment. Flowery flannel capri-length pyjama bottoms combined with a spaghetti strap top which barely covered her chest might be suitable for Belle—but for male house guests? In cold weather?

She had a sudden vision of what she must look like and almost squealed in horror.

Luckily her fleece jacket was hanging behind the door, and she quickly shrugged it on before turning back to face Kyle with a fixed smile as he threw a dog toy for Belle.

'Good morning. Did you sleep well?'

The Greek god covered a yawn with one hand, and then ran his fingers through what passed on him for bed hair. Totally relaxed.

'And good morning to you. I hope I didn't wake you up with my coughing? I had forgotten how hard it is to sneak downstairs in old houses with creaky floorboards.'

'I didn't hear a thing,' she replied truthfully. *Especially since she had not fitted her hearing aid yet.* 'Was Belle a pest?'

'Not at all. She was excellent company.'

It was only when he shuffled into a chair and dropped his head back, eyes closed, that Lulu noticed the dark shadows and pale skin and gasped.

'Have you been up all night?'

He gave her a wry smile as a reply. 'Not *all* night. I managed a few hours' sleep.' He must have noticed the concern in her voice. 'Kingsmede must be having a calming influence on me. I usually get by on a lot less. Why are you shaking your head like that?'

'I distinctly recall Mike Baxter telling you to rest.'

'Advising me to rest,' he replied, then startled her by reaching out and running his long slender fingers through her hair. She froze, unable to move and frightened to speak, until Kyle held up a long white feather with two fingers and waved it in front of her face. 'I think your pillow has sprung a leak.'

She smiled back, the tension broken. 'Old pillow. Old feathers. Thank you.'

'No problem,' he murmured. 'I am available for any kind of personal grooming duty you might have in mind for the next ten days. Just snap your fingers and I'll be there.' And with that he clicked his thumb and third finger together and locked eyes with her at the same time. 'Especially if you wear your hair like that.'

Her hand instinctively moved towards her head, which was a mess of unruly damp-frizzed curls, but he clasped hold of it instead and ran his thumb along the back of her knuckles.

'Don't change a thing.'

Then, releasing her hand, he pushed himself to his feet before she could reply.

'Since you made dinner yesterday, the least I can do is prepare your breakfast. I can see buttered toast and marmalade on the horizon. All you have to is sit where you are, looking gorgeous.' At this point he waggled his eyebrows a couple of times. 'And help me with the one question that has kept me awake in the night.'

Lulu took a breath. A twister had truly hit her little house in Kansas. 'Well, put like that, how can I resist? What would you like to know?'

Kyle had turned to the refrigerator, and she had to strain to hear what he said, but the words penetrated her heart and mind like a bullet.

'You've read your mother's diary and her letters. What did she say about me?'

Lulu sat stunned for a few seconds, and waited until

Kyle was cutting bread before focusing on what he was saying.

'Please don't think I'm arrogant, but studying has always come easily to me. Perhaps too easily in many ways. Medical school was hard, but I never felt challenged. When the chance came to go and work for the foundation I thought I was going to change the world. One country at a time.' He waved the breadknife in her direction, as though conducting an orchestra. 'Yes, I know. Young and foolish. Green as grass. All of my life to that point I had been told how clever and gifted I was. And here was my chance to do some good with all of that talent.'

Butter and preserves appeared on the table, then Kyle pressed both palms flat on the pine surface. 'I was an idiot. And it took Uganda to prove just how wrong I was. About everything.' A wry smile creased his mouth. 'I've just spent an hour reading through the records from my first month at the mission, and I am totally embarrassed by how unprepared I was. Ruth and the rest of the crew made sure that the patients didn't suffer, but looking back now it must have been a lot of extra work for them, with precious little gain.'

Lulu tried to focus on the movement of his hands as they set the table, willing him to continue, delaying the inevitable. She dared not look into his face.

'I'm not going to hide any of this. If the media company expect this book to be all about how great I was, then they are going to be disappointed.'

Lulu looked up in concern. 'You are going ahead with the project, aren't you? I've already told the hospice that they can expect a donation.'

His hand stilled, and he stared down at her with pain in

his eyes, brows twisted together as he replied in a low voice, 'Of course I'm going ahead with it. I made a commitment to my clinic, the foundation and your charity. I keep my promises. I'll finish the book—it's up to them whether they publish it or not. But it would make a difference if I thought Ruth believed that I had achieved something worthwhile by the end of those nine months.'

She breathed out a sigh of relief as he offered her a plate of crisp toast, but did not speak until he had taken a bite from a thickly buttered and marmaladed heavy crust. Watching his face contort with the simple pleasure of good food made her words seem foolish and pathetic.

'I wish I could answer your question, but there is a problem.' She waited until he was chewing before picking up her own piece of toast. 'You see, I have never read anything she sent home during the last year of her life. Not one word. So I have no clue what she thought about you. Or me. Can you pass the marmalade, please?'

His face paled and his toast hit the plate.

'Please tell me that the papers are not burnt or lost somewhere,' he said, in a decidedly less confident voice.

She shook her head. 'All the documents that came back from the mission are on the table in the dining room. I'm talking about the private letters and diaries. My dad kept everything safe while I was at university. They're all here, bundled up inside an old suitcase in my dad's studio.'

Kyle breathed out loudly, then stared at her. Hard.

'And you have never read them?'

'No.' She swallowed down her toast with a slug of hot tea. 'It was simply too painful after she died, and my dad never discussed it. He knew that I wasn't ready.'

Kyle sat back in his chair and nodded slowly. 'I can

understand that. Are you ready now? I *would* like to see her diaries, but it has to be your decision.'

I don't know. And I don't want to read any of it, but I know that I have to. 'As far as I know the diaries from her previous missions had a lot more to do with the day-to-day running of the clinics. That's where we need to start.'

'Are you okay with that?'

Lulu lifted her head and sniffed. She had known this moment was coming for the last week. No surprise. She simply had to face it and do the job she had promised. That was all.

'Yes. Those diaries will be fine. In fact, I can go back to the studio right now and find them for you.'

It was as though Kyle sensed that she had made her decision and they were back on track, and his mood seemed to lift immediately.

'Your studio? Ah. The Kingsmede centre of the art forgery trade.'

'Shush! I thought you said that your lips were sealed.'

She shot him a wide grin, and all the sunlight he had ever wanted was back in the room. Grey gone. This was what he needed. Wanted. This ray of sunshine. Perhaps that was why he heard himself saying, 'I've never been to an artist's studio. Do you mind if I make yours the first?'

Her mouth opened, then closed, before she answered him with a faint smile. 'If you like. There is not much to see at the moment. Come this way.'

Kyle glanced at Lulu as they strolled along the wide staircase side by side. She was clearly oblivious to how tantalising a prospect it was for any man to be walking behind her, and he decided to enjoy the moment for as long as possible.

She glanced sideways at him, as though a hidden sensor

had detected that she was being ogled. 'Before I forget, you can look forward to restaurant food for dinner tonight. My godmother has organised a welcoming committee in your honour at the Feathers this evening.'

'Excellent. I look forward to meeting your friends.'

'Before you get too comfortable, I should give you advance warning that Emma is responsible for raising funds for the hospice. I'm sure some cunning scheme has already been launched to make the best use of you while you are staying in Kingsmede. A naked doctors calendar, perhaps? The topless fire crew were very popular last year!'

She stopped outside what looked like a bedroom door and leant closer. 'Prepare to be dazzled.'

Without waiting for an answer, Lulu gently turned the brass handle, casually swung open the wooden door and stepped through.

It was the complete opposite of what he had been expecting.

Instead of the chaotic blend of startling bright colours that decorated the rest of the house, the walls and ceiling of this space were painted in a brilliant white. Light flooded in from the plain glass windows illuminating one single picture hanging over a large white fireplace. It was a life-size portrait of Ruth Taylor Hamilton, and it was so life-like that the impact of seeing her again knocked Kyle physically backwards.

He was so stunned that it took a few seconds for him to notice that Lulu had already started rummaging around inside a tall cupboard.

'Was this where your father worked?' Kyle asked, gasping in a long breath. He pressed both of his palms flat against the wall behind him, so that he could take in the entire space and regain his control.

'This was his studio for as long as I can remember. I used to play on a battered old sofa that was in the corner there, whilst he painted. In the winter we would light the fire and make toast whenever we felt like it. And sometimes we'd paint together, or just chat. This was always a happy room. He loved working here.'

'You must really miss him.'

Lulu looked into Kyle's face. 'I do. I know it sounds ridiculous, but after he died I used to come in here almost every day and just smell the paints. I only needed a whiff of linseed oil to bring him back to me. There are so many good memories of this place. I had some magical childhood moments here.'

Kyle Munroe moved closer to gaze at Ruth's portrait for a moment, hands on his hips before leaning forward and staring more closely at the signature.

'T. D. Hamilton? Is that your dad?' he asked, his voice low and business-like.

Lulu came and stood next to him, smiling up at the brightly coloured acrylic portrait of a very pretty young woman dressed in white against a landscape of blues and greens.

Her mother's energy beamed out from the canvas, her warm smile captured for eternity.

'He rarely did portraits. My mum was the exception.' She looked across at him and was surprised to find him still staring at the picture. 'Do you like it?'

He nodded. 'Very much. It's so lifelike. Ruth was a lot older when I met her for the first time, but there is no mistaking who it is.' He paused and turned towards her, so that they were only inches apart. 'There is a lot of love in that painting. He must have been extremely talented. Again, I am very sorry for your loss.'

Lulu looked into his face and saw something so intense that it took her breath away. A raw pain that brought tears pricking into her eyes. Just when she'd thought she had no more tears left to give.

'Are you also thinking of someone close? Lakshmi— that was her name, wasn't it?' she asked, her voice calm, low, as objective as she could make it.

He moved forward and gently wiped away the tear from her cheek.

His fingertips felt textured and rough on her skin. A soft smile lit his face from within. 'It was. But there have been so many. Friends who went to climb mountains and never came back. People I tried to help and couldn't. I get to know my patients as well as any doctor. It always hurts when you get there too late to make a difference— when clean water and a few simple medicines would have…' He swallowed hard. 'You are very intuitive, young lady.'

Then the moment was lost, and the big boyish grin came back like a mask and he closed down.

'You never forget them, you know. The patients who don't make it.' He shook his head. 'Far too many.' And with a final glance at Ruth's portrait, he squeezed Lulu's hand tight before turning to stroll out of the room.

'Kyle. Wait a moment.'

He whirled around to turn back into the room—only she walked faster and their bodies collided softly, surely, link-ing together so naturally that they seemed destined to be together.

It was pure reaction that drew his hands tight around her waist to steady her—but pure attraction that held them there for a lot longer than necessary. The only thing that he could concentrate on was the depth of the ice blue of her wide eyes and the gentle rise and fall of her chest against his shirt as their breathing became heavier. Hotter. He could have stayed there a lot longer, fuelled by his need to be close to this amazing woman, but Belle started barking outside, and in that instant he glanced over at the portrait over the fireplace.

Ruth. And Lulu was her daughter. What was he doing? Instantly he relaxed his grip.

'Steady, there. Why did you want me to wait?'

Lulu swallowed down the trembling dizziness that was rapidly taking her down the road to heartbreak. This was only their second day together, and Kyle was already turning out to be far more of a temptation than she ever could have predicted.

Every time he touched her it was becoming more and more difficult to look away and remind herself that he was only here to work. That was all. Except that if she had stayed in his arms one more second there was a very strong possibility that she would have wrapped her arms around his neck and done something very foolish.

And very regrettable.

'The suitcase is on the top shelf. Could you lift it down for me, please? It is rather heavy.' She pointed to the tall cupboard, delighted to have something to distract her from the bulk of him standing so close that she could smell the tang of his body. 'Then it's time to get back to the toast. You're going to need a lot more carbohydrate before you start reading all that.'

Kyle did not hesitate. 'And coffee. *Lots of coffee.* Now, tell me more about the Feathers. What exactly should I expect this evening?'

CHAPTER SEVEN

'I THINK you might have warned me that the entire village were going to turn out to see me last night! The children were a riot.'

'Not the *entire* village,' Lulu replied, as she waved to the occupants of a car as they hooted their way past them down the lane leading from Kingsmede towards Emma's cottage. 'Some of the babies stayed home with their fathers. You have to admit that the junior school had done a wonderful job with the welcome banner over the entrance. And the photographs should go very well with the question-and-answer session you gave in the bar. Especially that one with Emma's nieces in it.'

Much to Belle's disgust, Lulu stopped walking, leant closer, and brushed her hand over a stain on Kyle's jacket. 'I did tell you that Pip and Katy were high on cake and ice cream *before* you hoisted Pip onto your shoulders. I'm sure Emma can get that out.'

'No problem. I did notice one thing in the bar last night.' He pushed both hands deeper into his trouser pockets. 'Everyone I spoke to wanted to know about my clinic in Nepal, and how I was going to raise this money for the hospice, while you stayed in the background. Seeing as you are the reason I am in this village, I'm surprised that Emma didn't make *you* stand on the bar as the star of the show. Any explanation for that?'

Lulu shook her head. 'She knows that I don't like being the centre of attention. That's all. And of course they now have a new celebrity—you were a great hit! And it was your first public outing. They will soon get used to you.'

'I'm not so sure about that. The personal tour of the hotel and restaurant was brilliant. The book signing I could understand. But the autograph hunters? They were… different.'

'Ah…' Lulu hissed, drawing air through her teeth. 'The Bennett sisters. They run the newsagent and sweet shop on the main street. I admit they were a little over-enthusiastic about their new line in celebrity autographs, but when you reach their age any excitement in the village is welcome. Although, to be fair, it was *your* idea to offer to give them each a personal medical exam before you left town.'

Kyle shook his head with a sigh. 'I only want to make sure that your friends know how hard you've been working on this book. That's all.'

'Thank you for that, but I'm fine.' She paused and stared ahead before she spoke again, in a clear, confident voice. 'I know who I am, Kyle. I have done since I was sixteen. I live my life the way I want to and I'm quite happy to stay in the background.'

He turned and looked at her in silence—really looked at her, as though weighing something up in his mind. Then he startled her by presenting his strapped arm while keeping a tight control of Belle with the other.

'May I have the pleasure of escorting you to the home of Mrs Carmichael on this pleasant afternoon, Miss Hamilton?'

Lulu opened her mouth to give him a snarky reply, glanced at the half-smile on his face, and hesitated for a few seconds before nodding and threading her free hand through the crook of his arm. 'How gallant, Dr Munroe.' She looked up at the sky, where faint sunlight was trying to break through the heavy grey clouds. 'That would be splendid. If you can take the gossip, so can I.'

'Great. Because the cat is well and truly out of the bag. Your secret identity as an orchid painter has been revealed to the world. Forger or not, now you can tell me the truth about that painting you were struggling with in London that day. I want to know all about life as a famous artist.'

And with that he started strolling contentedly down the lane, under the shade of the great beech trees, with Lulu by his side, leaning into his shoulder.

'Famous artist?' She laughed. 'If only that were true and I had the income to show for it. The gallery owner on the South Bank was at art school in London with my dad, and he knows that I love painting flowers. Especially wild flowers.' She stopped walking, pulled back on his arm and gestured to the roadside, where a tiny clump of bright red flowers was almost hidden in the grass.

'Wild red poppies. They look wonderful with Herb Robert—those pink flowers higher up on the bank. Or even pink blackberry blossom and red rosehips.'

She leant in again as they continued walking and Belle became impatient to get going. 'Of course it is autumn now, so I have to rely on photographs that I took in the springtime. Primroses, daffodils. Wonderful spring flowers. I just adore them.'

There was so much joy and pleasure in her voice that it was infectious, and Kyle could only chuckle in reply as he pretended to scan the bushes. 'I don't see any wild yellow orchids! Can you point them out to me?'

She laughed out loud. 'Not down this particular lane.' Then she play-thumped him in the arm. 'It was a commission from a client who wanted a particular shade of yellow. A one-off. My usual work is a lot smaller and more detailed.'

'Why small? Why not just paint the flowers larger?'

'Because I paint life-size. That's why. No delusion. And here we are.'

Kyle felt her slide her arm from his, and the loss had already hit him before she bent down to pet Belle.

'Now, be a good girl for Uncle Kyle. Aunty Emma does not want you in the cottage—you're far too big and boisterous. And make sure that Uncle Kyle tells you a nice story all about his time in sunny Africa. See you back at the house.'

With one final finger wave she took a firmer grip on her cake box and strolled towards the small row of thatched cottages where Emma lived, leaving Kyle holding a dog lead attached to a mad beast who had just spotted ducks on the other side of the river.

Kyle Munroe sauntered slowly down the wet muddy footpath which ran along the riverbank, heading downstream away from Kingsmede, while Belle scampered on ahead. The light drizzle had turned into heavy rain and they were both drenched.

Which was not such a good idea with a chest infection. Right on cue, he choked on that dry cough he had learned to live with over the last few weeks.

Time to face up to his current dilemma. He was going to have to make a decision soon about the last chapter of the book.

The more he came to know Lulu, the more he realised that the pain of the truth would be one more thing for her to carry.

And *he* would be the one piling on the burden. How could he do it? How could he add to her problems? That would be the exact opposite of what he intended. He should be doing everything he could to make life easier for her.

Lulu was not only Ruth's daughter, but also a very special person, with an approach to life he had never seen before. Grounded, certainly. But something else. Something that had intrigued him from the first day when he saw her on that tube train. Lulu possessed an inner serenity, a self-contained calmness which acted like a lure. Drawing him to her.

In a few quiet moments last night in the Feathers, he had noticed the way she smiled at everyone she met without any hint of pretension or false emotion.

This was Lulu with the people who knew and cared about her as a valued member of their extended family, and she clearly cared about them in turn. Was it the village? Or was it Lulu herself?

Kyle looked around him at the picture-postcard thatched cottages that lined the footpath opposite the river. Their lovely gardens were bursting with late roses and apple trees heavy with fruit. Kingsmede and Lulu would always be linked together in his mind—she was just as much part of this village as the square-shaped ancient stone church, the Feathers and the winding river.

Perhaps Lulu's inner peace came from knowing who she was and where she wanted to be? Her sense of place. Was that it? It would certainly explain why he was lacking that perspective on his own life.

An hour later, just as Kyle was about to turn back towards the village, he glanced up and saw the very woman he had been thinking about walking towards him—only this time in heavy weather gear, carrying a golf umbrella.

He started jogging towards her, whistling for Belle as he did so.

She gingerly stepped towards him with a smile.

'Everything okay? I thought you were with Emma?' Kyle spoke calmly, matter of fact, trying desperately to suppress his concern.

She shook her head. 'We are both fine. It's you I'm worried about. I have an extra waterproof here for you, and warm gloves. This rain is getting heavier, and I have no intention of completing your book on my own. You, sir, are soaked.'

With that she pulled a long parka from her bag and passed it to Kyle, who thanked her and shrugged it on over his head.

She looked around. 'What have you done with my foolish dog? Has she run back home on her own without you?'

'Drat—she was here a second ago. You go that way. Meet back here in a few minutes.'

Lulu walked as fast as she could in the pouring rain, but it still took five minutes to reach the footpath that ran down the length of the river.

And there was Belle.

The ducks had been nesting on an island in the middle of the river that was swollen from weeks of autumn rain. The foolish dog had started swimming out to them, barking, only to find that the downstream current was too strong for her.

Lulu watched in absolute horror, calling Belle's name,

as her dog was slowly carried down the river by the power of the water. She was a strong dog, but inexperienced. The river widened in a few yards, and would probably be shallow enough for Belle to stand up in as long as she didn't panic.

But, to her horror, Belle started barking, out of control, and fought the current—which meant that she was swimming away from the shallows and into the fast-flowing deep water.

Lulu started to jog along the riverbank, calling to Belle to come to her. Come to the bank and be safe. Belle had been her constant companion since her father died. Nothing could happen to Belle. It simply couldn't. Even the thought of it was starting to give her palpitations.

Suddenly the ducks and swans lifted from the river, and Lulu turned to see what the problem was.

Kyle had started wading out into the water, and the fast-flowing river was already up to his thighs.

Without discussion or argument, Kyle simply crouched down in the water and waited until Belle had been carried to him by the current. He grasped her around the middle and hoisted the sodden animal over his right shoulder into a fireman's lift. His arm held on tight to her scrabbling legs as she wriggled like a fish from the waist.

Slowly, slowly, so as not to drop his precious cargo, Kyle turned around in the river and waded through the water and onto the riverbank.

'Oh, thank goodness. Are you both okay?' Lulu managed to get out, as Kyle bent his knees and allowed Belle to take her weight on her own feet as she slid from his shoulder. Lulu wrapped her arms around Belle, then repeated the process with Kyle.

They were rewarded by a full-body shower as Belle tried to shake herself dry.

'Oh, thanks a lot. Ingrate. Come on you two. *Home*.'

Lulu wandered back into her kitchen, where Kyle was stretched out, half-perched on a kitchen chair, back against the wall, sipping a steaming beaker of tea. His hair was still tousled from the rough drying it had received from the kitchen towel.

'She'll be fine now. Dry, clean and happy. Let that be a warning to us all about the dangers of chasing ducks across a fast flowing river.'

Kyle snorted. 'Looked to me like she was having the time of her life.'

Lulu grinned back, and fluttered his eyelashes at him. 'She was, but thank you all the same. Belle means a lot to me. You are officially our hero. There may be a medal.'

'I don't feel like much of a hero.'

'This is a small village. Standards are low. We'll take what we can get.'

Kyle saluted her with his drink. 'Faint praise, but I will accept it nevertheless. What made you decide to come looking for us?'

Lulu sat down opposite him. 'Emma and I were concerned when the rain started to get heavier.' She raised both hands in surrender. 'I know that you are the medic around here, but your coughing seems to have improved over these last few days. Of course that was *before* you decided to take a swim in the river . The future of Kingsmede as a spa town depends on your good recovery.'

'Well, I would hate to let the tourist trade down. Did Emma enjoy her cake?'

Lulu sniggered her reply. 'Loved it. Especially the sickly sweet icing, bursting with artificial colours. All washed down with *two* glasses of pink champagne.'

'Is it her birthday?'

'Not exactly. Long story.'

He cocked his head to one side. 'I have nothing else to do this evening except relive trauma in the African bush while Belle is snoring in front of the fire.'

'True.' Lulu sat down opposite Kyle. 'Have you ever heard of the Memory Book Project? It's one of the techniques they use at the hospice, and Emma asked me to help with hers. Basically the person creates a record of the life they have lived, their family history and customs, who their friends and relatives are. Anything they want their family to remember about them when they are gone.'

She smiled up at Kyle, and was humbled by the look of admiration on his face.

'Our generation is used to technology. Photographs, videos, digital images. Not so ladies like Emma. Photographs were expensive before the war. So these memory books can take their place.'

'So, *have* you helped Emma with her memory book?'

Lulu nodded. 'I made some copies of the only photograph Emma has left from her wedding. It was taken outside Kingsmede church. And she started telling me about her wedding day.'

There was a pause as Lulu looked out of her kitchen window at the lashing rain. 'It was a warm sunny morning. The whole family were walking back to the cottage where she still lives today for the wedding breakfast, and they had just reached the river when her new husband, Frank, slipped off his smart shoes and waded into the water with her in his arms, twirling her around and around, laughing and laughing, until they were both dizzy—with happiness and love. So much love.'

Lulu felt tears pricking at the corners of her eyes.

'He died of a brain haemorrhage. He was her soul-mate. Her one and only. They would have been married fifty years today.' She smiled across at Kyle, only he was focusing on the table, his brows tight with concentration.

'And I am babbling. Sorry.'

'You're not babbling. I'm so sorry for Emma's loss. She's a wonderful lady and deserves your love. What's more, you have just given me a clue to what I've been look-ing for!'

He clutched hold of her fingers, eyes bright, shining with energy and excitement.

'What you are talking about is a kind of scrapbook. A collection of pictures, thoughts, memories. Snapshots from the past that come together to make a complete story. Is that how you see it?'

Lulu simply nodded, bowled over by the change in Kyle. He was transformed. 'Yes. That's exactly right.'

'*That* is how my poor medical brain works. I see those separate parts, but I have a problem putting them all to-gether in a long piece of writing. What if I write the book in that way? Memories. Maps. Photographs. All the sep-arate pieces. I can do that, and I would enjoy it. What do you think? Would it work?'

She blew out, and made the mistake of looking at him— and was instantly swept away with his new-found passion and enthusiasm. A picture began to form in her artist's mind's-eye. 'A bright African collage. Oh, yes, I think it would work. It would work very well.'

'It's brilliant! You are brilliant.' And before Lulu knew what was happening Kyle had leant forward and kissed her heartily on the cheek as he clasped a tighter hold of her hands in his.

She pulled back her hands and smiled, trying to break the tension, but then moved back to rub Kyle's hand.

'Your hand is freezing! How stupid of me. You need a hot shower. I would never forgive myself if you caught a cold. Come on—off with your wet clothes.'

She was rewarded by the kind of seductive grin most girls would melt for.

It worked.

'Well, that's the best offer I've had all day.'

'It's the one and only offer you're going to *get* all day. Here. Let me help you.'

Even with Lulu's help it took five minutes to peel off Kyle's jacket and sweater over the strapping on his left wrist. He was drenched, and Lulu could see him shivering despite her central heating.

She grabbed a thick bath towel and came back into the room just as his shirt hit the floor. She leered, and despite her best intentions she lusted. Then lusted a lot more.

Kyle Munroe had the chest, shoulders and arms of a male model.

Not an ounce of spare flesh covered the well-defined body.

Lulu enjoyed a few more minutes of pleasure as he bent to remove his boots and socks, stretching the spectacular muscles across his broad shoulders, revealing an amazing expanse of taut, smooth skin with a covering of dark hair that was tantalising even before she noticed the waistband of his black underwear.

The reality of his work and life were only too evident from the sharp division lines between the dark brown of his lower arms and neck and the faint tan on the rest of his upper body. He looked as though he had plunged his head and arms into brown dye, and Lulu could not resist laughing out loud at the thought, helping to break up the sensual awkwardness of their situation.

'Well, *someone* has been working out!'

Kyle flexed his right bicep and heaved his boot to his chest in a joky demonstration of his weight-lifting skills, before lowering it back to the tiles.

'You need upper-body strength for the ice climbing. Not that I've done much of that recently. I've been way too busy at the clinic.'

Lulu gasped with horror as she gently touched one finger to the end of a jagged scar that ran over one shoulder and down his back. Smaller white lines were scattered across both of his arms, and across the bicep of his right.

'Is that what climbing does for you?'

He sniffed, not wanting to break her touch on his sensitive exposed skin. The delicious sensation of that single light fingertip had already set his heart racing and his body pulsing.

'A lifetime of accidents. Usually in the middle of nowhere. Pakistan—now, that was remote. When you have to stitch up your own skin one-handed, you can bet money the wound will be somewhere it's hard to reach.'

'Do you really expect me to believe that?' She looked at Kyle for a moment before exhaling loudly. 'You're *not* joking. Madness!' And then she looked at his strapped wrist. 'Can you manage in the shower?'

She was rewarded by a huge grin. 'Exactly what kind

of service are you offering, Miss Hamilton? Do artists receive special training to help in shower emergencies?'

'I was thinking of turning the water on for you, Dr Munroe, and finding you a plastic bag to cover your strapping. Possibly even finding you an extra towel. But of course that would be far too comfortable for a macho hero such as yourself.'

He looked around the room in pretend amazement. 'What did I say?'

'Had your chance. Blew it.' She pointed to the stairs. 'Shower! I'll get your wet clothes into the washing machine, and hope they don't disintegrate with the shock of hot water and detergent.'

'Can you use extra fabric softener?' Kyle asked in a pleading voice. 'I have such sensitive skin.'

Twenty minutes later Kyle walked into the dining room looking far better than any man had the right to, and Lulu's poor treacherous heart performed a double somersault with a twist.

She still had not recovered from the topless incident.

Vigorous use of the coal scuttle and log basket had created a pathetic excuse for her overheated cheeks and burning neck, and the open fire was already burning bright in the fading light, its orange-and-white flames licking up the chimney, creating shadows around the room. A single lamp glowed gently in the corner, and Lulu could hear the sharp crackling from her seasoned apple and beechwood logs.

It was the hair, of course. Any man would look edible with that length of tousled please-run-your-fingers-through-me curly hair. She could offer him a comb, but on second thoughts she decided she liked him just the way he was. Delicious.

He caught her staring, and glanced down at his clothing with a quizzical look, stroking the fine fabric of his Italian sweater. 'Will I pass?'

'For the moment. Perfect timing. The hot chocolate is almost ready. And help yourself to cookies.'

Kyle bent down to scratch Belle's head a couple of times, before collapsing down onto the sofa, his legs stretched out towards the open fire—where Belle had already dragged her fleecy bed before settling in for a snooze.

'That's better. I feel almost human again, and a lot warmer. That fire is gorgeous. Come and sit next to me and talk about Kingsmede. Anything you like. Tell me more about you and Emma.'

Lulu smiled as he patted the sofa cushion next to him and raised his eyebrows. She filled two beakers with hot chocolate from a saucepan on the hearth, and perched on the end of the sofa as far away from him as possible.

'As you wish, great hero! You drink. I talk. Deal? Was that a nod? Emma is so much more than my godmother. She gave me a refuge when I needed one. And then she gave me a job and a career! How about that for starters?'

'I need lots more details. Please carry on.'

'Okay. You already know that she has always lived in the village. She was born here. Emma knows everybody.'

Kyle blew on his steaming beaker to cool it marginally before taking a sip. 'So you were actually born here, as well—in Kingsmede? Mmm. This is good. Cinnamon?'

He took another sip as Lulu nodded. 'Cinnamon and a pinch of chilli. And, yes. Apart from a brief spell at university, I have lived in this village all of my life.'

'Wow! I didn't think that was possible any more. I have no idea how many flats and houses I lived in with my folks.'

Kyle frowned, as though trying to estimate how many homes he had used as a hotel over the years, before catching Lulu's eye.

'Please carry on. Emma has lived here all of her life. Got it. What happened to make her your refuge?'

'What happened was the annual arrival of the homeless and usually penniless waifs and strays from whichever far-off land my mother happened to be working in at that time. "Oh, just turn up," she would offer. "Tom will give you a warm welcome and somewhere to stay. Plenty of room in Taylor House."'

Lulu stopped, and realised that she had been gesticulating with her spoon.

'And so they came. Sometimes we picked them up from the airport; sometimes the docks. And still they came. At first it was the occasional nurse or medic who needed somewhere to rest and recuperate before going to see their family or start their next assignment. Then a few families started to appear. Perhaps a woman and a child who we had to take straight to the nearest hospital. Later whole families. Trying to escape a war zone.'

She stopped as Kyle sipped, his attention totally focused on her face.

'You know what's it like to arrive in a strange country where you don't know the culture. Often you can't speak the language, and the weather is something like today. Or colder.' She shook her head. 'The words *culture shock* do not even come close. But we managed. There was always something we could do, and they truly *did* need our help.

And sometimes they carried letters home from remote clinics.'

'So what went wrong?' Kyle asked, still totally focused on her.

'Drink up!' she said, then she nodded. 'Yes, it did go wrong. I remember having a bad day at school. I was studying hard for my exams. Oh, I loved school, but I had been teased. Again. I just wanted to go home and cry. Only when I got home…'

'You found a house full of strangers?' Kyle filled in the gap.

'The crying and yelling was so loud that I had to shout to ask where my dad was. I followed the loudest of the screaming to my own bedroom, where my dad was sharing out my clothes to the children who were running around him, throwing all my precious books and clothes around the room. My project work for school had been torn and trodden on.'

There was a pause as Lulu played with her cookie.

'I was seventeen years old, and suddenly, at that second, I just stood there, with the chaos and noise all around me, and realised that I wanted a normal life. With two parents and a home I could call my own.'

Lulu's voice dropped an octave as she brushed crumbs from her trousers.

'I know that sounds incredibly selfish, but I just picked up my books and stuffed them into my school rucksack, with the few clothes that I had left, and walked to Emma's cottage.'

Lulu brought the plate of cookies to the sofa, so that Kyle could finish them off, and sat down next to him, her legs under her, both hands wrapped around her beaker.

'I slept there every night for the next fourteen months. In exchange I worked in the hotel kitchens and learnt how to prepare accounts. Oh, I came here to the house every day, and checked that there was food in the cupboards and that the bills were paid and all the practical stuff. I didn't just leave Dad to cope on his own. Then I went to London to art college for a while. Apart from that, I lived with Emma.'

'What changed? What made you go back home? Did he start turning folk away?'

'Oh, no, he would never have done that. Never.'

Lulu sat back against the cushions and suddenly felt queasy at the smell of the hot milk.

'Lulu?'

'My mother died. But you already know all about that.'

She suddenly found the contents of her beaker quite fascinating.

'How did you find out? Did someone phone?'

'Mike Baxter came to see me at the college. All he could tell me was that her ambulance hit a land mine.' She looked up. 'He told me that it would have been very quick, but I always wondered how accurate he was about that.'

Kyle reached out and meshed the fingers of her left hand with his chocolate-smeared long fingers.

'It *was* instant. I'm so sorry—it must have been very hard to hear like that.'

Lulu sat up straight and took a breath. 'I moved back the day after Mike came to see me. As for Emma… She had a blood-pressure problem last year, but the Emma you saw in the Feathers is not so different from the Emma she has always been.'

'Then I'm glad to have met her. Do you miss them? Your parents?'

Lulu paused for a moment, before swinging out her legs. 'I think I've talked far too much for one afternoon. Now, we really should get back to work. At the moment I am up to month four, and things are not going too well....'

Then Kyle's hand was on her waist, the gentle pressure turning her towards him and closer, ever closer, so that they were looking at one other on the sofa, their faces only inches apart. His hand moved to her cheek, his thumb on her jaw as his eyes scanned her face back and forth.

'Don't lock me out. Please.' His voice was low, steady. 'Trust me, Lulu. Can you do that? Trust me?'

CHAPTER EIGHT

BEFORE she could answer, his hand moved to cup her chin, lifting it so that she looked into his eyes as he slowly moved his warm thumb over her soft lips. Side to side. No pressure. Just heat.

She felt his breathing grow heavier, hotter, and her own eyes started to close as she luxuriated in his touch.

Then he snatched his hand away to cover his mouth as a dry cough shook his upper body.

'Sorry. I think I swallowed some of your Kingsmede river water,' he gasped in a hoarse voice. 'Complete with duck feathers.'

He slid to the edge of the sofa and stretched up before reaching for his boots. 'Do you mind working later? Your wonderful crazy hound just cost me five hours.'

Lulu hissed at him as Belle lifted her head and thumped her tail hard against the floor, before settling down again, nose on paws in her comfy dog bed.

'Perhaps you should take the rest of the evening off? Being a hero must be *so* exhausting!'

There was a long sigh before Kyle replied. 'True. We *are* ahead of schedule, and I need to call my family some time today.'

'*Family* business? Now you really *do* have me intrigued.' Lulu rummaged around on the coffee table until she found a familiar book with a distinctive cover, and she waved it in front of Kyle's face before he had a chance to reply.

'I liked your book. But I do remember thinking that there were a few things missing. No mates, no ex-girlfriends—not even an anxious mum waiting at home.' She laughed. 'She must be very proud of what you have achieved.'

She looked up at his face and was taken aback by the sadness he displayed for a few seconds, before the smiling grin went back on.

Lulu broke the silence, her voice low to disguise her thumping heart.

'Sorry. I didn't mean to pry. It really is none of my business. Besides, you might spoil the surprise for the next book, when all will be revealed!'

Kyle answered by reaching out and taking Lulu's hand in his, startling her. He slowly splayed out each finger as she tried to clench her hand into a fist, and stared down at her palm.

'Long lifeline.' He looked up into her eyes. 'No, Lulu. I didn't leave a broken-hearted mother back in London. In fact, it was more like the other way around. She broke mine. As for girlfriends? Well, nothing serious.'

She didn't dare to breathe or speak at the sadness and regret in this precious man's voice. A sadness that almost overwhelmed her—a sadness that made her want to wrap her arms around him and share every ounce of heat in her body.

'After my parents' divorce my mother remarried and

moved to Australia with her new family. There was nothing for me there. I'd finished medical school here in England, so I took off to the most remote part of the world I could find.'

His eyes moved up to hers just long enough to check for understanding.

'Yes. I ran away to Africa to escape my parents' messy divorce. As for being proud of me? Well, I don't know about that. I get the occasional letter, and I know she's read the book. Maybe I'll ask her that question next time I see her?' He beamed a smile out to her. 'That should get the conversation off to a flying start.'

'When did you last meet up in person?'

'In the departure lounge of Singapore Airport,' Kyle whispered. 'About a month before her first minor stroke. She moved back to London soon afterwards with my half-brother, Alex, to start a new life as a twice-divorced woman. The second stroke was two weeks ago.'

Lulu took a sharp intake of breath. 'A stroke? Oh, Kyle. How is she?'

He smiled across at her. 'Recovering. Mother made it clear to Alex that she didn't want me to see her until she had better control of her speech and hand movements. Luckily for me, my half-brother is not someone who follows the rules, and he has been keeping me up to date. She should be discharged from hospital next week.'

'I hope it goes well for you,' Lulu replied, with a sincere sigh of regret.

'Do you believe that there is one person for each of us in this life, Lulu? One soul-mate, like for your Emma? My mother is already on her second divorce. It doesn't bode well for me.'

She looked into his face and saw something she had never seen before. Serious, yes. Concerned, yes. But more. This was fear.

Kyle was looking at her, holding her hand as though his very life depended on it. The flippant answer she had ready died on her lips, and she hesitated before speaking, her fingers moving to mesh with Kyle's, bonding them together.

'Yes, I do believe that. I have seen it.'

He lifted one hand and pushed her hair back from her forehead. 'I have no regrets. Once an adrenaline junkie, always an adrenaline junkie.'

Lulu looked up and raised her eyebrows, let him continue.

Kyle stopped and reached out for the copy of *Medicine Man* Lulu had left on the table.

'Do you see that photograph on the cover? I remember it like yesterday. The biting cold. Brilliant sunshine. I can still smell the smoke from the Buddhist offering to keep us safe on the mountain!' He looked up at Lulu and grinned. 'Those sorts of memories have to be earned. You can't buy them or trade them. You just have to be there, at that moment in time and space. That's special.'

Lulu found something fascinating in the bottom of her cup, then whipped around to face Kyle, her voice trembling.

'I've never understood it. *Never.* People in Kingsmede think that I've somehow come to terms with the danger of what my mother did for a living, but they are so wrong. If it was just adrenaline you wanted there are roller coasters, or any number of things that have thrills. Without the risk of killing yourself. And yet you still chose to climb mountains—by the most dangerous route, no doubt.'

She stretched out her hand towards Kyle as he started to shuffle closer.

'Your parents are probably just grateful that you lived this long and they still have you with them—even if it is for only a few weeks between missions. Sometimes family does have to come first. So don't expect the rest of us to feel grateful that you've lowered yourself to join our mundane existence. And—'

Before Lulu realised what was happening, he had wrapped his hand around the back of her neck, his fingers working into her hair as he pressed his mouth against hers, pushing open her full lips, moving back and forth, his breath fast and heavy on her face.

His mouth was tender—gentle, but firm. As though he was holding back the floodgates of a passion which was on the verge of breaking through and overwhelming them both.

She felt that potential, trembled at the thought of it, and at that moment she knew that she wanted it as much as he did.

Her eyes closed as she wrapped her arms around his back and leant into the kiss, kissing him back, revelling in the sensual heat of Kyle's body as it pressed against hers. Closer, closer, until his arms were taking the weight of her body, enclosing her in his loving sweet embrace. The pure physicality of the man was almost overpowering. The movement of his muscular body pressed against her combined with the heavenly scent that she now knew was unique to him alone and filled her senses with an intensity that she had never felt in the embrace of any other man in her life. He was totally overwhelming. Intoxicating. And totally, totally delicious.

Then, just when Lulu thought that there could be nothing more pleasurable in this world, his kiss deepened. It was as though he wanted to take everything that she was able to give him, and without a second of doubt she surrendered to the hot spice of the taste of his mouth and tongue. Cinnamon and chocolate. And Kyle.

This was the kind of kiss she had never known. The connection between them was part of it, but this went beyond friendship and common interests. This was a kiss to signal the start of something new. The kind of kiss where each of them were opening up their most intimate secrets and deepest feelings for the other person.

The heat, the intensity and the desire of this man were all there, exposed for her to see, when she eventually opened her eyes and broke the connection. Shuddering. Trembling.

He pulled away, the faint stubble on his chin grazing across her mouth as he lifted his face to kiss her eyes, brow and temple.

It took a second before she felt able to open her eyes—only to find Kyle was still looking at her, his forehead still pressed against hers. A smile warmed his face as he moved his hand down to stroke her cheek.

He knew. He knew the effect that his kiss was having on her body. Had to. Her face burned with the heat coming from the point of contact between them. His own heart was racing, just as hers was.

'Is that the way you usually silence women who ask you tough questions?' Lulu asked, trying to keep her voice casual and light as she tried to catch her breath. And failed.

He simply smiled a little wider in reply, one side of his mouth turning up more than the other before he answered in a low whisper, 'I save it for emergencies. And for when I need to know the answer to an important question.'

'Hmm?' He was nuzzling the side of her head now, his lips moving over her brow and into her hair as she spoke. 'Important question?'

Kyle pulled back and looked at her, eye to eye. 'I had to find out if you were holding on to a secret unrequited love. Now I know the answer I can do something about it. So. Would you care to risk being seen out in public again with me?'

Lulu leant back and took another breath, before grinning at Kyle. 'Well, I might.'

He bowed in her direction and pressed his forefinger onto his lips, as though considering his options. 'I happen to know that the Feathers has roast chicken on the menu this evening.' He dropped his hand and pushed it deep into the pocket of her father's best trousers. 'Would you care to join me for dinner, Miss Hamilton? No strings. Or do I have to use my emergency procedure again?'

'Dinner? That's it?' Lulu answered, knowing perfectly well that it was not the only thing he was offering.

'What do you think?' He winked.

And then she made the fatal mistake of looking into those eyes and was lost.

The words that came out of her mouth seemed to have no connection at all with the intentions of her brain. And everything to do with the desire burning in her heart.

'Thank you. I would love to have an evening out. In fact, I was wondering if you would like to be my guest at Emma's birthday party next week,' she said, giving him a polite smile, as though he had not just completely rocked her world. 'We always hold it here, and I'm in need of an escort. Since I'm between boyfriends at the moment, I suppose that you will have to do. If you're available?'

'An escort? Well, how could I resist such a tantalising invitation? I'm available. Assuming that nobody better comes along in the meantime, I presume?'

'Oh, yes.' She nodded and pursed her lips. 'I'd drop you straight away. But don't worry. I could probably pass you off to the Bennett sisters. They don't mind sharing.' A smile widened her mouth. 'I can be ready in ten minutes.'

A few minutes later Kyle was standing in the hallway in his coat, wondering how he'd got there and if he had truly just kissed Lulu Hamilton. Or had he merely dreamed that part of the last hour?

He had not planned to kiss her. Far from it. But the energy and passion of that woman was a flame, and he was the moth.

If ever he had lived for the moment, that had been it.

And, despite everything she had said, and the hurt he had unwittingly caused, when she'd kissed him back the intensity of the woman had made his heart soar.

She had pressed buttons in his body which had not been pressed for quite some time. The sweetness and intensity of that brief kiss had left him reeling—but his brain was still working.

This was no one-night stand. It was too deep, too special. Like her.

She had just told him what she thought about men like him—men who lived for the moment, not caring for the consequences. He had even admitted it himself.

It was true. He knew it, she knew it—and there was precious little he was going to be able to do to change her mind about that.

And yet…she had managed to do something he would have thought impossible. For the first time in years he was actually thinking about having something more. He *wanted* to try and convince her to give him a chance to prove that he was different. That he was going to be the exception to the others. That he would not break her heart when he took off to pastures new. That he was worth her time. Her affection. Her love, even?

And perhaps convince himself at the same time.

It was time to take another of those insane risks. And take an evening off. In the company of the only woman he wanted to be with.

Kyle stamped his feet on the welcome mat before strolling into the warm, bright and welcoming kitchen, still redolent of the breakfast bacon and tomato sandwiches he had shared with Lulu over several pots of tea while looking at the amazing party invitations Emma had sent out for her birthday celebration that evening.

They had laughed until they'd cried before setting to work for a few hours.

The memory book idea was working. Pictures, memories, facts and extracts from letters and diaries seemed to come together like magic to recreate a real place and time.

The book was going to be everything he wanted it to be and more. It would be a superb tribute to Ruth and the entire team he had worked with all those years ago.

And he could not have done it without Lulu.

The irony of that fact was starting to worry him more than a little. He had just spent the last-half hour by the riverbank, trying to work through the dilemma that would have to be decided in the next few days.

How was he going to end his book? With the truth? Or with the tributes and press statements the foundation had issued? Mike had no idea that there were two versions of the series of events. How could he? The only other person who knew was a paramedic working in Uganda who had probably forgotten all about it.

The more he worked with Lulu, laughed with Lulu, shared his life with Lulu, the more he wanted to be completely open and honest with her—just as she had been with him. She deserved to hear the truth from him, irrespective of whether he wrote about it in the book or not. No more lies and deception. Not with Lulu.

He cared about her far too much for that. Only if he was going to do it, it had better be soon—or not at all. And that was the problem.

Could he risk the relationship they had already built up? He knew that she cared about him. Would the truth destroy any chance they might have of taking things to the next level? Because one thing was for certain. Against the odds, he was falling for Lulu Hamilton.

Belle scampered up to his side with a gentle huff of a woof, as if to say *home at last*, her nails clattering on the polished floorboards either side of the rug before she attacked her food.

A delicious smell of hot coffee and burning logs wafted into the hallway as Kyle slowly raised himself on tiptoe and peeked into the dining room. Not that anyone would have heard him above the din of pop music bellowing out from the open door.

Lulu was standing on the top rung of a tall stepladder, apparently oblivious to the decibel level. Her hips were gently moving from side to side in line with her shoulders, and she was totally ignoring the swaying of the ladder and the impending doom which might accompany stretching upwards towards a high ceiling with both hands full of tools.

Lulu hummed along to the pop music blasting out from her sound system as she tightened the drill bit with her chuck key. The hammer drill made short work of the brick and plaster, and the plug fitted perfectly. Seconds later the picture hanging screw was in the wall and secure. She stepped down one rung on the ladder to measure the drop from the intricate plaster moulding of the dining room cornice. Exactly the same as the first. Excellent.

The pictures had been crooked for years. It was time.

Lulu was just about to move when she felt something touch the bare section of skin between her jeans and the bottom of her old T-shirt. It was icy cold, and running up and down her ribcage, and it was trying to tickle her under her arms. She squealed out loud.

As she whipped around in shock her left hand grabbed the ladder. At exactly the same time the heavy drill in her right hand swung around with the momentum of the movement. And made contact with Kyle Munroe's head.

'Ouch!' Kyle staggered back to sit on the sofa in a heap.

'Oh, no! I am *so* sorry.'

Lulu scrambled down the ladder and stood next to him as he clutched his head.

'I had no idea you were there.'

'My own fault for creeping up on unsuspecting females, I suppose. I did call out, by the way, but I can see now why you didn't hear me.' He pointed towards the drill, then to the sound system, where loud music was still belting out into the room. 'Having the music that loud can damage your hearing, you know.'

'Oh, really? Thanks for the advice. So can sneaking up on people.'

She moved her hands from her hips to look more closely at the side of his head, where he was rubbing vigorously. She started to reach forward to touch his hair, and pulled back, cautious. 'No sign of blood. How are you feeling?'

'I'll live. And I am the medic around here,' he mumbled under his breath as she tidied away the tools.

'I thought you would be out most of the morning. My dad used to say that a straight picture was a boring one. I don't think my party guests would agree. Sorry again.'

'No problem.' He chuckled. 'Belle disgraced herself with your local swans. They were not impressed, and... Lulu?'

No reaction. Strange. Unless... He snapped his fingers over to his left. Still no reaction.

Her hair was pulled back into a scrunched-up ponytail, and she was wearing her old working clothes again, but she somehow managed to look in control, calm and absolutely stunning. Her inner serenity shone out.

Kyle walked slowly over to Lulu's right side and helped her coil the drill cable before pulling a slip of paper out of his shirt pocket. 'I come with a message from the lovely Emma. The good news is that she has found the curtains you were looking for.' He raised his eyebrows high and gave her a quizzical look before going on. 'The bad news is that they have run out of lemon drizzle cake at the Feathers. So you will have to make do with chocolate muffins.'

'Well, she might have warned me.' Lulu paused. 'How

can I possibly hang pictures, fit curtains or type without lemon cake?'

She glanced up and caught him staring at the left hand side of her face, where her hair was barely covering her ears.

He knew.

She smiled and held out the sides of her overalls to create a skirt before bobbing him a short curtsey.

'Ah. You've noticed that I have a hearing problem. Well, I am impressed. Most people take a lot longer. So now you know. Stay on my right side and you'll be fine. Stay on my left and you can say whatever you like. There's a good chance I won't hear half of it.'

'Have you always had a problem in that ear?' Kyle asked, his eyes focused on her, intensely interested.

She paused just long enough for him to know that this was not something she talked about very often before she smiled up.

'It might surprise you to know that I have actually been to Africa. My dad and I visited Mum in the summer holiday I turned sixteen. She managed to get a few days' break on the coast at some medical conference or other, and we had a great time.'

Lulu busied herself unpacking Kyle's dictation machine, her head down.

'I came home with a very interesting souvenir—or at least that's what the tropical disease hospital in London called it. Encephalitis? Meningitis? They never did find out exactly what it was. But I was dosed with every antibiotic they could find, plus a few more experimental ones. I recovered with my brain intact and most of my organs doing what they were supposed to. Except one ear. So overall I would say I was very lucky.'

Kyle whistled and shook his head at her calm and matter-of-fact reply. 'I would say you were very, *very* lucky. Your parents must have been terrified.'

Lulu unwrapped the delicious-looking chocolate muffins before answering in a low voice. 'I was too far out of it to notice what was going on, but according to Emma my dad was hysterical.'

Lulu paused and looked up at Kyle with a smile. 'He actually sent a message to my mum and asked her to come home. Now, that was serious. He had never done that before.'

'Did Ruth come home?'

Lulu shook her head. 'There was no point. By the time the message reached the field station I was in recovery. She called from the nearest large town about four days later. I don't know what she said to him, but I know that was my one and only exotic holiday. Shame, really, but there was nothing else he could do. Fact.'

She passed the muffins across the table towards Kyle, skirting the plastic wallets of diary notes. 'I suppose you are well used to those sort of risks?'

He nibbled into the chocolate icing and tried hard to deflect the question. 'Mmm, this is good. And I seem to recall that it was your hearing that we were talking about. Does it still cause you a problem?'

She laughed and shook her head. 'You don't want to hear about that. Far too boring. And I know you have too much to do to chat to me.'

He held up his right hand. 'On the contrary. I do want to know. The work can wait a few minutes. Please. I'm interested.'

Lulu shuffled the paperwork a few seconds longer, but when she spoke, her voice was lower, calmer, slower.

'Okay. I'll start with a question. When you go climbing in the mountains, do you ever stop in the middle of no-where and just listen? And marvel that you cannot hear anything manmade? Just the sound of the wind, probably your own breathing. No planes. No cars. No radios or any-thing else from the modern world.'

Kyle nodded, not willing to break the fragile connec-tion held in her voice. 'It's a very special moment.'

Lulu rearranged the folders in front of her. 'That is what I miss. I miss the sound of silence. And, yes, I have been to specialists in hospitals all over the country, and tried the latest digital aids. They have no idea what caused it, or how to stop the tinnitus I get now and again. So I've learnt to compensate. But I'll probably never hear the sound of si-lence again.'

She smiled at him with the kind of tilted head, crinkly smile that melted his heart. 'On the plus side, my right ear is fine—so I still hear birds and ocean waves. Telephones. I love listening to music, and if I listen really hard and over-come my fear of calling attention to myself I can still hear a lot of what people say. Even if it is only one or two at a time.'

She glanced away to look out of the long windows at the open fields which stretched beyond the trees. 'So, yes, I would say that it *does* bother me. But it could have been a lot worse. I almost didn't make it.'

Kyle started to rise from his chair—only Lulu whipped back to face him so quickly that he caught her off balance, and he had to grab her around the waist and pull her to-wards him to steady her.

Lulu pushed down on his shoulders to steady herself, and made the mistake of looking into his face. And was lost, drowning in the deep pools of his eyes which seemed to magically bind her so tight that resistance was futile. She tried to focus on the tanned creased forehead above the mouth that was soft and wide.

Lush.

He already had the slightest hint of stubble at noon, so the rest of his body must be… No, she couldn't think about what was below the chest hairs curling out from the V of his shirt.

Sitting in her chair, she could see his head and throat were only inches from her face. Her bosom was pressed against the fine fabric of his sky-blue shirt. In a fraction of a second Lulu was conscious that his hand had taken a firmer grip around her waist, moving over her old overall as though it was the finest lingerie, so that she could sense the heat of his fingertips on her warm skin below.

She felt something connect in her gut, took a deep breath, and watched words form in that amazing mouth.

'I think we make our own destiny…' Kyle tried to join words together in a sensible sentence.

He gave up, because Lulu had slowly closed the gap between their bodies, drawn towards him by invisible ropes of steel.

'Destiny…?' she whispered.

'Who dares wins. Don't you take chances, Lulu?'

'Only with you…' Lulu replied, but the words were driven from her mind as Kyle's fingers wound up into her hair. Drawing her closer, he slanted his head so that his warm, soft lips gently glided over hers, then firmer, hotter.

CHAPTER NINE

THE sensation blew away any vague idea that might have been forming in her head that she could resist this man for one second longer. Her eyes closed as heat rushed from her toes to the tips of her ears and everything else in the world was lost in giddy sensation.

She wanted the earth to stop spinning, so that this moment could last for ever.

Before she could change her mind, Lulu Hamilton closed her eyes and kissed Kyle Munroe back, tasting the heat of his mouth, breathing in the heady smell of coffee, chocolate crumbs and a musky aftershave, sensing his resistance melt as he moved deeper into the kiss.

Her own arms lifted to wrap around his neck. She let the pressure of his lips and the scent and sensation of his body against hers warm every cell in her being before she finally pulled her head back.

Kyle looked up at her with those wonderful hazel eyes, his chest responding to his faster breathing, and whispered, 'Here's to taking chances,' before sliding his hand down the whole length of her back and onto her waist, drawing her forward as he moved his head to her neck and throat, kissing her on the collarbone, then in the warm hollow below her ears, his fingers moving in wide circles around her back.

'Oops. Perhaps those curtains can wait.'

Lulu opened her eyes in time to see the back of Emma's coat, and in one single movement she pulled back and smoothed down her overall with one hand as she gathered up her hair which had mysteriously become untied with the other.

'I…er…need to check on a painting. A present. For your mother.' Lulu just about managed to stammer out, and waved her hand towards the hallway. 'Painting. Studio.'

Kyle nodded. 'Great idea. Me too. Photos. Yes, photos. Catch up with you later. Right. Later.'

'Okay, this is new!' Emma stood at the end of Lulu's bed with her arms folded.

'Yes,' Lulu said, still feeling slightly giddy. 'It was a moment of reckless madness. He made the move and I decided to go along with it.'

Emma breathed out with a shake of her head. 'Oh, Lulu. I can see that he is very good-looking, but Kyle is a tourist. He will be gone in a few days. Are you ready for that?'

'Yes. I know,' Lulu said. 'If only he wasn't so amazing.' She closed her eyes and tried to recreate the heat of his mouth, his fingers running up and down her spine, and could not resist grinning like a fool.

'Well,' Emma said, 'you are old enough to make your own decisions, young lady, and if he makes you happy, good luck to you both. In the meantime, I have a party in a few hours. See you later.'

Lulu slid down the duvet and pulled the pillow over her head. She groaned out loud. Emma was only repeating what she already knew in her head. She did know the risks—better than most people.

It would probably be a lot easier if she didn't need him so badly.

Kyle leant back in the hard chair at the dining table, opened a computer file, and tried to focus on his memories of a distant place in a country he had last visited ten years earlier. Pity that all he could think about was Lulu.

He hadn't planned to kiss her, touch her.

She had kissed him back.

Where had that come from?

His eyes squeezed tight with frustration. *When had he become such an idiot? Just who was he trying to protect here?*

Lulu knew the score, and had been honest with him from day one. If anyone was being selfish, it certainly wasn't Lulu.

In a few short days Lulu had become his closest friend—the person he wanted to be with. Laugh with. Confide in. He had told her things about his past that not even his family would know about until they read the book. How had that happened?

Idiot.

Except that when he touched her face… Wow. Lulu was…so right. Beautiful. Hot.

And a lot more than that.

She had invaded his dreams day and night. Dreams of a life away from the stress and pain of the work he had chosen. Work where his only goal was to make a difference to other people's lives. Not his own. That was the legacy that Ruth Taylor Hamilton had left him, and he had to live up to that. Only now Ruth had given him something more—something so precious he was almost afraid to grasp hold of it, in case it fractured like a thin piece of crystal glass between his fingers.

So where did that leave him now?

This was Ruth Taylor Hamilton's daughter. He should go to her right now, tell her about her mother and take the consequences.

Big mistake. He needed to sort this out and do it now. Because what he was feeling was something new. And more terrifying than facing the highest mountain.

Yet he knew in his heart that this was one risk that he needed to take or die trying. Because he would never have this chance again.

His cellphone rang and Kyle casually flipped it open, his mind full of possibilities.

'Kyle Munroe,' he said, and then closed his eyes. 'Alex?'

His half-brother. The man he had only met once in his life.

'Hi, Alex. Sorry to sound so slow. I'm just in the middle of something. Thanks for getting back to me. Please go ahead.' He picked up a pen and started tapping it onto the smooth surface of the table before writing down an address. 'She'll be ready to be discharged from hospital next week? Fantastic. Yes, that would be great. Early afternoon would be fine.'

Kyle lowered the pen and pressed his forefinger and thumb hard into his forehead in fierce concentration before speaking again.

'No. I told you that I would respect her wishes. I'll make sure that I keep out of sight until you tell me she is ready to see me. Okay. See you then. Thanks, mate. Thanks for your help.'

With a great sigh, he leant back and closed his eyes. His mother was going to make a good recovery. That was one more thing to be thankful for.

Kyle was so preoccupied with dates and timings that he barely noticed that someone had come into the dining room and was talking to him.

'Hello, Kyle. Want to keep an old lady company for a few minutes?' Emma laughed and pointed to the window seat. 'It would make my day!'

Kyle leant forward and grinned. 'Show me an old lady and I'll answer your question.'

He raised his eyebrows a couple of times before giving her a suggestive wink.

That really got Emma going, her shoulders moving up and down with laughter as she wriggled down in the cushions. She waved a finger at Kyle as he positioned himself so that he was facing her.

'Lulu warned me about you, young man. You can save your charm for my only goddaughter. Although…'

'Although?' Kyle repeated, cocking his head to one side.

'I'm pleased that you are working on this book together.' Emma nodded her head. 'Ruth was a good friend to me over the years. She would have been proud of Lulu and what she has achieved. Yes, very proud. You will be working for a very good cause.'

'So you've known the Taylor and Hamilton families a long time?'

Emma narrowed her eyes and looked hard at Kyle. 'I was born in this village. Spent my life here. There aren't many folk I don't know one way or another. But why do you want to know?'

Kyle looked into Emma's face and recognised that she wanted a real answer. 'Well, for one thing, I admired Ruth Taylor Hamilton a very great deal. To do her memory justice, I'd like to know more about the lady before she became a pioneering surgeon.'

Emma sat back in silence, clearly sizing Kyle up.

'I knew Ruth very well. Eccentric, you might say, but bright! Sharp as a knife! And driven. I don't need to tell you that war surgeons like Ruth were not doing it for the wages.'

Kyle nodded. 'Well, that hasn't changed.'

She cocked her head to one side and stared at Kyle through narrow eyes.

'You married, handsome boy? Engaged?'

Kyle drew back and gave Emma a look.

'Me? No, Emma. Nobody is daft enough to have me. Or should that be brave enough?'

Emma blew out a puff of air. 'Daft. Courage is only part of it.'

She leant forward and grabbed Kyle by his right shoulder, looked into his face.

'Want some advice from someone old enough to be your grandmother? Because you are going to get it whether you like it or not. Don't leave the people you love to face the loneliness Tom and Lulu Hamilton had to look forward to every day. Stay single. Although…' she patted his face before sitting back '…there might be a few broken hearts along the way, a good-looking boy like you. Am I right?'

'Not too many, I hope.' He sat back, slightly stunned by the intensity of her words, and fought to change the subject. 'How about you, Emma? From what I see at the Feathers, there is a lot of mischief going on in a village this size.'

She smiled. 'I was lucky. I had some wonderful years. Sometimes it seems like yesterday.'

She looked down, her eyes glistening. 'It doesn't happen like that twice. Now, get yourself to that studio and talk to Lulu. I need my beauty sleep before the party. Remember to save a dance for me.'

'Wouldn't miss it for the world.'

Lulu pulled open the blinds on the studio windows and was dazzled by the sunlight flooding into the long, narrow room. Slipping off her shoes, Lulu slid down the wall to sit cross-legged, facing the windows.

She was exhausted.

Lulu brought her fists down onto her knees. Hard. *Stupid! Stupid girl!*

Had she not learnt anything?

How was Kyle any different from any of the other handsome young medics who had stayed in this house for a few days or even weeks over the years, until boredom set in, the next job came along and they were gone as fast as their legs could carry them?

Every one hooked on the rush. The adrenaline. The excitement. The thrill of exotic locations and hardship.

So what if he is gorgeous looking, charming and caring? When did that become so unusual?

She was stupid to think he was any different from the others.

Stupid to think he was special.

She took a breath. Stupid to think that he might actually come to care about her. Love her. Want to share his life with her.

Lulu dropped her head as tears pricked the corners of her eyes, burning.

Stupid to think that she could trust him to want to be with her instead of his work.

To dream for just a moment that he would come home and live in this village. Come back and stay.

Her parents had loved each other. But it had not been enough to make her mother want to stay. Ruth Taylor Hamilton had abandoned her husband, just as she had left her daughter behind to face her loneliness.

A tear rolled down her cheek and Lulu choked back others. She had always promised herself she would not cry about things she could not control. And now look at her.

Kyle stood transfixed and gazed in wonder as Lulu dropped her head back against the white walls of the artist's studio, her joy and serene calm acting like a spotlight, so that the entire room seemed to come to life when she was in it. How could he ever get tired of looking at her?

This was the image he would have to store away for those days when the satellite phone and the webcam failed and he was down to a photo—an imprint of a cheeky smile and those stunning whirls of long, blond, corkscrew curls. But all he wanted to do now was throw his rucksack into a corner of this room and tell her that he was not going anywhere. And keep on telling her, over and over again, until she finally believed him.

Perhaps then, at last, she would trust him enough to let him into her heart.

Except of course he might not be able to keep that promise. The TV company had planned to film in Uganda for a week. Fly in, fly out. But he knew precisely what would happen. A few days into the clinic and he would be stuck there until another medic could take over. Where would that leave Lulu?

What could he offer her? A short-term affair would be wonderful, amazing and unforgettable. But then what? A tearful farewell at some airport and six months of misery, during which he would work himself senseless every day to block out the loss?

While Lulu got on with her life in Kingsmede. Alone again, deserted by yet another medic on a mission.

Kyle looked away as he saw her mouth twist into her tears, torn between wanting to be with her and wanting to quell the fire in his belly he felt whenever they were in touching distance.

Emma Carmichael knew what she was talking about. He had a choice to make. Stay single and go back to the work that had been his refuge for the last ten years. Or change his life and find a new direction which was even more terrifying and uncertain.

Because one thing was clear.

He was infatuated with Lulu Hamilton and there was not a thing he could do about it. There was one task, however, he *could* help her with.

Lulu quickly swallowed down her tears when the door opened a little wider and she looked up to see Kyle standing there, leaning against the doorframe, filling the space.

He looked so handsome he must belong to another woman, another country and another life. He could not possibly want to be hers. She had been kidding herself with a silly teenage crush. How pathetic was that?

He shuffled down next to her, so that he could wrap his arm around her shoulders.

Lulu closed her eyes for a second, to luxuriate in the sensation of his hair and his stubbly chin on her skin. The smell of a citrus shampoo. His smell.

She could not help but instinctively snuggle closer, so that she could lean against him as he stretched out his long legs and crossed his ankles.

He drew a folder of papers onto her lap, and the air between them seemed to freeze. It was the folder of her mother's letters and personal documents from the suitcase, which Kyle had put to one side as they went through her diaries.

His arm tightened around her shoulder and his lips pressed against the top of her head.

'I want to thank you for showing me the diaries. You were right—they *were* full of technical details about the mission, but also I found what I was looking for. Apparently Ruth thought that I was doing okay. And that means a lot.'

'I'm pleased,' she managed to squeeze out through a tight throat.

'Now it's your turn to look at some photographs and choose some for the book. It's time.'

She swallowed down hard in pain, aware of his hot breath on the side of her face.

'I'll be right here next to you. We can go through them together. Okay? Here goes.'

And without another word, Kyle turned the package upside down so that the contents spilled out onto their laps.

She could only watch as he casually started rummaging through the jumble of envelopes, single sheets of paper, and something she had not expected.

Her mother had taken photographs. Lots of photographs.

And not just of the stunning countryside and the animals, but of the field hospital itself, and the patients she had treated. In many cases the name of the person had been written on the back, making them even more personal. Smiling men, women and children, some of them clearly very ill or wounded.

And of course she had taken photos of the people he worked with. Paramedics, orderlies, nurses whose names she recognised. There was one of a younger version of Kyle in a white coat, inside a fabric tent. She looked at it for a few seconds before passing it to him with a smile. 'This would be perfect.'

He smiled back and nodded. 'Book cover perfect.' And then he looked down and picked up another. 'How about this for the dedication page?'

It was her mother. The mission leader.

Lulu took the simple crinkly print from his fingers. Centre stage was Ruth Taylor Hamilton, walking with grinning children along a dusty dirt road below a clear blue sky. She was laughing, and she looked so happy as her arms swung wide to lift one of the children up from the ground.

Tears pricked the back of Lulu's eyes and she wiped them away, aware of Kyle's gentle touch.

'I'm sorry this is so hard for you. I truly am.'

Lulu shook her head as she ran her fingertip across the image. 'You don't understand. I'm not crying for Mum. I'm crying because I am so pathetic. Don't you see? I'm jealous. I keep thinking that it should have been *me* in that photograph. *I* should have been the little girl with her, playing and laughing and enjoying life. *I* was her daughter—not these children.'

Her shoulders were heaving with the pain in her chest.

'Can you understand how guilty that makes me feel? How pathetic? These children had suffered so much; they deserved some happiness. I have no right to be envious of that. None at all.'

He was holding her in his arms now, pressing her closer and closer to his chest, drawing her to him. 'Yes, you do. You wanted your mother and she wasn't here for you when you needed her. You deserved happiness as much as they did, Lulu. But you have the rest of your life to look forward to now. And quite a few letters to read. You can do it. I know that you can.'

'Don't do this, Kyle. Please. Don't make this worse than it is.' The quiver in her voice betrayed her and she was forced to stop. To gulp down her panic.

'It's going to be all right now.' His voice was low. Caring. Concerned. Everything she wanted but knew she could never have.

'And, in case you're wondering, you don't get rid of me that easily. Not a chance. You had better get used to that idea. So, now we're clear about that, I would like to hear what's on your mind, Lulu. Tell me why you were crying when I came in. Is it me? Have I been an idiot?'

Lulu tried to shake her head, but found Kyle in the way.

'No. No, it is not you. You have always made it clear that you want to go back to Nepal as soon as you can. Your work is important there. They need you.' Her head dropped forward a little. 'I knew that from day one. I'm the one who made the mistake of hoping that I might change your mind, Kyle. I'm the one who is being ridiculous.'

Lulu lifted Kyle's arm from around her shoulder and turned to face him. Their noses were only inches apart. She placed one of her hands on each side of his face and her eyes looked deep into forest pools reflecting every shade of amber and green as she forced him to look at her.

'I love my life and my work here in the village. I want to share that life with someone special. But that person has to want to be here. It's totally unfair for me to expect that from you. I am selfish. I know that. I want to wake up with the same person every morning. In the same bed. That's why I wanted you to leave, Kyle. Before…'

Kyle leant his head forward so that their brows were touching. 'Before?'

She smiled. 'I was going to say before we make promises and commitments we want to keep but know in ourselves that we can't.'

There was a huge sigh from the man whose lips were moving across her temple. He slowly pulled away and brought his hand up to push back the wisps of hair which had fallen onto her brow. His fingers stroked through the tight curls, revelling in the unique sensation.

'Is this what the quiet life does? Puts a wise head on such pretty young shoulders? In Nepal you would be called a shaman—a *jhankri*. A witch doctor. Someone who is not afraid to recognise the truth, even when it is hard to hear. But even witch doctors can only heal other people, Lulu. Not themselves.'

Kyle stopped messing with her hair and brought his hand down to cup her cheek as he looked into her face.

'Not many people have come to know me like you do.

Know me from the inside. Not even my own family. That is a rare gift.'

Her face creased into a wide grin before her head dropped. 'You're so easy to like.' *So easy to love.* She had to change the subject—quick. 'Now that I've chosen your photos, here's something I painted which *your* mother might like as a present.'

Her fingers creased around the edges of a watercolour sketch of spring flowers that looked so lifelike to Kyle he could almost smell their sweet fragrance lifting from the heavy cream paper.

Her forefinger stroked the edge of the paper, and when Lulu spoke her voice was low and sad. 'Dad never liked my flower paintings. They were too small and too commercial for his taste. Not the kind of work a real artist would do. That's why he wanted me to go to art college. So that I could learn to be a true painter and put this amateur stuff behind me.'

'You really mean that, don't you?' Kyle shook his head in amazement. 'You are so talented, and it's obvious that you love what you do. This is wonderful work, and I know my mother would treasure an original painting like this. You're a very special person, Lulu Hamilton.' He touched her forehead with his. 'So very special. And so beautiful.'

'Kyle? About earlier…'

The telephone rang in the hall.

'It's okay. I have an answer-machine.'

'*What* about earlier?' Kyle mumbled. He was caressing her face now, moving down to her neck, nudging open her blouse with his chin, trying to distract her from listening to the telephone—only to hear Emma's voice echo across the empty space.

'Hi, Lulu. Just to let you know that the party goodies should be with you in about half an hour. See you soon!'

'Half an hour!' Lulu shouted in horror, trying to wriggle herself free from Kyle's grip.

'Relax, sweetheart. You would be amazed at what we can get done in half an hour.'

'Did you just call me sweetheart?' Lulu's eyes widened like a schoolgirl's as Kyle nodded, his eyes never breaking their hold on hers. 'You did?'

'I'll call you sweetheart as many times as you like if it makes you look happy. And you *do* look happy. I can only hope I have played some small part in that.'

'Idiot. You have shown me what happiness feels like— I could get addicted to it. Addicted to *you*. Do you have a cure for that, Dr Munroe?'

He answered by kissing her forehead and neck. Luxuriating in the touch of her skin on his. 'And what if I'm addicted to you? Have you thought of that? A pair of hopeless addicts together.'

'A sad case,' she answered, kissing him back at the corners of his mouth as he tried to speak.

His hand came up and pressed against her lips. His voice was intense. Fraught. 'I can't lose you. It's taken me a lifetime to find you, Lulu. I want to be with you. Can you do that? Let me be part of your life?'

She closed her eyes and revelled in the warmth of his sweet embrace, which was so full of love and compassion. He meant it. There was no doubt. He wanted her as much as she wanted him. But did he need her?

'You have such a big heart,' she whispered as her fingertips ran across the muscles of his chest and collarbone to his jawline. 'I know that you mean those words now, at this minute and in this place, but some time soon you are going to take a telephone call, and then I'll be driving you to the airport.'

Kyle sighed and nodded before replying. 'You're right. I've been assigned to Nepal for another month before the winter closes in. Then there is Africa.'

She smiled as she stroked his face. 'I have good reason to know what it feels like to be left behind by the only person you truly care about in the world.'

'What about the person who's leaving their love behind?' He smiled back, his fingers playing with the curls in her hair. 'Do you have any idea how hard it is to smile and wave and know that you are going to miss everything about them? Especially when I have moments like this to remember.'

Her smile faded. 'Yes. I know that it would hard for both of us.'

She looked at Kyle, and there was so much pain in her eyes that he reached out with both arms and she fell into them.

'My mother broke my heart. And the pain was so terrible that I blamed her for it for a very long time. I never want to feel that way about you, Kyle. That wouldn't be fair on you.'

Kyle cuddled her closer, his hands stroking her back in wide circles. 'It doesn't have to be that way with us.'

He pulled back from her just enough so that she could see one side of his face, illuminated by the sunlight streaming into the room. The sculpted curved lines of his cheeks and jaw had not been created by some Renaissance master but through a hard life of years of work. Shame that it made absolutely no difference to how much she wanted to run her fingers along that skin and feel the man beneath.

With the kind of smile that would have saved her a fortune in central heating, Kyle said, 'Now—it is probably time to get back to work. You have a birthday party to organize, and I have to write the last two chapters of my book. Although I do have one request.'

He grinned down at Lulu as he slowly drew her to her feet. 'Any chance you could dig out that grey suit? As passion killers go, it was a winner. Otherwise there is absolutely no guarantee that I will be able to keep my hands off you.'

CHAPTER TEN

KYLE glanced around the brightly lit hallway of Taylor House and waved as he was recognised by many of the jovial people in the crowd.

Show tunes from Hollywood musicals were playing in the background, just loud enough to be heard against the laughter and contented chatter of the old friends and neighbours around him. He had helped some of the men from the Feathers string fairy lights along the trees leading up to the porch and hallway, and now at seven in the evening, they looked terrific.

He quickly scanned the hallway and sitting room for Lulu. Then he heard her distinctive laughter echo out from the kitchen and slowly made his way towards the source, acknowledging warm greetings from people he had only met a few days earlier, who had taken the time to make him feel welcome. Part of their community.

Lulu was standing at the makeshift bar spread out on the long pine table, her attention focused on Emma Carmichael, who had taken up residence at one end with her hand firmly clutched around what looked like a champagne bottle. More Christmas lights had been strung around the kitchen windows, but they paled into a dull glow compared to the woman he was looking at.

It could only be Lulu.

Her long, sensitive fingers were stretched out around a wide bottle, pouring golden sparkling liquid into champagne glasses. Her slender wrists jangled and sparkled with rows of gold bracelets. Bright yellow. Some inset with coloured stones.

A pale green and gold top in shining silk fitted her upper body and highlighted her tiny waist, where a band of pale skin was exposed just at the curve of her back. It was only a few inches wide, but it was enough.

Kyle stopped short, trying to record the image.

An elegant green silk sari was wrapped around her body, heavily embroidered with gold flowers and just short enough to reveal thin gold sandals. He could not help but stare at the gold ankle chains decorated with tiny bells that emerged as Lulu stepped forward on the terra cotta tiled flooring to return the champagne to the ice bucket.

Lulu half turned towards Kyle just as he was about to say hello, and he stalled, stunned by the woman he could not drag his eyes away from.

Three heavy gold necklaces of varying lengths hung below her face, drawing his attention to her fitted bodice and the tantalising curves of what lay beneath.

Then her earrings moved, sparkling in the coloured lights, making him focus on her face. Stunning make-up illuminated her blue eyes, which matched the colour of the silk cloth. Her lips were full, moist, her face radiant.

She had never looked more beautiful. Or more magical.

This was the Lulu he remembered working in her garden the very first time he had come to this house. This was the real Lulu.

The Lulu he had fallen in love with as she sawed wood and played with her dog.

The fact that he had not realised that fact until this moment shocked him so much that he could only stand and stare as she turned and spotted him.

He was in love with Lulu Hamilton. Not Ruth's little girl, but this unique, amazing woman who was grinning at him from across the room.

'Hello, Kyle,' she said, although his brain was telling him that her radiant smile was more than just a simple hello. 'I'm pleased that you could make it. There are lots of people from the hospice team who would love to meet you. The Bennett sisters have even brought their autograph book.'

Her voice, her smiling face. The way her eyes met his without hesitation or excuse. Welcoming. She wanted him to be here, with her.

Kyle swallowed down a lump in his throat. If this was what being in a real home meant, he had been missing out all of his life.

'Wouldn't miss it for the world,' he answered, well aware that he had a stupid teenage-crush grin plastered all over his face as he walked slowly over to her and inhaled her exotic perfume, half closing his eyes at the intensity of the spicy floral scent. Roses, vanilla, sandalwood. And Lulu.

'That perfume is perfect.'

She tilted her head at him so that he could sniff closer to her neck without the rest of the village calling the police. 'A present from Emma. I'm glad you like it.'

'Have I told you yet that you look…' he breathed in and raised his eyebrows '…totally amazing?' He whispered in her right ear, 'And seriously hot. You should never wear grey again.'

She reared back and stared into his face. 'Seriously?'

He nodded, and silently mouthed the word 'hot' before taking her hand. 'I am now officially on chaperon duty. Because in that outfit you need one.'

Lulu laughed and grabbed his hand. 'How gallant. Oh, and for the record, you don't look too bad yourself. You should wear a dinner jacket more often. Is it one of your dad's?'

She had the great pleasure of seeing Kyle's neck flush red with the truth.

Of course there was no way that she was going to tell him that he looked so gorgeous that she had almost fainted when she saw him strolling like a male model into her kitchen. She might have guessed that Kyle was one of those men who had been born to wear evening dress. The broad shoulders and slim waist were divine.

James Bond did not even come close.

His short hair had been waxed into a shiny mass swept back above a clean-shaven face. The cleft in his broad chin widened as he grinned back at her, revealing the laughter creases around his mouth and at the corners of both eyes. And then there were his eyes. No, she couldn't look into those eyes.

She would drown and not come up for air. And be happy to do it.

She would snatch at this chance to find a little happiness in her life.

To save herself from doing something foolish, like

patting his bottom or suggesting they take a tour of the bedrooms, Lulu started walking from group to group, introducing Kyle to those friends and neighbours he was on nodding acquaintance with from the Feathers and his walks.

'Of course there is one thing I haven't tried yet,' Kyle said between half-closed lips, as his hand moved down to wrap itself around the bare skin at Lulu's waist, his fingers lingering just a second too long before moving to her silk skirt as he drew her into the living room.

He turned and looked into her eyes with that special look for the first time that evening. And her heart melted. The intensity, the need, the loneliness were all there.

In that one single look.

'Dancing,' he whispered into her ear, 'is the only way a poor bloke like me can move closer to a lady without getting his face slapped.'

'Oh, don't be so sure of that,' Lulu said. 'The night is still young.' And with a beaming smile, she raised her left hand to his shoulder.

In seconds his hand was splayed out on her bare waist, pulling her to his body as the music changed to a big orchestra sound.

'Ready to strut your funky stuff?' he asked. 'With a poor wounded medic? I shall try not to step on your dainty toes. Are you willing to risk it?'

Lulu looked into his grinning face.

Daring to risk it, more like! Daring to be pressed against his chest. With her flat sandals she only came up to his chin. How ridiculous was that? How amazing. How…wonderful.

A second later and Kyle had swept her into the room, and he had yet another skill at which he excelled.

'Not bad. Not bad at all,' Lulu reported, as they completed a tour of the room in harmony with the music and each other.

To her eternal embarrassment, at that precise moment she looked over Kyle's shoulder just in time to see Emma staring at them. If that was not bad enough, Emma gave her a knowing nod as she raised one thumb. With a wink. As subtle as ever.

Well aware that her face was warming the room, as well as her neck, Lulu leant forward to get out of eyeshot and found herself peering into Kyle's black bow tie, sensing the masculinity of the man who was holding her in his arms. *Oh, boy.*

'Not too much for you, is it? Want to take a break and catch your breath?'

His hand moved up an inch from the waistband of her silk skirt until it was resting on bare skin, the rough fingertips light and tender. As she looked up into his face the music and chatter in the room faded away, until she felt that they were alone in a private room.

A room dedicated to just the two of them.

Lulu resisted the urge to close her eyes and succumb to the luxury of the moment.

Suddenly she lurched forward as a pair of small arms wrapped around her leg and tried to drag her away to the open French windows.

'Aunty Lulu, Aunty Lulu—Belle ran away, Aunty Lulu. Come quick. Come quick.'

Lulu glanced up at Kyle with a mischievous look before answering. 'It's okay, Pip. Uncle Kyle is going to find her for you. Aren't you, Uncle Kyle?'

Uncle Kyle said something under his breath about a

certain dog that was not suitable for the ears of small persons and released Lulu with a heavy sigh.

Pip immediately grabbed his right hand and dragged him out of the room. Kyle could only manage one half glance back towards Lulu, with a shrug of his shoulders, before he disappeared into the night.

That dog had an agenda. She had thought so before, but now she was sure of it. Lulu stared after Kyle for a few seconds, before the local grocer tapped her on the shoulder and she was off dancing once more.

It was a party.

Why not let her hair down and have some fun for once in her life?

Lulu stood in the front porch of her house and waved as the last of the guests staggered away down the lane towards the village, guided by the lovely fairy lights.

Thank goodness most of them lived within walking distance. Despite the gusting wind, the clear, dry weather had lasted. Unlike her bar. Although nobody seemed to have noticed that she had run out of everything except fruit juice almost an hour ago, when Kyle had taken over from Emma as head barman.

Emma's party was over. And this time next year Lulu would be a student at art school. She would have to rent out the house to pay for it, of course. This truly was the end of an era.

Stars were appearing between the light clouds above the trees as she looked out across the garden. Despite the cold, and her silk sari, Lulu stepped out onto the patio and walked slowly around to the main French windows which led into the living room.

Only to find that she had one guest still in place.

Kyle was stretched out on the sofa by the fireplace. She could just see his face in the glow from the dying fire. Music from Emma's favourite musicals still played softly from the incongruous ghetto blaster borrowed from one of her nephews who worked as a disc jockey at the Feathers, the sound amplified by the silence of the night air so that Lulu could just make out the individual song lyrics.

She stood at the patio door and watched him for a moment. His eyes were closed and his long legs were stretched out over the arm of the sofa, ankles crossed, so that his trousers had ridden up, revealing a tantalising strip of muscular leg above his smart black socks. It would be so very, very tempting to tiptoe across in her sandals and run her fingers up and down that skin and find out if he was ticklish or not.

And then do the same with other areas of his body. Such as the wonderful chest she had seen a few days earlier after his soaking in the river. That was one image had been seared into her brain.

A broad, open-mouthed grin of delight popped across her face as she tried to imagine what her father would have said if he had strolled into this room to find an adrenaline junkie dozing on his sofa. The very thought made her want to giggle, and she pressed her hand across her mouth to stop herself waking Kyle.

Because she wanted this moment to last as long as possible.

She wanted to remember what these little bubbles of happiness felt like when she looked into that tanned stubbly face above those spectacular broad shoulders and… Oh, she would have no problem remembering the touch of his hand on her waist as they danced together. No problem at all.

There went another little bubble of joy.

Making her grin again.

The scar on his upper lip was more pronounced this evening. Dark eyelashes fluttered below heavy eyebrows.

This man had pressed buttons she hadn't known that she even had. He had shown her what being in love could be truly like. She tilted her head so that she could look more closely at the movement of his chest rising and falling.

She was willing to take that risk with this man.

Watching him lying there, his face relaxed, warm, handsome, she knew it would be so easy to be seduced by the sweet and tender kisses of the man she loved.

Tonight had swept away any lingering unspoken doubts she might have had.

This was what she had been frightened of—what she had always feared would happen when she gave her heart. And she *had* truly given her heart. No doubt about it. They had become attached with bonds you could not cut with a sharp tongue or a kitchen knife.

How was she going to walk away from this man? When she wanted him so much? She knew that she was setting herself up for loneliness and pain if she walked down that road.

Kyle stirred slightly and she grinned at him. 'You did a wonderful job with the lights. It was a super idea, Kyle. Thank you for that.'

The hazel eyes remained tight shut as he replied. 'You are most welcome. Remind me not to volunteer to be barman again, would you? Those people can drink.'

There was a sigh from the sofa, and Lulu turned her

back to the room and wandered out onto the patio so that he could rest.

In the clear, crisp air, the faint streetlights from the village gave a background glow as one by one the familiar lights from the farmhouses on the other side of the fields blinked out, leaving the garden dark in the cool breeze that moved the trees.

One of the family of barn owls which roosted in the next copse sounded out, ready to begin its night flight.

There was a faint rustling noise from the room behind her, and Lulu felt soft, warm cloth being draped around her shoulders. Kyle's jacket.

'Is that better?'

Lulu could only manage a nod, and wrapped her arms together across her body to stop the shivers running down her spine.

Only this was not the cold. It was Kyle's body pressed against her back.

She could feel the warmth of his chest through her clothing, and without thinking or hesitating she leant backwards, daring to test the comfort she knew she would find there. His left arm draped around her waist and Kyle rested his head gently on top of hers as he looked out into the garden, then skywards.

'Do you know that the people I work with still follow a calendar controlled by the moon and the stars?' Kyle pointed over to the far right, where a thin silver disc had appeared above the horizon. 'Do you see that new moon? In Nepal it marks the start of a new beginning. A time for festivals. Processions with dancing and singing. It is great fun.'

'You must really miss your life in Nepal. Your patients,' Lulu answered, without moving position.

Kyle hesitated for a moment before answering. 'The people. That's who I miss. The work is the same no matter where I go, whether it is London or Nepal, but the people are special.'

She slowly twisted her body around so that there were only inches between them, so close she could sense the pounding of his heart in tune with her own.

Kyle raised his hand and stroked her cheek with the knuckles, from temple to neck and then back again, forcing her to look into his eyes.

'They love celebrations for a new beginning. A new start. You have chosen a very auspicious day to hold a party for the birthday girl.'

'And what about you? Are you looking for a new start, Kyle? A new beginning?'

Lulu looked up into Kyle's face as he gently stroked hers before replying.

'Maybe I am. Maybe we all are. Would you like to have one last dance to celebrate, pretty girl?' He pressed her fingers to his lips, his eyes never leaving hers.

Lulu leant into his broad shoulder, cuddling into his warmth, sensing and hearing the pounding of his heart as she slid her own arms around his neck.

She had no need of hearing.

No need of sight.

Just the smell of his body. His own unique aroma.

She closed her eyes and revelled in the sensation of his hand on the bare skin at her waist, pressing her even closer to his chest as he moved to the music, his hard-muscled body swaying to the beat.

Her head moved closer, so that she could touch her face against his. Content.

She sensed his arm moving away, then slowly, slowly, he stepped back so that his hand could take hold of hers, their fingers intermeshing.

She opened her eyes to focus on the man so close, so very close to her body. And felt the power of that rush of heat. Kyle was breathing heavily, its pace matching her own, his eyes darting all over her face.

It was Lulu who had the courage to say the words. 'Can you stay a little longer?'

His reply was a long exhale, followed by a hoarse whisper. 'I'm not going anywhere tonight. But there is something I need to tell you. It can't wait until morning.'

His hands closed around her cool, slender fingers and he led her slowly back into the dining room, the warmth of his smile hotter than the log fire burning in the grate.

She could only grin back in return as he released her hand so that she could wrap it around his waist and press her head into his shoulder.

'Now you really have me intrigued. What is it? What do you have to tell me?'

Kyle slowly turned her around, so that they were facing each other, and suddenly Lulu felt the air between them grow cold. The look on his face told her everything she needed to know. This was not going to be good news.

'Please? I would like to know what is going on.'

He nodded. 'I've decided to leave early. I'll be going in the morning.'

Lulu stared out of the French windows, her eyes fixed on the movement of the wind in the trees she could just make out in the light from the house and the drive. The gentle waving of branches to and fro in the breeze was no match to the tornado spinning inside her head.

It felt as though she had been strapped onto a horse on a childhood nightmare of a merry-go-round which had started whirling faster and faster, until all she could do was hang on for dear life, knowing that if she even tried to get off she would be seriously hurt.

Only to be slammed to a crushing stop into a large solid object called life.

He was leaving. Just as her mother had, and then her father. She had always known that this was a temporary arrangement. A few weeks out of her life. It wasn't meant to be so hard to say goodbye. She just wanted him to stay so badly.

Kyle snuggled next to her in silence, so that the left side of his body was pressed against her right. Leg to leg, hip to hip, arm to arm. Her body instinctively yearned to lean closer, so that her head could rest against that broad shoulder, but she fought the delicious sensation.

She had to.

It was almost a physical pain when the fingers of his left hand started to slowly unclench the fist she had not even realised was there. Slowly, slowly, she looked up into the most amazing hazel eyes she had ever seen. The dark flecks of cinnamon and forest-green seemed warmer tonight, in the soft light, but in that moment she could see there was something more. Something she had never seen before. Something different. His unsmiling eyes scanned her face for a few minutes, as though searching for an answer to some unasked question he had not the words to speak.

Uncertainty. Concern. Regret, even.

It was all there in the hard lines of his remarkable face, the shadows and planes highlighted by the flickering fire-

light. His fingertips clenched around hers just tight enough
to draw her attention away from his darkening eyes—only
their bodies were so close that she could feel the beat of
his heart through the thin fabric of his shirt against her
blouse. Her breathing seemed to increase, to match the
pace of his, and as she looked up his lips parted so he could
take in a deep, shuddering breath.

Was it possible that Kyle was hurting as much as she
was?

The voice that came from his lips was low, harsh and
barely above a whisper. Trembling. Uncertain. 'There is
one final request. I would like you to read the last few
pages of my diary before I leave.'

His right hand came up and gently lifted a coil of her
hair behind her ear in a gesture so tender and loving that
she closed her eyes in the pleasure of it.

'It's not going to be easy for you. For one thing the
handwriting is even worse than usual, but I do have a
feeble excuse.' The sides of his mouth twisted for a second,
but there was no laughter. 'I wrote them in the back of the
ancient truck sent to evacuate us from the clinic. It was the
first time I'd had a chance to sit down for days, and somehow it seemed right to—well, to try and make some sense
of the mess we were in after Ruth's death.'

His fingers started teasing out individual coils of hair,
as though that was the most important thing in the world
to do at that moment.

Lulu's heart fluttered. This was it. There was some terrible truth about her mother's death and he didn't know
how to tell her. He was trying to be gentle.

She tried desperately to remind herself of all of the terrible options she had imagined and dreamt up over the

years. Surely nothing he could tell her now would come close to the horror of those nightmares?

Lulu clasped her fingers around his.

'Kyle? Are you telling me that you saw her at the clinic on the day she was killed?'

He nodded, once, and then his head dropped for a second before he looked up and stared directly into her startled blue eyes.

'I was probably the last person to see her alive.'

CHAPTER ELEVEN

'THEN I don't want to read what happened in the pages of your diary or this new book. I want you to tell me in person. Now. To my face. What happened, Kyle? You are the only one who can tell me the truth. Can you do that?'

The powerful legs shifted, and he released her to run his fingers through his hair and walk slowly back to the table spread with papers. He slowly reached out and lifted up the photograph of her mother standing with the local children. One finger traced across the image in silence.

'It had been a hard couple of weeks. We were all exhausted.'

He lowered the photograph to the table and rested his hands, palms down, on the flat surface. But he turned slightly, so that there was no doubt that Lulu could hear precisely what he was saying.

'Ruth had promised the local chiefs that we would get to the village medical stations once a week. So we'd agreed a timetable. No matter what happened, I would go out in the ambulance every Tuesday morning and Ruth would stay at the hospital.'

After one sideways glance at her, he focused back on the photograph and gave a small shrug.

'You know what she was like—once she had made a promise there was no compromise. It actually seemed to work for a couple of months, but then the fighting started to get closer, and fresh casualties were coming in almost every day. Every bed in the clinic was taken and we had patients in corridors. It was relentless.'

He paused and suddenly found something quite fascinating to look at on the table.

'Go on,' she whispered under her breath. 'It was relentless and you were all exhausted?'

'Lulu, I…'

With one smooth movement, she took a few faltering steps closer, so that she could press the palms of both hands flat against his chest. The fast, hard beating of the heart that lay beneath told her everything she needed to know.

'It's okay,' she murmured, her eyes locked onto his. 'You can do this. I know you can. Just close your eyes and say the words and it will be over. I'm not afraid. I trust you.'

A shuddering long breath blew across her skin, and her eyes scanned his face in concern until his shoulders relaxed a little.

'It was a nightmare. You know how green I was. They don't teach you how to deal with situations like that in medical school. They can't. The wounded were being carried in by their families on carts and donkeys. All day and then all night. It seemed never-ending. The paramedics did amazing work, but Ruth and I were the only two surgeons, so we both had to work flat out, taking turns to catch a few hours' sleep whenever we could.'

He raised one hand and slid his fingers through her hair

until he found the base of her neck. Drawing her closer, he lowered his forehead to hers so that each hot breath fanned her face with its intensity.

'The fighting was getting closer, and we had been working thirty-six hours non-stop. I came out of surgery just before dawn, and Ruth insisted I get some sleep before I dropped.'

He paused and raised his head away from her, to look at the ceiling. When he lowered it to look at her there were tears glinting in the corners.

'I came out of my tent just in time to see Ruth jump into our rackety old ambulance. I shouted out for her to wait for me, but she just gave me a wave and took off down the track in a cloud of red dust.' His voice faltered, and the Adam's apple in his throat twisted hard as he swallowed down the tears and the grief that threatened to engulf them both. 'It was the last time I saw her. '

'Oh, Kyle.' The words closed her throat, and she dropped her head to the comfort and safety and warmth of his broad chest, unable to speak.

How long they stayed like that she didn't know, but it was Kyle who broke the silence, his lips pressed into her hair as he spoke.

'Don't feel sorry for me, Lulu. I am not telling you what happened because I want you to feel sorry for me. *You* are the one who deserves sympathy. You and your father were the ones she left behind. If only she had waited a few more minutes. You have no idea how guilty I feel every time I think about it.'

A cold shiver seemed to wave across Lulu's shoulders.

'Guilty? Why should you feel guilty? What difference would a few minutes have made? She was doing the work she loved.'

Kyle's hand pressed harder to the back of her head, as though getting ready to cushion her from the blow to come.

'You don't understand, Lulu. It was a *Tuesday* morning. *I* should have been the one in that ambulance. Not your mother. *I* should have been the one who was killed that day.'

Lulu pushed away from Kyle and staggered towards the table.

'Lulu? Talk to me. Let me explain.'

She held up one hand as she forced air down into her frozen lungs, a maelstrom of emotions welling up inside her chest and threatening to explode.

'*It was a Tuesday*. It was *your* turn to go out in the ambulance. Is that what you are telling me?'

The voice that came out of her mouth sounded like that of another woman. A woman who had just flung open the doors behind which every nightmare she had ever had were stored and hidden.

'Yes. It was my turn. Ruth told the nurse not to wake me and she took my place that day. Oh, Lulu, I am so sorry.'

Kyle reached out to take Lulu's hands, but she lifted them up and away from him.

'Don't do this, Lulu. Give me your worst—because nothing could be as bad as the guilt I feel every time I even think about that morning. Have you any idea how many times I have asked myself, *What if?* What if I hadn't been so exhausted and fallen asleep that morning? What if Ruth had waited another ten minutes? Or not been so stubborn? Or here's a good one. What if we had called the army to check whether they knew about the landmines on that road?'

'Stop. Stop it, Kyle. I don't want to hear any more.' Lulu wrapped her arms around her body to try and control the violent shivering. 'Is that the real reason why you are here right now? Why you agreed to write this book when it is obviously the very last thing that you want to do? It is, isn't it? You feel that you have to make amends for dodging a land mine? Was that how Mike blackmailed you to come here? By using your guilt that you survived?'

'Far from it. You see, Mike doesn't know that it should have been me who died that day. You are the only person I have ever told. The only person I ever would tell.'

'Me?' She stared at him for a few seconds, wide-eyed, before nodding her head.

'Of course. I see it now. That is why you agreed to come to this house instead of working in London. You are trying to compensate for your own guilt by being nice to me. Taking care of me. Is that it, Kyle? You think that you have some obligation to look out for me because you survived and she didn't?'

She was shouting now and she didn't care. Fists clenched, she strode up to him and stared into his shocked and pale face.

'How much do you like *me*? Or are you only interested in Ruth Taylor Hamilton's daughter? Please—I'd like to know the answer to that question before I throw you out.'

'So what if I do feel obligated?' Kyle snatched up the photograph of her mother laughing under the hot African sun. 'I owe her my life and I had no idea that she had a child. What is so wrong with my wanting to make sure that you have everything you need?'

He moved forward to clasp hold of both of her forearms, only she stepped away and crossed her arms tight, blocking any contact at all.

'But that was two weeks ago. Since then everything has changed. I had no way of knowing how much I would come to care about you. Want to be with you. And, no, *not* as Ruth's little girl. You are an amazing woman in your own right, Lulu Hamilton. You have to know that. Ruth would have been so proud.'

'Thank you for answering my question,' Lulu replied in a calmer voice, her eyes fixed on something fascinating on the carpet. 'But she's gone. And there is not one thing either of us can do to bring her back.'

She slowly raised her head and locked eyes with Kyle through her blurred tears.

'She took the decision to leave you behind that day—just as she took the decision to leave me behind every time she walked out of the door en route to some airport—any airport.' Lulu raised one hand. 'That was her choice. She was head of the clinic and she had a job to do. It was her decision to go out that day. Not yours. And certainly not mine.' She shook her head before stepping back. 'I've had to live with those decisions all my life. Now it's your turn. So if that is the reason you are here, you can consider yourself officially off the hook. Duty done.'

'What are you saying?'

'My part in this project is over. I've done everything I promised.' She waved one hand towards the boxes of paperwork. 'You can have the diaries and letters. Whatever you want. Just take them and go back to Nepal, or wherever it is you have to go back to so urgently. And allow me to get back to my life.'

'Lulu—please. Let's talk this through. I don't want to leave you like this.'

She looked hard at Kyle, lifted her head, and spoke in a clear, distinct voice.

'I don't want to talk about it. I want you to leave now. Please close the door behind you on the way out.'

And with that, she turned her back on him and walked with as much control as she could to the French windows. It was only when the curtains were almost closed that she saw the headlights of his car swing out of the drive and head off down the lane.

Dropping her hands away from the cords, she collapsed down on the window seat and put her head in her hands, let the shock take over. How long she sat there sobbing she did not know, but the air grew cold around her and she did not care.

Slowly, she became aware that a red-brown shape was standing patiently by her side, and as she sat up Belle gently laid her head on Lulu's lap and sat quietly, her deep brown eyes looking up at her. She wrapped her arms around the dog's head and let the tears stream down her face and into the dog's fur.

'Looks like it's back to just you and me, Belle. On our own again. Just you and me.'

Early the next morning over a half-hearted breakfast, Emma rubbed Lulu's shoulder as she dropped her head onto her outstretched arms.

'You knew it was going to be hard. But you can do this.' She dragged Lulu to her feet. 'Right? Right. Come on, girl, I'll make the coffee and you get back to work. Those paintings won't paint themselves. It will help.'

Lulu shrugged an ancient sweater over her overalls. Emma was right. She needed to work on something—

anything—to focus her mind and control the turmoil that raged inside her.

She had to get back to her old life.

The past two weeks working with Kyle had been a disaster for her painting projects. The gallery had already called to find out how many watercolours of local wild flowers she could provide. They were always in demand as Christmas gifts and hand-painted greeting cards—she was going to have to work fast if she had any chance of making the Christmas deadline now that the book project was behind her.

Over and done with.

Finished.

I don't want it to be over, she thought. *I don't want to be without him in my life.* But she dared not form those words. She had tasted something so wonderful it was hard to imagine life without that flavour again.

How could she have fallen so deeply, so fast?

In another world they might even have had a chance to make a life together. She knew what his world was like without any complicated excuses. They understood one another without having to explain.

Except, of course, he had not been honest with her.

Lulu dropped her shoulders and closed her eyes tight shut for a moment, before slowly twisting around in her chair to look at her mother's portrait.

This was where her father had sat, day after day. Joined for ever to the woman who still had the power to control their lives.

Ten years ago that woman had decided to let her exhausted new surgeon sleep after working through an African night. One single decision, made for the best of reasons. And Kyle had been punishing himself ever since.

'Oh, Mum,' she whispered. 'Look what you did. You gave me someone to love. Thank you for that. Any chance you can find a way to get him back for me?'

With a fast shiver, and a shake of her head for being so ridiculous as to talk to a painting, Lulu turned back to her work and wiped away the salty tears from her eyes.

Her painting was her refuge. Her solace.

And she had never needed that solace more than today.

She quickly pulled out her portfolio and lifted the first drawing onto the table in front of the window. A cluster of spring primroses peeked out from wide, fleshy leaves. It was a pretty still-life, in delicate shades of pale yellow and green that would sell well. There was nothing daring or brave or exciting about it, but it was true to life and simple. Natural and attractive.

Except that as she examined it more closely under natural daylight she saw that the original pencil drawing was too dark for the pale watercolours she had used, not daring to be too bold, and the leaves were out of proportion with the flowers.

The whole symmetry of the piece seemed wrong to her now.

It would take hours of work with layers of paint and tiny brushes to correct the mistakes and give the painting shadow, depth and texture. To make it come alive.

Suddenly the whole piece looked flat, boring, dull and mediocre.

Where was the life? The wonderful rich and vibrant colour and texture she thought she had created? How had she failed so miserably?

No one would notice the flaws from a distance. The actual painting was no bigger than a hardback book, with a huge white border that would be hidden beneath the mount and the picture frame. But *she* knew they were there.

What she been satisfied to accept a few days earlier was no longer good enough.

Which was why Lulu grabbed the top edge of the sheet of heavy paper with both hands and ripped it down the middle with all of the strength in her body, then again and again, until the table was littered with torn fragments of white and coloured paper.

Heart thumping, she stared down at the pieces with a smile on her face as a sense of freedom pulsed through her. *Liberated.*

She didn't want to go to art college and paint botanical drawings—she could already do that. She was going to art college to find out what she was capable of.

In an instant she had swept her watercolour box and portfolio off the table and replaced it with her father's large sketchpad. Twice the size of her own. Well used. And just what she needed.

Lulu could only smile as she flicked through the old sketchpad she remembered from being a girl. The spine was almost broken, and as she flicked to the next clean page a loose piece of paper fluttered out.

Swooping it up, she suddenly took a sharp intake of breath. This was not a sketch or a drawing, but a single sheet of familiar thin airmail paper covered in pale blue ink.

It was her mother's writing.

Her legs threatened to give way and Lulu collapsed at the table. She certainly had not seen this letter before.

She turned the sheet over in her hands. It looked like a page from one of her mum's letters, except their address had been scribbled on the reverse. That was unusual; she'd usually tried to fill both sides of the pages with tiny thin letters, so she could cram as much as possible into the mailing.

Not this time.

The writing was thin and wobbly, disordered, but with a sense of energy and urgency Lulu did not recognise. There was no date or address to indicate where or when it had been written.

Taking a breath, she read through the words, and then read them again.

There are only the four of us left now. We have already moved three times during the night, carrying patients and whatever we could save to higher ground, but they are moving faster than we can. The villagers have fled into the hills.

We're all too exhausted to go any further, so we sit here waiting for the inevitable. Too tired to talk.

I wonder what you are doing in Kingsmede? Working in the garden, perhaps, with Lulu by your side? Or filling the world with colour and light in the happy home I left behind? It must be so pretty now that summer is here.

You told me once that our lives are our greatest treasure, our most precious possession. Far too precious to waste on anything which is not capable of breaking our hearts. How very right you were. As always. I am looking at the photograph you sent me from our little girl's last birthday party and my heart is breaking.

It is too painful, and the crew are looking for me to get them out of this.

I think you are the only person in this world who knows that I could not even try to do what I do, in these hard places, without the knowledge that you are both safe back home.

You are my heart. My foundation. Without my family I would not have the strength to get up every day, to work to make things better for these people, knowing that I will probably fail. You are the ones who make this possible for me. And I know you pay the price.

At the clinic someone had left behind a book of poetry. I wrote down one of the lines: 'If you love somebody, let them go, for if they return, they were always yours. And if they don't, they never were'.

You are strong enough to let me go. Time and time again.

I'm going to leave this note in my medical bag. If anything happens to me, someone might post it. Kiss our little girl for me. I love you both. Never forget that.

There was no signature. No familiar kisses at the bottom. Only a faint mark of the pen as though she had started to write something and been interrupted.

Along the margin, next to the quotation, her dad had written in pencil, 'Quote from Khalil Gibran.'

Lulu slid back against her chair and let the tears flow down her cheeks.

Terrified, Ruth Taylor Hamilton had held this very piece of paper in her own sweaty hand. She had wanted them to know what she was thinking while she waited for the local militia to arrive and execute her, with the crew and the patients.

Was that why her father had taken it from the box of letters and tucked it between the pages of the sketchbook that had never left his side? To remind himself of that great love? A love which was worth breaking his heart over? A love worth that huge risk?

No. *More than that.*

Lulu closed her eyes and inhaled deeply.

Her father had sacrificed his own happiness to make sure that her mother had a stable base to come home to.

He had let her mother go time and time again in the hope that she would return to him.

Knowing that they belonged together.

Knowing that their love was capable of breaking their hearts.

Her father had stayed married to her because that was what her mother had needed. No matter the cost.

'Lulu? What is it?' Emma had come in and was staring down at her, her face anxious and caring. 'What's happened, little girl?'

'She spent so much time away on missions and he was so lonely,' Lulu gulped. 'I always thought that he regretted marrying someone who didn't want to be with us. But I was wrong. I simply never saw it before today.'

Lulu stared down at the page between her fingers, blinking away tears so that she could focus on the faint blue words written so many years ago.

'I've been such a fool. He loved her so much he was willing to let her go. Even if she broke his heart. Their love was so precious. I can see that now.'

'Well, of course it was. They were two sides of the same coin.'

Emma stood back and turned to one side, to gaze up at the portrait of Ruth Taylor Hamilton over the mantel.

'You only have to look at this painting to know how he felt about her. Your father was a clever man, Lulu, and he did love your mother—very much. He knew that Ruth would never be happy with a nine-to-five job in Kingsmede. And he was willing to make the sacrifice so that she could be happy. Every single time she stepped out of that door it broke his heart. But their love kept him going when they were apart. Kept them both going. Because I know that she felt the same way about him. They adored each other.'

Emma looked back with her head tilted and smiled.

'Why am I getting the feeling that this is not just about your parents? Am I right?'

Lulu suddenly sat up straight, blinking away her tears as she stared out of the window into the brightening sky.

'I'm in love with Kyle Munroe and I don't want to lose him. I need him so much, but I know now that I have to let him go. Even if he does break my heart.'

Emma sucked in a sharp breath of air, then grasped Lulu by both arms.

'Then go and tell him how you feel. Or regret it for the rest of your life. Go. As fast as your legs can carry you. I'll lock up here and follow you with Belle. Go! Scoot! You might just be able to catch him in time.'

CHAPTER TWELVE

PLEASE let him still be here. Please. He could not have left yet, could he?

She pedalled faster, and the arms of her old painting overalls puffed out in the cold wind which lifted the chestnut leaves up into loose whirls either side of the lane.

Lulu's heart soared as she saw a flash of dark green in the car park next to the Feathers. *His car was here!*

In one swift movement she swung her legs from her old cycle and leant it against the nearest tree, before running into the reception area, her eyes scanning for Kyle in the lunchtime crowd.

It took Lulu three seconds to bounce up the steps to the bedrooms and stand puffing and panting outside the only closed bedroom door. Emma's best guestroom.

Her hand stretched out towards the door handle. And then she snatched it back.

Eyes closed, she blew out a long deep breath, her head suddenly dizzy with doubt as the blood surged in her veins.

What was she doing here? What if he said thanks, but no thanks? This was crazy.

What had her mother said in her letter? If you love somebody, let them go? She loved this man and yet she was going to let him go free to live his life? Away from her? Mad. Yet she knew deep in her heart that it was absolutely the right thing to do.

She was risking her future happiness on a crazy decision to trust her heart instead of her head.

And what if he said yes? On the one hand she could be committing herself to the life of loneliness that her father had endured—or, on the other, to loving a man who had shown her how to love.

She had to do it now. Or never. Perhaps that was why she felt so naked? Exposed?

After ten seconds of agonised waiting, she straightened her back and prepared to knock—and at the very second she did so there was movement on the other side of the door. The handle turned on its own and cracked open an inch, then wider, braced by a familiar khaki rucksack.

She was stunned into silence as the door opened and her eyes locked onto his. He looked at her with the kind of intensity that seemed to knock the oxygen from her lungs.

Then those eyes smiled, and she took in the full effect of that handsome face. He grinned straight at her with the kind of smile that turned her legs to jelly. No camera could have captured the look on his face at that moment.

She felt as though the air would explode with the electricity in the air between them.

'Hi.' He smiled. 'You look nice. Although you didn't need to dress up to see me off.'

Lulu glanced down at her oldest pair of painting overalls and smiled back at him, desperate to break the tension so that she could put the words together that she needed to say. Wanted to say.

So much had changed.

'Oh, this little old thing?' she managed in half-breaths.

'I was planning to drive up and see you. I've been pretty busy in the last few hours.' He paused. 'Has something happened? Are you okay?' There was so much love and concern in his voice that any doubts Lulu had had about what she had to do next were wiped away.

'I—I found a note from my mother,' she faltered. 'It was inside Dad's old sketchbook. It said that…' Her throat was so choked the words refused to co-operate.

'Hey. Come and sit down.'

He wrapped his arm around her shoulder and shoved the rucksack aside so that he could draw her inside the room, where he lowered her gently on the bed while he sat on the quilt and held her hand.

'Now, talk to me. And take it slow. Tell me what this letter said that was so important you dragged yourself away from your painting to tell me about it.'

'What did it say?' she replied, stroking his hand as her eyes locked onto his, and all the words she had practised on the cycle ride spilled out in a rush. 'It said that I have been a complete fool. I have been so wrong, Kyle. About so many things.'

She reached up and stroked his cheek, her eyes never leaving his.

'I haven't stopped thinking about what you said. And you were right. This is the biggest risk of my life—your life—anyone's life.'

She breathed in, her heart thudding so loudly she suspected that he must hear it from where he was sitting so quietly.

'I know now that I will always love you, Kyle Munroe, and it doesn't matter where you are in the world. And if that means that I have to let you go—to be free to do your work…' She licked her lips. 'Then that is the way it has to be. I want to be with you. Love you. If you still want me to wait for you?'

Kyle sat very still, staring at her, and she bit her lower lip in fear. She might have just made the biggest mistake of her life, but this was the way it had to be.

'I could be away for six or seven months at a time, you know,' he told her gently, his voice low, sensual and intimate.

'Probably longer. But I am going to let you go and do what you have to do—wherever that is. Because just maybe we can get back together one day. I love you, Kyle, and that is not going to change whether you are in Nepal or Uganda or down the road.'

Kyle did not answer, but slid her fingers from his so that he could caress her face, his eyes scanning from her nose to her roughly tied-back, out-of-control hair.

'You love me but you are willing to let me go and do the work which means so much to me? Is that right?'

She nodded, afraid to trust her voice. 'As long as you are somewhere in this world, loving me, then I shall be complete. My heart will be your beacon home to my love.'

'Then there's only one answer to your question. No. I don't want you to wait for me.'

Her heart caught in her throat, but he pressed one finger on her lips and smiled, breaking the terror.

'You see, I'm not as brave as you are. As soon as I left you this morning I knew that I couldn't leave the woman I have fallen in love with without trying to come up with some options.'

He grinned at her and slid forward, so that both his

hands were cupped around her face as tears pricked her eyes.

'I love you way too much to let you go. I need you, Lulu. I need you so much. Nothing else comes close. What would you say if I told you that I will be working out of London for the next twelve months?'

She shuddered out a chuckle of delight and relief. 'I would say, yes, please, and then I would ask how you have managed it.'

'They love what we've done, Lulu. Not me. The two of us. It seems that we make a pretty good team. Mike Baxter wants me to finish the book over the winter, then work with the media company on a series of follow-on books and documentaries. The Nepal mission is going to be fully funded for the next five years, and I have a job managing the missions in Africa and Asia any time I want one.'

Kyle grinned back and took her hands in his, ready and willing to tease out the delicious moment when she heard the surprise he had planned.

'I did insist on one extra condition before they agreed to double their donation to the foundation. I told them that I would only do it if I could bring my fiancée with me to Nepal next May, so that she could paint the rhododendron forests in bloom. She might be at art college, but she'd deserve first-class travel all of the way.'

'Your fiancée…' She breathed out the words, tears pricking her wide eyes, scarcely daring to believe what he was saying.

'You have given me the greatest compliment a man could wish. You've offered me your love and the freedom to live my life. I never imagined I would find a woman who could love me as much as I loved her. I told you last night that I wasn't going anywhere, and I meant it. Not without you.'

Kyle's voice faltered as he pressed his forehead to her flushed brow.

'Last night, when I held you in my arms, I had the unbelievable feeling that I had come home. That this was where I belonged. I have travelled all over the world, Lulu. I might have kidded myself that it was for work, but the truth is hard to accept. I needed to prove to myself that there was some reason why I survived and Ruth perished. To prove that I could make a difference to people's lives. Just as she had done.'

'Oh, Kyle. It was never your fault. Just as it wasn't mine. I know that now. And you *have* made a difference.' She was stroking the hair back from his forehead now, her fingertips moving through the short curls as she stared into the depths of those stunning eyes.

'I have never felt such an overwhelming sense of homecoming than in these last few weeks I have spent with you. I didn't even realise that I was looking for it. Your heart is my beacon home. Wherever you are is where I want to be. Bring me home, Lulu. Bring me home.' He knelt in front of her as he whispered, in a husky, intimate voice that she had only heard before in her dreams, 'I love you and I want you to be part of my life, Lulu. If you'll have me?'

Lulu looked into a face so full of love that her heart broke.

'Have you? Oh, my sweet darling. How can you ask that after last night? You have to know that I love you. I will love you for the rest of my life. You are the centre of my world.'

She choked with emotion as Kyle stood, then swung her up into the air, whirling her around and around until her feet connected with the bedroom lampshade.

In an instant Kyle had lowered her to the floor and grabbed her hand. She had to skip down the stairs to keep up with him as they ran out together into the faint sunshine, laughing and squealing in joy. Oblivious to the people around them.

Emma Carmichael stepped out of her car just in time to see Kyle grab Lulu behind the knees and throw her over his right shoulder.

Kyle was almost in the middle of the river before she managed to wriggle free, and then, holding hands, they pulled and twirled each other round and round, heads back, laughing and shouting in pleasure, water splashing up around them, before collapsing into each other's arms, their heads pressed together into a passionate kiss.

At that moment Belle leapt out of the backseat of Emma's car and charged into the water to dance and play around the happy couple, barking and scampering in the shallows.

Emma turned to the rest of the village, who had crowded in to look over her shoulder, and shooed them back inside the Feathers.

'Those Taylor girls always end up with the best-looking boys! Now, who's ready for a nice glass of champagne? There is far too much excitement around here.'

EPILOGUE

KYLE strolled into the spacious art gallery and looked over the heads of the glamorous patrons to catch a glimpse of the only person he needed to see.

And there she was. The centre of attention, chatting away to friends and buyers as though she attended an exhibition of her own paintings every day of the week.

Incredibly beautiful. Confident. Unique.

Looking at her now, it was hard to imagine that only an hour ago he had been fighting to pin back her corkscrew curls to display the African tribal jewellery that had been her wedding gift from their friends in Uganda.

She looked wonderful.

By some sixth sense, at that precise moment she turned her head towards him and grinned right back across the room. The familiar heat of attraction flashed through his body. He did not want to be apart from the woman he loved for one moment longer than necessary!

Clusters of people were gathered in front of a wall of brilliantly coloured paintings of exotic blooms. Rhododendron bushes in full bloom, magnolia trees and stunning African blossoms shone out from the walls.

Glowing and vibrant. Just like the amazing and beautiful woman who had painted them.

He casually wrapped one arm around the waist of her simple aquamarine silk satin shift dress and was rewarded with a tender kiss on the side of his neck as he drew her closer.

'Have I told you this evening that you look stunning, Mrs Munroe?'

'Um… Once or twice. Thank you, anyway—and you clean up pretty well yourself, Dr Munroe.' She reached up and smoothed down the lapel of his black cashmere suit. 'Although I do have a certain preference for khaki green.' Her mouth lifted into a personal smile that still hit him hard.

'Kyle—glad you could make it.' The beaming gallery owner strolled forward to shake his hand. 'Thank you for delaying your plans for a few days. The exhibition has been a huge success, but we couldn't have done it without Lulu being here. When are you flying out this time?'

'We're leaving for Kampala tomorrow, then Delhi,' Kyle replied, and laughed out loud. 'But don't worry. We shouldn't be gone for more than a few weeks. Unless, of course, my wife decides to take off on yet another botanical expedition of her own. In which case—' he threw his hands up and shrugged in defeat '—who knows where we'll end up? There is no holding this girl back.'

Lulu squeezed his arm as she smiled up into his face. 'Well, there have to be some perks for marrying the director of the foundation responsible for all of Africa and Asia! But then we are going home to Kingsmede. Together. To start the most amazing journey of our lives.'

A sneaky peek at next month...

By Request

RELIVE THE ROMANCE WITH THE BEST OF THE BEST

My wish list for next month's titles...

In stores from 15th February 2013:

❑ His Defiant Mistress – Catherine George, Carole Mortimer & Sandra Field

❑ Baby on Board – Liz Fielding, Patricia Thayer & Raye Morgan

3 stories in each book - only £5.99!

In stores from 1st March 2013:

❑ The Wilders – Marie Ferrarella, Mary J. Forbes & Teresa Southwick

Available at WHSmith, Tesco, Asda, Eason, Amazon and Apple

Just can't wait?

Visit us Online

You can buy our books online a month before they hit the shops! **www.millsandboon.co.uk**

0213/05

The World of Mills & Boon®

There's a Mills & Boon® series that's perfect for you. We publish ten series and, with new titles every month, you never have to wait long for your favourite to come along.

Blaze.
Scorching hot, sexy reads
4 new stories every month

By Request
Relive the romance with the best of the best
9 new stories every month

Cherish™
Romance to melt the heart every time
12 new stories every month

Desire™
Passionate and dramatic love stories
8 new stories every month

Mills & Boon® Online

Discover more romance at
www.millsandboon.co.uk

- 🌹 **FREE** online reads
- 🌹 **Books** up to one month before shops
- 🌹 **Browse our books** before you buy

...and much more!

For exclusive competitions and instant updates:

 Like us on **facebook.com/romancehq**

 Follow us on **twitter.com/millsandboonuk**

 Join us on **community.millsandboon.co.uk**

| *Visit us Online* | Sign up for our FREE eNewsletter at **www.millsandboon.co.uk** |